I whipped through this twisty mystery that takes place in one of my favorite settings, a newsroom full of curious characters. As Deborah Kalb's protagonist tries to figure out who killed the journalist whose body she discovered on her first day at a new job, she's also trying to regain her confidence after being abruptly dumped by her fiancé. A layered romp with a dash of suspenseful romance, *Everything She Most Admired* is an admirably tricky whodunnit.

— Karen Dukess, author of *Welcome to Murder Week*

Everything She Most Admired, Deborah Kalb's new novel, is a lively mystery with a full cast of colorful suspects. Set in a news magazine office in Washington D.C.—Kalb's familiar turf—it's packed with amusing details, including a Transylvanian alibi and ornamental goats. Appealing amateur sleuth Lauren Green complicates the murder investigation by falling in love with one of the suspects. Kalb keeps readers in suspense, then treats them to a delightful denouement. *Everything She Most Admired* is a perfect book to curl up with on a dark and stormy night.

— Corinne Demas, author of *Daughters* and *The Road Towards Home*

Imagine: it is your first day at a new job, and you find the body of a freshly murdered colleague lying next to the copier machine. Such is the intriguing kick off to Deborah Kalb's delicious murder mystery, *Everything She Most Admired.* Kalb masterfully mashes together the mechanics of mystery procedurals, the gossipy culture of office politics, the competitive milieu of Washington, D.C., journalism, and a touching love story. With a colorful cast of characters hiding all sorts of juicy secrets, *Everything She Most Admired* builds to a suspenseful climax that will keep readers turning the pages.

— Len Kruger, author of the novel *Bad Questions*, winner of the 2023 Washington Writers' Publishing House Fiction Award

In this fast-paced whodunit, you'll root for the heroine who goes far beyond her job description by becoming an unlikely sleuth.

— Lorna Landvik, author of many novels, including *Chronicles of a Radical Hag (with Recipes)* and *Last Circle of Love*

Lauren Green, jilted by her fiancé without warning, is rebuilding her literary life at the "Most Admired Unit" of Lens magazine. Then, the unimaginable – she stumbles across the dead body of a co-worker on her very first day of employment. Her life, already seriously sideways, now lurches forward through the fun house mirror of her mind, her personal, cinematic world of intrigue and discovery. And, yes, maybe there's a well-deserved romance along the way. *Everything She Most Admired* is a deftly written whodunit populated by humorously drawn characters who propel the plot forward to a very satisfying conclusion. Lauren's imaginative internal video replays keep the reader guessing (and smiling) all along until the very end. Agatha Christie would have been proud to have written this one! Highly recommended!

— J. Paul Rieger, author of *Clonk!, Sunscreen Shower* and *A Most Unlikely Man: A Tale of Resistance*

Blends the cozy procedural vibes of an eccentric office, bumbling cops, and romantic tension with an entertaining locked-room whodunit. *Everything She Most Admired* is a "must read."

— Suzanne Chazin, author of *Land of Careful Shadows*

Everything She Most Admired is a fun and well-written mystery that will keep you guessing until the end. The story follows Lauren Green as she begins a career conducting surveys for a fictional D.C.-based magazine, Lens. Imagine showing up to work on your first day and finding a dead body. Using her experience as a former journalist, Kalb takes you inside the newsroom and gives the reader a story with depth and relatable characters to root for. What I admired most is the subtle humor throughout the novel. Kalb's expert light touch isn't over the top. It's just enough for a slight chuckle all while taking in the clues of this murder mystery.

— Michelle Paris, author of *New Normal* and *Eat Dessert First*

In *Everything She Most Admired,* Deborah Kalb transforms an ordinary workplace into a stage for suspicion, ambition, and quietly simmering tensions. Lauren Green arrives at Lens magazine hoping for a reset — a temporary refuge from a shattered engagement and a drifting career — only to find herself at the center of a murder investigation before her first day of work even begins. As colleagues trade pleasantries, defensiveness, and veiled anxieties, Lauren navigates a world where professional reputations mask private fears and loyalties shift with unnerving ease. Kalb deftly balances psychological insight with mounting suspense, capturing the fragile dance of office politics while tracing Lauren's gradual rediscovery of confidence and instinct. The result is a smart, character-rich mystery that is as much about perception and reinvention as it is about solving a crime.

— Eric D. Goodman, author of *The Color of Jadeite*

"*Everything She Most Admired* is a lively, fast-paced whodunnit set in the high-pressure world of a D.C. magazine—full of sharp wit and a heroine readers will root for."

— Aggie Blum Thompson, author of *You Deserve to Know*

Everything She Most Admired

Everything She Most Admired

A Mystery Novel

Deborah Kalb

First Edition

Library of Congress Control Number: 2025948856

Hardcover ISBN: 978-1-62720-641-9
Paperback ISBN: 978-1-62720-642-6
Ebook ISBN: 978-1-62720-643-3

Design by Eleanor Salvatore
Editorial Development by Sarah McKoy

Published by Apprentice House Press

Loyola University Maryland
4501 N. Charles Street, Baltimore, MD 21210
410.617.5265
www.ApprenticeHouse.com
info@ApprenticeHouse.com

To my family

One

Was it normal to feel this nervous on the first day of a new job? Lauren wasn't sure. Her heart was pounding and her mouth felt dry. She swallowed and looked around the second-floor room that she had thought was the office. It was completely deserted. But it was 8:45 a.m. Was she in the wrong part of the building? She noticed that the staircase continued upward. So she ascended the steps one more level, to the third floor.

And the first thing she saw, as she peered around the corner, was something that looked like her ex-fiancé Eric's running shoes. She shook her head to clear it of Eric, who had broken their engagement five months earlier and shattered her life into incomprehensible pieces that didn't fit together anymore. She shouldn't be thinking of him.

All was quiet on the third floor, too. Almost unnaturally so. She approached the shoes and realized that they were on the feet of a dark-haired man, maybe thirty-ish, about her age, who was lying on the floor next to an antiquated copier.

"Hello?" she asked tentatively. There was no response. Lauren stepped a little closer still and gasped in horror. This couldn't be real. He was most definitely not moving. His eyes were open and unblinking. Was he hurt? Was he conscious? Could he possibly be...dead? What was she supposed to do? She looked helplessly around the room. Call the police, that's right. She should call the police.

Suddenly the full impact of what she was seeing hit her, and she screamed and ran out of the room, her legs feeling rubbery. She stumbled down the stairs, and charged into a woman who was about to enter the second-floor office.

"Help," Lauren yelled. "We have to call the police. Or an ambulance. I think he might be dead." She started rummaging through her bag to find her phone.

The woman pursed her lips. "Who are you? And what are you talking about?"

"Lauren Green," Lauren whispered. Her voice had suddenly disappeared. "But we have to call the police. There's someone up there and I think he's possibly dead."

The woman ran up the stairs, her shoes clicking on the concrete. Lauren followed. The woman gasped. "Oh, my god. It's Tony." She bent over the prone figure. "I just can't tell if there's a pulse." She pulled her phone out of her pocket and ran back down the stairs, Lauren—who still hadn't found her own phone—again in tow.

Tony? Did he work here at Lens magazine? Lauren tried to recall what Amanda—her best friend, who worked at Lens and in whose apartment Lauren was currently staying—had told her about her future colleagues, but found she was incapable of remembering anything.

The woman snapped impatiently at the person at the other end of the phone, and disconnected. "I'm Louisa Bates, by the way." She stretched her hand in Lauren's direction, and Lauren automatically shook it.

Footsteps sounded on the stairway. "Louisa?" a male voice said hesitantly, as if unsure of the reception it would get. "I think we have to be at a meeting with Natasha." A pale thin man stepped into the room. "Oh, you must be Lauren. I'm Wade Wood. Nice to meet you, Lauren, nice to meet you."

"Shut up and listen to me, Wade," Louisa snapped. "Tony's lying up there by the copier. I think he might be dead."

Wade started shaking. "Dead? Dead? How do you know?"

"I don't know." Louisa tapped her foot up and down. "That's why I called 911. I can't imagine what's taking them so long."

Lauren felt numb. She never should have moved back here, to her hometown of Washington, D.C., in the wake of the broken engagement. She should have stayed in Boston, despite the awkwardness of possibly running into Eric, who still resided there. She should walk right out of this office and return northward, Eric and the last few hellish months be damned. She should go back to academia, her natural habitat.

She watched as various people came in and out of the room, including one who started screaming and ran out again, followed by another. Then Lauren heard a siren.

"Louis," Louisa said wearily, turning to a young man who had remained behind. "Could you let them in, please?"

"Sure." Louis, his bespectacled face looking queasy, gulped and disappeared down the stairs.

"I don't understand it. Who could have done such a terrible thing, who?" Louisa walked over to a desk at the far side of the room, presumably her own, and absently picked up a clipboard, which she clutched to her chest.

"Obviously some criminal broke in here." Wade rubbed one hand over the top of his balding head. "Obviously some criminal broke in here."

"Up here," Lauren heard Louis calling, and footsteps clattered past them to the third floor. Wade and Louisa followed, and Lauren thought she should too. She didn't want to be alone. She scrambled up the stairs behind the rest of them, and then found that her legs were unable to hold her up anymore. She sat down on the steps next to the open door to the third floor. Two medics were bent over the victim.

Wade was blinking and gulping convulsively. He had turned quite chartreuse in color, Lauren noticed. And then she shivered. How could she even be noticing things like that when someone was lying there, possibly dead, in front of her? She had never seen anything like this before.

It seemed, understandably, that none of the others had either. Everyone appeared to be equally overwhelmed.

"Excuse us, excuse us," one of the paramedics said. They had lifted Tony onto a stretcher and were trying to maneuver toward the stairs.

The stretcher and its bearers moved out, and a moment later Lauren heard the siren start to sound. Everyone trooped back to the second floor.

Lauren leaned on an empty desk. She'd have to get out of here. Soon.

"Well." Louisa sat down next to her. "What a day to start working here, my god." She cradled her head in her hands. "I just don't understand it. Who could have done such a thing?"

"Okay, folks," a voice boomed. Everyone jumped. "Detective Tucker, MPD. So what do we have here?"

"One of our staffers appears to have been attacked," Louisa said. "In the room upstairs. Where the copier is. I just can't imagine who could have done such a thing."

"Okay." Tucker leaned out the door. "Upstairs, Mac, in the copier room. Third floor. And now." He turned back to Louisa. "The victim's name?"

"Tony Mandel. He's a reporter here."

A reporter at Lens. Suddenly Lauren came up with a dim memory of Amanda discussing Tony Mandel. Something negative.

Hadn't they both covered Congress, and, what else? She shook her head. She just couldn't think right now.

"Tony Mandel." Tucker rolled the name slowly around on his tongue. "All right. And who discovered Mr. Mandel?"

"She did," Louisa said, gesturing at Lauren. A suspicious expression appeared on Louisa's face. "Lauren Green. She started working here today. And I'm Louisa Bates."

Oh my god, Lauren thought. She must think I did it. Here I am, this new person, and I find...

"Uh-huh." Tucker pulled out a small notebook. "And what time did you find the victim, Ms. Green?"

"I think it was about eight-forty-five." Lauren's voice was emerging unevenly. She cleared her throat.

"Okay," Tucker said. "And then?"

"I arrived and called 911," Louisa said, retrieving control of the conversation. "I couldn't tell if he was still breathing."

Lauren heard more footsteps tromping up and down the stairs.

"And you folks were all here when Ms. Green discovered Mr. Mandel?" Tucker continued.

Lauren opened her mouth to say that they hadn't been, but nothing came out. She stood there gaping like a fish, feeling ridiculous.

"No. But I arrived first," Louisa said. "After Lauren, that is. And then Wade, and Louis, and then Jim and Cecily."

"How many entrances are there to this part of the building?" Tucker queried.

"Just the one. Where you came in."

"And who's in charge here?"

"I am," Wade and Louisa said simultaneously. They glared viciously at each other.

Louisa frowned. "If you have any questions, Detective, you

certainly shouldn't talk to him."

The detective looked skeptical. "I'll have to talk to everyone, ma'am, if you don't mind. Now, you all work for a separate unit of the magazine? That's why you're all over here in this part of the building? I've gotta say, it's much nicer in the main part." He peered at the dingy off-white walls and the threadbare brown carpet.

"The Most Admired Unit," Louisa said, nodding. "I'm Louisa Bates, as I mentioned. I am the director of this unit."

"But..." Wade began.

"Wade Wood," Louisa continued. "My co-director." She shot him a look of scorn. "Louis Dubois, our intern who works on computer data. And Lauren, whom I've already mentioned."

Tucker looked around as each was introduced, and made notations in his notebook.

"Small staff, Ms. Bates." Tucker chewed on his pen with apparent satisfaction.

"Oh, well, that's certainly not the entire staff," Louisa said, sounding peeved that Tucker was accusing her of ruling only a tiny empire. "We have several other people. Jim Alvarez-Chao and Cecily Bartleby, our reporter-researchers, are right here. Or they were, until a minute ago. I have absolutely no idea where they could have gotten to."

"Bartleby?" Tucker's brow furrowed. "As in, owners of Lens magazine?"

Louisa nodded. "Great-niece. And then there's..."

"Hoo boy." Tucker looked up from his notebook. "Well, that gets into a whole nother ball game here. TV and all. Big-time press coverage."

"TV? Press coverage?" Louisa snapped. "Certainly not. Surely you realize that the Bartlebys haven't been seen in public in more than twenty years? They never come out of their house."

Tucker shrugged. "So what is most admired about your unit, anyway, Ms. Bates? Why is it called that?"

"We work on polling. Surveys. We ask people what their most admired whatever-it-might-be is. It's a new direction for Lens. The Bartlebys want to diversify, given all the problems facing the magazine industry these days. So they came up with this idea, and we just started the unit a couple of months ago."

"Most Admired Unit." Tucker tapped his pen on his notebook. "I see."

Footsteps sounded, from the stairs, and a tall broad-shouldered man, maybe fortyish, strode into the room. "Detective McDonald. I work with Detective Tucker." Detective McDonald, Lauren noticed through the waves of shock still pounding through her, looked quite glum, in contrast to his partner, who was looking more exhilarated by the minute.

"Hey, Mac." Tucker slapped McDonald on the back. "The Bartlebys' niece works in this part of the magazine. What do you think about that?"

McDonald sighed. His long, dark, bearded face drooped. "Just another complication."

"I was about to say," Louisa noted, "that then there's Nick Belotserkovsky, another reporter, who hasn't come in yet."

Nick Belotserkovsky. The name sounded familiar to Lauren, but she wasn't sure why. It was an unusual name.

"Hmmm," said Tucker. "Well, as I mentioned, we'll have to question everybody, so we'll have to find out where he is, won't we."

McDonald gestured toward his partner. "I need to talk to you a second."

McDonald pulled Tucker over toward the stairway and out of Lauren's view. It was frustrating not to be able to see or hear them. This whole experience was too horrible. Too unbelievable. She shouldn't be here. Her life wasn't supposed to be like this. And while she had mostly stopped blaming Eric for everything that went wrong in her day-to-day existence, she felt a sudden flash of anger toward him. What kind of person proclaimed undying love and affection for two years and then ended an engagement in a series of texts right before the wedding, anyway?

"Excuse me." Detective McDonald strode back into the room, Tucker following. "I have a few words to say to all of you." He narrowed his eyes and scrutinized the whole group of them, still looking rather dissatisfied. "We have examined the entrance, which is the only one, correct?"

"Yes," said Louisa and Wade together.

"City fire code violation?" Tucker smiled pleasantly.

"We're in the process of renovation," Louisa said. "We usually come in through the main entrance, but for the time being the passageway's blocked up."

"The elevator for this part of the building also appears to be broken," Tucker said. "Not very accessible."

"They're working on it," Louisa replied snappishly. "Is that really what you're here to investigate?"

"Yeah." Louis peered at them through his glasses. "Why don't you tell us what's going on here?"

"Yes, sir," McDonald said stolidly. "That's what we're planning to do. As I was saying, we are examining the door for signs of tampering." He glanced around at them, raising one eyebrow. "Now, who has a key to this entrance?"

"Just what are you getting at, Detective?" Louisa snapped. "You can't seriously suspect us."

"It must have been..." Wade began.

"Someone who broke in? We're checking that, Mr. Wood,"

Tucker said dismissively.

So was it was one of us, Lauren thought, or, more correctly, one of them? And she was standing here in a room with them? And with two police officers, but still.

"Why couldn't Tony have let the person in?" Louisa argued.

"We'll look into that possibility, of course, Ms. Bates," Tucker said. "Now, does anyone besides your staff here have a key to this entrance?"

Louisa, looking affronted, shook her head. "Just us, and Fred and Natasha, of course. They were new keys. We just got them yesterday, late afternoon, actually. They put in a new door and new locks because of the renovation."

"Fred and Natasha?" Tucker repeated, as McDonald left the room.

"Fred Biggs, the managing editor, and Natasha Wise, the editor," Louisa said. Lauren had met Natasha the previous summer in Prague. She was the one other person besides Amanda whom Lauren knew before taking the job at Lens. But Natasha hadn't been working at Lens yet.

Loud sobs sounded from outside the room, echoing up the bare stairwell. "I don't want to go back in there, Jim," came a plaintive voice.

"Ah." Tucker beamed. "Ms. Bartleby, I presume?" He turned in the direction of the approaching duo. A young woman, her large blue eyes wide, was clutching the arm of a young man. "And Mr. Alvarez-Chao?"

They nodded. Jim Alvarez-Chao scratched at his scruffy beard.

"Ms. Bates." Tucker turned back to Louisa. "You seem like a reasonable person. So I don't mind telling you that my partner and I would like to question each of you in turn. I'm sure you won't have any problem with that."

"Well," Louisa was saying, when McDonald returned, a grim look on his face.

"Mr. Mandel," he announced, interrupting Louisa, "was pronounced dead at the hospital."

Several gasps sounded from around the room.

"No!" Cecily started crying and collapsed into a chair. "This can't be happening. There must be some mistake." She reached for a handful of tissues from a box on her desk, as Jim put his arm around her.

"And now we'd like to speak to each one of you," McDonald continued over the sound of Cecily's sobs. "You are not to leave this building until you have spoken to me or Detective Tucker."

Lauren, trapped in a room full of murder suspects, felt a shiver run down her back.

Two

"So, Ms. Green." Detective Tucker leaned forward in his chair. "Tell me what happened this morning."

It was some hours later, afternoon, and Lauren was sitting with the detective in a small storage room located in the main part of the building, which, as Tucker had noted, was much nicer. Plush carpets, clean white walls, relatively new-looking office furniture. The Most Admired Unit's wing was temporarily off-limits, except to police; the third floor, where Tony had been lying, had been sealed off with yellow police tape, and Lauren had seen uniformed officers swarming around before she and the others were escorted out of the area.

Lauren gulped. "I came up the stairs. And I looked in the room on the second floor, and no one was there, so then I figured maybe the office was upstairs, on the third floor. So I went up there, and there he was." The image of Tony Mandel, motionless on the floor, swam through her mind, and she suddenly felt like vomiting.

"What time did you get here this morning?"

"Pretty early." Lauren fought the queasiness. What if he thought she had done it? "About eight-forty, maybe? I talked to the security guard downstairs because I didn't realize I needed to go in the other entrance. You can ask him."

Tucker nodded and made a note in his notebook. "We will be talking to him, Ms. Green, yes indeed. And why were you here at that exact time?"

Lauren took a deep breath and tried to remember what had

happened after her alarm had gone off at four that morning. It seemed a lifetime ago. "I had to get up early to drive a friend to the airport, for a six-thirty flight. And we got stuck in traffic once we got into Virginia." It had been frustrating. Andreea, her friend, was frantic about possibly missing her plane home to Romania, and had babbled away in a combination of Romanian and English. Lauren, who normally knew both of those languages, hadn't been able to cope with such a bilingual conversation at that hour of the morning.

Tucker nodded sympathetically.

"So you see, I was on my way to Dulles when all this must have happened."

"Oh?" Tucker gave her a shrewd look from his smallish brown eyes. "And what were you doing between the time you drove this person to the airport and the time you arrived here?"

"I was changing my clothes." Lauren felt almost ready to cry. She had gone back to Amanda's apartment, where she was staying, and changed out of her sweatshirt and yoga pants into the newest of her few professional-looking outfits. To her disappointment, Amanda, on whom she relied for fashion advice, was still at her brother's house, where she'd been babysitting the previous night. And then Lauren had paced around the apartment getting more and more stressed out about starting her new job, until finally she had put on her warmest winter jacket—it was surprisingly cold for early spring—and driven over to the Lens office.

Tucker was eyeing her skeptically. Why didn't he believe her? "Really, I was. I hadn't ever seen Tony Mandel before in my life. Honestly."

"Okay, Ms. Green." Tucker suddenly looked quite benevolent. "So we'll try to get in touch with this person you were driving to the airport. What was the individual's name?"

"Andreea Ionescu." Lauren took another deep breath. "She was on her way to Transylvania."

Tucker's brow furrowed and his benevolent look vanished. "To where?" He shot a sharp glance at her.

"Transylvania." It sounded perfectly normal to her, but then again, not everyone was an expert on Romanian politics like she was. "You know, Romania. She's a Romanian writer, but she's here on a fellowship." Andreea, thin, blonde, and generally swathed in floaty scarves, was one of Lauren's oldest Romanian friends.

"Ah." Tucker smiled broadly at her. "Of course. Romania." He chuckled, while Lauren squirmed in her chair, feeling ridiculous. Did he think she would make up such a story? If only Andreea had been going to Florida or New Jersey.

"Okay." Tucker wrote something in his notebook. "So you were driving Ms. Ionescu to the airport so she could fly to Transylvania. We'll check into all this, Ms. Green."

"Well, she might have missed the plane. You know, because of the traffic jam."

"You don't happen to know the flight number." Tucker's eyes narrowed again.

"No." Lauren started to panic. "I don't. But it was Lufthansa. And I know she was changing planes in Frankfurt or Munich or somewhere like that, okay?"

"Okay. Look, don't worry, Ms. Green. This is all routine. We have to find out what you all were doing this morning. Now, this is your first day at work here?"

Lauren nodded.

"So I hear you're from Boston? And why did you come down to D.C.?"

Obviously for the express purpose of killing Tony Mandel, Lauren wanted to reply, but she didn't. "I needed a change."

Was she supposed to reveal her disastrous engagement story to Detective Tucker? No. It wasn't any of his business, and it didn't have anything to do with Tony Mandel. "And I'm from here, originally, I mean, I haven't lived here for a long time now, but I grew up here. I've been living in Boston for a couple of years, teaching, and I went to college up there, too, but I've never considered that I'm from there." She realized she was blathering on incoherently.

"Uh-huh." Tucker sounded less than enthralled by Lauren's explanation. "So would you happen to have some contact information for Ms. Ionescu?"

Lauren retrieved her phone from her bag, finding it relatively quickly this time, and located Andreea's information. "I'm not sure the number will work because I don't know if that phone takes international calls. I know she was switching phones. And her mom just moved, so I'm not sure exactly what her address is. And Andreea's really bad about checking her email, and..."

The thought of Andreea's mom suddenly reminded her of her own parents, who were on an all-expenses-paid cruise around Southeast Asia for three weeks. Also political scientists, recently retired, they had been offered an opportunity to deliver daily lectures to the cruise-goers about various topics relating to the countries they would be visiting. She could only hope they were occupied with their lecture preparations and wouldn't hear about any of this and start worrying about her. Since Eric had abruptly ended the engagement, her parents had become somewhat overprotective. It had been a minor miracle that they had agreed to leave her and venture so far away.

Tucker was still scribbling in his notebook. "Anything else?"

"Not really."

A knock sounded at the door, and McDonald poked his head in. "I finished with Ms. Wise and Mr. Biggs. Anyone left over here?"

"Yeah, Mr. Alvarez-Chao, Mr. Dubois, and Ms. Bartleby."

"How's everything with you, Ms. Green?" McDonald looked gloomily in Lauren's direction.

"She's just telling me about a Transylvanian friend of hers," Tucker said.

"Oh, yeah?" McDonald's eyes brightened. "I just read a book about that part of the world. Young guy travels around on a bike."

"Mac's a big travel buff." Tucker turned towards Lauren. "Always reading one of those memoirs. Me, I watch the news. CNN, local news, whatever. So why don't you go home now, Ms. Green? Take it easy, okay? Oh, and I wouldn't take any trips right now if I were you."

Lauren nodded and departed. She got into her old Toyota Corolla, vaguely noticing a crowd of people—reporters?—surrounding the building. A couple of them saw her as she pulled out of the parking lot next to the office, and started waving at her, but she ignored them. She checked the time. Three-thirty. She should contact Andreea. Maybe Andreea would be in an airport and would be able to reply.

Once she was a few blocks away, she pulled over. "Where r u?" she texted. "Pls reply, emergency." She thought about it, and added, "Hope u r OK & made flight." She sent a similar message via email, and sighed. Andreea was probably on a plane anyway and wouldn't get any of these messages for hours.

She pushed open the door to Amanda's Dupont Circle apartment shortly thereafter. It was strange living with Amanda DeLuca again after so many years. The two had first met at the start of freshman year of college, when they were assigned, with two other roommates, to share a suite. She and Amanda had quickly bonded, especially when they both decided to join the newspaper and spent many hours hanging around the newsroom. Amanda had stuck with it, becoming managing editor, while Lauren had drifted away, preferring to spend time listening to visiting speakers at the school's international affairs center. But they had continued rooming together all through college and had remained in close contact since.

Lauren glanced around nervously, taking in much of Amanda's goat collection, which dominated the apartment. Stuffed toys, decorative plates, wall hangings, cushions. Amanda had started collecting goats at age eight, and in the intervening decades, the assemblage had multiplied. While being here surrounded by goats was certainly better than being in the office surrounded by suspects, the goats weren't offering much comfort. Amanda's apartment just didn't compare to Lauren's old apartment back in Brookline, Massachusetts, with her tall bookshelves and Romanian souvenirs.

She wondered whether Amanda even cared about goats anymore, or if it was something she had long outgrown but people didn't realize it. When Lauren was in middle school, she started a classic movie-watching club. Every Friday night, she and a group of her friends gathered at her house to watch something she had chosen. For her bat mitzvah party, her mom decorated the temple's social hall with old movie posters, Lauren's choice of decor. The club eventually disbanded when a few of the cooler kids decided they'd rather do something else on Friday nights. But Lauren's old friends still sent her cards and memorabilia related to Bette Davis, Humphrey Bogart, and other stars of the silver screen. She still loved those movies, but she'd moved on. To Romanian politics. But lately, she wondered if that, too, was fading as an interest.

Tony Mandel's face floated through her mind again, and she tried desperately to banish it. Why don't you think about your book? she told herself. But try as she might, she couldn't, although she knew that if she didn't finish it soon, her academic career would be in even worse trouble than it already was.

She sighed, sat down on Amanda's blue-and-white-striped sofa, and reflected on her situation. Single, basically homeless, and no longer working in her field. It had been early November, a month before the wedding would have been, when everything unraveled. She had thought she understood Eric Miller. After all, they had known each other for five years, since she was in graduate school at Stanford and he—an investigative reporter for The Boston Globe—was out there on a journalism fellowship. They had stayed in touch and had resumed their friendship once she moved to Boston two and a half years ago to teach. And after the friendship turned into a relationship, she had never worried about Eric's commitment to her. Clearly, she should have.

As the date for the wedding approached, Eric suggested that Lauren move into his apartment because he owned his and she was only renting. She had agreed, though she liked her apartment much better. She had already given notice to the management of her building and was standing amidst piles of packing boxes when she got a series of texts from Eric informing her that they should break things off. No relationship, no engagement, no wedding. No chance he'd change his mind. She hadn't believed it. She had tried to call him, leaving increasingly hysterical messages on his voice mail. She had emailed, texted, and even written a series of letters that she mailed to his apartment. Was there some misunderstanding? Something she had done wrong? Something she could put right somehow? But he hadn't replied, despite repeated, futile efforts on her part over the next several weeks to talk to him. She had parked herself in the lobby of his building on various occasions, but he never seemed to be home. Her friend Sonya, who lived in the same building as Eric, had managed to speak with him once, but the conversation had been unsatisfactory. He just kept saying that his decision was final.

Now, as she sat in Amanda's apartment, Lauren's phone, which she had been checking periodically, started ringing, startling her out of her reverie. It was Amanda. "Lauren? Are you okay?"

At the sound of an even mildly sympathetic voice, Lauren almost started to cry again. "I don't know. They think I did it. I found him. He was just lying there. I mean, it was so awful."

"I know. I wanted to call you earlier, but Fred said we shouldn't because the police were busy questioning people. So I thought maybe you'd be home now. You want to hear something interesting? I assume you've checked online about the latest developments? Or you have the news on?"

"No," Lauren admitted. She knew that Amanda tended to think she, Lauren, was a little spacy at times. "Dreamy and impractical" was how Amanda tended to put it. This characterization, Lauren believed, had started because Amanda's brother Adam was three years ahead of them at the same university, so Amanda felt she knew the ropes from day one, whereas Lauren didn't. Amanda was more practical than Lauren, that was true. But Lauren also knew that Amanda appreciated her, impracticality and all. And vice versa.

"Well, anyway, we're the lead story on all the local news shows. Tragedy strikes Lens magazine. The police are currently questioning all the staffers of the magazine's new Most Admired Unit."

"I knew that already."

"But there's some new stuff. Did you know about the heavy object?"

"No." What now?

"Apparently the police think Tony was hit over the head with a heavy object. And, at least so far, they've found no signs of unauthorized people going into your part of the building. No tampering, no breaking and entering. Everyone thinks Cecily did it." Amanda lowered her voice. "You know, because she threatened to kill him a couple of weeks ago. Did I tell you about that? They've been dating for months, but he cheats, I mean, cheated, on her constantly."

Lauren shivered. "Wait a minute. So one of those people in the office definitely did it? They hit Tony Mandel over the head with a heavy object?"

"It seems like it. Although it's hard to imagine."

A grainy black-and-white image of the waiflike Cecily, hoisting the as-yet-unseen heavy object into the air and hitting Tony over the head, popped into Lauren's head. It then popped out fairly quickly. "But how could she have picked up the heavy object then? She's so..."

"I don't know. I just know what I told you. And then I also happen to know that Jim has an incredible crush on Cecily. Really incredible. He follows her around all over the place."

The image in Lauren's mind of Cecily lifting the object was replaced by footage of Jim, his messy man-bun atop his head, doing the same. He raised the object and hit Tony hard on the head. Tony, a look of disbelief crossing his face, collapsed in a heap by the copier...

"I told you about the time Tony had that accident in Rock Creek Park, didn't I?" Amanda said.

"No." Lauren didn't feel like thinking about Tony anymore, although she couldn't stop. It was so, so horrible.

She wouldn't even be here if Amanda hadn't mentioned the job at Lens and encouraged Lauren to take it. Lauren's year-to-year contract at a small college in the Boston area had not been renewed.

"We love your teaching, and you've done so much for the school, but the budget crunch, you know..." the academic dean had told her last spring. They would extend her through December because they liked her so much, but that would have to be it.

Eric had come up with what, at the time, seemed the perfect solution. She would finish her book on Romanian politics and then look for a job. After all, they would be married by then, right?

Of course, in hindsight, following Eric's advice had been, like everything else in recent months, a disaster. She couldn't get her apartment back when Eric abandoned her, and had to put all her possessions in storage and stay with her childhood next-door neighbor Melanie and her boyfriend in their minuscule Cambridge apartment. Staying with Sonya was of course out of the question.

After somehow managing to finish the semester—she wasn't sure how given that she had stopped eating and sleeping and was mired in a zombie-like haze of despair—she had retreated to her parents' house in the D.C. suburbs where she spent her days unable to think about anything but Eric and what had gone wrong between them. Sure, there had been disagreements, but nothing that seemed irrevocable. She just couldn't understand it.

And then one day Amanda—who would have been the maid of honor had the wedding taken place—showed up at the house in Chevy Chase and demanded that Lauren get her life back in order. She could stay in Amanda's tiny guest room for a while. She could work at Lens—there was an opening in this new polling unit that she was sure Lauren could get. The job was far from ideal, some phone survey work, some writing, way beneath Lauren's qualifications, Amanda had said, but the Bartlebys paid decently. And now here it was, several months into 2017, and...

"Are you listening to me?" Amanda was saying now.

"Oh, sorry," Lauren said, feeling mingled annoyance and

gratitude toward Amanda.

"You know how the roads through the park are really twisty? And knowing Tony he was probably driving like ninety miles an hour. So he came in to work the next day muttering about how someone was trying to kill him, how he couldn't control his brakes. It's really ridiculous. Except"—and here Amanda took a deep, shuddering breath— "that Cecily threatened him a few days before that." She paused for a moment. "And then there's Nick. He had a reason to..."

"Why does his name sound so familiar?" Lauren interrupted. She racked her brain. Graduate school? Her work in Boston?

"I told you about him. Just like I told you about everyone else you'd be working with."

"No." It was an earlier memory. Lauren definitely remembered something about the name Nick Belotserkovsky. Something...but she couldn't recall exactly what it was.

"I've never really been able to figure him out, even though I've worked with him for years now," Amanda said. "And he's been especially moody the last year or so, since his wife left him."

"Oh," Lauren said absently. "That's too bad." Maybe this Nick Belotserkovsky person had done it. And then the detectives wouldn't suspect her anymore.

"I have to go now. But I'll be home soon. See you later." And Amanda hung up.

Lauren pictured Amanda at work, communicating with her sources, her glossy dark hair looking perfect. "Have you been using that anti-frizz cream I gave you?" Amanda, casting a critically appraising eye on Lauren's hair, had asked her a week ago, when Lauren had been moving her clothes into Amanda's spare room. Amanda had been giving Lauren those appraising looks, like a jeweler examining a gem for flaws, since college, and Lauren always had to brace herself. Generally, whatever Amanda came up with had at least a grain of truth.

Tony Mandel's face reappeared, replacing the image of Amanda, and Lauren tried to make it go away but once again failed. She needed to do something different. She should check her email and texts again.

There was, of course, nothing from Andreea, but she did see a text from Sonya. "Fascinating news on the research front!" Sonya had written in her characteristically exuberant style. "Poet muse surfaced on the East Coast!! Very excited. Cousin may be in DC, will tell him get in touch w/u if so. No sighting of Eric. Hope all is well."

Lauren deciphered the message as best she could. Sonya, who taught Russian literature at the college where Lauren had worked, was writing a book on an obscure mid-20th-century Russian poet who had met his demise as a result of a tragic love triangle. As for the cousin, Lauren was somewhat confused about whether the message referred to the poet's cousin or Sonya's own cousin. Sonya had a huge, international family, and relatives were constantly turning up for unexpected visits.

But she wasn't sure what to write back. "Murder at new office, am suspect" seemed inappropriate. So she didn't write back. She was sitting in a daze when her phone rang.

"Hello?" she quavered into the phone without looking at it. It was probably Amanda again.

"Hello, Lauren. It's Meryl."

It wasn't Amanda, it was Professor Meryl Segal. Lauren's former thesis advisor. Of all the out-of-context people, Lauren thought. Here she was, in the middle of a horrendous murder investigation, and Professor Segal was calling?

"Hi," she managed to say. An image of the professor, sitting in her book-lined office in Palo Alto, flashed into Lauren's mind. Her birdlike dark eyes peering over her reading glasses, her graying hair pulled back haphazardly around her face. She was probably splashing her overly-full mug of tea onto the piles of paper that covered her desk.

"I do hope things are going well. I wanted to call and let you know that I'll be in D.C. next week for the Association of Comparative Political Scientists conference, and perhaps we could meet at some point?"

Yes, if I haven't been murdered by then, she thought. "Yes. Great." She and the professor had always gotten along well. While Lauren had sometimes managed in recent years to call the professor "Meryl," she still thought of her as "Professor Segal." It suited her.

"Yes, yes." Professor Segal sounded delighted. "And Ethan's planning to come too."

Ethan was Lauren's grad school classmate, and the two of them had maintained a friendly competition for years. Clearly, Ethan—who had a tenure-track job at Berkeley and was already starting his second book—had pulled far ahead at this point. And he even had a long-term relationship, with a law student named Jose. She had received a save-the-date message for Ethan and Jose's wedding and had mentally filed it away amidst various other friends' good news. Weddings, new jobs, babies. After her entire life had melted down, she had a hard time processing any of these missives. She was happy for her friends, of course, but couldn't help feeling envious. And then there was the shame. That everyone knew what had happened to her. That everyone was talking about her. It was so humiliating.

"He's presenting a paper," Professor Segal continued. Lauren frowned, thinking about Ethan. The consensus in the political science department had been that Ethan was the best-looking grad student to grace its halls in years. His thick blond hair framed a finely chiseled face with deep blue eyes. The problem with Ethan was that what he said tended to annoy her. Lauren had decided long ago that the best way to treat Ethan was to pretend he was a silent movie. That way she could look at him without necessarily listening to him.

"So I know you're not presenting anything this time, but you've registered to attend, right?"

Actually, no, Lauren hadn't. This would be the first year she'd miss the conference, despite the fact that she was currently residing in the city where it would take place. She hadn't had the motivation to register, and the thought of networking with various potentially helpful people in an effort to get a new job was too much to contemplate. "Well, not really."

"I can get you in to some of the sessions. Don't worry. Oh, and have you heard about the fellowship yet?" The fellowship, which Lauren had applied for in October, was to enable her to go to Romania for a month in the summer to finish her research. It had come through. But she didn't want to go to Romania, that was the problem. She had no desire to get any work done at all.

"Yes, I got it," Lauren said distractedly, not even listening to the professor's congratulatory words.

"Now, what was it I meant to tell you about Lens magazine?" Professor Segal was saying. "Something rather strange, I believe." Lauren pictured her shaking her head. "Well, it will come to me, I'm sure. And as it happens, I think the son of an old friend of mine is also working there. We'll all have to have dinner. So how is the job coming along?"

"Oh, fine, fine." The job was great. Life was wonderful. "Look, um, I really have to..."

"Oh, yes, quite. It's almost dinnertime there already, isn't it? Well, I'll be calling you soon, then. Goodbye."

"Bye." Lauren wandered into the kitchen and pulled out some leftover slices of pizza from the refrigerator, which was decorated with charming little goat magnets.

Her phone rang again. "You want to hear the latest?" This time, it actually was Amanda. "Okay, you know the building has this new alarm system at night that records the time people come in and out? It's not totally high-tech, because we don't each have our own card, so it can't tell specifically who came in, but it's pretty good anyway."

"Isn't there a guard there at night?"

"No. Winston's there from six in the morning till about two or so, and then Antonio comes in. He stays till about ten at night, and then the alarm system automatically goes on. It's a real pain. You have to use your key to get in, right? And then to get out, here's the thing, you have to punch a code in, and then the door opens. It seems totally backwards to have a code for getting out and not for getting in, but I guess the Bartlebys must have wanted it that way. They have their own weird reasons for doing everything. So do you understand so far?"

"I think so." Lauren remembered Fred explaining it to her over the phone after she had accepted the job. Amanda had brought home Lauren's key the previous night, before heading out to her brother's to babysit for his two-year-old twins, and Lauren had used it this morning.

"So this was the side door, the one that leads to the Most Admired Unit," Amanda continued. "You know, the passageway to the main building's blocked off because of the renovation? So the police checked the records. And they found that someone came in that door at four-thirty, and then someone else came in about four-forty-five. And someone punched in the code to leave at five-fifteen or so. And that was it. Two people came in, but only one person came out."

"So that should prove to them that I didn't do it. Thank god. I mean, that's when I was driving Andreea to the airport."

"Well, of course you didn't do it. But that proves that somebody from the office did do it. If Tony had let someone from the outside into the building, then they wouldn't have been able to get out again. You have to know the code to get out. So it had to be someone from your unit or Fred or Natasha, because they were the only ones who knew the code for that door, and who had keys. Actually, I had a key for a while because I brought it home for you, so they questioned me too, but Adam and Stacy confirmed I was there all night."

"You guys didn't know the code?"

"No. Nobody ever uses that side door except the Most Admired Unit people. Plus it was a new system, remember? So that means it's either the six people in the Most Admired Unit, or Natasha. One of them killed Tony. It turns out Fred didn't do it. He has this unshakable alibi. You want to hear about it?"

"Okay." Lauren stared down at her pizza. At least someone had a good alibi.

"His son woke up in the middle of the night with a really bad stomach ache, and they were worried it was his appendix. So Fred and his wife were at the emergency room at Sibley from one a.m. to six this morning. His son's okay now, fortunately. Nobody else has much of an alibi, though, as far as I can tell."

"How do you know all this?" Lauren asked, amazed.

"It's a news organization, okay? Things get around. I probably should be back on the Hill, but I sort of felt like I should come over here to the office given everything. Oh, and you might be wondering whether a security camera caught who was coming in and out?"

Lauren hadn't, but it was a good question.

"Well, the camera at that entrance was being replaced as part of the renovation. So there isn't one there right now. Not great timing. The police must be pissed."

Lauren agreed. "Are the police still over there? I have to call and tell them about my alibi."

"Oh, yeah, they're all over here. Tucker, McDonald, and a bunch of others. So I'll see you later."

The detectives had handed out business cards to everyone, and Lauren located Detective Tucker's card.

"Yes, Ms. Green? You have something to tell me?" He sounded as if he expected her to confess on the spot.

"Yes. I heard you've narrowed down the time when it could have happened? So during that time I was driving my friend to the airport."

"Look, Ms. Green, we've had someone trying to locate Ms. Ionescu for a couple of hours now," Tucker said, a hint of weariness in his voice. "Apparently, she missed her plane at Dulles and we've been trying to trace which plane she eventually took, but the airline's having some computer problems right now."

"What? You mean you can't find Andreea?"

"We're trying, Ms. Green. But your friend could be anywhere from Munich to Transylvania at this point, and once she gets to Romania it could take a while to reach her anyway, depending on her phone situation and the Romanian police's level of cooperation. We'll do our best, but until then, keep calm and carry on." And he hung up.

Three

The alarm on her phone sounded at six-thirty the next morning, rousing Lauren from a fitful slumber. The events of the previous day came flooding back. Tony Mandel's motionless face. The paramedics. The detectives. The infuriating unavailability of Andreea, her alibi.

She dreaded returning to the office. But Amanda had informed her that the Bartlebys expected everyone to be at work at the usual time. Lauren checked her messages—nothing from Andreea—and emerged from her room to find Amanda, standing in front of the bathroom mirror, applying mascara. Being around Amanda, who was about five-two, half a foot shorter than Lauren, always made Lauren feel fashion-challenged and messy, as well as extremely tall.

"I really can't believe," Amanda said, pausing momentarily to put on her lipstick, "we'll get anything done today at work. Especially in the Most Admired Unit. But apparently the Bartlebys don't want to create the impression that anything's wrong. So you have to keep on going with the surveys."

"But that's crazy."

"Well, this magazine is crazy." Amanda frowned at herself in the mirror. "You take your unit, okay? Why don't they just hire a pollster to do these surveys? Because the Bartlebys want an in-house group to test things out first. That's fine, but the whole unit is completely disorganized. Why don't they get more up-to-date equipment for the surveys? Because the Bartlebys are scared of modern technology. Why do they put two people who hate each other in charge of the unit? Because the Bartlebys want it that way. It's ridiculous."

"The Bartlebys chose Louisa and Wade? Did they both work at Lens before the unit started?"

"Yeah. Everyone worked there before, except you. And they only added your position because they thought they weren't getting enough done. Anyway, the Bartlebys like Louisa because she has a Ph.D., even though she's kind of unpleasant. And no one can figure out why they chose Wade. He's really incompetent."

Lauren headed toward the kitchen to get some cereal, and Amanda followed her, still talking. "So are Jim and Cecily. Louis isn't incompetent, he's smart, but he can be a little obnoxious about his tech skills. And Tony, I mean..." her voice trailed off, but then picked up steam. "I don't want to say bad things about him, but he was hard to deal with. I had to work with him covering Congress, and he was always insinuating things about people. I was relieved when he went over to the Most Admired Unit. I was surprised, though, because it's sort of out of the way. Not where you'd think he'd want to be, given how ambitious he was. I think that's why he was dating Cecily. Because of her family."

"So why did he want to work in the Most Admired Unit, then?"

"My theory is that he wanted to keep an eye on Cecily. Especially once he knew Jim would be working there. And I don't know what to think about Nick. He can be so weird sometimes. I mean, he actually volunteered to work in that unit. The rest of us were basically hiding under our desks so Natasha wouldn't send us over there."

Lauren nodded, staring down at her bowl of cereal. What was it that she remembered about Nick Belotserkovsky? Something nudged at the back of her mind. College? No, Amanda hadn't mentioned any connection like that. Something to do with Eastern Europe? It was a Russian name, after all, and she knew some Russian. Professor Segal had advised her early on to broaden her expertise beyond Romania. But she couldn't remember anything about Nick Belotserkovsky that was connected to her trips back and forth to that part of the world. What could it be, then?

"So," Amanda said, retrieving an English muffin from the toaster. "Andreea should be in Romania by now, right?"

"She should be. But I still haven't heard from her. And the problem is that I don't know exactly where in Transylvania she was going. I'm sure she told me, but it was four-thirty in the morning."

"Well, the police should find her eventually. At least you have some sort of alibi. Most of them don't. Natasha says she was home alone, and so do Wade, Jim, and Cecily. Louisa says her husband would have noticed if she'd left in the middle of the night, and Louis says the same thing about his parents. And I don't know about Nick, since he was out sick."

All of a sudden Lauren remembered the significance of the name Nick Belotserkovsky. During her junior year in high school, her parents had taken sabbaticals from their teaching jobs in Washington, and the family had moved to the Boston area for the year. And Nick Belotserkovsky had been the academic superstar of the grade ahead of hers. All the teachers, before assigning a paper to her class, had read them something Nick Belotserkovsky had written the year before and told them what a wonderful student he had been. Nick Belotserkovsky had been the editor of the school paper, the valedictorian, and the star of the track team. He had volunteered for numerous organizations, winning an array of awards for good citizenship. Of course, he had gotten into about ten top colleges. The local paper had even done a feature story about him. Not that Lauren hadn't done pretty well in high school herself, but she certainly hadn't been in that league. It was all coming back now. In addition to everything else, she'd have to work with the former paragon of Brookline High School? Well, maybe it was someone else with the same name. Although that seemed unlikely.

"Remember the story about that paragon, the genius writer who was a year ahead of me when I went to high school in Brookline?" she said to Amanda. Surely she had told Amanda about it in college. It had made an impression on her teenage self. "At least, the teachers seemed to think he was a genius writer." She recounted the whole thing to refresh Amanda's memory.

"That was Nick?" Amanda looked surprised. "Wow, I never put two and two together."

"How old is he? The guy who works at Lens, I mean."

"About our age. Early thirties. And he's definitely from Boston." Amanda's lip curled slightly. "I certainly wouldn't consider Nick much of a paragon. Although I have to say, he's a good writer. He's writing a novel, did I tell you? So he just sits there looking at the rest of us with this half-smile on his face, as if he's storing up everything we say to put into his book. It's really infuriating. But maybe you're thinking of someone else. I mentioned your name to him the other day, and he didn't seem to react."

He wouldn't have, though, Lauren thought. Her name didn't exactly stand out. And she had been one of the anonymous masses, while he had been famous. But there was no point in getting into this with Amanda now. She'd have to wait till they got to the office, to see if it was the same person. Assuming Nick Belotserkovsky came in today.

By nine o'clock, Lauren and Amanda had arrived at the Lens building. The weather was much warmer today. Much more springlike. It wouldn't be this warm yet in Boston.

"Why don't I come into your part of the office with you?"

Amanda's eyes gleamed reportorially. "Just to take a look?"

Lauren nodded. She had no desire to go up the stairs, back into that office, ever again. Especially by herself.

They approached the door to the Most Admired Unit, where a security guard was standing. "We work here." Amanda flashed what looked like a Capitol Hill press pass at the guard, who motioned them inside. "God, this is creepy," Amanda whispered, their footsteps echoing on the concrete steps. "Just think, Tony walked up these very steps early yesterday morning."

Lauren shivered. "Could you please be quiet?"

"Well, I don't see why." They emerged on the second floor. Police tape blocked the way up to the third level. "Look, nobody's here." Sure enough, the office was empty.

Lauren put her bag down on the desk that had been designated amidst the chaos of the previous day as hers. Most of the furniture consisted of mismatched scuffed metal desks probably dating back to the 1970s. A row of windows lined the back of the room, the blinds still drawn. Amanda pulled the blinds open and switched the lights on. The elongated fluorescent overhead bulbs cast a harsh glare.

"This was Tony's desk." Amanda pointed at a bare desk just in front of Lauren's.

Lauren winced, another shiver running through her. The whole office had a temporary look to it. No artwork decorated the dingy walls. It felt sinister. But maybe that was because of what had happened yesterday.

"Hi, there," came a voice from the door, and Jim sauntered in, seeming quite unconcerned about anything.

Lauren gave him a curious look. "Hi."

Amanda, still focused on Tony's desk, nodded.

Jim shrugged off his long black coat. "You know, one time

when I was in college, something fell on this guy in my dorm and like totally knocked him out," he said, throwing the coat over the back of his chair. He sat down, pushed his hair out of his face, and pulled a pair of portable speakers out of his backpack, setting them on his desk and connecting them to his phone.

"Well, what happened to him?" Lauren asked.

"Oh, you know," Jim said, as a blast of loud music emanated from the speakers. He started chanting along.

No, Lauren didn't know. But obviously, nothing more was forthcoming from Jim, who seemed lost in his own musical world. What had Amanda said? That Jim had no alibi for the previous morning? She glanced over at Amanda, who was being uncharacteristically quiet.

More footsteps sounded from the doorway, and Lauren turned to see a guy about her age. He was maybe a couple of inches taller than Lauren, with light brown hair, a large slightly uneven nose, and a quizzical expression on his face. This was definitely Nick Belotserkovsky. More than a dozen years older, more filled-out, but basically the same person. How strange.

"Hi, Nick," Amanda said. "Nick, this is Lauren. So I hear you were sick yesterday?"

Lauren surveyed him. She should say something about high school.

"Yeah." He sat down at the desk next to Lauren's and leaned back in his chair. "My stomach was kind of screwed up." He switched his gaze from Amanda to Lauren. "Hi, Lauren, good to meet you." He seemed preoccupied, she noticed. As if his thoughts were a million miles away. She wondered if he was thinking about Tony.

"Thanks, you too." She pondered whether her observations of him in high school counted as "meeting" him. Probably not.

"Are you feeling better?" Amanda gave him a skeptical look.

Nick shrugged. "Not really. It's hard to feel better when someone just got murdered right here, you know?"

Lauren shivered yet again.

"Oh, he didn't," Jim said suddenly, his brown eyes opening wide.

"What?" the others said in unison.

"I mean, the guy I was talking about before. In my dorm. He didn't get murdered. It's just that this heavy brass thing fell on him. So they took him to the hospital. But he was okay. I just wanted to let you know."

"Okay," Lauren said, somewhat bemused.

Amanda shook her head, as Jim returned to contemplating his music.

Lauren turned her attention back to Nick, trying to reconcile him with his younger self, and an image appeared in her mind of a skinny kid lugging a huge fat tuba around the high school. "You used to play the tuba, didn't you?" she blurted out. She had forgotten this aspect of Nick Belotserkovsky's high school career.

"Well, I tried to." He smiled at Lauren. His smile, she noticed, actually reached his eyes, transforming his quizzical, preoccupied expression into something warmer. "But how did you know that?"

"The tuba?" Amanda shot Lauren a glance. "Interesting."

Lauren explained her brief stint in the suburban Boston public schools.

"That's pretty funny," he said. "What a coincidence."

"Hey, guys," a voice sounded from the door. It was Louis. He deposited his M.I.T. backpack by his desk and peered at his large computer screen. "I don't know about you all, but I didn't get much sleep last night. And then Louisa? She texted me at eight this morning and told me to get my butt in here and start looking over the data on Our Most Admired Foreign Leader. And shortly thereafter, Wade emailed. He told me to input the data on Our Most Admired Animal Friend."

"So which are you going to do?" Amanda asked.

"Neither," Louis said. "That's what I usually do when I get these conflicting orders. I think I'll do Our Most Admired Electronic Device." He clicked away at his keyboard. "So, I was checking the news, and they said the police were coming close to making an arrest in this case."

"Already?" Lauren asked.

"Apparently the police think it's a major high-priority case," said Louis. "You know, because of the Bartlebys."

Jim abruptly leaped from his chair and ran out of the room. "You should have called," Lauren heard him saying, and then a faint murmur in response.

"The lovely Cecily," said Louis, as Jim and Cecily entered the room.

"How are you doing, Cecily?" Amanda asked.

"Oh, all right." Cecily sat down at her desk next to Jim's, huddled in her expensive-looking black leather coat. The music was still blaring from the speakers.

"They went into all this detail," Louis said, returning to his earlier subject. "About Tony and all."

Cecily pulled her coat tighter around her.

"Oh, sorry, Cecily." Louis turned toward her. "I mean, I can shut up now."

"No, what else did they say?" she whispered.

"That the custodian cleaned the doorknob on the side door at 8 p.m. Monday night, and that when the police checked the door, there were no fingerprints on the inside of the doorknob that matched up with Tony's. Like, Tony's fingerprints were only on the outside knob. And if Tony had let someone into the building, his fingerprints would probably have been on the inside knob too."

"I heard a lot of that last night," Amanda said dismissively. "They said someone, most likely Tony, came in at 4:30, and someone else at 4:45, and someone punched in the code to leave at 5:15."

"Apparently the preliminary medical evidence, like when they think Tony was attacked, fits with those times that people came in and out," Louis said.

"Maybe Tony gave the person a duplicate key and told them the combination," Nick said.

"But that combination was so tricky," Louis said. "Like, it wasn't just a question of punching in four numbers or something. Remember when we were practicing it? You had to know how to turn the door at just the right moment, right?"

Everyone else nodded, as Lauren shuddered.

Amanda glanced at the clock on the wall. "Okay, I'm out of here. I have to get up to the Hill. See you later." And she hurried toward the stairs, leaving Lauren with her new colleagues.

Jim was staring at Cecily, who was looking down at her desk. Louis was absorbed with his computer. Nick was resting his chin on one hand, apparently deep in contemplation. Could one of these people really have killed Tony Mandel? None seemed a likely murderer, but...someone must have done it. She really should call the police and find out the latest about Andreea.

"Turn that music off at once," came a commanding voice from the stairs, and Louisa, followed by Wade, strode into the room. She was holding her clipboard, and Wade was brushing nervously at his fringe of hair. "Are you all working on your surveys?" Louisa snapped. "The only person I see working is Louis. Lauren, I'd like to see you at my desk, please."

"Okay, people," Wade said. "I know there's been a tragedy here, but that doesn't mean we shouldn't hit the ground running on this project. We do have a lot of calls to make, don't we?" He looked at Cecily, who seemed about to cry. "Now, Cecily, if you want to take it easy today, that's all right. But the rest of you, work, work, work. If you run out of survey forms, there are more by my desk." And he headed for his own desk next to Louisa's.

Lauren approached Louisa's desk. "I'd really like to call the police now, and..." Lauren began. Would Louisa get upset if she, Lauren, wasn't at her desk working on a survey?

"Of course I can't stop you from calling the police," Louisa interrupted, "but we are starting on a new project titled Our Most Admired Religious Figure."

Lauren nodded.

"Now, with this project, we will not be contacting experts, as we usually do. Instead, we will be calling typical people in the D.C. area." She pulled out a piece of paper bearing a computerized list of phone numbers, and handed it to Lauren, along with a stack of stapled survey forms. "We will be using this script. Do not deviate from it. Record all answers in the spaces provided. And high productivity levels are important, so get those surveys completed." Her eyes, a surprisingly bright green in color, bored into Lauren's.

Lauren tried to look appropriately respectful.

"And remember to read your questions distinctly, with the proper enunciation," Louisa said, tapping her pen against her clipboard.

"Of course." Lauren returned to her own desk. She glanced down at the survey form, which was five pages long, consisting of about fifty questions. How she'd be able to keep people on the phone for long enough to get through this, she couldn't even begin to imagine. She sighed. Maybe she could call the police later, if

Louisa ever left the room.

"Hello, my name is (fill in your name)," she read to herself. "I'm calling from the Most Admired Unit at Lens magazine, and we're doing a survey today on Our Most Admired Religious Figure. Could I ask you to spend a few minutes completing our survey? Let's begin with your attitude towards religion. When it comes to religion, do you find it, A, very important, B, somewhat important, C, somewhat not important, or D, very not important."

Here, Lauren paused. "Very not important?" How could she say that? She glanced up to find Nick looking at her.

"Go ahead and say it in a different way on the phone," he said helpfully. "I mean, if it sounds too ridiculous, say something that sounds more normal. I guess Louisa never got to edit this survey. Usually she catches stuff like that."

"Do they really expect us to read this?" She felt torn between totally cracking up and being totally appalled.

"This job is pretty funny sometimes," Nick said. "I'm actually trying to write a novel, and a lot of things I hear around this office kind of find their way into the manuscript." He paused, and then quickly shook his head. "How I can think about all this writing stuff when Tony was just killed is beyond me. I mean, I find that I'm thinking about Tony, and then all of a sudden I start remembering something I want to put into the novel, and then I feel guilty. You know?"

"Yeah, that's exactly how I feel," Lauren said, glad to find someone who seemed to understand. "Except I didn't even know him. And I'm not writing a novel. Not that that means anything," she added hastily.

"But you must have them," Lauren heard Louisa say from across the room. "Oh, I don't believe this."

"Well, Louisa, I didn't see them yesterday," Wade was

protesting. "I didn't see them all day yesterday. I had other things to think about."

"Yes, we all did," snapped Louisa. "Louis?"

By this point, everyone in the room was looking up except Louis, who was seemingly entranced by his computer. He was tapping away rapidly at the keyboard and smiling to himself.

"Louis!" Louisa barked. "Pay attention, please."

"What?" Louis snapped to attention. "You called?"

"Where," Louisa said, approaching Louis's desk, "is the data for that survey on Our Most Admired Senator or Congressperson?"

"Oh, yeah. I have absolutely no idea."

"Well?" Louisa looked around the room. "We seem to be missing an important set of data. It was supposed to be our first survey in the magazine, and it was scheduled to run sometime within the next couple of weeks. I can't imagine what Natasha will have to say about this."

"Maybe it just got misplaced, Louisa," Wade said placatingly. "Maybe it's in a pile somewhere in the room."

"Maybe the police misplaced it," Nick said under his breath.

"I would like each of you," Louisa declared, "to search in and around your desks. We will not proceed until we have found this data, do you hear me?" And she stalked over to her own desk and started rummaging through it.

Lauren was puzzled. Why wouldn't this data be in the computer? Were they working entirely off of sheets of paper? She leaned over toward Nick's desk. "Why..." she began.

"Yeah. Welcome to Lens. Archaic beyond belief. Even with this new unit that the Bartlebys are so excited about." He shrugged. "Part of it is that what we're doing here is sort of preliminary. To give Natasha and the Bartlebys an idea of what might work. Then the actual pollsters take over. At least, that's how they explained it to us. And the Bartlebys like to have things on paper. Eventually it all ends up in the computer, but they prefer paper. They're kind of elderly, and sometimes their eyes get tired if they spend too much time on the computer."

"Oh. Thanks." Lauren's college had been out of date in some ways, at least compared to the schools where her friends taught, so she understood. Although this seemed more so.

"No problem." And Nick paused, his dark brown eyes thoughtful. "Just let me know if you have any more questions. It's a weird place. Especially right now. I mean, having us doing these surveys this week after what's happened is completely insane. You must be wondering why on earth you decided to work here, right?"

"Well..." She didn't want to sound rude or anything.

"Come on, admit it." He gave her a half-smile. "It's okay."

"Yeah." She smiled back at him. "I wonder that all the time." She felt a flutter as she looked at him, as a dormant emotion darted through her. Attraction? Was that even possible? No, she must be imagining things. She couldn't feel attracted to anyone anymore. What was the point?

She glanced around the room. Everyone seemed to be searching for the missing data. Even Nick started looking through the papers on his desk. She had nothing much to search through, so she checked her phone. Nothing. She had tried contacting Andreea in every way she could think of, every form of social media and app. She had been avoiding social media for months, and was daunted by the number of messages, notifications, and likes that had piled up. Thousands of them. But it was too much to deal with. Too many explanations. And Andreea seemed to have vanished into the dark Transylvanian night.

Louisa was looking more and more harried, pushing wisps of hair back into their knot on her head. From across the room,

Lauren caught a glimpse of flashing diamond from Louisa's ring. Lately she noticed rings all the time, although she had been oblivious before the engagement. But Eric had been determined to buy her a beautiful engagement ring and had done copious research on the subject.

She remembered the day the two of them had gone to the jeweler's. And Eric had been upset because the one they had settled upon was in stock only in white gold, not platinum, and platinum, the shop owner had told them, would last longer. Eric, therefore, was quite insistent upon platinum. "This has to last forever," he had said, pulling Lauren in for an embrace.

As it turned out, the ring could have been made of plastic, because soon after they had picked it up, Eric had made his still-inexplicable decision to disappear from her life. And after it became painfully clear that Eric didn't want to talk to her again, she had mailed back the ring and all of his possessions that he'd left behind at her apartment, in a huge box. Despite its short tenure on her finger, there were moments when she missed the ring's presence. The only thing she had kept of Eric's was a shapeless old Red Sox t-shirt, which she liked to wear because the fabric was incredibly soft.

Lauren frowned, pulled a new book about Romania from her bag, and settled down to read. The book, a heavy hardback tome by a well-respected husband-and-wife team named Sandor and Margot Kis, was filled with tables and charts, and the writing was dense. Still, she knew she had to read it because it related to her work on Romanian political participation. So she slogged onward.

Hours and hours went by, but no data was found. "All right," Louisa announced, sighing angrily. "If anyone wants a lunch break, you can go ahead, since it's past twelve-thirty."

"Man, I'm hungry," Jim exclaimed. "You want to go, Cecily?"

"Hang on just a second," someone said. Feet thudded, and

Tucker and McDonald hovered into view. "Hello, folks," Tucker said. "Not to get alarmed, but we'd like Ms. Bartleby to come down to the station with us for a little more questioning. Of course, you can bring your lunch with you, Ms. Bartleby."

Everyone turned toward Cecily and gasped.

Four

Cecily screamed, a piercing wail. "I didn't do it, I wasn't there, I didn't do it. I have to call my lawyer. I didn't do it."

Lauren felt a surge of relief, followed quickly by skepticism. Maybe now the police would believe that she, Lauren, had nothing to do with it. But Cecily did seem an unlikely murderer.

Lauren glanced around, finding that most people's expressions mirrored her own confused feelings.

Louisa reached for her phone. "Fred should know what's going on here."

"Ms. Bates," McDonald interjected, "this is only a routine inquiry. We are not arresting anyone at this time."

Fred came rushing into the room, mopping his streaming brow with a tissue. Lauren felt a pang of sympathy for Fred, who had seemed like a really nice guy in her brief dealings with him. "Detectives, I'm afraid you're making a terrible mistake."

"Yes, really." Louisa glared at her clipboard. "The whole thing is ridiculous."

"Mr. Biggs?" Tucker smiled and nodded at Fred. "It's good to see you again. And I'm glad your son's doing better. You certainly did a good job on the news last night, yes, sir."

Fred shook his head in frustration. "Detective Tucker. Would you please explain exactly what is going on here?"

"Oh, certainly, Mr. Biggs," said Tucker, a trace of obsequiousness in his voice. "We're just making routine inquiries, and we'd like to bring Ms. Bartleby down to the station for a little more questioning. Nothing to get alarmed about."

"But I don't understand." Fred wiped his forehead again. "Why Cecily? I mean, why are you so sure it was someone in this building anyway?"

"Of course, Mr. Biggs. Certainly. We'd like to explain. Take it away, Mac." And Tucker gestured with a flourish toward his partner, who looked gloomily back at him.

"Mr. Biggs," McDonald said slowly, as if speaking to someone who couldn't possibly understand. "We are still investigating this incident. We are attempting to provide you, and the public, with the appropriate information at the appropriate time. This is a very complicated investigation, and..."

"Any more questions?" Tucker broke in. "I'll tell you people, this isn't an easy thing to do, to bring Ms. Bartleby in. Such a fine family and all."

McDonald shifted around as if embarrassed. "So let's get going. Ms. Bartleby?"

"Just one minute," Louisa snapped. "I'd like to report some missing documents. We have recently discovered that data from a very important project has disappeared. Nobody has seen this data since Monday night."

"The night before Tony was killed," Wade contributed.

"Yes?" said Tucker. "And so?"

"There may be some connection," Louisa said.

"To Mr. Mandel's death?" Tucker said, an expression of supreme patience settling upon his broad features. "Look, Ms. Bates, I understand your problem with your missing material. And if it doesn't turn up, you let us know. Maybe one of our officers misplaced it."

McDonald gestured toward Cecily. "And now, Ms. Bartleby? I'd appreciate it if you'd come along with us."

Cecily, who had remained remarkably silent, started crying again.

"She didn't do it." Jim leapt from his chair. "Why can't you leave her alone?"

"We're not accusing anyone of doing anything at the moment," Tucker said, as McDonald gently but firmly led the hysterical Cecily down the stairs and out the door. Jim raced out the door after them, with Fred following more slowly behind, and the cries gradually faded away.

"Now," Tucker said, turning the volume up on a large TV that was mounted on the wall near Louisa's desk. "I just want to see the latest. You people realize there's a whole mob of reporters outside the building, don't you?"

Lauren watched as Tucker settled into a chair. "Detective Tucker?" she asked. "Have you managed to get in touch with..."

"No." Tucker's eyes were fixed on the TV. "One minute, please, Ms. Green."

"There really are a lot of reporters out there," Louis noted. He was almost hanging out the window.

"Please." Tucker waved at Louis as if shooing away an annoying insect, and focused on the TV.

"An unexpected development in the Lens murder case this afternoon," a reporter, who was standing outside the Lens building, was saying. "As we speak, police are taking Cecily Bartleby, the twenty-three-year-old heiress to the Bartleby fortune, in to police headquarters for further questioning. Cecily Bartleby, sources tell us, was involved in a romantic relationship with the victim, Tony Mandel, a reporter for the magazine.

A few weeks ago, according to sources, Bartleby threatened to kill Mandel after she heard he had been seeing other women. We don't know if this latest development means an arrest is imminent, but we have learned that witnesses claim to have seen Bartleby and her car at the scene of the crime early yesterday morning."

Lauren started paying more attention to the TV. This was new.

"Dave," the anchor was asking the reporter. "I understand the murder weapon has been found?"

"Yes, Pete. A brass vase, hidden in a trash dumpster outside the Lens building. Sources describe it as relatively heavy, but able to be picked up by most adults. And we learned this afternoon that the vase sat on Cecily Bartleby's desk in the Lens office."

"The vase," Lauren heard Nick, who was standing next to her, whisper. "Oh, my god." She glanced at him. He had turned pale and had a stricken look on his face. "This is like being trapped in an awful nightmare," he said quietly. "I just keep thinking about what happened. And hearing the details now..." and he stopped.

She nodded. "I know." She thought again of Tony lying by the copier. "It's so horrible."

"...also learned that fingerprint evidence has so far been inconclusive," Dave was continuing. "Sources say, Pete, that the door into the Most Admired Unit office was handled by many people after the murder was discovered, and many of these people were wearing gloves because of the cold weather yesterday, smudging any fingerprints. Police sources do believe, however, that Tony Mandel's fingerprints were not on the inside of the door, Pete, indicating he did not open the door to his killer."

Tucker shut the TV off. "All right!" He slammed one fist into the other opened palm. "Way to go!" He stood up and smiled.

Lauren needed to find out about Andreea. "What about..." she began again.

"Ms. Green. We know that your friend is in the city of Cluj, in Transylvania. We've contacted the Romanian police. And in fact we managed to get through to someone in the house where she's staying. But your friend was not in the house at the time, and her cell phone does not appear to be working. We did leave an urgent message, however."

"Thanks," Lauren muttered, retreating to her chair. Nick, she noticed, was looking speculatively at her.

"So I'll be heading on out now, folks." Tucker lumbered over to the door. "If anyone has anything to tell me, please feel free to call. You all have my number." And he strode out of the office.

Five

Lauren put down her phone the next morning and sighed. It was eight-thirty, and she had been trying unsuccessfully for the past hour to reach Andreea.

"No luck?" Amanda asked, hovering in the kitchen doorway.

"No. And I'm sure all those people at the office think I did it. They don't seem to think Cecily did it. I mean, I arrive that day and find the body? And this ridiculous disappearing alibi I have? It must look really suspicious."

"Oh, I don't think so," Amanda said reassuringly. She was wearing a chic-looking flowered dress with a black jacket over it. Lauren, in contrast, was wearing a wrinkled pair of black pants and a somewhat less wrinkled blue sweater. Amanda had lent her a purple-and-blue scarf, which, when draped about Lauren's neck, made her feel like an untidily wrapped present. She had never quite mastered the art of scarf-tying. "This might sound callous, but I don't think any of them are too sad about Tony's death. Except Cecily. And I'm sure they don't think you did it. You didn't even know Tony, for god's sake. And the point isn't whether or not they think you did it, it's that one of them did it. Now let's get going."

Lauren proceeded reluctantly up the stairs to the Most Admired Unit half an hour later. She didn't want to be here. But, she had to admit, she was curious about Cecily. Were the police really about to arrest her? The door to the second-floor office was open, and she found Nick at his desk, occupied with his laptop. The rest of the space was empty.

"Hi," Lauren said, feeling uncomfortable. He probably thought she was the murderer, despite what Amanda had said. And the possible attraction sensation that had emerged the previous day had returned. But to what end? She tried to dismiss it.

"Hi, so we haven't driven you away yet. That's good." He seemed perfectly friendly. Well, maybe he didn't suspect her. Or maybe he was just being polite? "I'm working on my editing." He gestured at the laptop. "My manuscript. So how's everything going?"

Lauren frowned. "Not so well. You know, my alibi?"

"Yeah, I've heard about it. She flew off to Transylvania, right?"

She nodded. "And I can't get in touch with her."

"At least you have an alibi." Nick picked up a pen and twirled it around. "I don't. And I have a lot more of a motive than you do, I guess. You know." He looked down at his desk.

"What do you mean?"

"Oh, nothing." Nick glanced back over at her. "So I'm thinking of changing the name of one of my characters. I don't think it works too well. Chuck Hefflefinger."

What had he meant about having a lot more of a motive, Lauren wondered. She'd have to ask Amanda.

"It's too large-sounding," Nick continued, putting the pen back down on the desk. "This guy is supposed to be small and skinny."

Lauren focused on what Nick was saying. Names said a lot about people. She often wished she had a more interesting name. Lauren Jennifer Green was about as boring as you could get.

Lauren's office phone rang. "Is this Lauren Green?" a voice asked. "This is Joanna from Natasha Wise's office. She'd like to see you now." Lauren agreed and hung up.

She noticed that Nick was looking at her questioningly. "That was Joanna from Natasha's office. Natasha wants to talk to me."

"Oh, that's right, you guys know each other. Amanda mentioned something about that."

"Yeah, I met her last summer. I spent a week hanging around with her and some mutual friends in Prague." Lauren had been on a long-anticipated vacation, and Natasha had been conducting interviews for a series of articles she was writing for her former publication, Synthesis magazine in New York. Eric hadn't been able to come along to Prague, pleading an overload of work. A workaholic, he almost never took vacations, even long weekends, something Lauren had found frustrating. "Maybe she's heard something from the police. About my alibi."

"I hope so." And Nick returned to his manuscript.

Lauren headed down the stairs and over to the main entrance. Meeting Natasha again would be strange, especially because the last time she'd seen her, in Prague, they had been relative equals, and now Natasha was running this entire magazine.

But in a sense, they were equals now, too. They were both suspects. And Natasha was a suspect with no alibi, according to Amanda. But had Natasha even known Tony Mandel? From what Amanda had said, Natasha had been at Lens for only a few months, and much of that time Tony had been in the Most Admired Unit.

Lauren walked into the lobby, where the security guard reigned behind his massive teak desk, which bore a nameplate reading Winston Johnston. A white dusting of hair clung to his head, and he was looking into one of the TV monitors next to his desk.

"Hello, young lady," he said, turning and smiling as she approached. "I bet you're here to see Natasha, right?"

"Right."

"Third floor. I just can't believe them suspecting that little Cecily." And Winston shook his head sadly.

"Yeah." Lauren nodded. "It is hard to believe." She pushed

the elevator button. One of the four large chrome elevator doors opened, a bell chiming as it did so. This was pretty fancy, she thought. But at least the still-unrenovated Most Admired Unit didn't smell of new carpet.

She entered the elevator, mirrored all around, and was forced to confront her reflection. Her longish brown hair was experiencing one of its frizzier days, despite her frequent applications of Amanda's frizz-reduction cream, and her clothes looked appalling. Her students and her fellow faculty members had rarely commented on what she wore, nor had Eric, so in recent years she'd tended to ignore her wardrobe. She'd have to get Amanda to take her shopping, she thought, as the elevator door dinged open on the third floor and released her from her looking-glass prison.

Lauren stepped out, into a scene of total chaos. People were rushing around frantically.

"What's up with McCloskey, damn it?" one red-faced man was grumbling into his phone as he headed down the hallway. "He needs to file something now. The Post had the latest development up an hour ago. We can't keep being behind all the time!" He stopped, noticing Lauren. "You look lost."

"Yeah, um, where's Natasha Wise's office?"

"Down the hall to the right," the man said, returning to his phone call.

Lauren followed his directions, down a freshly painted white hallway with plush beige carpeting past various other stressed-out-looking people. Finally, she came to a corner office with a red-headed woman sitting at a desk in front of it. "I told you ten-thirty," the woman was yelling into the phone while clicking away with long, red-lacquered nails at her keyboard. "We need that information by ten-thirty at the latest." She stopped typing and banged the phone down. "Lauren?" she asked briskly, glancing up. "Go right in, Natasha's waiting for you."

Lauren entered the office, which stretched on endlessly. Natasha was perched on top of a paper-covered desk in the corner, talking to Fred. Her thick, wavy brown hair cascaded down her back, and she was wearing a black dress, cinched in with a fancy belt of some kind, and complicated-looking black shoes with incredibly high heels. Lauren was conscious once again of her own rumpled appearance. In Prague, Natasha had always attracted throngs of men, who would listen, entranced, as she expounded upon life in New York.

"Hey, Lauren!" Natasha said in her familiar smoky voice, jumping off the desk. "Fred, you know Lauren, don't you?"

The black-and-white images started running in Lauren's head again. Natasha was creeping into the room that housed the copier, vase in hand. Tony looked up, surprised, as the vase descended upon his head...and the video stopped abruptly.

"Of course." Fred gave Lauren a weary smile. "Look, Natasha, I'm going back over to the police station now, and then I'll call the Bartlebys again."

"Man." Natasha shook her head at Lauren and sat back down on the desk, as Fred headed out. "Sit down, why don't you? Things around here are like an absolute fucking disaster. So, how did you end up working here?" she continued, as Lauren sat down in a nearby chair. "I thought you were one of those perpetual academics. There was some problem, right?"

Lauren told Natasha an abbreviated version of the Eric saga. "So I decided to try something different for a while."

"Damn, that sucks. Men can be total assholes, and I'm sure you've heard a million times already that you're better off without him. I've met my share of jerks, too. But I'm still hoping to meet the right person." Natasha picked up a paper clip and started tapping it against her desk. "But it's hard right now. That's the one thing about being an editor. It takes up all my time. I can't meet anyone outside this building, you know?"

She paused, fiddling with the paper clip. She untwisted it and then bent it again, before tossing it aside. "Shit," she said, her green eyes narrowing. She picked up a roll of mints and popped one in her mouth. "Playing with paper clips sure as hell doesn't make up for quitting smoking, you know?"

"You quit?" Lauren was impressed. "Good for you." Lauren had always been allergic to smoke, and that had been one of the problems about spending time with Natasha. It was also one of the problems with being an expert on Eastern Europe, because many of the Eastern Europeans of her acquaintance smoked incessantly.

"Yeah," Natasha said ruefully, holding out the roll of mints to Lauren, who helped herself. "It's part of my new Washington persona. The Bartlebys have a no-smoking policy here, even right outside the building. So, when they interviewed me—it was on the phone, because they don't see people—they asked me if I smoked, and I said, Oh, no, of course not, as I guiltily put out my cigarette. It's probably illegal for them to even ask me that, but they're kind of a law unto themselves. And then, since I couldn't smoke anywhere around the office, I decided to try not to smoke at all. It's tough, let me tell you."

"Wait a minute. You mean you've never met the Bartlebys either?"

"That's right." Natasha nodded. "It was all done over the phone. Pretty damn weird, huh?"

"Yeah." The Bartlebys were a local legend. The three billionaire nonagenarian siblings hadn't been seen in public in decades. They lived in a mansion in Chevy Chase that was quite well-known to Lauren because she had passed it every day on her way to elementary school. She remembered peering through the hedge, trying to spot a Bartleby.

"And the way they make new employees start on Tuesdays?" Natasha said. "I mean, why Tuesdays? Why not Mondays? But no, that's the Bartleby way of doing things. Totally weird."

Lauren nodded. Fred had mentioned to her that the Bartlebys only allowed people to start working on Tuesdays. If only they had had a fixation with Wednesdays. Then she wouldn't have been the one to find...

"And then there are all these areas in the building where the cell phone reception is awful? The lobby, and some random sections of the newsroom? I've told them that's not workable for a news magazine. But I can't really do anything about the way they handle that kind of thing," Natasha continued. "Although I'm certainly trying."

"So how does it feel to be the editor of a major magazine, anyway?"

"It's a big change from Synthesis. And Washington sure as hell isn't New York. But I really like the job. I mean, dealing with the Bartlebys is a pain in the ass, and that's why most editors leave the job after about a year. I've only been here for a few months so far, but I hope I'll stay a lot longer. I think I can deal with the Bartlebys all right." She stopped and looked closely at Lauren. "Look, Lauren, I really need your help."

"You do?"

"The Bartlebys, as you can imagine, are like up shit's creek about this whole Cecily thing." Natasha started to pace around the room. "You know, the police are really hovering around her. They'll probably arrest her sooner or later. I mean, they've heard all about the fights she and Tony used to have..." Her voice trailed off for a moment, and Lauren glanced at her. "So the Bartlebys asked me to find out what really happened to Tony. Cecily apparently told them she had nothing to do with it, that she must have been framed by someone on the staff who was jealous of her, etcetera, etcetera. So basically, my job's on the line. If I don't exonerate Cecily, I'm going to be out of here. And I really like this job. So I know you're incredibly smart, and I thought maybe you could help me."

"But..." Lauren began. Why on earth would Natasha think she, Lauren, could help exonerate Cecily? After being at Lens for all of two days, she certainly didn't know the ins and outs of the magazine's office politics.

"You probably think I'm crazy." Natasha smiled sheepishly at Lauren and sat down again, this time in the chair behind her desk. "See, the thing is, they want written progress reports, and I just don't have time to deal with that." She picked up a stack of papers and flipped through them. "So that's where you could help. Find out what people thought about Tony, you know? Talk to all of them. Get to know them. Don't make it obvious what you're doing, but just pick up information. And then give it to me so I can pass it on to the Bartlebys. Okay? You know the kind of thing I mean."

Lauren, who wasn't entirely sure she did know the sort of thing Natasha meant, nodded. Maybe it wasn't a bad idea. If she found out what had happened, maybe she could clear her own name. The vanishing Andreea certainly wasn't much help in that regard.

"Let me tell you a few things, okay?" Natasha said. "Things the Bartlebys told me, that they heard from someone in the police department. Apparently that vase, you know?"

Lauren nodded again.

"It had Cecily's fingerprints all over it. And Tony's. But nobody else's. Plus, it had bloodstains that matched Tony's blood type."

Natasha shuddered. "This whole thing is just too awful. All these police officers roaming around the building. McDonald wasn't too bad, but Tucker drove me up the fucking wall. He kept asking me what it felt like to appear regularly on TV. That's the last thing I wanted to think about. My god, someone was dead, and all that asshole cared about was the goddamned TV?" Natasha's voice rose.

"Did you know Tony?"

"Oh, not really." Natasha looked down, picking up her paper clip again and starting to twist it around. "He was over in your part of the building most of the time I've been here, and I never go over there, really. That's what I told the police, too. But I mean, he's dead, you know?" And she glanced back up at Lauren.

Lauren nodded.

"Look, I'll give you till tomorrow to decide if you want to help out." Natasha put the paper clip down again. "But I'd really appreciate it if you would. I just feel sort of overwhelmed here." There was a catch in Natasha's voice. Fine lines were etched into her forehead and the large dark circles under her eyes were only partially hidden by makeup. She did look exhausted. "And I know you didn't do it. Even though you do look suspicious, to the police at least. Because you found the body and all. I'm really sorry about that, Lauren, really. So, do you have any questions?"

Lauren thought quickly. "What if Cecily did do it? I mean, people saw her here that night."

"Yeah, I guess it's possible. She did threaten to kill him at one point. But frankly, that's not what I'm supposed to find out, as far as the Bartlebys are concerned. You know, if that's what really happened, I guess that's what we'll have to report to the Bartlebys. But that's not what they want to hear. And I don't know if you've heard about the missing documents?"

"The data from that survey?"

"That's right. Louisa thinks maybe there's some mysterious connection between Tony's death and the disappearance of some of that data. It dealt with politicians, I think. So if you could find out about that, too, I'd appreciate it. Maybe it does tie in somehow."

"Could you tell me something about Tony's background?" Lauren asked, growing more and more interested in the possibility of helping Natasha. "So I have a better sense of him."

Natasha frowned. "Okay, well, from what I know, he could be a real asshole. He used to threaten people, accuse them of doing various unsavory things, you know. Fred knows a lot more it, because he's been here for longer."

"What about his family?"

"So his dad died a long time ago, and his mom remarried and lives in Florida, I think, and he has a sister and brother in Chicago. The funeral's in Florida. Immediate family only. They might have a memorial service at some later point." She paused for a moment. "He wasn't too close to any of them. The police checked them out and they weren't anywhere around here when it happened." She picked up a pen, which she started flipping around in her hand.

"What about Cecily's family? I know that she's the great-niece of the owners, but..."

"Oh." Natasha put the pen down and looked more relaxed. "It's like one of those old British novels, except they're American. The names, I mean. Her grandfather, Bertie Bartleby, was the one Bartleby who died young, back in 1970 or so. He and the two other brothers, John and Roderick, and their sister, Margaret, are the ones who founded the magazine. The family's money originally came from the oil business, but they wanted to get involved in publishing. So, anyway, Bertie had one son, Reggie, who's Cecily's father. None of the others ever got married. Cecily's parents are divorced, and she grew up with her mother and her younger brother in California."

"Does Cecily live with her aunt and uncles?"

"No, she has her own apartment in Georgetown. They wanted her to be close to the office." Natasha's phone rang, and she picked it up. "Hi, Fred. No luck? Damn. Well, call the Bartlebys again, then, okay? Yeah, bye." She put the phone down and started fiddling around with the pen again. "Damned police. Tucker and McDonald keep giving us all this shit about routine inquiries and nobody's being arrested yet, and so on, and meanwhile the Bartlebys are putting all this pressure on us to find out what the police are going to do with Cecily. So," she concluded, looking at Lauren. "I should get back to work. But let me know by tomorrow, okay?"

"Actually," Lauren said, her mind made up, "I'll do it."

"Great." Natasha let out a deep sigh. "I'll get together some things for you to look at. Just some background information, okay? You've probably noticed that a lot of things here aren't exactly up-to-date, thanks to the Bartlebys, so some of these are paper files. I wish I could just email them to you, but I can't. So you can stop by early tomorrow morning and pick the stuff up, and then you can read through it before everyone else comes in. If I'm not in yet, I'll just leave it in my top drawer in an envelope. So thanks a lot, Lauren. We'll figure this whole thing out, I know it."

As Lauren left Natasha's office, she was struck by something ironic. One of Eric's biggest stories, years ago now, before she knew him, had unfolded when he had been assigned a routine story on a long-unsolved murder case in Boston. He had plunged into it with his usual tenacity, and had uncovered enough information to make it clear who had committed the murder. The police had reopened the case, the perpetrator had eventually been put away for life, and Eric had written a well-received book about the whole thing.

The book had come out around the time she met him, the year he had been on the fellowship in California. They had first encountered each other in a class on Russian politics and had started getting together periodically for meals. At the time, Eric had been in an on-again-off-again relationship with another reporter at the Globe, and Lauren had been pining away for a Romanian grad student who didn't seem to notice her. But she and Eric had become close friends, confiding in each other about career and relationship conundrums.

He was an incredibly good listener, which undoubtedly worked to his advantage in obtaining all his journalistic scoops. Exuding his characteristic intensity, he would fixate on her, as if what she was saying was the only thing going on in the entire world, the only thing he cared about. He would pose questions that somehow made her say things she hadn't even realized she wanted to say. She had seen him do the same thing with pretty much anyone he ran across, and it was quite incredible to watch. She found their conversations extremely satisfying.

They never lost touch, and when she moved to Boston, he was the first person she wanted to talk to. So they picked up where they had left off in California, except that by then the on-again-off-again girlfriend had taken a job in London and things were permanently off, and the Romanian student had long since departed for Romania, still never having noticed Lauren, except for one night when he had had too much to drink. And gradually Lauren realized that she and Eric seemed to find excuses not to end their dinners, even after they had ordered coffee and dessert, and their friendly goodbye hugs started to linger a little longer than they ever had before.

It was on a Friday night, about six months after she had moved to Boston, when everything changed. Eric wasn't on deadline, having just handed in another major investigative exclusive, this one exposing a corrupt police officer, and seemed more relaxed than usual. They had gone out for dinner in Coolidge Corner, and had returned to her apartment to drink tea and talk some more.

She had been telling him a long, convoluted story about how she had been offered a fellowship back in California for a semester, and maybe she should take it because her job in Boston was only year-to-year, and about how she wasn't sure if she could keep up with Ethan and maybe she was disappointing Professor Segal, and he had been giving her his usual attention, when all of a sudden, a sad look had crossed his face. "Oh, Lauren, please don't go back to California," he had said. "I'll miss you too much."

And the two of them had fallen into each other's arms, and had not emerged from her apartment for the rest of the weekend. She had turned down the fellowship, opting instead to stay on at the college. Remembering all of this now, she felt even more bewildered. How could things have ended the way they did? She shook her head.

Eric undoubtedly could figure out who had killed Tony. But of course, she couldn't ask Eric for help. She'd do her own investigating. Even though the thought of interrogating everyone in her new office made her feel uncomfortable. She often felt shy around unfamiliar people.

But maybe it was good that she didn't know them. Maybe it would be harder if they were people she knew. And how difficult could it be? Three of them were more or less the age of her students, so that wasn't too intimidating. One of them was someone she had been in school with, even if their interaction had been completely one-sided. And, well, two of them were her bosses, and one of those bosses seemed quite formidable. But she could manage to talk to Louisa, right?

It couldn't be that hard. She, Lauren, just needed to blend into the office. Quickly. As if she'd been there for a while. Maybe if she were enough a part of things, but still kind of a novelty, they'd feel comfortable talking to her. It seemed to make sense.

It was only when Lauren arrived back at her desk a few minutes later that she realized the obvious: If she investigated Tony's death, and if Cecily hadn't killed him, the real murderer would be none too eager to have someone poking around. And if they'd killed one person, they probably wouldn't hesitate to murder again. Feeling comfortable talking with her new colleagues would be the least of her concerns.

Six

"Natasha asked you to help her? You? But you're not a detective. I mean, you're not even a reporter." Amanda looked stunned.

"Maybe that's why. Maybe she wanted the perspective of a confused would-be expert on Romania." It was about eight that night, and Amanda had just come home from work.

"So you're going to do it?" Amanda looked envious.

Lauren nodded.

"Can I help you?" Amanda took a container of yogurt from the refrigerator and opened it up. "I was looking at some of those police officers the other day and a couple of the guys, the ones in uniform, you know? They were kind of cute. You know, in books, when there's a murder or something, and the heroine has to solve it, and she falls in love with the detective?"

Lauren tried to picture Amanda falling in love with Detective Tucker, and snickered. "Well, here's your chance."

"All right!" Amanda high-fived Lauren. "Let's solve it! I never thought Cecily did it anyway."

"But you have to be subtle. You know? This isn't some typical news story. This is a murder investigation."

"I know, I know. I am perfectly capable of being subtle, thank you. So the first thing we'll do is interrogate them all on Saturday night."

"What's happening Saturday night?"

"I had invited people from the office to come over. Before all this happened. And maybe they'll still come. I should reextend the invitation."

"That's subtle?" Lauren asked, somewhat appalled. "Having a party right after there's been this horrible murder? I think it's really inappropriate."

"Well, I originally invited them before this. And it's all in the service of our investigation. We might be able to get more out of them here than in the office, you know?"

Lauren didn't say anything.

"I wonder if Cecily'll come," Amanda continued. "She wasn't at work today, was she?"

"No."

"So I think we need to do a systematic search on each of them. Social media, Googling, the whole nine yards. I can do that part of it. I'll fill you in if I find anything that seems relevant. Oh, and I heard some more stuff about Tony today." Amanda swallowed a spoonful of yogurt. "From Raoul, this reporter I know at the AP who went to college with him. He said a woman must have done it."

"Why?"

"He said it was just so typical that Tony was dating the owners' niece. That his girlfriends always had these connections. They'd help him get summer jobs and things. He really thinks Cecily did it. I mean, what if he's right? And if you follow his logic, then maybe Natasha and the Bartlebys are trying to pin it on some innocent person who probably had nothing to do with it."

"But Cecily just seems kind of spineless. It's hard to imagine her doing something like that."

"I agree. Maybe it's one of the other women, then. Maybe Tony was having a secret affair with one of them. Or maybe it was more of a professional thing." Amanda squinted thoughtfully into her yogurt container, scooping out the last of its contents.

Lauren reflected on this idea. Somehow, she couldn't imagine Louisa having a secret affair with anyone. And Natasha? But Natasha was the one who told her to investigate. Would she have done that if she herself were guilty? Wouldn't she just let Cecily take the blame?

Okay, so what about the professional side? All of a sudden, Lauren remembered Nick's cryptic remark about having a stronger motive to kill Tony than she had. But would Nick Belotserkovsky kill someone? It was hard to imagine. As for the others in the office, Lauren had no idea.

"Raoul said that their freshman year, Tony copied his paper and passed it off as his own," Amanda said. "He said he never quite understood Tony's motivation, because apparently Tony was a much better writer than Raoul anyway."

"That's weird." Lauren should find out what Nick had meant. "So..." she began, when Amanda's phone rang, causing Lauren to jump.

"Oh, hi," Amanda said after picking it up. "Adam's outside," she mouthed at Lauren.

Amanda's brother Adam, his wife, Stacy, and their twins lived in Silver Spring, just outside D.C., to the dismay of Amanda's parents, who kept trying to get them all to move back to New Jersey. Adam and Stacy were in a constant search to fix Amanda up with suitable men, whom Amanda generally found boring.

"He and Stacy and the kids are going back home for a wedding this weekend, so I told him to come by and pick up some stuff I want to give my parents," Amanda said, heading for the door to let Adam in. "I forgot to bring it the other day when I was babysitting."

Lauren sighed. Whenever she heard anything about weddings lately, she couldn't help wondering. She'd hear people talking about their fiancé, and their dress, and their invitations, and she'd want to warn them. She, too, had sent out wedding invitations, bought a dress, obtained a marriage license. She and Eric had met with the rabbi. They'd been enveloped in that pre-bridal cloud of congratulatory good wishes. And then Eric had waved his magic wand, and, poof! it had all gone away. But most engaged people really did end up getting married. Of course, half of them then got divorced.

"Hi, Lauren," said Adam. He and Amanda definitely looked like siblings, both being on the short side with bright blue eyes and brown hair. "So, Amanda, Stacy says to tell you there's this guy at her office she wants you to meet." They all sat down. "He's supposedly very interesting. Almost as interesting as the famous Peter O'Reilly."

Amanda frowned at him. Peter O'Reilly, Lauren knew, had been the one true love of Amanda's life. He had met her requirement of being interesting. In fact, he had been so interesting that he had gone off to Central America with the Peace Corps, after fruitlessly trying to convince Amanda to do the same. And after a couple of years, he announced that he had decided to move to Nicaragua permanently. Would she join him there? This was not something Amanda was willing to do, and the subsequent end of their long-distance relationship had been traumatic. Lauren had come down from Boston for a few days to make sure Amanda was okay. And two years later, no one else had measured up in Amanda's mind.

Adam turned his attention from his sister to Lauren. "So, what do your parents think about their beloved only child being a suspect?"

"They're away, on a cruise ship somewhere in Southeast Asia, so they haven't heard about it yet. At least, I don't think so." She hadn't heard from her parents for several days now. She assumed the communications on the ship must be faulty, because it wasn't like them to be out of touch. Especially since November.

"Well," Adam said. "I've heard some things about Tony from my friend Brad. You know, Senator Fogerty's chief of staff." Adam, who worked at a lobbying firm, had been the chief of staff for a congressman from New Jersey, and always knew a lot of Capitol Hill gossip.

"Brad's Louisa's husband," Amanda told Lauren, as they both looked expectantly at Adam.

"Right," Adam said. "You know, Tony used to work for Fogerty before he started at Lens. I never met him, but Brad told me some pretty bad stories." And Adam shook his head. "Of course, Brad's in a bad way in general at this point."

"Senator Fogerty's involved in a huge federal investigation." Amanda curled up in her chair and turned toward Lauren. "He hasn't been tied directly to it yet, but it has to do with this big transportation project that's under investigation. It's part of the story I've been working on for the past couple of weeks."

"It's really unfortunate," Adam said. "Fogerty's one of the best-respected Democrats on the Hill. He was a real prospect for at least the number-two spot on the presidential ticket down the road. And now that's probably all shot to hell."

"Wow, that's too bad." Lauren paused. Not that she didn't care about Senator Fogerty's problems or those of the Democratic Party, but she needed to steer the conversation back to Tony Mandel. "So why did Tony leave his job?"

"He was fired." Adam smirked. "At least according to Brad. Tony would always go around making insinuations about people. Going behind people's backs. You know. He probably did the same thing at Lens."

"Absolutely." Amanda's eyes narrowed.

"The thing with Tony, though," Adam continued, "is that

he bit off more than he could chew. His big mistake was to go to Fogerty with accusations about Brad. Fogerty couldn't live without Brad. I mean, he's worked for Fogerty for almost twenty years now, since Fogerty was a state representative and Brad was just out of college. So Fogerty and Brad fired Tony. But they didn't want to provoke him, so they gave him a decent recommendation. I guess that's how he got the job at Lens."

This was interesting. If Louisa's husband worked for a senator who might be caught up in a federal investigation, a senator for whom Tony Mandel also used to work, wasn't that significant? Lauren pictured Louisa, standing in the Most Admired Unit's office, all upset. "Where is that data on Our Most Admired Senator or Congressperson?" Louisa was snapping at someone. What if that data had something to do with Senator Fogerty? She told Amanda and Adam about the missing data.

"Score one for Louisa," Adam said. "Any other suspicious tales going around the office?"

Amanda nodded vigorously. "I could tell you some stories. Like the story I told you about Nick, right, Lauren?"

"What story?" Could this have to do with...

"Who's Nick?" Adam asked at the same time.

"I told you about this," Amanda said to Lauren. "I know I did. Nick's a reporter I work with, okay?" she told Adam. "And he and Tony had this whole feud going on. I think it started when the Justice Department beat opened up, and they both applied for it, and Nick got it. And Tony ended up covering the Hill with me. But he kept badmouthing Nick all the time, saying Nick had stolen his story ideas, saying he was doing all this unethical stuff, that his sources shouldn't trust him, you know. Things like that."

Lauren found this hard to believe. Except that Nick had made that cryptic comment earlier. "So what did Nick do when Tony said those things?"

"Nothing, really. He seemed to brush it off. Except finally, I guess it got to him, so about a year ago, when Tony accused him of stealing yet another story idea, Nick went to the editors and complained. It turned into a whole big internal investigation, and Nick was exonerated. But he was upset."

"I can imagine." Lauren felt somewhat indignant on his behalf. For some reason, although she hardly knew him, he seemed quite trustworthy.

"It's not like the article was so interesting anyway," Amanda said. "It was something about once-famous writers who dropped out of sight."

"Why was he writing about that if he covered the Justice Department?" Lauren asked, puzzled.

"He asked to be switched to general assignment last year. That way he could work on more of a variety of stories. Actually, he wrote something you'd be interested in, Lauren, right before he went over to the Most Admired Unit. It had to do with Eastern Europe."

Seven

It was just past seven when Lauren walked into Natasha's office the following morning. The room was bathed in shades of gray. A large envelope with Lauren's name on it was in the desk drawer. Suddenly, the phone on the desk started ringing. Lauren jumped. She picked up the envelope, hastily withdrew from the empty, darkened office, and headed back down the hall to the elevator. Everything was silent, in shocking contrast to the normal daylight activity. The elevator chimed loudly, and she got on and descended.

Winston smiled at her as she passed his desk, and Lauren smiled back. "It's warming up out there, isn't it? Nice to see someone else around here. Usually it's just Natasha and me and a few other people this early in the morning. I do the early shift, you know, so I leave at two in the afternoon. But I don't know when she ever leaves. Nice young lady like that, when does she ever have time to herself?" And he tsk-ed over his newspaper.

Natasha did seem very overworked. "I'm not sure. Maybe she doesn't?"

"Maybe not." Winston shook his head.

The Most Admired Unit office was dark, the same faint morning light coming in through the windows along the back of the room. Lauren quickly opened the blinds before sitting down with her material. At least if someone approached, she'd be able to hear them coming up the stairs. And then she could hide the papers in her desk.

The first item in the file folder she pulled from the envelope was a Post Style section article about Natasha. "Natasha Wise: Can a hot young New York writer turn Lens magazine around?" the article queried. It detailed Natasha's career as a writer at Synthesis magazine and ran through her assignments, ranging from a series about problems faced by rural American women seeking abortions to her recent articles on Prague and the Czech Republic. Both series were apparently up for major national magazine awards. Natasha, at age 32, the Style piece continued, was the youngest Lens editor-in-chief ever.

The article then described the problems Lens had faced in recent years, including the revolving-door progression of editors the Bartlebys had selected. Lauren, who had heard much of this from Amanda, skimmed quickly over the page. The magazine had been in turmoil for years, even before the downturn that had devastated the entire industry more than a decade ago. Editors came and went like so many replaceable machine parts, resulting in a confused, demoralized, and increasingly small staff. Founded in the 1950s as a weekly photo magazine, a sickly stepsister to Life and Look, Lens in subsequent years had been reincarnated as a monthly investigative journal. Several decades ago it had returned to a weekly format, attempting to compete, rather unsuccessfully, with Time, Newsweek, and U.S. News. And now the magazine seemed to be on its last legs. The Bartlebys were pumping money into it, but how long, the piece asked, could that continue? After all, they were in their nineties.

Lauren wasn't quite sure why—except for self-promotional reasons—Natasha had included the article, but it was interesting. She moved on to the next item, which proved to be Natasha's resume. Freelance writing from Europe for travel magazines, editor at a travel magazine in New York, writer for Synthesis, Lens editor. Several national magazine awards. Quite impressive.

Suddenly, a banging noise sounded from the stairway, and Lauren flinched. Was someone coming up? Maybe being alone in the office wasn't such a good idea. She stood up in alarm. But no. It was just the heat, or the air conditioning, or whatever the building's ventilation system produced in early springtime. It wasn't a person at all. She sank back into her chair, still shaking a little.

A brief queasy flutter hit her stomach. It was already Friday, and, despite major efforts, at least on her part, neither she nor the police had been able to get through to Andreea. Lauren had come to the conclusion that her old friend was a figment of her imagination. She had dreamed the entire ride to the airport.

She turned back to the file. The next resume was Tony's. He had worked at a couple of communications firms, and then had worked for Senator Charles Fogerty for three years before starting at Lens. Clipped to the back of the resume were evaluation forms, signed by Fred. He had given Tony excellent ratings in everything except cooperation. "Tony, while working hard on his own stories and displaying superior intelligence, is very hard to get along with," Fred had written in the most recent evaluation, dated about six months ago. "He causes unnecessary trouble and friction with his coworkers."

Next was Louisa's resume. She did in fact have a Ph.D., in political science, which she had obtained while working as a political reporter in Connecticut. That must have been difficult, Lauren thought. Louisa had moved to Washington five years ago to work for the Post, and then there was a year's gap in her resume before she had taken a political reporting job at Lens. Strange, Lauren reflected. Why would Louisa have taken time off at that point? She turned the resume over to find an evaluation. Fred had given Louisa excellent ratings in everything. Nothing too surprising there.

Lauren moved on. Nick's resume. She set it aside. For some reason, she felt she shouldn't look at it without his permission. But that was stupid, she told herself. He was a suspect just like everyone else. Yet somehow it seemed different.

She turned to the next resume, that of Louis. A couple of years ago, he'd won a scholarship awarded to students of color excelling in technology. He was taking a year off from M.I.T. to intern at Lens. No evaluations yet.

Cecily's resume was next. First job out of college. Again, there were no evaluations. Who would want the job of evaluating the owners' niece anyway?

She turned Cecily's life history over, to find Wade's beneath it. Eight years at Lens. Covered law, business, and the environment. Before that, nine years as a freelance writer. This was bizarre, Lauren thought. Wade's work history covered only seventeen years? He looked at least forty-five, about a decade older than Louisa. Maybe he had been in graduate school, or traveling, or something. But there was no such indication on the resume. Was he trying to seem younger by cutting some years out? She shrugged and turned to Wade's evaluations. Here, Fred had been less than enthusiastic. Wade had been given mediocre ratings each year, getting excellents only in cooperation. "Very slow to complete assignments, no original story ideas," Fred had written. So why, then, had Wade been named co-director of the Most Admired Unit?

Next came Jim's resume. At the magazine for almost a year. Before that, temped for a year. No evaluation for him either.

Well, this was not proving to be a gold mine of information. She had reached the bottom of the pile. Nick's resume still sat off to the side. Why was she hesitant to read it? She was supposed to find out what was going on around here, and he was one of the people she was investigating. So. She picked it up. Researcher for a Pulitzer Prize-winning investigative reporter. Research assistant for a best-selling book about the New York literary world in the 1960s. Master's degree in English from Georgetown University. Six years at Lens. Excellent ratings on everything. Not very suspicious. She slipped the resume into the pile with the others.

She knew Amanda was handling the social media/Googling end of things, which was fine with her. But maybe she could check on a couple of things. For one, she was curious about Louisa's husband. Brad. She Googled "brad chief of staff senator fogerty," and a stream of stories appeared. One of them was a profile that had appeared in Politico a while back. She skimmed through it. Brad Wilkins. One of the top-ranking Black staffers on the Hill. Right-hand man to up-and-coming senator who might be on the national ticket one day. Married to Washington Post reporter Louisa Bates. She read through a few more articles. Nothing very incriminating. Nothing relating to Tony.

She switched over to Facebook and typed in Brad's name, eventually locating the correct Brad Wilkins. He didn't have much on his page that was public, but there were a couple of photos of himself with Louisa, and a few with the senator. Various people had sent him birthday greetings a month ago.

She clicked on Louisa's photo, noting as her page popped up that they had three mutual friends: Amanda and a couple of people Lauren had known in grad school. Once again, there was little to see due to privacy settings. Amanda would do better, being connected on social media with everyone at Lens, most likely, and able to see more of what they'd posted. She tried Cecily, but again didn't come up with much. Same with Louis and Wade.

But Jim's Facebook page was completely public. Most of it consisted of pictures of Jim surrounded by other people, all of them holding guitars and seemingly in the process of singing. "Open mic night at the Lounge!" one of the posts said. "Can't believe I met my musical idol!!!!" another one exulted. The photo depicted Jim with a man Lauren didn't recognize. He had long blond hair and was eating an apple. Okay. This wasn't very useful.

She tried Natasha. She actually was Facebook friends with Natasha, so more photos came up. None of anyone she recognized. And some posts, mostly about Lens articles Natasha was touting. "Check out Frank McCloskey's intriguing new angle on the Russia connection," she had written last week, with a link to a piece about the latest Russia-related news. Lauren scanned through them. There weren't any relating to Most Admired Unit staffers.

She might as well check Nick's Facebook page, as long as she was on here. She typed his name in, feeling a little stalkerish. Five mutual friends, including Amanda and several people Lauren had gone to high school with in Brookline but had lost touch with outside of Facebook. The only even somewhat recent photo was from September. Hannah Belotserkovsky-Lin with Nick Belotserkovsky, it said. "Look who I dragged out of his writer's garret! Happy 31st, little bro!" It showed Nick, who was smiling, next to a woman with an identical smile, in what looked like a restaurant. Underneath the photo, he had commented, "Thanks, Hannah. Best sister ever!" She checked further back to see if there was anything else—maybe a photo of his ex-wife? But no. She'd have to sign in as Amanda at some point and see if she could find out more.

Maybe she should look for that article he'd written. The idea Tony had accused him of stealing. She checked the magazine's website. There it was.

"...really hit the ground running," she heard. Hastily, she emailed herself the link. "I don't mind telling you, Nick, that I've been a little thrown by this whole thing," Wade was saying. "But as I always say, prioritize, prioritize, prioritize." He and Nick entered the room, followed a minute later by Louisa, Jim, and Louis.

Louisa, who seemed upset, pulled Wade into the stairway, where Lauren couldn't hear them. Everyone else sat down. Jim, who had his earphones on, started singing something, and Louis became engrossed in his computer.

"What do you think they're talking about?" Nick asked Lauren, gesturing toward the stairway as he took out his laptop. "Do you think it has to do with the missing survey forms? She's probably screaming at him about whatever it is, and he's probably repeating the same thing over and over. You know?"

"Yeah." Lauren thought about the unlikeliness of Louisa and Wade's partnership. "Do they ever get along at all? I mean, can they ever cooperate on anything?"

Nick shook his head. "No, at least not that I've ever seen. It's an incredible dynamic. It's as if the Bartlebys, and our old editor Bonnie, sat there and thought, how can we make this place even more dysfunctional than it already is? Oh, yeah, let's put these two completely incompatible people in charge of this new unit. That should do it." He looked at her, a smile flickering across his face. "And then Bonnie left, so she didn't have to deal with it anyway."

Lauren nodded, finding that she was sort of smiling too. Despite having heard years' worth of Amanda's stories about Lens, she hadn't quite realized the extent of its bizarreness. Nick seemed to be taking it in stride, although maybe after all this time, it just didn't get to him that much. But why had he chosen to work in the Most Admired Unit anyway? It didn't seem like something he would want to do.

"So why did you..." she began.

She was interrupted by the return of Louisa and Wade, who were glaring at each other. "Cecily will not be coming in today," Louisa announced. "She told me she was too upset to concentrate.

But we do have to complete Our Most Admired Religious Figure as soon as possible, and we'll have to entirely redo Our Most Admired Senator." She picked up her clipboard and studied it angrily. "So I'd like everyone to work on the phones today. Wade and I will also be making calls."

Senator Fogerty. Maybe he could be Our Most Admired Senator and that somehow would help his career. And then Louisa's husband's career would also be helped. And that was why Louisa was so upset about the surveys' disappearance. Maybe. But could a survey really make that much difference in the face of possible indictment? The whole thing didn't make sense.

After two hours, Lauren put down her phone, feeling thoroughly exhausted and in need of water. Her voice, she realized, was almost gone.

She reached into her bag for her water bottle and noticed that a text had come through. "Simon here," it said. Not Andreea. Damn. "Sonya's cousin. In town doing research, she suggested I get in touch."

Well, she should reply. "Hi," she texted back. "Welcome to DC."

A reply pinged back immediately. "Visiting from South Africa via NYC. Dinner? Lunch? Will be here 1 week."

Dinner? Lunch? She wasn't sure she felt up to meeting new people. But then she had a thought. "Roommate having party Saturday night, feel free to stop by?" she texted. If he was as annoying as most of Sonya's relatives, at least he'd be diluted in the crowd.

"Yes, thx, great," he texted back. "Where?"

She sent him Amanda's address. He thanked her and said he'd see her soon.

Another text came through. Again, not Andreea. It was Sonya. "Assume Simon's been in touch?"

"Yes," Lauren texted back.

"Super-excited re new work development!!" Sonya texted enthusiastically. "Might be heading your way next week. Glimpsed Eric in lobby, he said hi, I growled at him. How r u anyway?"

Lauren wasn't sure what to respond. Was Sonya talking about the repercussions from Tony, or from Eric? Did Sonya, wrapped up in her Russian-Bostonian literary world, have any idea that Lauren was involved in a murder investigation?

"R u still thinking abt him a lot?" Sonya continued, answering Lauren's question. "U need realize wasn't ur fault. Eric scared of marriage, changing life, not self-aware enough to realize. U did nothing wrong. OK?" Sonya had said the same thing to her hundreds of times by now, but it never hurt to hear it again.

"Thx," Lauren texted back. Part of her agreed with Sonya's conclusion, but part of her still wondered. Could she have done anything differently to make things work out? Were there problems she should have noticed? And if she had failed in a relationship with a friend of five years' standing whom she had loved so much, how could she ever try again with someone new?

"And am even more sure no other woman involved," Sonya continued. "Haven't seen him w/anyone."

"OK," Lauren replied. Another woman was one thing she hadn't worried about. Eric was so wrapped up in his work that he wouldn't have had time to enmesh himself with another woman. In his case, work was the other woman.

"Will keep u posted," Sonya concluded.

"I am going to a lunch appointment." Louisa rose from her chair, clipboard in hand. "I'm terribly sorry to be leaving right now, but it can't be helped. I don't want any slacking off while I'm gone, Wade." And she shot him a nasty look, put on her coat, and left.

Lauren seized the opportunity to read Nick's controversial

article. His writing was good, she thought, with some clever turns of phrase. But overall, Amanda had been right. The piece wasn't especially noteworthy. It quoted a number of formerly famous writers, most of whom seemed to be living reclusively in Vermont. She couldn't understand why Tony would claim to have written it himself.

Eight

Lauren looked around. Louis's eyes met hers. "Do you want to go to lunch now?" she asked him. She might as well plunge in.

"Sure," he said, picking up his M.I.T. backpack. They both stood up. He was a couple of inches shorter than she was, and seemed very young and scrawny. Not a good candidate to hit Tony Mandel over the head. Or was he? Maybe there was some side to Louis she hadn't noticed.

"Man," Louis said as the two of them headed out the door. "Am I glad I don't have to work the phones most days. The computer's a lot easier. It doesn't talk back to you and tell you its baby's crying so it has to get off."

Lauren nodded. "I know what you mean." She paused. "So where should we eat?"

"Pizza?"

Lauren agreed, and they started walking down Wisconsin Avenue, the sun drifting in and out behind the clouds.

"Do you know anything about IT?" Louis asked. "How everything works and all?"

Lauren shook her head. She had no clue.

"Oh." Louis sounded disappointed. "I keep hoping someone else around here will turn out to be a techie, but so far, no luck. It's probably just as well. Sometimes knowing a lot about tech can lead to real problems."

"Why?"

"Oh, well." Louis shrugged. "See, people ask for your help, and you end up feeling totally taken advantage of."

"How?"

"Well..." Louis took a deep breath, and then a Metrobus belched to a stop next to them, expelling fumes and people before starting up again. Whatever Louis was saying was inaudible.

"What?"

"...Tony. So I just felt really stupid."

"Wait a second. I couldn't hear you."

"Right. Okay, let's try it again." Louis grinned. Lauren smiled back. He reminded her of some of her best students. He couldn't have...but yes, he could. A chill ran through her. She should listen to what he was saying.

"So, I was naive at first," Louis continued, as they entered the pizza place and sat down. "Being an intern and all. And I thought I was hot shit with my tech skills. And Tony was being really nice to me. He'd take me out for lunch, he'd introduce me to all his friends, if—and of course, there was a condition involved, it being Tony—I showed him how to do some stuff."

A waiter came by and they ordered—half veggie, for Lauren, and half pepperoni, for Louis—and he continued. "This was before the Most Admired Unit started, and my job was to help the computer-assisted reporting editor, but she's a control freak and wouldn't let me do all that much. I was pretty bored, in other words. So I had a lot of free time, and I showed Tony some things that maybe I shouldn't have. Not really illegal, but you know."

Lauren didn't know. "Like what?"

"Tech stuff." Louis shook his head. "Nothing specifically to do with the office or anything. Okay, so it was really dumb of me. But I thought Tony was my friend."

But why did he feel taken advantage of? He still hadn't said.

The pizza arrived, its warm tomatoey aroma wafting towards

Lauren. She suddenly felt exceedingly hungry, and helped herself to a large slice.

"You still haven't heard from that Transylvanian yet, have you?" Louis asked. "That must be really frustrating. Of course, I have an alibi." He bit into his pizza with a self-satisfied smile.

"Oh, really?"

"Of sorts. I mean, I live with my parents. So I told Detective Tucker that if I had stirred as much as a toe in the early morning hours, my mom would have jumped out of bed. I swear, I come in past midnight and they wake up and start asking me where I was. It's like being in high school again."

"Did the police question your parents too?"

"Oh, yeah. My dad got in this big philosophical discussion with Detective Tucker about criminal justice and Black Lives Matter. My parents are both teachers, and they're into philosophical discussions."

"Mine are similar." But Lauren didn't want to discuss her parents. She needed to get the discussion back on track. "You mentioned teaching Tony something, and feeling stupid?" She tried lifting one eyebrow, as Detective McDonald had done the other day, but succeeded only in lifting both of them, which ruined the effect.

A guarded look appeared on Louis's face. "Yeah, Tony. Right. You know, it was really strange when I was talking to the police the other day. I didn't want to admit I didn't like Tony. But mostly they just asked me where I had been that night."

"Mm-hmm," said Lauren encouragingly.

"After work that night I had dinner with some friends from college who were in town. Including this girl I kind of like." Louis sighed. "Not that I think it's reciprocated at all. They all think I'm crazy to work for a magazine. I mean, dying industry and all that.

So we had this long conversation about life in general, and I didn't get home till past twelve-thirty, and then I didn't leave again till work the next day." He looked at his empty plate. "You know, I was thinking of getting some ice cream, but I don't think I can eat any more."

Neither could Lauren. As they waited for the check, she watched as Louis shifted around in his chair, looking more and more uncomfortable. He pulled out his phone, apparently checking his messages, and put it back in his pocket. He seemed to be on the verge of saying something. She waited. Eric had mentioned on various occasions that often the best strategy with sources was to sit and wait. Eventually they would break the silence.

"What do you think of Nick?" Louis finally asked.

"Nick? Why?"

"I was just wondering. You went to high school with him, right?"

"Yeah, but it was only for one year, so I didn't really know him. I heard about him a lot, though. He was the academic superstar of the class ahead of mine."

"Oh." Louis relaxed somewhat. A contented expression spread across his face. "I was the academic superstar of my high school class too."

Lauren wasn't surprised. "But why do you want to know about Nick?"

"Okay. Here's the story. You know about that whole thing from last year with Nick and Tony? It was before my time, but I've heard all about it."

Tony accusing Nick of stealing his ideas? Lauren nodded.

Louis took a deep breath. "Well, I think Tony was about to accuse him again. Of stealing another idea."

"What? Really?" This was disturbing.

"Like, a month or so ago, we ran this piece Nick did on new trends in European literature. It focused mostly on Eastern Europe because Nick had been there recently. Last year sometime, I think. You know, he wrote this thing before the unit started, but they held it for a really long time."

Lauren nodded again. She'd have to take a look at it.

"And just last week Tony muttered something to me about 'that piece about Eastern Europe' and how he'd 'do it right this time and not fuck it up like last time.'" Louis sketched Tony's words in air quotes.

"Well, so? Why..."

"Well, then," Louis interrupted, "I was checking my email, this account I don't really use very much, and I saw this message Tony had sent me by mistake. He meant to send it to himself. It was a draft of a memo he had written last year about Nick's article. It was all about how Nick had stolen that story idea from Tony. And then right below it was another notation."

"What did it say?" Lauren leaned forward in her chair.

"Talk to N. about Eastern Europe story. This time I'll know what to do." Louis quoted solemnly.

"And it was right under the memo about Nick's first story?"

"Yeah." Louis nodded. "And he had indicated the date right next to it. A week ago. Last Friday. I just didn't know what to do. I like Nick. And I didn't like Tony. I felt bad about it, but I decided to tell the police." He sighed. "But they didn't seem too interested. I guess they're focused on Cecily."

"Wait a minute. Why would Tony send you something that he meant to send himself? And wouldn't he have noticed that he never got it?"

Louis looked embarrassed. He shifted around in his chair again. "Okay, so don't think any less of me. I have this email account

I first got seven years ago. When I was in middle school. Tmandc, that's the address. Tmandc, like Tmandel. Kind of similar, right?"

"Tmandc?"

Louis sighed. "Tech man. T-man. That's what everyone called me in middle school. I thought it was totally cool. Obviously, not so much now. That's why I hardly ever use that account."

Lauren tried not to smile. Some of her students had equally embarrassing old email addresses that they were reluctant to share with her.

"And Tony probably just thought he hadn't sent it to himself after all." Louis shook his head. "He wasn't always so great on the follow-up. That's why a lot of his schemes came to nothing."

"Did you find anything else interesting in your email?"

"No. After I found this new thing about Nick, I was sort of shaken up, you know? I didn't look at it anymore. See, I kept thinking, what if Tony went to Nick and told him about this? And what if, this time, Nick got so mad that he went into the office, followed Tony that night, say, and took that vase and, well, you know."

Lauren nodded. The same black-and-white screen reappeared in her mind, only this time it was Nick and Tony standing by the copier in the fluorescent nighttime glow, arguing. And Nick picked up the vase and...but the picture stopped there. She just couldn't imagine Nick bashing Tony over the head.

"It's hard to believe," Louis said, as they started rummaging around in their wallets to pay the bill. "But I also find it hard to believe Cecily did it. So that's why I was willing to entertain other possibilities."

"How did Nick get along with Tony in general?"

"Oh, Nick handled Tony pretty well. I never would have known about the whole thing if Cecily hadn't told me about it. Nick never acted resentful or anything. But I guess underneath he must have been pissed. At least, I would be."

"What about Wade and Louisa? Do you think they liked Tony?"

"I don't think anybody except Cecily liked Tony."

Lauren could understand why. Tony sounded like a nightmare.

"Okay," she said. "So maybe we should be getting back now."

Louis got up, as did Lauren. "Yeah," he said. "Louisa will be telling us our productivity level has hit bottom."

But by the time the two of them arrived back at the office, nobody else was there except Jim. He had his music cranked way up, and he was leaning back, his feet on his desk, drinking a Coke. "Hey, guys." He waved lazily at them.

"Your productivity level, James," Louis said loudly. "Turn that shit down immediately, do you hear me?" Louis and Jim both started laughing. Lauren smiled. "Well," Louis continued. "As long as she's not around, I'm going to run over to the other building and talk to some people over there about this conference that's coming up." And he was gone.

Lauren was alone in the office with Jim. "So," she said, seizing the opportunity. "It's good that Cecily's coming back on Monday, isn't it?"

Jim nodded dreamily. "Yeah. But she shouldn't have to go through all that questioning, you know? Like, Cecily couldn't have killed someone. No way, man."

"Who could have then?" Maybe the direct approach was best with Jim.

"Like."

"Like, what?"

"Like, do you sometimes have trouble falling asleep at night?"

"What?" Lauren said, taken aback.

"I was just talking to Nick about that. I'm having trouble

falling asleep at night."

"Since the murder, you mean?" Lauren queried, trying to turn the subject back to her investigation

"Last night. I couldn't sleep. I kept playing this music, and it didn't help at all."

Lauren wasn't surprised. Nobody could sleep through that music. Her own favorite music in recent years had been Bulgarian. But for some reason, for the past few months, she found the Bulgarian music irritating. It reminded her of her unfinished book, and of Eric. He used to download Bulgarian music for her because he knew she liked it.

He really had been nice about buying quirky gifts for her. At one point, she remembered, a toy company had put out a series of small plush bears, one for each country. Eric had found the Romanian bear, which apparently was one of the hardest to obtain, and had given it to her one day when she was feeling especially discouraged about her book. The bear was yellow, and was holding a small blue, yellow and red Romanian flag. It had made Lauren feel much better.

And the Romanian bear, which had become her book's good-luck charm, was now in storage, along with most of her other possessions. In fact, one whole storage box was filled with gifts from Eric. She wondered if she'd ever open it again, or if the memories would remain too painful.

She shouldn't be thinking of Eric. Whatever may have happened with him, she needed to finish the book. She had published a number of articles, and had co-edited a volume on Central and Southeastern European politics, but she needed more if she wanted a job that would lead toward tenure.

"...so I called Cecily," Jim was continuing. "It's funny. Like, Cecily and me, we're just really good friends. And we kept talking all night. I guess she couldn't sleep either."

"Uh-huh. So how's she doing?"

"Last night, okay? This just totally blew my mind, she's like, My uncles and aunt want me to go back to work Monday." He paused and looked at Lauren, his eyes widening. "They act as if nothing had happened, you know? She doesn't want to go out of her apartment. I said, I'll go over and make sure nobody bothers you. But she's like, no, I don't want anyone to come over right now. Not even you." He shrugged.

"Hmmm. So who do you think really did it? I mean, attacked Tony?"

"Tony?" Jim seemed startled. "I'll have to think about that one."

Lauren returned to her desk.

Nick came in a few minutes later, and Lauren looked at him curiously. Why would Tony have been about to accuse him of stealing again? Especially when the first accusation had come to nothing? Maybe there was something behind it after all.

"I was just taking a walk," he said, sitting down. "I needed some literary inspiration, and somehow or other I wasn't finding it in this room."

"Where do you usually find it? In other parts of the office?" Lauren asked, somewhat sharply. She was surprised at herself.

Apparently he was too. He glanced at her, a wary look on his face. "What do you mean? No, I usually go for a walk and then I think about things."

"Sorry. I was just in a bad mood about something."

"Okay." And he frowned and picked up his phone.

Why had she said that? Did she believe that Nick went around stealing ideas from other people in the building? Of course not. But still. Why would the issue reemerge? How confusing. She shook her head.

"Lauren?" It was Jim.

"Uh-huh?" She looked over at Jim, who was beckoning her to his desk, a conspiratorial look on his face. She approached him. "What?"

"Louisa," he whispered.

"What about Louisa?" Things had turned even worse in the past few minutes.

"You asked me who I thought had really killed Tony. So I think it was Louisa."

Nick hung up his phone and walked out of the office.

"I think it was Louisa," Jim said, louder.

"Why?" Lauren reflected that at least Jim meant it when he said he'd think about something. It was just that his time lapses were disconcerting.

"Okay. Like, Brad and Tony hate each other's guts. Hated, I mean. Brad and Tony hated each other's..."

"What? Brad who? You mean, Louisa's husband? Senator Fogerty's chief of staff?"

"Brad." Jim nodded, as if there were no other Brads in the world. "Right. Tony went to the senator and told him Brad was trying to sabotage him. Totally sabotage him. And the senator didn't believe it because Brad was just, like, really loyal. So Tony got fired."

It was the same story she'd heard from Adam the night before. But how did Jim know it? "Did Tony tell you this?"

"Huh?"

"How do you know this?"

Jim shrugged. "It was hard to miss. I would overhear Brad talking to someone on the phone about it, his wife. And then there was an office party and it turned out his wife was Louisa. Like, she didn't work here yet."

Lauren was thoroughly confused. "Wait a minute. I know where she worked then. What I want to know is, where did you work?" She tried to recall details from his resume, but they eluded her.

Louisa and Wade reappeared. "Where is everyone?" Louisa surveyed the room. "I have an important announcement to make."

"Where did you work?" Lauren hissed at Jim.

"Work?" he said, as if it were a foreign term.

I can't deal with this, Lauren thought, as Nick and Louis filed back in. She went back to her own desk and sat down.

"All right." Louisa tapped her pen against her clipboard. "Wade and I"—she gestured at her co-director, who opened his mouth as if to speak—"have just been in conference with Natasha. She says that next week all the information for Our Most Admired Senator or Congressperson and Our Most Admired Religious Figure must be ready, because it's going to the pollster."

"She knows about the missing data," Wade contributed. "But..."

Louisa glared at him. "I told her that Louis had started organizing the data, and so it wasn't a total loss. That some of it was in the computer. Right, Louis?" And she swiveled around to face Louis, who looked smaller than ever between her and his computer monitor.

"Well," he said. "Um."

"Well, what? I most distinctly asked you to start inputting that data last Thursday. Over a week ago. And you told me you were doing it. Correct?"

"Um," Louis said again.

"Uh, Louisa," Wade said. "I asked Louie last week to start on Our Most Admired Holiday Meal. So maybe he was doing that instead. Right, Louie?"

"Well. Um."

"Can't you say anything more than that?" Louisa said. "What were you doing last week?"

Louis mumbled something.

"What?" both Wade and Louisa inquired.

"...football player," Louis said, a little louder.

"Damn," Louisa said. "The football survey isn't supposed to run for months. Now we have double the amount of work. And this is a very important survey."

"So," Louis began. "You tell me to do one thing. Wade tells me to do another thing. So I don't know what to do, right? So I go ahead and do something else. If the two of you could ever get your..."

"I don't believe this," Louisa said. "Listen to me, Louis, I'd like a complete accounting of exactly what you've been doing for the past month. Come over to my desk, right now!" And she marched deskward, a chastened Louis following behind.

"Well," Wade said to his remaining audience of Lauren, Jim, and Nick. "I guess we should get going. Prioritize, prioritize, prioritize..." his voice faded away as he crossed the room.

Lauren looked at Jim, who was staring open-mouthed across the room towards Louisa and Louis, who were arguing, and then she glanced over at Nick, who seemed lost in thought. She wondered what he was thinking about, and picked up her phone with a sigh.

"Senator Fogerty's office," Jim said loudly, causing both Lauren and Nick to turn around and focus on him. "I mean, that's where I was working then, Lauren, okay?"

"Oh." Had that been part of his resume? "So what did you..."

"Please, people," Wade said from across the room. "Keep the non-survey-related conversations down, all right?"

"I'll tell you later," Jim said, picking up his phone.

Too many surveys could drive a person to distraction, Lauren realized a couple of hours later. Was she, A, very tired of this, B, somewhat tired of this, C, ready to quit, D...

"No," Jim was saying into his phone. "Like, I never thought about religion that way. I tend to think that maybe there's some form of deity up there somewhere, but I don't really tend to...yeah, like, that's cool."

At least someone was getting something out of these phone calls. Lauren had hoped to talk to some interesting people, but those who had been willing to do the survey—a small fraction—had spent their time complaining about how long it took.

"Wade," she heard Louisa say. "We have a meeting with the art department people in five minutes. Put your phone down and let's go. And Louis, I want you to come along. It might be good for you to see how the data will be presented. And the rest of you, keep working. We'll be back in half an hour." And, almost dragging Wade and Louis behind her, Louisa stalked out and down the stairway.

Lauren looked over again at Nick, who was now apparently editing his manuscript. He was typing away and seemed very absorbed in what he was doing. Why had she said what she did? Maybe she had been assuming he was perfect. Not only because of his annoying, distant, high-school past, but also because—despite that high-school past—she thought he was a decent person. And she often tended to ascribe qualities of perfection to people she instinctively liked. And when she had heard all these stories about the problem between him and Tony, she had overreacted. Was that it?

She wasn't sure.

To be honest, there was probably more to it than that. There was something about him that stirred up those emotions she had been experiencing, emotions she had thought were gone forever. He was thoughtful, and intelligent—well, that she had already known—and seemed to understand when things were funny or bizarre. And he had turned out, all these years later, to be surprisingly good-looking. But he was a suspect, so...that made the whole thing kind of weird, didn't it?

"Pretty cool lady." Jim had finally disengaged himself from the phone. "She thinks about religion all the time, she says. You really can get into some interesting conversations." He plugged his speakers into his phone and some music that Lauren didn't recognize blared forth. "So, Lauren, you ever think about converting? I mean, sometimes I sit there and think, like, why stick to one religion? I might as well be something totally different. I might as well be, like, Baha'i or something, you know?"

"Mmm." Lauren had never thought about being anything other than Jewish. She went over to his desk. "So. What were you doing in Senator Fogerty's office?"

"I was an intern. Like, helping out, you know? It was a blast. Lots of parties and stuff."

"So you knew Tony from there?"

"Sure," Jim said, beating time to the music. His ancient metal desk was wobbling back and forth drunkenly.

Lauren pondered this latest piece of information. Maybe Tony had antagonized Jim back then, and Jim had taken a few years to think about it, and all of a sudden something made him remember his dislike of Tony, and he had abruptly picked up the vase... "What did you think of him?" Lauren asked, trying to keep the conversation going.

"Huh? Who?"

"Tony," Lauren said louder, over the sounds of the music.

"What did you think of Tony."

"He was okay."

"Did he do anything you didn't especially like?"

"I'll think about that. Like, overall, I'd have to say that internship was okay. It wasn't that different working there from a lot of my other internships. I was an intern at an environmental group one summer, and that was pretty cool."

"Okay, you let me know." She returned to her desk.

Nick didn't seem to be typing anymore. He looked so sad. What had come over her? She never should have said that to him. He glanced over at her.

"I'm really sorry," she started to say.

"Look," he said at the same time.

They both stopped. She felt embarrassed.

"Go ahead," he said.

"All right." Lauren took a deep breath. "I'm really sorry about what I said. I didn't mean that I thought you stole anything from Tony. Or from anyone else. Honestly. I never say things like that normally."

"Yeah. Okay. I figured that's what you were talking about. And it didn't sound like something you would say. I mean, not that I really know what you would say. I mean, this is sounding really stupid, you know?" He smiled. She really did like his smile. It was genuine, lighting up his entire face.

Lauren smiled back, feeling a lot better. "Um, do you want to have dinner or something? We could talk about it."

"When? You mean tonight?"

"Oh, whenever." She waved her hand in the air in what she hoped was a casual manner. Of course, he wouldn't be able to have dinner tonight. It was Friday night. The start of the weekend. He was probably busy. And so what if he were? It didn't matter. He was just another one of her suspects, anyway.

"I think I can tonight," he said. "But it would have to be an early evening because I have to revise three pages of my novel tonight. I have this schedule, three pages every night. I either have to stick to this really rigid schedule, or I feel as if I won't end up doing anything at all. Even if I'm turning out total garbage, at least it's three pages. Anyway, sorry. You probably don't want to hear about this." He looked more nervous than she felt, Lauren thought.

Which made her feel more in control. "Okay, so whenever we get out of here, then we'll figure out where to go," she said, sounding almost authoritative.

"Great." And he returned to his editing.

He did seem very dedicated to his fiction-writing, Lauren thought, reflecting on the idea of really rigid schedules. Eric had been obsessive about his daily routines. Every day, even when snow or ice clogged the sidewalks, he ran seven miles along the Charles. It helped him think about the story he was working on, he explained. And every morning he ate a piece of toast and a banana, and many nights he ate at this late-night diner in the Square. Unless he was eating at his desk in the office, or eating in his car on the way to talk to a source or stake out someone's home or workplace. His car had been disgusting, filled with old food wrappers and empty water bottles and crumpled napkins. She had always insisted that they take her car when they were driving somewhere.

She sighed. In her alternate reality, she would have been married to Eric for several months already. They would be living in his apartment. She would be finished with her book. It was surreal to think about how quickly things could change. Here she was, back to wondering what the object of her no-doubt-unrequited attraction thought of her, a phase of life she had thought was mercifully over. Her signal-reading antenna, never that strong to begin with, had been knocked completely out of commission in November. And even before November, she'd been terrible at figuring out such things, leading to missed and crossed signals. Amanda had always ascribed this antenna problem to a disturbing lack of self-confidence on Lauren's part. As usual, she was probably correct.

But did the ability to read those signals really matter? Probably no one would ever like her in that way again. Why should they? And if anyone ever did, and really got to know her, he'd probably dump her. Just like Eric had. Because clearly there was something wrong with her. So there was no point to any of it. No point in making herself vulnerable again.

She started sinking into what, since November, had become a repeating, self-pitying mental litany. She was a reject. A freak. The jilted bride left at the altar. Well, not literally, but close enough. She knew from all her classic-movie-watching that it wasn't the dumper who was the figure of mockery. It was the dumpee. And layered over the humiliation and accompanying anger was the sadness. The emptiness. The times when she'd think of something she'd like to tell Eric, and then remember that she couldn't anymore.

Lauren's phone rang, breaking into her dispiriting thoughts, and she answered it. "Ms. Green?" a deep voice queried. "Detective McDonald. We've just located Ms. Ionescu, and she confirms that you were, in fact, driving her to the airport between four-thirty and six-thirty Monday morning."

Nine

"You did?" Lauren shrieked. "Oh, that's amazing. That's wonderful." She felt her emotions zooming upward again, as she noticed Nick and Jim staring at her.

"We thought you'd be pleased." McDonald's voice betrayed no sign of pleasure. "You know, Ms. Green, Romania's a crazy country. I've been reading up on it. So have a relaxing weekend." And he hung up.

Lauren put the phone down, relief sweeping over her.

"What happened?" Nick asked.

"My alibi. She appeared at last."

"Hey, cool," Jim called over the sound of his music. "Good job."

"Yeah, congratulations," Louis added.

"That's great," Nick said, nodding. "The Transylvanian alibi resurfaces. It sounds like an old horror movie, doesn't it? Except in this case it's a force for good."

She smiled at that, and then she heard voices on the stairway.

"Well?" Louisa looked around. "Have any of you been working? And Jim, turn that music off. I don't know how many times I have to tell you. Now, Cecily will be coming back to work Monday, and I'm sure I don't have to remind you to treat her well. She's under a lot of stress."

"Sure." Jim nodded in agreement. "No question about it. So Lauren's alibi came through. Did you hear?"

"Oh." Louisa frowned in Lauren's direction. "Good."

Wade nodded and rubbed his head.

"It's almost six," Louis said. "Can we leave now?"

"Very well," Louisa snapped. "You're obviously not getting anything done."

"Remember, people, bright and early Monday morning, hit the ground running," Wade said, his pale eyes shifting around the room. "Lots of work to do."

Louis was out of the building within about ten seconds, followed more slowly by Jim. Wade and Louisa returned to their desks.

"So," said Nick. "Where would you like to go?"

Lauren pondered for a minute. "Where do you live?"

"Oh, do you want to come over for dinner? Yeah, we could do that."

"No." She felt completely mortified. God, could she be any more awkward? "I just meant, to be convenient for you to get back so you could finish your writing."

"Oh. In Bethesda. But we could eat around here, that's okay."

"Why don't we just go to Georgetown then." They left the building and started down Wisconsin Avenue, passing clumps of people waiting for buses, heading into shops and restaurants, hurrying homeward with briefcases and backpacks.

"You must feel really relieved," Nick said. "About your alibi. I wish I had an alibi."

Lauren tried not to feel sorry for him. Maybe he was the one who had done it. Maybe he really had stolen Tony's idea. No, he hadn't.

"So you probably want to know about this whole thing with Tony, right?" he asked, as if reading her mind.

"We don't have to talk about it right now. I mean, we could wait till we get to the restaurant."

"Why don't we just get it over with. Then maybe we can talk

about something slightly more enjoyable." He gave her a half-smile.

"Okay." Lauren was curious, after all.

"Well, so I suggested this piece on forgotten writers. The editors are pretty good about running offbeat cultural stories—as long as I did whatever else they wanted, of course. It was last year, right after I switched off the Justice Department beat to more general assignment stuff. I had been trying to do that for a while. Switch, I mean."

Lauren nodded. Wasn't the Justice Department a more prestigious beat? Why would he have...

"I wanted more time for my writing," Nick said, again seeming to know what she was thinking. "And I was going through some difficult personal stuff, too, you've probably heard about that."

His wife leaving him? "Yeah. I'm sorry."

"It's probably for the best. She, well, anyway, I mean, I guess you've gone through something similar yourself, Amanda said, so..." he trailed off.

"Well, we never even got as far as getting married." That terrible day in November suddenly flooded her brain. She had been weeping as she left messages on Eric's phone, one after another, hoping that somehow he would answer this time. That he would reassure her and tell her she had misunderstood and he couldn't imagine his life without her. That he'd turn up at her apartment and say he hadn't meant what he'd texted her, and then repeat over and over again that she was the most wonderful thing that had ever happened to him. Which was something he had said, quite often.

And as he kept not answering, she had wondered if this was all just a bad dream and she would wake up with Eric wrapped around her the way he tended to sleep, as if he would never let her go, and things would return to how they had been. "What could have happened that's serious enough to end this?" she had sobbed into his voice mail. "This can't be happening. Not if we love each other as much as we do." And he had loved her, she knew it. So what had happened? She found tears welling up in her eyes right now, thinking about it. She should get the subject back to Tony. "Um," she began quaveringly.

"Right, I was supposed to tell you about Tony. Not about Alissa. My ex, that is." Nick cleared his throat. "So anyway, Tony had been badmouthing me to everyone at the magazine, plus a bunch of my sources, trying to imply that I wasn't trustworthy, that I stole his story ideas, all kinds of things that weren't true."

Lauren nodded, trying to get her voice under control. "Why did he do that?"

Nick shrugged. "I'm not sure. He liked to cause trouble. And I got the Justice Department beat, and he really wanted it, so I guess that's how I got on his radar. I tried to ignore it, but one day it got to be too much. This was after I had switched off the Justice beat anyway, so you'd think he would have stopped, but he didn't. And I got the sense that maybe some people were starting to believe him." He paused.

They were approaching M Street, and, it being Friday night, the sidewalks were jammed with pedestrians, mostly talking on their phones.

"We could go to this Afghan place on M Street," Nick said. "If you like Afghan food, that is."

"Okay." Lauren found that she was feeling a little better. She really liked Afghan food. It came in second to Chinese on her international food list. "Keep going."

"So the editor at that point was Bonnie Atlas. She's at CBS now, covering the White House. She only lasted about six months here before she quit. I don't think she could deal with the Bartlebys. So I went to her and complained about everything Tony had been saying. I probably should have done that a lot sooner. Not let it get that far."

They had arrived at the light at Wisconsin and M. "So what happened then?" Would he mention the second allegation?

"I'm just trying to remember which direction the restaurant is. I think it's to the left." And they started down M Street. "Anyway, it turned into this big internal investigation, with everyone involved. Bonnie, and Fred, and even the Bartlebys. Not that they actually came out of their house or anything. But Bonnie and Fred would keep them informed about every little detail. It was awful, you know?" He looked over at her.

Lauren nodded sympathetically, feeling a sudden urge to... something. She didn't know exactly what. Something involving some sort of physical contact. A physical connection. He was really attractive. But, as she had reminded herself before, he was a suspect. And she had no wish to become vulnerable again. She had to pull herself together.

"Here it is." He stopped in front of the restaurant. "Look, I'm sorry to go on about this. I try not to talk about it that much." They entered the restaurant, which was not too crowded, and sat down. A waiter appeared with menus, and Lauren and Nick discussed Afghan food until the waiter returned to take their order.

"The police asked me about the whole thing from last year the other day." Nick said once the waiter had departed, returning to the topic of Tony. "When Tony...you know. And I said I had this stomach problem that night and I wouldn't have been able to come in."

"So what's wrong with your stomach?" Lauren asked, as their food arrived. It smelled delicious. Spicy dumplings topped with yogurt. Shish kebab. Could someone with a stomach problem really eat this?

"It all started when I was traveling in Central America a few years ago, on vacation. We went to a few different countries, and I got this parasite and since then I've had these periodic problems with my stomach. It usually goes away again in a day or so."

"I'm sorry. That sounds difficult."

He nodded. "But let's not talk about that. It's not very interesting."

"Okay. So have you ever been to Romania? Or anywhere else in that part of the world?" Would he mention his recent article? "You know, that's what I work on."

"Right. I haven't been to Romania, but I've been to some other Eastern European countries. I was trying to track down the town, or village, or shtetl, or whatever it was where my family originally came from. Apparently our last name comes from the name of this village. But I wasn't sure if I found the right place."

Lauren was intrigued. "Where was it?"

"In what's now Ukraine. You know, everyone always assumes my family came over here recently, because a hundred years ago, names like Belotserkovsky tended to get shortened. To make them sound more American."

Lauren nodded. She assumed her last name had been shortened from something, but her father was never exactly sure from what. There were differing family stories.

"Well, actually they came through Ellis Island before World War I, and someone shortened it to Bell. But my dad, this was in the seventies when people started looking into their roots? He decided to change it back. So there you have it."

"Wow, that's really interesting." She should try to figure out more about her family's history. Especially given that they had come from the same general part of the world where she spent a lot of time. "So when did you go on this trip?"

"Last year. A few months after Alissa left."

Lauren wondered why Alissa had left. Amanda would probably know.

"I had a few weeks of vacation time stored up, so I traveled around," Nick was saying. "You know, I wrote an article pretty recently about European literature, especially Eastern European, since I had just been there."

"I know." Would he say anything about Tony? She looked closely at him, to see if he was betraying any signs of a bad conscience. He had a far-away look on his face and was paying no attention to his food. "Who did you talk to?" She helped herself to some more dumplings. "For the story, I mean."

"Oh." Nick focused on her again. "Actually, some people here in Washington. Karel Halama, Andreea Ionescu..."

"Andreea? She was my alibi."

Nick smiled. "Oh, really? I didn't realize that. I liked her. Karel Halama, though, well...." He stopped. "Sorry, I mean, maybe he's one of your best friends or something."

"No." Karel Halama was a grumpy Czech literary figure who had been a young dissident during the later years of the Cold War and then became part of the government's inner circle after the fall of communism. These days, he seemed to commute between Washington and Prague. She had met him a few times last year in Prague, as had Natasha. She remembered Natasha complaining about how hard he had been to interview; his English wasn't too good but he insisted on using it.

She asked if Nick had had the same experience.

"Yeah. But what he said was fascinating."

"I'll have to take a look at your article."

"Oh, it's no big deal." Nick absent-mindedly took some more food, which he then proceeded to ignore. "Not compared to what you're doing. I'd really like to go back some time. To Eastern Europe. But it was hard not knowing the languages, even though so many people spoke English. I always study the wrong languages."

"What do you mean?"

"I really like taking beginning languages. It's sort of my hobby. But it doesn't correspond to what I do. Say I decide to go to Eastern Europe. Do I take beginning Russian or beginning Czech or something? No, I take beginning Chinese. I mean, that's the way it tends to work out. I went to all these countries last year, and then I came back and signed up for beginning Italian when I hadn't been anywhere near Italy. It makes no sense. Plus I always end up missing half the classes because of work."

"What if you get beyond the beginning stage?" Lauren was something of an expert at taking language classes, but they usually corresponded at least vaguely to the places she was visiting or studying.

"I never seem to. I get the catalog and instead of signing up for Beginning Chinese II, I see something like Beginning Dutch I, you know? And then I sign up for that instead. The thing is, beginning language classes are just really funny. You get these amazingly disjointed conversations. I think if I ever try to write another novel, it'll be about a guy who teaches a beginning language."

"What's your novel about, anyway?"

"It's about all these people here in D.C. who are trying to figure out what to do with their lives. Sort of early mid-career crises. And one of the characters is from Prague. He's starting to take over the book, which is too bad because I've never been to Prague and I don't know any Czech. The main character was supposed to be this other guy who's trying to be a trumpet player. Not that I've ever played the trumpet either. Just the tuba, and that was too uncool to write about."

"I used to play the flute."

"Were you in band the year you lived in Brookline? You'd think I would have remembered you." He gave her a look that was hard to figure out. She shook her head. It hadn't fit with her schedule that year. "I'm curious, how did you get so interested in Romania, anyway?"

Lauren told him. It had all started with her AP European History teacher, Mrs. Codrescu, a native of Romania who focused more than the curriculum required on her home country. Lauren had become fascinated by the idea of a Romance-language-speaking country sandwiched among Slavic-speaking lands. Her interest had only increased over the years.

"But you also know about Prague, right?"

Lauren did. In addition to her vacation the previous summer, she had spent several months there on a fellowship during grad school, and had learned some Czech. They started talking about various places in Central and Southeastern Europe, and about high school, and about Lens, and about politics, and eventually Lauren noticed that it was past ten o'clock. "Oh, no. Your three pages."

Nick shrugged. "That's okay. It's been a while since I've had such an interesting conversation. I'll just revise six pages tomorrow then." He paused, and looked at her, his expression turning more serious. "So, Lauren, I, um." He stopped again. "Maybe I shouldn't say this, but I sort of wanted to tell you. Your, you know, Eric? I mean, he's a hell of a reporter, I read the Globe pretty much every day, but that was a really awful thing he did to you. I can't even imagine how he, well, you're just so..." He looked down at his plate and then back at her, shaking his head. "It's hard to understand people sometimes."

She nodded, a mixture of feelings swirling through her. That was nice of him to say. But how did he know that Eric was her ex-fiancé? How many details of the broken engagement fiasco had Amanda told him? She felt exposed.

And she still had to find out about the second incident. Had Tony confronted Nick with his new allegations? Maybe she should wait and find out some other time. She didn't feel like thinking about Tony right now. But that's very unprofessional of you, her conscience said.

The restaurant was almost empty, and their waiter was hovering nearby, having left the check on the table a couple of hours earlier. "I think he probably wants us to leave now," Nick said quietly. "Even though I'd be fine staying here and talking for a while more. But I guess he needs to clean things up and get home or something." He reached for the check. "I'll get this."

"Oh, that's all right." After all, she had invited him to dinner. "You don't have to..."

"No, I know that, but I want to." He sent her one of his amazing smiles. The idea of physical contact floated into her head again, stronger than ever. She was picturing all kinds of things she probably shouldn't be. He really was so good-looking. "Okay?"

She tried to stop thinking about any sort of physical contact. No good could come of such thoughts anyway. She took a deep breath and smiled back at him. "Okay. Thanks." She definitely didn't want to ask him anything about Tony at this point, but she felt she must. "Did Tony ever do this again?" she asked, as they were leaving the restaurant. "Accuse you of stealing story ideas from him, I mean?"

"Oh, no." He sounded shocked. "After that whole investigation, we got along pretty well."

Ten

It was after eleven when Lauren returned home, and there was no sign of Amanda. Lauren, feeling nervous, put all the lights on and was huddled on the living room sofa draped in a blanket embroidered with goats, when she heard Amanda coming in. "Lauren! Guess what happened."

Lauren sighed with relief. "What?"

"Well." Amanda fell onto the sofa and pulled her shoes off. "I was at work till just now."

"Why? Did it have to do with Tony?"

"No, it's the Fogerty story. At about six o'clock, we found out Fogerty was about to be indicted. So Natasha decided to make that the cover story for the weekly, since Fogerty's such a political superstar. The editors are still at the office, but they finally sent the rest of us home because there wasn't anything more we could do. I am so exhausted. And I went on a couple of radio shows to talk about it. I kind of like doing radio. Better than TV, anyway."

Lauren was impressed. "Congrats. But that's really late, to change the cover. I mean, tonight's the deadline for this issue, isn't it?"

"Yeah, it's almost unprecedented. The Bartlebys aren't really into last-minute changes, even if it's major breaking news that everyone else has. But Natasha talked them into it—she decided it was do-able because we already had a four-pager ready to go. So it was just a question of making up the actual cover, which the art department did, and updating the story with today's news. But it was still a hell of a lot of work. So how was your evening?"

"Interesting. I went to an Afghan restaurant in Georgetown with Nick."

"Well, how did it go?" Amanda asked, a skeptical look in her eye.

"It went well."

"So let's hear it," Amanda said, reviving somewhat. "Oh, and it got so busy today that I didn't have much time to Google everyone and check their social media. But I did do some of that in the morning, and I didn't really find anything all that helpful." She padded into the kitchen, Lauren following her. Amanda took a box of Girl Scout cookies from a cabinet and they each had a few while Lauren filled Amanda in on the day's events.

"Okay, so what have we learned today?" Amanda said, once Lauren had finished. "First, that Jim may have known Tony before. Second, that Louisa knew Tony before, which we already knew. Third," she continued, biting into another cookie, "that Louis disliked Tony. Fourth, that Louisa's all upset about the loss of that senator data, and I can imagine why. With today's news about Fogerty, that is. I'm sure anything to do with Fogerty would upset her. Fifth, that Nick denies Tony asked him about this second suspicious article. And sixth, that you're not a suspect anymore. Congratulations, by the way. So am I leaving anything out?"

"Not that I can think of. But Nick didn't deny anything. I never specifically asked him about the second allegation. He just said Tony hadn't made any more accusations."

"I don't know. I mean, there you go, off on a dinner date with a murder suspect, and you just sit there and believe him?"

Dinner date? Had the dinner actually been a date? That was an overwhelming concept. And Nick didn't seem like a murder suspect. Even though she knew he was.

"What else would he tell you?" Amanda was continuing. "You're just so gullible sometimes, Lauren."

"I am not." But was she? She wasn't sure. "So why did Nick's wife leave him, anyway?"

Amanda shook her head. "I don't know all the details, but I think she just got frustrated with him. She's a lawyer at one of those top firms, and from what I heard, she assumed his career would keep pace with hers and it didn't. So finally she walked out."

"Had they been married a long time?" Lauren felt even more sorry for Nick.

Amanda nodded. "About five years. And they'd been together for years before that. I think they met freshman year of college. Of course, it's too bad. But he must be really hard to live with."

"So how much did you tell him about me and Eric? He seemed to know all about it."

"Just that you had been through this whole awful thing. Maybe I said your ex was Eric, I can't remember. Should I not have?"

"I don't know." Somehow, having Nick know that Eric was the one who had dumped her made the whole thing even more humiliating. They were in the same field, after all. And Eric was well-known in the world of journalism. Well-respected. And had Amanda mentioned that Eric had ended things via a series of text messages? Lauren sighed.

"I'm going to sleep now." Amanda headed down the hallway. "I don't think it's a problem. If Nick wanted to find out who you were engaged to, he could, regardless of what I said or didn't say. I mean, he's a reporter, right?"

"Wait." Lauren intercepted Amanda before she reached her room. "Do you think this really was, like, a date? I mean, tonight?"

Amanda stopped. "Hmm. I wasn't thinking specifically when I described it as a dinner date. But maybe it was!"

Lauren wasn't sure what to think. What if it was? Would that be a good thing?

"I need some more info. How did this dinner come about?"

"I invited him. Because of the investigation."

"And who ended up paying?"

"He did."

"What happened at the end?"

Lauren thought back. "We walked up the hill to the office. And then we were in the parking lot, and we were standing near my car."

"And?"

They had stood there for a moment, sort of looking at each other. And then Nick had given her a quick hug and said he would see her soon, and she had said thanks for dinner. And then she had gotten into her car and driven back home. "So what do you think?"

"Ambiguous. I'm not sure. But please be careful, Lauren. You know he's a suspect. Please don't be gullible." And Amanda went off to bed, yawning hugely.

Lauren headed back to the living room sofa and the goat blanket. Was she gullible? Had she been gullible with Eric? She hadn't had that many long-term relationships before Eric, so it was hard to make comparisons. Her previous serious boyfriends had been Romanian, and the romances had ended when they returned to Romania or she returned home.

What she really wanted to do was find out more about Nick and Alissa. But was that actually germane to her investigation? Didn't her curiosity come from a somewhat different motive? She considered this for a minute, and concluded that since Nick was a suspect, anything relating to him must therefore be relevant.

So she typed "nick belotserkovsky alissa," not being exactly sure how to spell Alissa. Was it with an I, or maybe a Y? Alyssa?

And also not knowing what her last name was. Had she changed it?

What popped up, to her fascination, was a New York Times wedding announcement from six years earlier. With a photo. The two of them looked like one entity. Which, of course would be expected, if they'd been together since freshman year of college. And they both looked very young. Nick, in fact, looked closer to his high-school self than to his current incarnation, although his smile was the same. Alissa had long, straight, dark brown hair and dark eyes, and although she was smiling in the photo, she somehow came across as extremely serious. She was attractive, in an intense kind of way.

"Alissa Jordan Wachtel and Nicholas Evan Belotserkovsky were married Saturday night at the home of the bride's parents, Marilyn Goodman and Theodore Wachtel, in Winnetka, Illinois," Lauren read. "Rabbi Richard Weinberg officiated. The bride and groom, both 25, met as freshmen during their first week of classes at Yale University, from which they both graduated magna cum laude. The bride, also a graduate of Georgetown Law School, is an associate at the law firm of Casper, Moulton, and Slotsky, in Washington, D.C. She will be keeping her name. Her mother is a psychologist and her father teaches at Northwestern University's law school. The groom is completing a master's degree in English at Georgetown University and is about to start working at Lens magazine in Washington as a reporter. He is the son of Anita and Michael Belotserkovsky of Brookline, Massachusetts. His mother is a real estate agent and his father is a partner with the law firm of Hogarth, Wilson, and Belotserkovsky in Boston."

Lauren read through this announcement several times, before turning back to the photo. What could possibly have gone wrong here? They seemed so well-suited. But then, people must have thought the same thing about her and Eric. It was hard to figure anything out. About engagements, about marriages, about investigations. She shut off the laptop, got into bed, and reflected on all of this, perplexed, until she finally fell asleep.

The next day was spent preparing for Amanda's party, about which Lauren still had her doubts. She wasn't sure anyone would show up, although Amanda had assured her they would. So she helped Amanda clean the apartment and bake vast quantities of desserts and buy even vaster quantities of beverages.

After Amanda had picked out her own outfit—a striped maxi-dress with thin spaghetti straps, and high-heeled sandals—she started going through Lauren's clothes, muttering about how she really would need to take Lauren shopping. "Didn't you ever go to any parties in Boston?" she asked, before finally settling on a sleeveless, flowered dress that Lauren had never worn, thinking it was too low-cut and not very flattering. "This will look good on you," Amanda pronounced. "Let me help you with your makeup, okay?" Lauren agreed. She needed all the help she could get.

Finally, it was eight p.m. and the two of them sat, completely drained of energy, on the sofa awaiting their guests. Trays of cookies, brownies, and lemon squares filled Amanda's dinner table, along with bowls of fruit salad, various types of potato chips, and an assortment of drinks.

And then Lauren watched as people kept pouring in. She had never seen most of them before. Could they all be from the office? Finally, Lauren caught sight of Jim, clad in a lurid tie-dyed t-shirt and ripped jeans.

He was waving his hands—one of which was holding a plastic cup and the other a cookie—around rhythmically in the air and singing something. "Hi, Lauren," he shouted. "I was just, like, demonstrating my voice for Lisa. From the art department." He pointed his plastic cup at a woman about Lauren's age, with long straight blond hair and pale blue eyes, standing next to him. She was wearing a short black leather skirt, a tight-fitting black sleeveless top with a deep V-neck, black tights, and high-heeled black boots. Small tattoos of dragons or serpents of some sort adorned her shoulders. She was really tall and skinny, although somehow curvaceous at the same time. She looked like a model. Or maybe an updated version of a Norse goddess.

"Hi," Lauren said.

Lisa took a sip from her beer bottle and nodded coolly at her.

"Did you see Wade yet?" Jim asked Lauren. "He's getting some food, I think."

"Maybe I'll go talk to him," Lauren said. "I'll see you later." She had yet to question Wade. Actually, she was surprised he had shown up. Neither he nor Louisa—nor anyone else from the office—had said a word to her about Amanda's party.

Wade was pouring himself some wine. "Hi, there, Lauren," he said in a jovial tone, nodding in her direction. "Pretty nice spread here, pretty nice spread." He glanced around shiftily. "So, Lauren. Is Cecily coming?"

"I don't know," Lauren yelled, over the noise of the assembled guests. She should ask Wade his opinion of Cecily. "Do you really think Cecily did it?" She leaned towards him. Nobody was paying any attention to them, fortunately.

"Cecily? Hard to believe, isn't it?" He sipped at his wine and gave her a conspiratorial glance, brushing his free hand across his head. "Another unlikely suspect is Louie."

"Louis? Why?"

"I don't mean Louie did it," Wade shouted. "But Tony did steal his invention. And when something like that happens, a person can get kind of angry. And of course there's Louisa. Her husband

and Tony were enemies from way back. But of course we all know Louie wouldn't kill someone. As for Louisa, well," and he grimaced.

"What invention? What are you talking about?"

But Wade had already moved away, out of earshot. Lauren would have to ask Louis about this mysterious invention. That must be what he had referred to at lunch. About being taken advantage of. She looked around the crowded room but couldn't find him. She also didn't see Nick. Maybe he wasn't going to show up. He hadn't mentioned anything the previous night about the party.

"Well, hello, Lauren." It was Louisa, accompanied by a fit-looking man. "Lauren, this is my husband, Brad." The sharp tone that Louisa used in the office was gone, as was the pulled-back hair. Instead, her hair was down and she was wearing a dress similar to Amanda's. She looked a lot younger. And a lot more relaxed. Maybe Amanda was right about this party.

"Hi, there." Brad extended a friendly hand. "I've heard a lot about all you folks in the unit, but I've never had the pleasure of meeting any of you before, except Jim over there. We go way back." He grinned, laugh lines extending from the corners of his eyes. "You know, I really needed to escape from the office for a while tonight. And so did Louisa, right, Lou?"

"You're not kidding." Louisa smiled back at him. "This was a bad week for everyone, I think."

Was this really Louisa? Lauren was fascinated.

Jim came over, still holding his plastic cup. "Hey, Brad. Tough luck about the senator."

"Yeah." Brad clapped Jim on the shoulder. "So how are you, kiddo? Still into music?"

"Oh, absolutely."

Lauren murmured an excuse and went to search for Louis. She

really had to find out about this invention.

"Did you meet Brad?" Amanda hissed into her ear as Lauren passed by. "He's really nice."

"I know. It's interesting." Now, where was Louis? And where was Nick? She looked around the room and caught sight of Natasha, in a chic-looking black and white outfit, surrounded by a group of men. She was laughing, her long hair thrown back. Lauren approached her.

"Hi, Lauren. This is really a great party," Natasha shouted to her. "I've just been telling everyone about the piece I did on Lady Gaga for Synthesis last year."

The circle of men nodded eagerly, their eyes fixated on Natasha. It reminded Lauren of Prague. But she wanted to get Natasha away from her admirers and tell her about the investigation. "Could I talk to you for a minute?"

"Oh, sure." Natasha took a step toward Lauren. "What is it?"

"I just wanted to tell you about some of the things I found out."

"Well, maybe this isn't the best time. I can't really hear you too well. But have you found some stuff that'll help us get Cecily off the hook?"

"Yes. At least I think so."

"Good. We'll talk about it at work then. So is Cecily coming tonight?"

"I don't know." Lauren felt somewhat impatient. She wasn't Cecily's secretary, after all.

"Okay." And Natasha returned to her acolytes.

"Lauren." It was Jim, shouting into her ear. "I've thought about why I didn't like Tony, okay? You want to hear why?"

Jim's unerring timing once again astounded her. "Okay, let's hear it."

"Seeing Brad again reminded me. See, I was working with Tony on this project, and he took all the credit for it. And then I was working with Tony on another project, and he took all the credit for that one too. He, like, told people I was just a spacy kid and I wasn't capable of doing anything. And I was totally pissed off. So then he starts doing the same thing at Lens. I mean, I was really freaked when I started working here. I walk in my first day, and there's Tony. And he started talking about me that way to everyone here too."

Lauren nodded.

"Plus then I noticed how he was treating Cecily like a total object. And I really care about Cecily. So, I just couldn't deal with it anymore. I saw him that night, and I really yelled at him. I said, stop treating Cecily like an object, okay?"

"Wait. When was this?"

"That night. You know I told you I've been having trouble sleeping. So I went over to the office just to walk around. I live kind of nearby, you know."

"The night Tony was killed? You were in the building?"

"Huh?" Apparently, five minutes of coherence was all Jim could manage.

"Oh, forget it. Let me know if you think about it some more, okay?"

"Sure thing. I'll go get some more Sprite."

She was left with even more questions than before. Had Jim been in the office that night? Maybe he had seen what had happened. Maybe he had actually killed Tony himself? This was all too much. She looked around, and, finally spotting Louis, headed towards him. Like the others, he was not in office attire. Instead, he was wearing an M.I.T. sweatshirt and jeans.

"Oh, hey, Lauren," he said. "Lots of people here, huh."

"Yeah. Look, Louis, I have to ask you about something."

"What? Anything important?"

"Well, it's about an invention." She realized she was holding a cookie that she hadn't even started eating. She took a bite of it.

A brief look of surprise passed over Louis's face. "Invention? Yeah, well. Um. Look, I have to get something to eat now. I'll talk to you later, Lauren, okay? Oh, is Cecily coming, do you know?"

She shook her head, and Louis rushed off in the direction of the food.

Amanda hurried over to her. "You didn't tell me about Simon. He's great."

"I didn't tell you about who?" Lauren was baffled. "What are you talking about?"

"Your friend from New York. Simon."

"Oh, right." Lauren remembered the texts from Sonya's cousin. She had completely forgotten about him. "Is he here?"

"Yeah. Right over there."

Lauren looked where Amanda was pointing, at a guy about Lauren's own height. He was wearing black-framed glasses, and his wavy brown hair had a few streaks of gray running through it, as did his beard. She felt a shock run through her. For a moment she thought it was Eric. She looked more closely. No, it was only a very superficial resemblance.

"What's wrong?" Amanda asked.

"Nothing."

Simon, who was talking to Louisa and Brad, was smiling. He looked quite pleased with himself. He really didn't look anything like Eric at all. Eric had an intense, stressed-out air about him.

Amanda had slipped away, and Wade took her place. "I was thinking maybe Monday we could have lunch," he said. "I usually try to have lunch with new employees to find out what they think about the magazine."

Lauren looked up at him. She needed to find out more about his career. "How long have you worked at Lens anyway?"

"Oh, for years. It's a great place, really. And the Most Admired Unit is a true stroke of genius, a true stroke of genius."

"Mmm," said Lauren noncommittally. "And what did you do before that?"

"Freelancing." Wade gobbled up a lemon square. "For a long time. But I'll tell you all about that at lunch. Excuse me." And he vanished into the crowd.

Well, Monday was certainly time enough to question him. Maybe she should meet Simon. She went over towards him and Louisa and Brad.

"Hey, there, Lauren," Brad said heartily. "You know Simon?"

"You're Lauren, then?" Simon asked. "Well, it's a pleasure to meet you at last. Sonya speaks very highly of you indeed. She's told me all sorts of wonderful things about you." He raised his beer bottle. "Cheers."

"It's nice to meet you too," Lauren said politely. Was Sonya trying to fix her up with her cousin? Over the last couple of months, various friends had mentioned guys they thought she should meet. But she had always put them off, saying it was still too soon.

"So where exactly do you work?" Louisa asked Simon. "You were just about to tell us."

"I teach economics back in South Africa, but I'm in New York now on a fellowship. I just arrived last month. A pleasant place to be, I think. So." He turned back to Lauren. "We've been talking about that poor guy Tony. Quite a shame, really."

"Did you know him too?" It wouldn't surprise her. The way things were going, Simon would probably inform her that Tony had spent some time in South Africa or New York and had ruined an important project dear to Simon's heart.

"I don't think so." Simon's forehead wrinkled. "Of course, I do know quite a number of people, so it's possible, but I don't think so, no."

Out of the corner of her eye, Lauren caught sight of Nick, talking to Lisa from the art department. He hadn't even come over to say hello? Why not? How long had he been here, anyway? The two of them seemed to be having an animated discussion. Or rather, she was, and he seemed to be listening intently and nodding. Then he bestowed one of his incredible smiles on her, and she put her hand on his arm and said something to him and they both started laughing. They seemed so...connected. Lauren felt something shrivel up inside her. The hope that maybe...that maybe...well, there was no point in ever getting her hopes up about anything, was there? She had let down her post-November guard, just a little. It had been a mistake. She sighed.

"...not very popular," Louisa was telling Simon. "He tended to antagonize people."

"And did you two like this Tony?" Simon inquired.

"Well," Brad said, frowning, "let's say Tony and I were on each other's shit lists."

"Tony was not my favorite person," Louisa contributed. "But he wasn't anyone's favorite person. In fact, I think he was truly evil."

"Oh, I don't know about that," Brad said. "He wasn't evil. He was just extremely hard to take." A phone started ringing. "Damn." Brad reached into his pocket. "I'm being summoned." Lauren watched as he retreated toward the kitchen, where she couldn't hear what he was saying. She wished she could follow him but figured it would be too obvious.

"...investigation," Louisa was saying. She must be telling Simon about the problems at Brad's office. "Plus this horrible business with Tony. It's all too awful."

Brad reemerged from the kitchen. "Trouble at the office. It's your former employers." He turned to Louisa. "The Post. They have a story they're about to post on their website with some new allegations. Banner headline tomorrow morning, front-page treatment." He shook his head. "I have to leave."

And he and Louisa said their farewells and headed off.

"Well. And what about this Cecily?" Simon's brown eyes gleamed behind his glasses. "I assume she's coming tonight? I understand she'll be back at the office on Monday. And speaking of Monday, what are you doing then?"

"Maybe we could do something after work Monday. You could come by and meet some of the people from the office, if you wanted." He did seem quite interested in them.

"That would be awfully good. I'll be in touch. And now I must go and talk to that young chap from M.I.T. The tech guy, you know? We were having a fascinating talk about comparative race relations."

"Okay." Lauren watched him go in search of Louis.

Natasha tapped Lauren on the shoulder. "Wonderful party, Lauren. I have to go, though. The Bartlebys will probably call me tonight, so I'd better be prepared." And she pushed through the crowd towards the door.

"Hi, Lauren." It was Nick, finally detached from Lisa from the art department.

"Hi." Lauren could tell she sounded sort of annoyed. It was probably not good to sound that way, but she couldn't help it. She also couldn't help eyeing him more closely. And she realized to her dismay that despite her annoyance and her decision to draw her guard back in, she wanted nothing more than to keep staring at him. He was wearing jeans and a faded green polo shirt that looked really good on him, and she hadn't seen him in non-work clothes before. Well, not since high school. But he hadn't struck her as exceptionally attractive back then, and now he had matured into someone who was. And, unlike some good-looking guys, he seemed to have no clue that he was attractive at all. She wondered why.

"Sorry, I meant to find you and say hello to you first, but then I ran into Lisa. You know, we started at Lens the same day, like six years ago now, so we've always shared a kind of bond."

What kind of bond? Lauren asked herself.

"I wasn't really planning to come over here," Nick continued. "To Amanda's, I mean, your apartment. Because I thought it was sort of inappropriate to have a party when Tony's dead."

Lauren nodded. She agreed with him.

"But, well, I'm glad I did. I'm glad I came over here, I mean." He gave her a look that, like the one the previous night, she couldn't really figure out. Maybe something was wrong with her dress? Had she spilled something on it? And it probably was too low-cut after all. She felt a little self-conscious. "I was just wondering, is Cecily coming?"

"Please don't ask me that! Everyone keeps asking me that, and I just don't know!"

"Okay, I rescind the question." A hint of a smile crossed his face.

"Thanks. Did you get your six pages done?"

"Yes, actually. That's why I was late getting over here. And then I was talking to Lisa about the last-minute cover they did for this week's magazine." He launched into a description of what Lisa and her colleagues had managed to accomplish, while Lauren grew increasingly resentful. Nick, despite his attractiveness, wasn't very interesting anyway, she thought spitefully. Maybe he had copied Tony's story ideas after all.

A hush suddenly settled over the crowd, and only Simon's voice was audible. "Yes, the fellowship is in New York, but I'm here doing research," he was saying. "And...what? Oh." And his voice, too, fell silent.

Cecily had just walked into the room.

Eleven

Cecily looked around, her eyes larger than ever. "Jim? I really need to talk to you."

Jim ran over to her. "What's wrong, Cecily? Just let me know, and I'll do whatever I can."

"I was standing there leaning over the balcony," Cecily whispered, a tear running down her cheek. "Just leaning. And for a second I almost... I mean, then I stopped, and I realized I would never really do that, but I just need to talk to you. I think..." and her voice faded away.

Jim put his arm around her and led her toward the kitchen. After a few minutes, they still hadn't emerged, and people started flocking out the door, offering vague words of thanks. And soon almost nobody was left, except for Amanda, Lauren, Wade, Nick, and Simon, who were all in the living room. And Jim and Cecily, in the kitchen. Everything was very quiet.

"I thought I'd stay, to see what was wrong," Wade murmured. "After all, these people are my employees."

Lauren considered what Cecily had indicated. That she had almost jumped off the balcony. And she remembered a day in late December, one of the darkest days of the year, a season when her depression flared up. She had just moved back to her parents' house from Boston and it was dusk and snow was covering the ground outside. She was lying on the cold bathroom floor in the near-dark, crying and crying until her head ached, and at one point she had looked up at her prescription tranquilizers on the bathroom counter and thought that no one would miss her if she took them all. But, like Cecily, something had stopped her from following through.

"Well," Simon said loudly. "Now, that was Cecily Bottomley who just came in, I presume?"

"Bartleby," Lauren muttered.

"Bottomley, yes."

What were they talking about in there anyway? Lauren's curiosity and worry were mounting.

Nobody was saying anything, except Simon, who had started discussing his research. "...I've been involved in an interdisciplinary task force that's studying your campaign finance system. Of course, I'm looking at it from an economic standpoint. Quite fascinating, really, yes. Did you know that..."

Lauren found that she couldn't focus on what he was saying. Could Cecily be confessing something to Jim? Or the other way around?

"Excuse me." She stood up. Amanda followed her toward the kitchen. Lauren tapped gently on the closed kitchen door. "Um, is everything okay?"

"Oh, yeah." Jim pushed the door open. "Cecily was just a little tired." Cecily was propped against the kitchen counter, like a fragile antique doll. "She, like, needed to talk."

"Jim, I think I should go home now," Cecily said. "But I'm too tired to drive. Could you drive me?"

"Absolutely. Can you make it over to the door?"

"I think so." Cecily turned and stared limpidly at Lauren and Amanda. "I'm really sorry." She seemed about to cry. "I'm under so much pressure now, and then there's my family, and I really needed to talk to Jim. The balcony thing, I mean, sometimes I get a little morbid. Since Tony, you know."

"I understand," Lauren said. She thought of a couple of her students who had expressed similar thoughts to her, and how she had referred them to the college's counseling services. She had made frequent use of the counseling services herself after Eric had left. "So, have you talked to anyone about these feelings? Besides us, I mean? Like, a therapist or something?"

Cecily nodded.

"You probably should make another appointment as soon as you can," Amanda said, frowning, as they returned to the living room. Lauren noticed that Simon had a look of curiosity on his face, Wade seemed fretful, and Nick appeared worried.

"Yes," Cecily said. "I will. Tomorrow."

"Absolutely," Jim said. "We're on it. Therapy appointment. Bye, everyone, like, see you Monday." And the two of them left, Jim half-propelling Cecily out the door.

"Well," Amanda said once the door had closed behind them. "Really."

"Such devotion." Wade shook his head. "I think if she asked him to kill someone, he'd do it in a minute." Lauren looked sharply at him, but he was getting up in preparation to leave. "Goodbye, there, Amanda and Lauren. Thanks." And he departed.

"How dramatic," Simon said. "When I first got to America, I thought you people were really quite stolid. Not too imaginative. But I've decided I was wrong."

"Of course you're wrong," Amanda said. "We always have a lot of drama going on, at least at the magazine. I mean, not like the really awful things from the past week, but just more normal drama." The two of them started discussing the situation at Lens. Lauren suddenly found herself unable to concentrate, much less participate in the discussion. There was too much information crowding into her head. She felt utterly overwhelmed.

Nick stood up and stretched. He hadn't said a word in about half an hour, Lauren noted through her haze. "Do you need any help with anything?" he asked her. "Cleaning up, or something?"

"Thanks, but that's okay." She tried to focus. She figured Amanda would want to be in charge of cleaning up, and wasn't sure she'd welcome additional help. Especially from a suspect. Although the thought of the amount of cleaning up that would need to be done was daunting.

"Well, then, I probably should leave now." He thanked Amanda and said goodbye to Simon before heading for the door.

She followed him. Part of her was somehow hoping he wouldn't leave. She was experiencing the same sensations she'd had the previous night. The need for physical contact. But she was undoubtedly making a fool of herself. She wondered again, fleetingly, what sort of bond he had with Lisa. She had left a while ago. Why was he still here?

"So," he said, standing by the door. He didn't seem in any hurry to go, now that he had reached it.

"Well," she said, not sure what to say but wanting to postpone his departure.

"Lauren. I wish...I mean, you just have this..." He stopped, and gave her another look, this time a searching kind of look that seemed charged with some sort of emotion. She wasn't sure what sort of emotion it was, but she found that once again she couldn't take her eyes off him. And she was finding it hard to breathe.

Then he reached out and lightly brushed one finger along her cheek. "So, take care of yourself." He sounded a little breathless himself. "Sometimes I worry about you." And he let himself out the door, leaving Lauren in an even more overwhelmed state than she'd been in a few minutes earlier. She couldn't even begin to figure out what all of that meant. Why would he worry about her?

Her brain seemed dysfunctional.

She returned to the living room and collapsed onto the sofa. Amanda and Simon were still talking about the murder case. Simon, for his part, showed no sign of leaving. He followed Amanda and Lauren back and forth to the kitchen, chattering away about New York, as they threw things in the trash and loaded the dishwasher.

"Would you like me to help?" he finally asked.

"Yes." Lauren handed him a dishtowel.

By the time the last of the dishes had been put away, Lauren had heard more than she ever wanted to about what it was like to see New York from the perspective of a White South African academic. And she was about to fall asleep. It was almost two in the morning. "I'm going to sleep now. I'll see you, okay?"

"It is rather late, isn't it?" Simon said. "I think I'll be getting back to my Airbnb now." And he finally left.

The next morning, Lauren didn't wake up until past ten. She settled down to eat breakfast and check the news headlines. Sure enough, the Fogerty investigation was the lead story on the Post's website.

She felt a pang of sadness. She and Eric had had a Sunday morning routine, at least on the Sundays he wasn't on deadline. They would sleep late and then eat lox and bagels and drink orange juice, and sit around talking and reading the Globe and the Times and watching the Sunday morning political interview shows on TV. It was the one day of the week when Eric broke away from his toast and banana. Sometimes one of his big front-page investigative pieces would be plastered all over the Globe's website, and she would feel quite proud of him.

"Good morning." Amanda entered the room still in her pajamas. "I was thinking we should do something interesting today. Like go to an exhibit downtown. Or I could take you shopping.

But first, I thought I'd bring you along to my yoga class."

"What kind of yoga class?" Amanda tended to do more intense things like hot yoga, which Lauren found too draining. She was really out of shape lately anyway. She used to go to a weekly yoga class in Boston, but hadn't done any yoga since November.

"Just a regular one. At the gym. Come on, it'll be good for us, given everything that's going on."

Lauren agreed, and they retreated to their rooms to change. Amanda emerged in a cute-looking sleeveless athletic top and yoga pants. Her hair was pulled back in a neat ponytail. "Nice yoga pants," she said approvingly, looking Lauren up and down.

"Well, you picked them out." It had been last summer, and Amanda had been up in Boston.

At the end of her visit, Amanda had pulled Lauren aside and given her one of those appraising looks. "Are you absolutely sure about this engagement?"

"Why?"

"He's incredibly charismatic. In a good way. I totally get what you see in him. And he seems to really love you. But I want to be sure everything's okay. He's almost 37 and never married and sort of set in his ways."

"No, it's okay. Don't worry."

"All right, then." And Amanda had given Lauren a big hug. "I'm really happy for you. And I'm psyched to be the maid of honor."

"I just wish we were more the same size," Amanda was saying now as she eyed Lauren's t-shirt. It was Eric's shapeless old Red Sox shirt, which still stirred up a lot of emotions. But the material was so soft. "I have all these things I could lend you. I mean, that t-shirt is huge on you. You might not be voluptuous or anything, but you actually have a really good body, Lauren. You can eat and eat and eat and not gain weight. I wish I could do that. You know, that dress looked great on you yesterday. You shouldn't always hide yourself under large garments. What is that, one of Eric's shirts?"

Lauren nodded, as they left the apartment en route to the gym. She agreed, it probably would be better if she and Amanda were the same size. But Amanda was considerably shorter and much curvier, so there wasn't much that would work. Except jewelry and other accessories, of course.

Before she knew it, she was in the midst of a bunch of people, many of them women about their age, all dressed like Amanda, all perfectly executing a series of seemingly impossible yoga poses. She tried her best, but her t-shirt kept flopping down around her head during downward-facing dog, which was very distracting. She finally tucked the shirt into her yoga pants, and was relieved when the yoga teacher had them all lie down for shavasana, Lauren's favorite. Before November, she had been able on occasion to let her mind go in shavasana and attain some degree of peacefulness. She needed peacefulness. Desperately. But she wasn't sure she'd be able to find it now. The teacher was talking about breathing deeply and attaining tranquility and removing all unnecessary thoughts, and Lauren attempted to empty her mind and relax, but found it impossible. Thoughts of Tony, of Eric, of Nick, of the entire unbelievable situation in which she found herself, kept filtering in. Frustrated, she gave up. It wasn't working.

"Just what we needed," Amanda said as they left the gym. "I was able to forget about things for a few minutes. Were you?"

Lauren shook her head. "Not really." Would she ever be able to? Would there be a time when she might actually feel peaceful? Not completely torn up inside?

It was a beautiful day, incredibly warm. Probably close to 80 degrees. "What about going for a walk?" Lauren asked, trying to switch her mind back to something productive. "I have all these things to tell you about the investigation." She loved taking walks. She used to walk every day on the treadmill at the college's gym when the weather was too bad for outdoor walks; after six years in California, she found Boston's chill inhospitable. And when she was living at her parents' house, she would wander around the neighborhood for hours, thinking about how sad she was. But the past week, since she'd started at Lens, she hadn't been walking at all.

"Simon's really quite charming," Amanda said, as they headed up Connecticut Avenue. "Don't you think?"

"He's nice, but he talks a lot."

"Yeah, well, better that than sitting there and not saying anything. Like Nick. We're all just material for that novel of his."

"Well, I think he talks to some people." Lauren felt a little flustered. Like Lisa from the art department, for example. Like herself, sometimes at least. She needed to find out about Lisa. "So, I know you thought the date situation was ambiguous, but do you think he might be, um, seeing anyone? I mean, someone else." She glanced around at the trees, which, seemingly overnight, had burst forth in their full pastel-blossomed glory, and then back at Amanda.

"I've been thinking about that since Friday night." Amanda assumed a thoughtful expression. "And I'm honestly not sure. At one point, I thought there might be something going on with Lisa. You know, from the art department."

Lauren felt her heart sink.

"But I just don't know," Amanda continued. "I still would have to say the whole thing confuses me. Nick has always been hard to figure out." She paused, as a noisy group of what looked like college students passed them on the sidewalk, laughing and joking around. Lauren looked at them, thinking of her own former students. Would she ever get another chance to teach again? She really missed it.

"...I'll repeat what I said before, that you need to watch out," Amanda was saying. "You don't want to get involved with a suspect. I mean it, Lauren. And you only met him a few days ago, anyway, so what do you know about him? This really isn't like you, you know? Usually you take forever to decide you like someone."

That was true, Eric being a prime example. But in this case... "I knew Nick before. Or it seemed as if I did. So it doesn't feel as if I just met him." He seemed like a known quantity, somehow. She thought for a minute. Really, Amanda was sounding uncharacteristically illogical. "You know him, though, right? I mean, you've worked with him for years and years. Do you seriously think he could have..."

"Look, I wouldn't have thought so, no. Of course not. But I wouldn't have expected Tony to be murdered, either. So I'm not sure what to think. The bottom line is, Nick is a suspect, and therefore you should stay away from him, end of story. And speaking of suspects, what did you find out last night? About the investigation? I have to say, I was so busy making sure everyone was having a good time that I didn't get a chance to ask them anything much."

"Well..." Lauren forced her thoughts back on track. "I think Jim might have been there that night. At the office, I mean. The night Tony was killed."

"What? How did you get that out of him?"

"It wasn't hard. He just came out and said it. So I said, You were there the night Tony was killed? And he just said, What?"

"Well, probably tomorrow he'll remember what you were talking about. So let's look at that possibility. Cecily and Tony have a huge fight Monday night. And Cecily calls Jim, all upset. Tony's going in to the office now, she says. Can't you go over and talk to him? So Jim goes over, and they get in a big fight and he ends up killing Tony."

"And then there's Louis and his invention. Did you know about that?"

"What invention? I assume some kind of invention that Tony wanted to steal?"

"I don't know. He wouldn't say."

"Hmph," Amanda sniffed. "Well, that certainly puts Louis right at the top of the list."

"Wade was the one who told me about it. But he wasn't too specific. And by the way, do you know what Wade was doing before he worked at Lens? I looked at his resume, and it seems as if all these years are missing. I know people don't always put everything down on their resumes, but it's just kind of weird. Like, maybe suspicious."

"Well, Wade's kind of weird in general. I could try to track down his old girlfriend and see if she'd tell me."

"Who's his old girlfriend?"

"She used to work on the copy desk. She was kind of nervous and fidgety and repetitive the way he is. I'm not sure why things ended. Maybe they drove each other crazy. And I'm not sure where she's working now. I think she moved to New York. I'll see if I can...oh, hold on, someone just texted me." Amanda pulled out her phone. "It's Fred. He wants to know if I can go on this radio show in a couple of hours to talk about the Fogerty story." She started texting as they continued walking up the street.

By this point, they had crossed the bridge over Rock Creek Park and were passing the Woodley Park Metro stop, located in the midst of apartment buildings and restaurants. Lauren was admiring an especially beautiful tree with bright pink puffy blossoms when she heard Amanda address someone. "Well," Amanda was saying, a hint of frostiness in her voice. "What a coincidence, seeing you twice in one weekend."

Lauren turned away from the tree to find Nick, who apparently had just emerged from the Metro. "Oh, hey, Amanda," he said, sounding distracted, as if Amanda had broken his train of thought. He shook his head, and seemed to snap out of whatever fog he had been in. He glanced at Lauren and smiled at her. "Hey, Lauren. Go Sox."

"Yeah," she replied weakly. She wasn't sure how to react to him at this point. He looked sort of rumpled and unshaven, which somehow made him seem even more attractive to her than he had the previous night. Lisa from the art department once again flashed into her mind. If Lisa were going to a yoga class, she probably would wear something tight-fitting. Sexy. Voluptuous-looking. Not an ancient Red Sox t-shirt handed down from the fiancé who had dumped her.

"And where might you be going?" Amanda asked Nick, breaking into Lauren's increasingly desperate musings.

"I needed a break from my writing. So I thought I'd go to the zoo." He gestured up Connecticut Avenue toward the National Zoo.

"The zoo." Amanda curled her lip. "Well, isn't that nice." She shot Lauren a glance. Lauren ignored her.

"Yeah, I really like going to the zoo. Actually, the last time I went there, it was with Tony. A few months ago."

"With Tony?" Amanda asked skeptically.

"Mm-hmm. We were running together, and we happened to pass the entrance to the zoo, and I said, why don't we go in and take a look? It was really cold out, so most of the animals were inside, but it was kind of fun."

Amanda was watching him, her perfectly shaped eyebrows raised. Lauren wished either Nick or Amanda would leave. She couldn't deal with their mutual presence. None of them said anything for a while as they progressed up the street.

Then Nick sighed. "I'm going to have to ask Louis about my laptop. It's really temperamental, you know? Sometimes all these lines start flashing all over the screen. But that's only when I'm writing fiction. When I'm writing nonfiction, it behaves really well. I think it's trying to tell me something."

Lauren smiled despite herself. "My laptop acts weird if it knows I'm doing anything connected to my book."

Nick smiled back at her, as Amanda stared at each of them in turn. "Maybe both of you should have your laptops taken in for service. I mean, that's ridiculous."

"Well," Nick said as they reached the zoo entrance. "I'll see you guys at work. And thanks again for the party." And he joined the stroller-pushing throngs on their way into the zoo.

"I don't know about him," Amanda said, as she and Lauren proceeded onward. "He's acting awfully suspicious. Why the hell would Tony Mandel go to the zoo?"

"Maybe he wanted to do something different for once. Besides messing things up for other people."

"Forget it. And Nick's acting like he and Tony were great pals? Come on."

Lauren wasn't sure. Maybe the next day would prove more enlightening.

Twelve

When Lauren arrived at the office Monday morning, the only person there was Nick. He still hadn't shaved, and his two-day stubble made him look yet more irresistible. She caught her breath, but decided to try to act as if he had no effect on her at all. He shouldn't be having an effect on her. He was a suspect, and she was a reject, and that was that. "So," she said. "How was your visit to the zoo?"

"Pretty good. I'd been wondering how to describe a certain character in my novel, and then I passed by these things, I think they were ostriches, and I knew that was it. You know, the little head with the heavy-lidded eyes on the long neck?"

Lauren tried to picture someone who looked like an ostrich and came up with a woman she'd met a few times in Romania. "Yeah, I know someone who looks like that." She sat down. What had she meant to ask him about? His second article, that was it. "Do you have a copy of your story that I could see?"

"The Central Europe one? Sure. I'll send you a link to it. Or wait, I think I have the hard copy in my desk." He opened a drawer and started going through it, and eventually handed her a magazine, folded back to the page with his article.

She skimmed the piece, which didn't even take up a full page. It referred to a number of writers, but quoted only Karel Halama and Andreea. Again, as with Nick's article about forgotten writers, she was baffled. This piece was so short. And it didn't say anything especially shocking. Why, then, was it the apparent subject of such controversy? Maybe she should talk to Karel Halama and find out whether he had noticed anything suspicious. Had he really been interviewed? And by whom? She frowned. Talking to Karel Halama would be a pain. Andreea would be better, but she wasn't about to try to find her again.

Lauren looked at Nick, who seemed to be editing his novel. She would need to go out in the hallway to call Karel Halama, or maybe outside, but then she'd probably run into someone else from the office. So she'd have to wait.

But there was one thing she could do. She could return that folder with the resumes and evaluations to Natasha. She got out her key and unlocked the drawer. The folder wasn't there. She pulled everything out of her desk drawers and even looked behind the desk. Nothing. Her folder had been taken. She felt a chill. What could have happened to it? She frantically searched through piles of completed surveys, tossing them onto the floor.

"What are you doing?" Nick asked.

"Oh, nothing. I'm just looking for something."

"You need any help?"

"No, thanks anyway." Had she left the drawer unlocked? Or had someone found her key? Was it just a bizarre coincidence? Or was the murderer going through people's drawers? She shivered.

Gradually, the entire Most Admired Unit staff filtered into the office, and she realized she'd have to postpone her search. The last to arrive was Wade. He crept into the room, clutching a brown paper bag and looking as if he had just robbed a bank and Tucker and McDonald were hot on his trail. Lauren watched him deposit the bag under his desk.

"Where have you been?" Louisa said sharply. "You know we have a lot of work today. I want to get this religion project out of the way."

"Oh, sorry, Louisa," Wade said. "I just had to go somewhere. It doesn't matter."

Louisa sniffed. "Very well. Oh, and I was to tell everyone that the passageway through to the main building is open again. So we can use the front door now. The door we've been using will be an emergency exit again, so please don't open it."

"Great," Jim said. "Like, I kind of miss talking to Winston. He's a cool old dude, you know?"

"Please get to work." Louisa pursed her lips. "You may talk to whomever you want, but not when you're supposed to be working."

As Lauren began her fifth survey of the morning, she saw Wade reach under his desk and surreptitiously remove something. Then he put whatever it was into his pocket and scurried out into the hallway. What was he doing? But she was in mid-survey and couldn't stop.

"Lauren?" She looked up a while later, having finished several more calls, to find Wade hovering by her desk. "Do you want to go to lunch now?"

"Okay." She set her pile of completed survey forms aside. Maybe now she could find something out about Louis. And about the missing folder. And about Wade's own peculiar behavior, for that matter.

"I was thinking," he said, once they were outside, "of going to the Italian restaurant up the street. Pasta might be just the thing."

"That sounds good."

"Lens magazine," Wade said, brushing at his hair with his hand, "is a wonderful place, don't you think so, Lauren? A wonderful place."

"Well," she began doubtfully. What had been in that brown paper bag anyway? Maybe it was a weapon. Or maybe he was an alcoholic and had committed some kind of awful crime while under the influence, and Tony had found out and threatened to tell everyone. The film started rolling in her head again. Wade was stealthily entering the office. He picked up the vase and hit an unsuspecting Tony over the head. But what had Tony been doing there in the middle of the night anyway? she asked herself as the video abruptly stopped.

"...ravioli?" Wade was saying.

"I'm sorry. Excuse me?"

They were at the door to the restaurant. "Do you like ravioli, I said. It's one of my favorites."

Lauren nodded, as they sat down. Wade, she noticed, was acting more fidgety than ever. He kept looking at the menu, and then wringing his hands and smoothing his hair. The waiter appeared and took their order. Neither Lauren nor Wade said anything for a while.

"So," Lauren finally began. "This is really nice of you, taking time out from work. Especially with so much going on."

"Oh, well." Wade's pale narrow eyes shifted around warily. "I like to see what our new employees think of Lens. I'm quite an old-timer now. I've been here for a long time."

"And before that, you said you were a freelance writer? How many years did you do that?"

"Uh. Yes, well, here comes my appetizer, and the bread." He started wolfing down his spaghetti and meatballs. Lauren picked up a piece of crusty bread and nibbled at it.

"Freelancing must be tough sometimes," Lauren said, trying to keep the conversation going.

Wade mumbled something around his food. He had already finished the spaghetti and was helping himself to some bread.

"In fact," Lauren said, "I've been in the academic world for a while now, and I realized I needed to try something different. Did you ever feel like that?"

"Well." Wade paused from his voracious eating for a minute. "Sometimes. Sometimes, Lauren."

The waiter arrived with the main courses. This lunch was progressing so rapidly, Lauren thought, taking a bite of lasagna. She hadn't gotten answers to any of her questions. What had happened to that folder, anyway?

Wade was thoroughly occupied with his food. He wasn't even looking at her.

"Why would someone want to kill Tony?" she blurted out.

"I don't know. I certainly wouldn't want to kill him," Wade said between quick mouthfuls of ravioli. "I do know that he'd had run-ins with practically everyone else on the Most Admired Unit staff, but I can't imagine who would want to kill him. Do you want some dessert?"

"No, thanks."

"Well, I think I do," Wade said. His hands were shaking. Lauren was getting really nervous. The combination of this odd behavior and the missing folder—the entire situation was getting out of control. "I can't believe this. Do you know what I bought this morning?"

A brass vase, extra-heavy variety? She glanced around the restaurant. Should she summon help? Was he about to...

"Candy." His voice was quavering. "An entire bag of candy. M&Ms. Hershey's kisses. Milky Ways. Three Musketeers. And then I ate most of it. And for breakfast I had eggs. A three-egg omelet, to be precise. For the third morning in a row. And then I came here. A little pasta would be okay, I thought. But I ordered meatballs. And meat ravioli. All this meat. All that candy. Too much pasta. I can't believe this."

Lauren looked at him. So that's what he had been doing out

there in the hallway? Sneaking pieces of candy? But he wasn't overweight. In fact, he was one of the thinnest people she'd ever met. What did it matter if he ate some candy?

"But you're not..." she started.

"Overweight? Oh, no, Lauren. Oh, no. I'll never be overweight. It's my cholesterol. What's your cholesterol level, Lauren?"

Lauren realized she had no idea. She knew it was pretty good, but couldn't remember anything more about it.

"Well, mine used to be two-fifty." He shook his head. "Two-fifty. And I just got it down under two hundred for the first time in years. I've been learning to eat properly. And then with all this Tony business I've started eating all the wrong foods again. Eggs. Red meat. Candy. I ate way too much bad stuff at Amanda's party. I spent all weekend eating high-cholesterol foods. I just can't even think about all of this."

"It's okay." Lauren tried to sound calming. "So you'll stop eating the wrong kinds of food once this all gets resolved, right?"

"But it might take weeks! And meantime my cholesterol level could go through the roof. And I don't know if Cecily did it. You take Louisa, for example. She hated Tony. Brad hated Tony. Nick hated Tony." Wade was counting the suspects off on his long thin fingers. His nails were bitten down to the quick.

"I thought Nick and Tony got along pretty well after the whole thing ended."

Wade shrugged. "I wouldn't know about that." He reached for a leftover piece of bread and bit into it. "And Louie hated Tony, too. He stole his invention."

"What invention?" Lauren fixed her eyes upon Wade's.

"Oh, well, Lauren. Oh, well."

Lauren leaned forward in her chair. "What invention are you talking about?"

"...video game," Wade mumbled. "He invented a new video game. And he showed it to Tony and Tony stole it. And Tony was about to talk to a lawyer about copyrighting it."

"How do you know?" She was surprised. A video game? Would Tony know enough about creating video games to pass off Louis's idea as his own? "Did Louis tell you about this?"

"Not exactly. Not exactly, Lauren. Good journalism, you know? You can find out a lot with good journalistic techniques." And he gave her a worried look.

Thirteen

Lauren put her phone down at around six-thirty, after several solid hours of calls, and stretched. The Most Admired Senator or Congressperson poll was an exhausting exercise. Her shoulders ached and her throat was dry and she hadn't had any further opportunity to search for her missing folder. Her phone buzzed with a text. "Seven pm OK?" She didn't recognize the number. Who could it be? Did she have dinner plans? Her mind wasn't working right. Another text came through. "It's Simon." Oh, of course. She had forgotten about him again.

"OK, do u know address?" she texted back.

"Yes, see u quite soon," he replied.

Whereupon her phone rang. "Lauren?" It was Professor Segal. "I arrived in town yesterday, and I was thinking perhaps we could have dinner tonight," she said. "And I would love to invite my friend's son, too, if only I could remember his name. Now, was it Daniel? She has four sons, and this is the youngest. And I know one of them is named Daniel."

"Do you remember his last name?"

"He has a different last name from his mother. But if I were to see him, I'm sure I would recognize him immediately. After all, he looks just like her. So I'll be at your office, Lauren, quite soon, then, quite soon." And she hung up.

Quite soon, then, quite soon? The professor and Simon both showing up at her office? But maybe they would get along. Maybe they could talk to each other and Lauren could think about her investigation. She called downstairs to Antonio the afternoon security guard and asked him to send the two of them up when they arrived.

"Can we go home now?" Louis inquired. Lauren looked over at him. So Tony had stolen his video game idea. But had Tony actually gone to a lawyer to discuss copyrighting it? Or had he been killed before he could do that?

The room had fallen silent. Everyone was off their phones. Jim was tapping out a rhythm on his desk, while Cecily snuffled quietly into a tissue. Louisa was organizing some papers on her desk. Nick appeared to be working on his manuscript, and Wade was reaching guiltily into his brown paper bag, which had made its way onto the top of his desk. Well, at least now she knew the story behind that.

Wade mumbled something indistinctly.

"Very well," Louisa said. "Good work, everyone. I really appreciate it."

Lauren sighed. Maybe if they all went home, then she could see what had happened to her folder. Not that she wanted to go through their desks, but…

"Well, I'm out of here." Louis hoisted his backpack over one shoulder and threw his jacket over his arm. "See you all tomorrow."

"Jim?" Cecily asked. "Will you take me out for dinner?"

"Oh, sure. Like, where?"

"I don't know. But let's go now, okay?" And they drifted out the door, followed by Wade.

"Aren't you leaving?" Nick asked as he gathered up his belongings.

"I think I'll just hang around for a while. Straighten some things up, you know?"

"Look, um, are you okay?" Nick seemed concerned. She sensed an echo of that same emotional charge from the night of the party. She remembered their brief moment of physical contact that night, and felt a shiver run through her. But maybe he had been expressing a purely platonic sentiment? "So maybe if you wanted... no, forget it. I mean, if you ever need someone to talk to about it, just let me know, all right?" And he left.

Well, that was thoughtful of him. Lauren took a deep breath. But what did it actually mean? And she wasn't about to tell him that her secret file of information about him and everyone else in the office was missing. Maybe he was the one who took it, a voice in her head warned. She shook her head, trying to ignore the voice. He couldn't have taken it.

The only other person left in the room was Louisa. And she didn't seem to be showing any signs of departing. She arranged the papers on her desk, and then rearranged them. She made a couple of phone calls.

Leave, Lauren thought, sending a telepathic message across the office to Louisa. Leave, leave, soon, please. As if in response, Louisa slowly raised her head from her desk and stared across the room at Lauren. "Well, Lauren, I have to talk to Natasha. So I'll be back in about half an hour. And if I might make a suggestion? It's all in your best interest, of course."

Lauren nodded.

"You may recall that a murder has just been committed here? So I wouldn't advise your staying around here by yourself." And she shot Lauren a peculiar look. "People might start wondering what you're doing."

Was Louisa threatening her in some way? "But you're going to be here by yourself if you come back and I'm gone." Lauren tried to keep her voice steady.

"I can take care of myself. Now take my advice and get out of here." And Louisa picked up her clipboard and left.

But she couldn't very well get out, could she? She had to look for that folder. And her dinner companions were supposed to arrive soon, so she wouldn't be alone. Everything would be okay. Lauren got up. Where to start? She felt squeamish about opening other people's drawers. But she could look on top of the desks, or even under them. She started with Wade's desk, then moved to Louisa's, Louis's, Jim's, Cecily's, and the empty desk that had been Tony's, with no success. There was nothing to discover except little clumps of dust on the threadbare brown-carpeted floor.

The last desk was Nick's. She checked the top of it, finding nothing but survey forms, and then sat down on the floor next to his chair to check under his desk. A pile of books lay in one corner. She brushed aside a piece of dust, and sneezed, before reaching for the books. They proved to be an eclectic group: a few novels, a couple of copies of the book about the New York literati that he had helped research, a dictionary, a book about jazz musicians, a beginning Chinese book, and...what was this? A Czech language textbook?

But hadn't Nick said he had never taken a Czech course? Lauren opened the book, suddenly chilled. The book looked well-worn, its spine broken in several places and various pages bent down at the corners. Certain phrases were underlined, and there was writing in the margins. Was that Nick's writing? She sat up and looked on his desk to find something to compare it to. Yes, there was his handwriting on one of the surveys. And it did look somewhat similar. She couldn't really tell. She crawled under his desk again to replace the book. Did Nick really know Czech after all? Why would he have lied to her about it? Maybe because of his article? Something to do with Karel Halama, perhaps? Or maybe it was just research for his novel. Maybe he just needed to make sure the character from Prague sounded authentic. Maybe...footsteps were coming up the stairs. She jumped up quickly, her legs shaking, her heart pounding, and in the process banged her head on the underside of the desk. "Ow," she shrieked, falling into her own chair.

"Hello?" she heard a voice calling, and then Simon came into view.

Lauren breathed a sigh of relief. "Simon. Hi."

"Lauren. How nice to see you again. And where are your fellow toilers?"

"They've all left." And she still hadn't found her file.

"So." Simon sat down at Nick's desk. "I think I'll just chill, then. I've been for a lengthy stroll around Georgetown. I thought of inviting you along, but I knew you'd be at work." And he gave Lauren what seemed like an admiring look. But of course she wasn't sure. Simon was enthusiastic about many things. "Perhaps we could go back sometime?"

"Well..." Lauren began, when she saw Professor Segal approaching. "Oh, Professor Segal, I mean, Meryl." Lauren stood up to give her mentor a hug.

The professor beamed, hugging her back. "Why, Lauren, how lovely to see you. And this is one of your office-mates?"

"Do you work here?" Simon asked at the same time, viewing Professor Segal with interest.

She was peering at him from over the top of her glasses. "Oh, no. Just visiting Lauren, and hoping to locate my friend's son." She turned to Lauren. "Is there a Daniel who works in this department?"

"No."

"Very well." The professor gave a little shrug. "I'll have to look for him some other time."

They ended up at the same Italian restaurant where Lauren

had eaten with Wade. It was starting to feel like her second home.

"Well," Simon was saying as they sat down. "When I was at university I considered myself something of a Marxist, really. But I find my position has gradually moderated somewhat. I find that..."

Lauren started tuning him out. Who could the professor's friend's son be? Oh, no. What if it was Tony, and the professor didn't know about the murder?

"...many of my friends have moved to New York, yes," Simon was saying once she tuned back in. "And...well, how extraordinary. Isn't that Cecily Bottomley over there behind you, Lauren?"

Lauren twisted around in her chair. Sure enough, a few tables away were Cecily and Jim, having an intense conversation.

"Yes. And Jim, too."

"Friends of yours?" the professor queried.

"They work with me. At the magazine."

"You know, they've had a rather shocking event there," Simon said. "Cecily over there is the main suspect in a murder inquiry."

"No." The professor's mouth formed a perfect O of surprise. "How horrible."

Lauren told her what had happened, wondering all along if Tony Mandel could have been the professor's friend's son. But his name didn't seem to ring any bells. Not that it necessarily would have, Lauren realized. At one point, early in her acquaintance with Professor Segal, Lauren had become quite concerned about the professor's forgetfulness. But Professor Segal's daughter, who was about Lauren's age, reassured her that her mother had always been like that. Her mind was just too full of information to be able to remember all of it at the appropriate time.

"Well, how awful." The professor made a clucking noise. "Terrible, terrible. The world is just full of awful things these days, isn't it. And it's so sad when it happens to a young person with his whole life ahead of him." She shook her head.

Lauren nodded in agreement. Professor Segal was absolutely right. But she found her mind turning to Jim and Cecily. What were they talking about? Could she casually walk by them on the way to the bathroom? But then they'd see her. Well, she could risk it. "Excuse me for a minute." She left the table and made her way slowly past Jim and Cecily, who were so caught up in their conversation they didn't even notice her.

"...that night," Jim was saying. "But I didn't see..."

That was all she could hear without becoming too obvious. And it wasn't very helpful. What night? And what hadn't he seen? Was he talking about the night Tony was killed? Or, far more likely, something completely unrelated? She turned around and tried to listen again on her way back to her table.

"...Natasha," Cecily was almost whispering. "And my uncle..."

Natasha? What about Natasha? Lauren was tempted to stop and hover over them. But she didn't.

The food—more pasta—had arrived. Lauren wished she were sitting the other way, facing Jim and Cecily. What could they be talking about? Maybe they had taken her folder. But how would anyone know she had it anyway? Natasha hadn't told anyone else, had she?

"How fascinating," the professor was saying, nibbling on her ravioli. "You know, one of our panels this week will be focusing on racism in Europe. It should be very interesting, yes, yes. And then I'm going to be discussing my recent trip to Hungary and the Czech Republic, of course."

The Czech Republic. That Czech language book. Lauren pictured Nick sitting at his desk in the Most Admired Unit. He was lost in thought. He was contemplating the complexities of the Czech language. All of a sudden Lauren couldn't eat anything else.

"...conference, Lauren?" the professor asked. "I'm scheduled to deliver an address at some point. And participate in a couple of panel discussions, I believe, so I hope you'll be able to attend."

"I hope so." Actually, she didn't hope so. She really didn't want to attend an academic conference.

"Ethan should be getting in this evening. Professor Segal nodded sagely. "I'm quite pleased with Ethan, really." Lauren felt a rush of jealousy. Here was Ethan, successful scholar, and what was she doing? Trying to solve an impossible murder case.

"Could I attend the conference?" Simon was asking.

"Why, yes, of course." Professor Segal smiled at Simon.

The professor and Simon started discussing the schedule, and Lauren took the opportunity to glance towards Jim and Cecily's table. But they had departed. Oh, well. She tried to pay attention as Professor Segal and Simon moved from the schedule to various scholars they both knew. Lauren, who knew some of these people too, found her mind wandering.

"I really should be heading back to my hotel," the professor said eventually. They had all finished their meals. "I must get an early start in the morning. But what was it that I meant to tell you, Lauren? Something important about something that someone at your magazine wrote."

"Perhaps it had to do with the murder inquiry?" Simon suggested.

"No, because I don't think I knew about that. But it will come to me, things usually do."

Lauren's phone buzzed. It was a text from Natasha. "Call me."

Fourteen

After bidding farewell to the professor and Simon, Lauren called Natasha on the way back to the magazine's parking lot. Could it relate to the missing folder? She should tell Natasha about it in any case. Obviously someone was interested in those resumes and evaluations.

"Lauren? Good to hear from you," Natasha said.

"Yeah. I wondered if I could just tell you..."

"I'm really busy right now, but I thought you should know about the latest development. I had an interesting little talk with the Bartlebys late this afternoon...No, just send the official application form. And make a couple more copies. Sorry, Lauren. I'm keeping poor Joanna here late tonight. We're entering some pieces in a competition."

"What about that Czech series you wrote for Synthesis? Did you..."

"I think that's been entered in enough contests at this point." Natasha sounded curt.

"Oh. So what did the Bartlebys say?" Lauren had reached the parking lot.

"That the police have some witness, a guy who just came forward today, who says he saw Wade outside the building that night."

"The night Tony was..."

"Right. The witness says he saw someone fitting Wade's description, walking out the side door at about quarter after five that morning. Tucker and McDonald were skeptical, but the guy stuck to his story. Yeah, Joanna, the address should be in my contact list. Sorry, Lauren."

"Well, that's amazing." Something didn't seem quite right, though. "So what about Cecily?"

"The police still have Cecily on the brain, so the Bartlebys aren't relaxing quite yet. So as far as your investigation goes, don't abandon it, okay? I mean, until they formally charge someone besides Cecily, we should be trying to uncover whatever we can."

"Do you want to hear about anything I've found out? This is important. You know that folder?" Lauren opened her car door and dumped her bag onto the passenger seat.

"Yeah, sometime. Right, Joanna. Yeah. Sorry, Lauren. Sure, we'll discuss it at some point. And, right, Joanna, it's that one. Bye, Lauren." And she hung up.

Natasha certainly hadn't sounded too interested in the investigation, Lauren thought, getting into the car. But if Wade was about to replace Cecily as chief suspect, Natasha's offhandedness was understandable. The Bartlebys probably couldn't care less about Wade. Still, she'd need to figure this out, soon. She ran through each person in her mind, hoping for an elusive flash of insight, and before she knew it she was back at the apartment.

It was empty. Trembling, she switched on the lights in the entryway and the living room. One of Amanda's little goat statues had fallen on its side on the coffee table, and the books in the living room bookcase looked different somehow. Rearranged. As if the person who had taken the folder had also violated the privacy of Amanda's apartment. Stop it, she told herself as she turned on every light in sight. It's just nerves.

She picked up Sandor and Margot Kis's book, prepared to try again with it. But she had forced her way through only one page when she heard the door open and then saw Amanda coming in.

"Damn," Amanda said edgily as she slammed the door and locked it. She sank onto the sofa next to Lauren and started to cry.

"What's wrong?" Lauren was worried. Amanda almost never cried.

"Things just aren't going well. Shit. Now my mascara's going to run all over the place." Amanda pulled a tissue from her bag and started dabbing at her eyes. "It's the whole situation. Everyone's so stressed out. I mean, I hated Tony, but it's awful beyond words that he's actually dead. I keep thinking about him all the time. And they never replaced him on the Hill when he went to the Most Admired Unit, so instead of three reporters, it's been just two of us, me and one of the reporter-researchers, doing all the congressional stuff and lots of the overall political stories too, and they've been working us so hard."

She sniffed and blew her nose. "I know Congress is out this week, but it's still been really busy with the Fogerty story, and the editors keep asking me to post updates to this new politics blog, and they're always on my back, and sometimes it just gets to be too much."

Lauren nodded sympathetically and gave Amanda a hug. "You're an amazing reporter. I'm just totally in awe of what you do." She thought about it. "But I can see how it could be exhausting. Especially on top of this horrible stuff going on."

"And, you know, I spend so much time at work, so I have no time to meet nice, interesting guys, and here we are, and we're 30 and we're not married, and if we don't find someone soon, who knows if we can ever have kids, and I guess I sort of thought that eventually Peter would get tired of living in Nicaragua and come back, but that's obviously not happening, and..." Amanda started crying again, and Lauren, feeling more depressed by the minute, patted her on the shoulder.

Her own situation was all Eric's fault. If she never got married and never had a child, it would all be because of him. Not that she wanted to have a baby right now anyway. She didn't feel ready. Her parents had been on the older side, in their late thirties, when she was born, and she'd always assumed that she would be older too by the time she got around to it. But what if she never ended up having kids at all? That would be awful. Not what she had expected. Eric had never expressed strong feelings one way or the other about kids, but had seemed fine with the idea of their having one, or maybe two, at some future point.

"Sometimes I wonder if I should keep working in journalism." Amanda blew her nose again. "You know? I mean, it's just so all-consuming. I never have any time to just enjoy myself."

"I know what you mean. I feel like I don't know what I'm doing anymore, either." It was as if being interested in Romania had identified her, given her a reason to justify her daily existence, but now she had come loose from her moorings and was floating around. She wasn't excited about her research. She didn't want to go to the conference, when even Simon was eager to go. And then Ethan was coming to present that paper of his, based on his new work-in-progress, which made her feel even more upset. She sighed.

"Well." Amanda sniffed and got up. "I'm sure that's just temporary. You can't be so fascinated by Romania for all these years and then just suddenly decide you don't care about it anymore. I'm going to sleep now." And she headed gloomily toward her room.

"Wait," Lauren called, hoping to distract her. "Natasha told me something interesting about Wade."

"I don't care right now. I'm tired of all that."

Lauren couldn't help but agree.

The next morning, Lauren arrived at the office at seven-thirty, having been unable to sleep the entire night. Perhaps she'd have a better chance of finding the folder this time around, she thought.

Winston greeted her. "So you all get to pass by my desk again, young lady. That renovation sure is taking a long time."

Lauren smiled blearily and went through the newly renovated passageway and up the stairs to her desk. She had been thinking about her investigation all night, especially the new information about Wade. It had surprised her. Wade seemed the least likely suspect.

She put her bag into the drawer and locked it, and looked around the room. Where could the folder be? Should she go so far as to look in other people's drawers? Open their file cabinets? Maybe Wade's file cabinet. She rested her chin on her hands and thought.

The video started again. Wade was picking up the vase in the harsh light over the copier and hitting Tony over the head. I can't stop eating high-cholesterol food, Wade was saying as he hit Tony. Can't stop. Can't stop. This is Our Most Admired Way To Die. Our Most Admired. The videotape was slowing down, the voices becoming blurred. It faded away. All was calm. Then she thought she heard someone saying, Wake up. Wake up.

Lauren opened her eyes and lifted her head off her desk, where she hadn't quite realized it was.

Cecily was standing over her. Lauren felt a shock of fear. How long had she been there, anyway?

"I was worried about you," Cecily said. "You wouldn't wake up, and I thought you might be..."

"Oh." The sun was shining brightly through the windows. Lauren checked the time. Nine o'clock. "No, I'm okay."

"Well, well, well, good morning to one and all," came a booming voice from the stairs.

"Oh, no." Cecily began to tremble. "It's the police again. What if they arrest me?"

"They're not going to do that." Lauren tried to sound reassuring. Although, for all she knew, maybe they were.

"Good morning, Ms. Bartleby." Detective Tucker marched into the room and looked around in a proprietary manner. "And Ms. Green, too. Ms. Green, I don't think I need to talk to you today. As far as I'm concerned, you can take the day off." And a satisfied smile spread across his face.

"Detective Tucker?" It was Louisa, obviously not at all pleased to see him. "What might you be doing here?"

"Just some routine matters, ma'am. I'd like to speak to you, if you don't mind."

"Excuse me, detective, but I'm trying to run an office here." Louisa threw her briefcase down on her desk. "We have a lot to get done today."

"I'm sure you do. This won't take long at all. And here's Mr. Wood." Wade was holding the brown paper bag partly concealed under his jacket. "I'd also like to speak to Ms. Bartleby, here, and the others. Any idea when they might be coming in?"

"They should be here right now," Louisa snapped. "I can't imagine where they are."

"Jim has a doctor's appointment," Cecily whispered, as Louis and Nick arrived. "He said he'd be in later."

"Ms. Bates, why don't we start with you, then," Tucker said, smiling beneficently at her and gesturing toward the supply room. She stalked after him.

Lauren picked up her phone reluctantly, as if it had a communicable disease. She heard her voice asking all the right questions, and saw the pile of completed surveys on her desk getting bigger and bigger, but she wasn't absorbing anything. Person after person went into the supply room with Detective Tucker, and she finally heard him announcing that he was going over to the other building. She came to the end of a survey and looked up to find only Cecily in the room.

"Would you like to go to lunch?" Cecily said timidly.

"Where did everyone go?" Lauren asked, slightly bewildered.

"Lunch. I guess you were kind of into your surveys."

"I guess so. Okay, let's go." Maybe she could, at long last, get a sense of what Cecily was really like.

They went down the stairs. "Are we going to the Italian restaurant, or...?" Lauren asked.

"I was thinking we could just go to my apartment and sit out on the balcony. I have some pasta salad." She looked questioningly at Lauren.

"That sounds nice." The balcony? Could that be the same balcony Cecily mentioned the night of the party?

"We'll have to drive, okay? It'll take too long to walk over there and get back on time."

"Sure."

"I'll drive, then." Cecily led the way over to a red Mercedes sportscar. "I just love to drive." She put on her sunglasses, unlocked the doors, and they got in. The car roared loudly, accompanied by an ear-shattering blast of music. "Sorry," she murmured, turning the volume down. She backed rapidly out of the parking space, and, barely stopping, shot forward into the Wisconsin Avenue traffic.

"Watch it, lady," a cab driver yelled from his open window.

Cecily ignored him and careened on past his taxi. She screeched to a halt at a green light at the intersection with R Street, causing the cars behind her to similarly apply their brakes. A few of them started honking. "Fucking bastards," said Cecily softly, and she floored the gas pedal. The car whizzed down the hill into Georgetown. Lauren, who by this point was clutching the armrest, let out her breath with relief once Cecily tore down a couple of side streets and turned the motor off.

"Driving's so much fun," Cecily said.

Lauren wasn't sure what an appropriate reply would be, so she didn't say anything. She was just glad to be alive.

"This is my house," Cecily continued. Lauren looked at the house, a skinny red-brick Georgetown abode that probably cost a few million dollars.

"I just have the top two floors." Cecily, followed by Lauren, proceeded up a flight of narrow, claustrophobic stairs to the second floor, where she opened the door. The apartment was very tastefully decorated. Antique furniture, well-preserved hardwood floors, and a surprising amount of light. Cecily disappeared around one corner, and emerged a moment later with forks, napkins, and plates heaped with pasta salad. "Here's the balcony." She waved toward the back of the room. Lauren followed her. The balcony was small, with a low wrought-iron railing around the sides.

Cecily pointed at two white wicker chairs that, together with a table, filled the entire balcony area. "Why don't you take that one?" She indicated the one closer to the railing. "The other one has a hole in it."

They sat down and started eating. "You know, Tony lived just down the street," Cecily said. "And Jim lives sort of nearby too."

She gazed at Lauren with her huge blue eyes. Lauren looked back at her. Cecily was wearing a worn jeans jacket over a white t-shirt, and a short plaid skirt, and could have passed for a twelve-year-old parochial school student. "You know, I didn't kill Tony," Cecily murmured around a bite of salad. "I really didn't. I really loved him." And she let out a small discreet sob.

Lauren nodded, and assumed what she hoped was a sympathetic face.

"Tony was just so wonderful. Not that he was perfect. I mean, he did some things I thought were horrible. But deep down underneath it all, he was a good person. And that's why I would get so upset when he'd do these horrible things. But I never would have done anything to hurt him."

"What kind of things would he do?" Lauren looked over the balcony railing at the small garden in back of the house, where a cherry tree was blooming.

"He would, like, see other women. And every time he'd tell me he was sorry. I said, then why do you do it when you know it upsets me so much? And he'd say, I just can't help it. But he'd look so sorry that I'd always forgive him."

"Hmm." At least Eric hadn't been doing anything like that, as far as Lauren knew. That would have been even worse. She frowned. Would she have forgiven him if he had?

"...and Jim has been really amazing," Cecily was saying. "I don't know how I'd have gotten through the past week without him. And whenever I was upset with Tony, I'd always know I could tell Jim about it and he'd understand. You know?"

"Jim? Yeah, he is a pretty amazing person." Lauren paused to take a bite of salad, reflecting that she might as well get the important question over with. "So who do you think did it, then?"

"I really don't know." Cecily's voice quavered. "I know a lot of people didn't like him, but I don't know who would have done that."

"Cecily, so why are there witnesses who say you and your car were there that night, if you say you weren't there?"

"I don't know." Cecily started to cry. "I just don't know."

"Sorry." Lauren felt guilty. "How are you doing, anyway?"

"Better than Saturday night. I went to my psychiatrist yesterday, and then again early this morning, and she's really helping. It was kind of a momentary thing."

"Good." A nearby bird sang out cheerily, and another one responded. Lauren and Cecily sat silently for several minutes, and finally Lauren checked the time.

"Do you think we should go back to the office now?" Cecily asked.

"Probably." The thought of returning to Cecily's car was not appealing, but Lauren fatalistically got back into it, putting on her seatbelt and holding onto the armrest before Cecily even turned the key. Cecily zoomed down the side streets leading to Wisconsin Avenue and turned left onto Wisconsin without even looking.

"Goddamned fucking idiots," Cecily murmured, as other drivers honked at her. "These stupid assholes don't even know how to drive." She shot up the hill towards the office. Lauren's knees felt weak when she and Cecily finally got out and walked up the stairs to the Most Admired Unit. It was as if Cecily were channeling some completely different personality behind the wheel.

"Who taught you how to drive, anyway?" she asked.

"Tony."

Fifteen

For some reason that didn't surprise Lauren. "When was that?" she asked, as they walked into the empty office.

"Just a few months ago. And I just got the car a month or so ago. Tony helped me pick it out." And she sniffed and reached for a tissue. "A lot of people tried to teach me to drive before, but I was always too scared. People have so many accidents. I only got my license last month." She sat down at her desk. "You know, Tony was in an awful accident in Rock Creek Park recently."

Lauren nodded.

"He thought there was something suspicious about the accident, but he got his car checked out and there was nothing wrong with the brakes. Maybe he was just driving a little too fast."

Undoubtedly. His driving style must have resembled that of his pupil. Could Cecily have killed someone with her car? Say a hit-and-run accident. And Tony threatened to tell someone about it? So Cecily picked up the brass vase...But what were they doing in the office in the middle of the night anyway?

"Cecily, what would Tony have been doing here in the middle of the night? I mean, did he do that all the time?"

"I wasn't here." Cecily pulled her denim jacket closer around her shoulders and shivered slightly.

"Yes, but," Lauren said, feeling like a large elephantine creature trampling through a field of butterflies, "why was Tony here?"

"Look." Cecily emitted a soft sob. "I don't know. I wasn't here. I don't know."

She sounded as if she were about to become hysterical again. Just then, Jim came in. "Cecily? Is everything all right?"

"Yes," Cecily murmured. "Can we just go outside for a second?"

"Absolutely. Let's go." And they left.

Lauren sat down, feeling frustrated. Getting any information from Jim or Cecily when they were together was proving impossible. And then there was her missing folder, which showed no signs of reappearing.

She picked up the phone to call Natasha again. Natasha really should know about the folder's disappearance. "Oh, Lauren," Natasha said distractedly, once Lauren had launched into her story. "Yeah, I'd like to hear about this problem, but I have people in my office now. Why don't I call you back." And she hung up.

Great, Lauren thought. Maybe she should try Karel Halama. She knew he was based most of the time at the Institute for International Affairs near Dupont Circle. Lauren knew the place well; she'd been an intern there one summer. She dialed the Institute's main number and asked to be connected to Halama's office. A woman answered, someone Lauren didn't know. "Oh, no," she said. "Karel never comes in till late afternoon. Can I take a message?" Lauren declined, and hung up. She really wasn't getting anywhere, was she?

Nick wandered in and sat down at his desk.

Lauren looked at him. Did he know Czech? Why did he have to be so infuriatingly confusing? She suddenly directed a Czech sentence in his direction, the rough equivalent of "Hi, how's it going?"

"What?" He stared at her with what looked like genuine bewilderment.

"Sorry. I was just testing my Czech. It's a little rusty."

"But I don't know Czech. I told you that." He paused. "So I

was thinking. You and Amanda should come over for dinner sometime this week. I'd like to reciprocate for the party."

"Oh." Lauren was surprised. "Okay. I'll check with her and see what day might be good."

"You know what I've really been wondering about," Nick continued.

"What?"

"What was Tony doing here in the middle of the night anyway. I sit there wondering that all the time, when I'm supposed to be working on my writing. Even when we were over in the main part of the magazine, it was really unusual to pull an all-nighter. It's actually just a few people who are here on the night shift. A couple of copy editors and some web people. If I had to go somewhere in the middle of the night, this would be the last place I'd think of going."

Lauren nodded.

"Plus, they shut off most of the heat or air-conditioning at night, except for the areas where the overnight staff works, so it's kind of uncomfortable. I was here once late at night when it was cold out, and I had to wear my jacket the whole time. I remember wishing I had some gloves with me."

"Yeah. I've been wondering the same thing myself. Did Tony do this a lot? Or was it just this one particular night?"

Nick shrugged. "I don't know. Tony never really told me that much about what he was doing outside of work. Every now and then we'd go running, or go for a drink after work or something, but he was pretty secretive about what he was up to."

This was fascinating, Lauren thought. How could Nick tolerate the company of someone who had treated him so badly? Either Nick was just too nice to be believed; or he was oblivious, which she didn't think was the case; or...

"Once you got to know Tony, he wasn't all that villainous," Nick was saying. He had picked up a pen and was tapping it absently against a pile of papers on his desk. "I mean, he'd never be a close friend of mine or anything, but he was interesting. Writers try to seek out interesting people. And I think he felt kind of bad about the whole thing."

Apparently not bad enough to stop him from trying again, Lauren said to herself.

"Sometimes when you go through an ordeal with someone, you get to be a little closer to them," Nick said.

"I guess." Maybe Amanda was right, and Nick was making up this whole thing about being friendly with Tony. It did sound implausible. But somehow, she still couldn't imagine Nick murdering someone. The idea was absurd.

"How do you think Lens magazine compares to an old-style Eastern European government?" Nick put the pen down and looked at her, his dark eyes contemplative. "All the intrigue going on. People being suspicious of one another. Struggles for power. Secret romances."

"What secret romances?" Was he having a secret romance with someone? Lisa, perhaps?

"Well, there usually are a couple of secret romances going on in an office."

"How do you know?" What was he trying to tell her? It had been a year since his wife left him, after all. Had he spent that whole time monastically working on his novel?

"I don't." He gave her a half-smile. "Not specifically. I mean, I'm not having a secret romance. But probably somebody is, wouldn't you think?"

He wasn't having a secret romance. That was good. Unless that meant he was having a not-secret romance that she just didn't happen to know about. But how likely was that? Wouldn't he have been spending time with this hypothetical woman on Friday and Saturday night? Well, maybe the woman lived out of town. A long-distance thing. That was possible. She shook her head. What she should be thinking about was Tony's secret romances, not Nick's.

"What about..." she started to say, when Wade came in.

"I don't believe this day." Wade smoothed his fringe of hair nervously. "Nick, Lauren, I don't believe what's happening to me." He shook his head and sighed. "First I wake up and consume more eggs. And then I arrive here and Detective Tucker tells me they've come up with a witness who saw me coming out of the office around five-fifteen in the morning that day." He reached into his pocket and pulled out a Reese's peanut butter cup. "I don't even like these things." He gestured at the offending orange wrapper. "The morning Tony was killed, that's what I'm referring to." He unwrapped the candy and bit into it.

"Someone saw you?" Nick looked skeptical.

"But I wasn't there. I wasn't there! I wasn't there!" His voice got louder and louder, and he stuffed the rest of the peanut butter cup into his mouth.

"Well," Lauren said, trying to be reassuring. "If you weren't there, you can try to convince them of that, right?"

"I tried," Wade said stickily around his mouthful of candy. "I told them the same thing I told them last week. I went home from work Monday night. I watched a show on Netflix. I went to sleep after the eleven o'clock local news. I came in to work on Tuesday morning." He was sounding more and more agitated as this recitation continued. "I went up the stairs. And you know what happened after that. I told Detective Tucker everything. And he said, Can anyone verify that? And I said, Not the part at my apartment because I live alone. It was the same conversation I had last week. Except then I think he believed me, and now he doesn't. This witness just isn't telling the truth."

"Did you call anyone?" Lauren asked. "Or go online? During the night, I mean. Maybe the police could check some records on that."

"I don't usually call people or go online when I'm sleeping, Lauren." Wade sounded aggrieved. "And in the middle of the night I usually am sleeping. And then I just had a meeting with Natasha. Louisa wasn't there. She was at another meeting with the art people. And Natasha kept asking, So, is the data ready from the religion survey? Is the data ready from the political survey? And I didn't know what to say." And he drifted off toward his desk.

Lauren's phone rang a few minutes later. "Hello, Lauren. I wanted to let you know that my little presentation is going to be tonight, and if you wanted to come, you'd be quite welcome."

Professor Segal's presentation. She really should go.

"Okay, sure. I'd like to."

"It's at the Institute. At seven, in the auditorium."

At the Institute? Maybe she could talk to Karel Halama at the same time.

"Simon and Ethan and I have been having quite an enjoyable day, yes, yes," the professor was continuing. "What was that, Simon? Ah, yes. Simon says to say hello. Oh, and Lauren, I found Daniel, who works in your office. Except that his name isn't Daniel at all, that's his brother. And he doesn't work in your office. His name is Zach, and he's a college intern at Time magazine's bureau here, doing research for one of the journalists, who asked him to cover this conference. I'm sure you'll enjoy meeting him. And Ethan also says to say hello and he'll see you tonight. Well, the next panel is beginning, so we must be going. Goodbye," and the professor hung up.

"Who was that?" Nick asked.

"My thesis advisor. She's giving a talk tonight and she wants me to come." She told Nick about Professor Segal, and about the mysterious Daniel, and he started laughing.

"That's great. I wonder how she finally identified him, then? You'll have to let me know."

Wade had wandered back towards them. "I don't even have the heart to make you people work. And I don't even care that Jim and Cecily and Louie aren't here. I can just feel my cholesterol level soaring." He started wringing his hands. "My parents both have high cholesterol levels too. And I even look like my mother. Not that that's relevant of course."

Daniel/Zach looks like his mother too, so maybe that's how Professor Segal tracked him down, Lauren thought.

"...just like old John Bartleby. Except that he has a lot more wrinkles," Wade was saying. "And he's her great-uncle. I've never seen such a strong resemblance."

"How do you know that?" Nick asked. "John Bartleby hasn't come out of his house in twenty years."

"Oh, I know what he looks like." Wade bobbed his head up and down.

"From old photos?" Nick queried. "Or have you actually seen the Bartlebys?"

Wade suddenly looked quite startled. "Oh, no. Oh, no. I haven't seen the Bartlebys, no. It's from pictures, Nick, from pictures." And he scuttled back across the room on his long skinny legs.

"That was weird," Nick muttered. "Did you hear that?"

"It sounds like he's really seen them." Lauren was puzzled.

"Yeah. And nobody ever lays eyes on them. So why would Wade, of all people, have seen them?"

It was an intriguing question, to which Lauren, unfortunately, had no response. She returned to the equally intriguing question of secret romances. "Do you know anything about Tony's secret romances?"

"Tony's romances? I don't know. We didn't talk about that a whole lot." He looked a little embarrassed.

Her phone buzzed. "In Baltimore!" the text said. It was from Sonya.

Lauren was amazed. First Professor Segal and Ethan, here in D.C., and now Sonya, an hour's drive away. She couldn't escape academia. "Really? Why?" she texted back.

"Anna Slinsky here temporarily & agreed speak w/me. So excited as u can imagine!" Sonya replied.

Lauren couldn't imagine, because she wasn't sure who Anna Slinsky was. "Great!"

"Yes, it is!" Lauren could picture Sonya, her ever-present black clothing, the wooden earrings shaped like little Russian dolls dangling amidst her wavy dark hair. "Anna has never spoken about Petrovich to anyone. A little concerned, she 99 years old, recollections could be faulty. But certainly hoping to get a lot out of her!"

Lauren had a sudden image of Sonya shaking a piggy bank shaped like a ninety-nine-year-old Russian woman, and watching the coins fall out. Except that they weren't coins, they were recollections about the obscure mid-20th-century Russian poet Petrovich, the subject of Sonya's research. Now she realized who Anna Slinsky must be—one of the women in Petrovich's fateful love triangle that Sonya was writing about.

"Going to Institute to hear Meryl Segal tonight. U should come, bring Anna," Lauren texted. "7 pm. Simon there too."

"Yay! Simon one of fave cousins. Will try!"

"My friend Sonya just texted me," Lauren told Nick. "She's

in Baltimore interviewing a ninety-nine-year-old Russian woman who knew this poet Sonya's writing about." She sighed. Why wasn't Natasha calling her back?

"Wow. You know a lot of really fascinating people."

Lauren's phone rang. It was Natasha. "Look, Lauren, I'm sure you just misplaced the folder somewhere. It'll turn up."

"But don't you think someone..."

"No. I wouldn't worry about it, okay?" And Natasha hung up.

Lauren shrugged. She had done all she could. So she located some blank political surveys and picked up her phone. She was in the middle of interviewing a famous Harvard political expert when Louis strolled into the office.

"Where have you been?" Louisa snapped. "You're supposed to be inputting the data for Our Most Admired Religious Figure."

"I was talking to my lawyer," Louis said, hanging up his jacket.

Lauren's ears perked up.

"Your lawyer?" Louisa said disbelievingly.

"The level of political discourse in Washington is lower than I've seen it in my entire career," the political expert on the other end of the line was saying. "Can anyone agree on anything? You take health care, okay? Are there any prospects for bipartisanship? No. The quality of our elected officials..."

"Yes," Louis said, beaming as he sat down at his desk. Lauren frowned. Did this have to do with Louis's mysterious video game? Had he succeeded in copyrighting it, now that Tony was dead?

"Did I say you could do that today?" Louisa said sharply.

"I asked Wade, right, Wade?" Louis looked in Wade's direction.

"I think Louie did ask me for permission to leave the office today," Wade said hazily. He popped a Hershey's kiss into his mouth.

"Well, all right," Louisa said. "So get to work, Louis, now, please."

"...as I remarked on MSNBC the other night," the expert was saying, "it's several years away, but when you look at the potential Democratic presidential candidates, you think about Fogerty's problems now, and..."

"The doctor was like totally excellent, man." It was Jim, followed by Cecily. They ambled into the room, toward their desks. "He said I should get glasses, but just for distance. Like, my vision's not as good as it used to be."

"I think you should get those really cool glasses with the blue frames," Cecily said.

"Please." Louisa tapped ominously at her clipboard. "I would appreciate it if you two could do some work?"

"Yeah." Jim sounded pleased. "Let's go after work and check out those glasses." He sat down and plugged his earphones in. "This is just too cool," he said blissfully.

"Jim?" Louisa's voice was getting louder.

"...never seen anything like this administration," the expert on Lauren's phone was expounding. "Chaos. Dysfunction. As I mentioned to the minority leader a few weeks ago, what the country really needs is..."

Louisa marched over to Jim's desk. Jim was leaning back in his chair, earphones on, oblivious to her presence. She reached over and unplugged the speakers.

"Hey," he said, apparently surprised. "Why'd you do that?"

"Because I am your boss, and this is your office, and you are supposed to be working," Louisa yelled.

"Is something going on in your office?" the political expert queried.

"Oh, um," Lauren said.

"I can't take this anymore," Louisa shouted, her voice breaking.

"Look, I should be going anyway," the expert said. "I have the Post and CNN waiting to speak with me. Bye."

"Okay, bye." Lauren hung up and turned towards Louisa.

"I try to keep this office going, but first someone gets murdered, and then the surveys disappear, and nobody can ever seem to do anything without me standing over them. And meanwhile, and meanwhile...oh, forget it." And Louisa rushed out of the room.

"All I wanted to do was listen to some music." Jim looked around in bewilderment. "I don't see why she got so upset."

Sixteen

It was a little before seven when Lauren arrived at the Institute, which occupied an ornate mansion off Dupont Circle, a short walk from Amanda's apartment. The front lobby was crowded with people, all milling around and talking loudly. She slipped through the crowd and down the hallway to the stairs. Karel Halama's office was probably on the second floor, she figured, with those of the other visiting fellows.

She crept down the deserted second-floor corridor, past posters from various art galleries around the world, and finally she heard a querulous Czech voice that sounded like Halama's, coming from a half-open door. He was complaining, apparently on the phone, about how he had to share an office with an annoying woman who insisted on talking to him all the time. Probably the woman Lauren had spoken with earlier. Halama obviously hadn't modified his behavior for his American sojourn. He was as irascible as ever.

She waited till he'd hung up, and then tapped at his door.

"What?" he grunted.

Lauren pushed the door open. Sure enough, there he was. His white hair stuck out in wisps around his head, his corpulent body was stuffed into a straight-backed wooden armchair, and his large lower lip stuck out truculently.

"What do you want?" he demanded in heavily accented English, shooting an unpleasant look in her direction.

Lauren explained who she was, that she'd met him in Prague,

and that she worked at Lens magazine now. "So I thought I'd stop by, since I was going to the conference downstairs."

Halama seemed to get even angrier. "Lens? Pah," he spat, his face turning red.

"What?"

"I have to get some work done," Halama said in Czech. "I have no time to talk to you now. But maybe later I'll go down to the conference. Not that I especially want to talk to you there either." And he made a shooing motion at her.

So Lauren went back downstairs. Halama had never been pleasant, but this was ridiculous. Natasha, she recalled, had been very good at imitating him. She would send Lauren into hysterics by sticking out her lower lip and saying something incredibly rude.

Lauren approached the lobby, and suddenly found herself face-to-face with Braden Finney, one of her former students. He had taken her International Relations course, as well as her seminar on Russian politics, and he had graduated a year ago. "Braden!" she cried, feeling a wave of nostalgia for the college and her students.

"Dr. Green, I mean, Lauren." His freckled face lit up. "Wow, it's great to see you. I didn't know you were coming."

She smiled, noting that Braden was going through the same name-confusion with her that she did with Professor Segal. She had told the students who'd stayed in touch after graduating that they could abandon title formalities, but she knew that old habits were hard to break. "It's great to see you, too," she said, noting that Braden was wearing a nametag reading, "Hi, my name is BRADEN. Braden Finney, Institute staff." She hadn't realized he was working there.

"I just started here a few weeks ago," he said. "I tried to get in touch with you and let you know, but the email bounced back. What's up?"

"They ran out of funding for my position. So I left after fall semester."

"Aw, man, that sucks. You were like my favorite professor. And I know a lot of other people felt like that, too."

"Thanks," Lauren said sadly.

"Why don't you have some dinner?" Braden led her over to a buffet table laden with various cold cuts, rolls, and salads. "It's not bad."

Lauren, who found she was quite hungry, fixed herself a sandwich.

"Let me make you a nametag." Braden reached for one. "Hi, my name is..." the nametag said, incompletely. Lauren hated nametags. They made her feel overly conspicuous. "LAUREN," Braden was writing in block letters with a black marker, and then underneath, "Lauren Green." He looked at her. "Where are you working now?"

"Lens magazine."

At Braden's look of surprise, Lauren added, "It's a long story." She imagined what the nametag really should say. "Hi, my name is LAUREN. Lauren Green, confused person." And then other people's might say things like, "Hi, my name is WADE. Wade Wood, secret egg-and-red-meat eater." Or, "Hi, my name is (FILL IN THE BLANK). (Fill in the blank), murderer."

"Lauren!" It was Professor Segal, with Simon, Ethan, and a large young man in tow. He was wearing a fedora, was holding a reporter's notebook, and had a pen tucked behind his ear. "I do so love nametags," The professor beamed and gestured at her own nametag, which hung askew on her jacket. "Normally I'm so bad with names."

"Lauren, it's great to see you," Ethan gave her a hug. "Let me tell you about my flight. It left San Francisco four hours late, okay? Four hours late. And then I missed my connection in Chicago, so

I had to wait five more hours for the next one. And then I was bumped off that one, so I didn't get in till this afternoon."

Lauren was starting to feel that familiar impatience. She glanced over at Professor Segal, who was busily chatting with Braden.

"And then," Ethan continued, lowering his voice only slightly, "Meryl told me I was giving my presentation Thursday, and then it got moved to tomorrow. Can you believe that? And what did you think of her article in the L.A. Times the other day on the Russia situation? I myself found it to be a little overstated. I found..."

"So you're a friend of Mrs. Segal's too?" the large young man broke in, turning to Lauren. She looked at his nametag, and found that his name was ZACH, Zach Cohen, Time magazine. He had an aggressive look on his round moonlike face. She pictured an older female version of him, telling Professor Segal what her four sons were up to.

Lauren nodded. Although she had never thought of the professor as "Mrs. Segal." Professor Segal didn't even have the same last name as her husband. And why was Zach Cohen wearing a fedora, anyway? And that pen behind his ear? He looked like something out of the movie The Front Page. Or maybe His Girl Friday. Both great movies, but still.

"Well?" Zach leaned toward Lauren and pulled the pen out from behind his ear. "Let's hear the real scoop, okay?"

"On what?" She noted that Ethan had drifted off to talk to a group of other people. She should be doing that, too, she told herself. Sandor and Margot Kis were off in the distance. She thought of their book and shuddered.

"On what." Zach snickered. "And you call yourself a newswoman?"

"No, I don't, actually." Zach reminded her of a few students she had taught over the years. Try as she might, she couldn't bring herself to like them.

"Give me the scoop on Mandel," he said, pen poised over notebook. "I want to know what really happened. Did Cecily do it? Or did this Wade guy do it?"

So everyone knew that Wade was the new star suspect. How strange.

"Cecily Bottomley couldn't have done it," said Simon, who had reappeared. "She's far too namby-pamby."

"Oh?" Zach turned abruptly toward Simon. "How do you know?"

"I've seen her a couple of times." Simon shrugged. "She couldn't even lift that vase, much less hit someone over the head with it."

Lauren, finishing the last bite of her sandwich, wondered whether Simon's impression of Cecily would change if he saw her in her Tony-channeling daredevil driving persona.

"Well, Lauren?" Zach asked. "Do you agree with this assessment?"

"Why should I tell you?" Lauren felt rather disagreeable. "You work for the competition, right?"

"Hey, Lauren, come on. Mrs. Segal and my mom go way back. If I break this story, I'll get hired for sure once I graduate. And then I can do more interesting things than covering conferences like this."

"Simon! Lauren!" a voice sounded behind her. She turned to find Sonya, leading in a tiny old lady. Sonya wrapped Lauren and Simon, in turn, in enthusiastic embraces, after which Lauren looked down to find the nametag on Sonya's companion. "Hi, my name is ANNA," it said. "Anna Slinsky, muse." Muse?

"Lauren, Simon, this is Anna Slinsky," Sonya said, her face flushed with professional well-being. "Our interview was going so well, Anna decided to come along to the conference with me. And of course I know Braden over there, so he let us right in." Sonya took two plates and filled them up, handing one to Anna Slinsky. Both Sonya and Anna Slinsky were wrapped in Russian scarves patterned with brightly colored flowers.

"Very pleased to meet you," Anna Slinsky said in a cracked accented voice. "Please, to the chairs now?"

"I think she wants to sit down. We'll see you at the break, okay, Lauren?"

"Okay." Lauren wished Nick had come along. He would have thought this was funny. But then the thought of Nick reminded her of the article, and of Karel Halama. Was he really going to show up? Or would she have to brave his office again?

"Muse?" Zach seemed baffled. "I don't get it."

"How absolutely fascinating," Simon said. "I assume she's some sort of Russian muse?"

"I would assume she was the muse of a Russian poet from the middle of the twentieth century called Petrovich," Lauren said.

"How does she tie in?" Zach asked. "Is she one of the speakers or something?"

"No," Lauren said, about to explain, when a man started talking into the microphone at the front of the auditorium, imploring the conferees to sit down. As everyone, including Lauren, settled into their seats, he introduced Professor Segal, who launched into a comparison of political conditions in various Eastern European countries. But the excitement Lauren usually felt when listening to someone talk about that part of the world was absent. It was as if she were someone else who just happened to be attending a lecture. Her brain was not involved.

The moderator had regained the podium. "Many thanks to our esteemed colleague Meryl Segal," he said, and everyone applauded. "And now I'm pleased to announce the start of our annual meeting."

About three-quarters of the audience got up and started leaving the auditorium, talking and laughing as they did so.

Sonya moved over to sit in front of Lauren, Anna Slinsky tottering behind her.

"Hey," Zach said loudly. "Who is she?" He gestured at Anna Slinsky, who was about to sit down next to Sonya. "What does she do, anyway?"

Anna Slinsky turned to face Zach, as Sonya frowned reprovingly at him. "I was friend of great poet," she said, pausing carefully between each word. "Great poet known by pseudonym of Petrovich. In fact, I was present at death of Petrovich. Many years ago." And she turned around again.

"Petrovich?" Zach said accusingly. "I've never heard of him."

"How did this Petrovich chap die?" Simon asked.

Lauren didn't feel like listening. She wasn't sure she could bear hearing anymore about how people died. First Tony Mandel, now Petrovich.

"Petrovich had been living with Anna for several years," Sonya began. "He referred to her as his muse. She inspired some of his greatest poems. And then another woman entered the picture. Petrovich's poems from that time become more confused, more angry, more elemental. The imagery becomes more violent. You see, Petrovich was a true genius. And I have been selected to translate a volume of his poems into English for the first time, and write a biography too. My research indicates..."

Lauren started tuning out. She spotted Ethan across the room, deep in conversation with a couple of his colleagues from Berkeley.

"...so Lyubov, the other woman, that is, killed Petrovich in a tragic love triangle," Sonya was saying. "And Anna was there when it happened. Weren't you, Anna?" Sonya tapped Anna Slinsky on the back.

"Yes," Anna said.

Simon shook his head pleasurably. "What a gripping tale. I need to talk to you some more about your research, Sonya. Absolutely fascinating."

"I still don't get what she has to do with the conference," Zach said, tucking his pen behind his ear.

"Well, as the muse of an esteemed Russian poet, she has her place at any gathering," Sonya said indignantly.

"Hear, hear," Simon said.

Lauren sighed. Her feeling of exasperation was increasing rapidly.

"I'm getting the hell out of here," Zach muttered. "I have to come back tomorrow, and I can't stand this anymore." He stood up and pushed his way down the aisle past Simon and Lauren, shooting a puzzled glance over his shoulder in the direction of Anna Slinsky.

Lauren wanted to leave too. But she felt she should stay to tell the professor she'd enjoyed the speech. And the thought of returning to Karel Halama's office wasn't too palatable either.

"Why don't we go stand in the lobby?" Simon suggested.

Lauren agreed.

"I think Anna and I will leave now," Sonya stage-whispered toward Lauren and Simon, as the noise from the crowd subsided. "I'll try to be in touch tomorrow."

Anna Slinsky smiled and nodded, her hooded eyes crinkling.

Out in the lobby, Lauren saw Ethan heading toward her.

"So, Lauren, the wedding invitations are going out in a few weeks," he said. "You're coming, aren't you? I mean, I know weddings might stress you out after everything with Eric, but Jose and I would really like it if you could make it." He paused. "But of course we'd understand if it's just too much for you right now."

Lauren considered the options. Going to a wedding would be very difficult. Not going might be the easier path to follow. But she should go. She had known Ethan for almost a decade, after all. And she was fond of him, despite his often-annoying tendencies. Plus, it would be nice to return to the Bay Area for a visit. "Sure. Yes. I'll be there." She mustered up a smile.

"Oh, good. I'll let Jose know. And I wanted to tell you, Jose finally finished that project of his. The one about the libel case." Ethan had described the case to Lauren in excruciating detail far too many times.

Finally, Lauren thought, nodding pleasantly at Ethan. It would be nice not to have to hear about that case anymore.

"Of course, I feel libel is totally unimportant when contrasted with the issue of press coverage of Central and Southeastern Europe, don't you think so, Lauren? And furthermore, I feel..."

Lauren tried to concentrate. She knew that the whole issue of libeling someone was important. So she would have to disagree with Ethan. But she really wasn't in the frame of mind to engage in that kind of discussion right now.

Simon had joined Lauren and Ethan, and started discussing his research again. "...many more people from quite prominent families are involved," he was saying. "And I've been given access to some information that I think is quite new, really, quite new."

Maybe she should leave without seeing Professor Segal, Lauren thought. She just couldn't deal with the world of academia anymore. Not that the world of Lens magazine was any better, of course.

Her mind drifted back to a time when she thought she knew what she was doing. When other people also seemed to think she knew what she was doing. There was the time in graduate school when she had won the teaching award. The time at the college when she and Sonya had been recognized for organizing a new interdisciplinary seminar on Russian politics and cinema. And the time when her European politics course had been voted most popular in the college newspaper's annual survey. And then it had all fallen apart. The personal as well as the professional. Her life was a total disaster, any way you looked at it.

"Lauren, Simon, Ethan, I just had to get out of there," said the professor, bustling towards them. "The meeting seemed about to degenerate into a shouting match, so I made a hasty departure."

"That was a great presentation," Lauren said.

"Quite good, really," said Simon.

Ethan nodded.

"Well, I am delighted you thought so," said the professor. "And where has Daniel disappeared to?"

"He had to leave," Lauren said. "But he said he'd be back tomorrow. And actually, I should be leaving too." She turned to Ethan. "I'll try to be there for your presentation. What time is it going to be?"

"Tomorrow morning," Ethan said. "Right, Meryl?"

"Oh, dear." The professor wrinkled her brow. "I just heard the panels had been shifted again. They moved your panel, Ethan. To Friday, I believe?"

Ethan took a deep breath.

"Well, we'll be seeing you, Lauren," the professor said. "Perhaps tomorrow, then?"

"Maybe. I mean, I hope so." Lauren waved at the professor and Simon and Ethan, and hurried through the lobby to the stairs.

Halama's door was open, a shaft of light shining out. The second-floor hallway was silent. Lauren knocked softly on the door, and he looked up. "What do you want?" he said, his lip jutting out. It seemed to be his customary greeting.

"I wanted," said Lauren, trying to maintain as much dignity as possible, "to talk to you about an article in Lens magazine."

"Article in Lens?" Halama glowered at her. "I know nothing about article in Lens."

She pulled out Nick's article from her bag and handed it to him.

Halama took the article, glanced at it for a split second, and recoiled. "Lens," he said ferociously. He switched into Czech. "I would never have agreed to be interviewed for that article if I had known what I know now," he muttered, his eyes shooting waves of fury at her. "The sort of people who work at that magazine," and he shook his head. "Totally irresponsible."

"What do you mean? Is something wrong with the article? Who interviewed you? Was it Nick Belotserkovsky? Or someone else?"

But Halama refused to say anymore. "Out," he suddenly yelled in English, his face turning even redder than it had earlier. "That is all I say now."

Lauren left.

Seventeen

Still determined to find her missing folder, Lauren got to work at eight the next day. "Morning," said Winston. "You're an early riser, aren't you."

"Not usually, actually." Lauren paused to glance at Winston's set of monitors.

"Pretty quiet this morning. At least those workmen are finished with that renovation right in back of my desk. All that banging around, it was too much. I told that to the police. I told them maybe one of those workmen did it." And Winston gave her a meaningful look and nodded.

"What else did you tell them, anyway?"

"Well, now. I told them I got here at six, that I didn't see anybody coming in, and then I saw Natasha coming in around seven." He paused and shook his head. "I don't know how that young woman ever has any time to herself. And it's too bad, if you ask me."

"Did they ask you about anything else?"

"Then I saw Fred coming in a little later. Early meeting, he told me." Winston shook his head. "It's those Bartlebys again."

"What, they have meetings early in the morning?" Maybe that's what Tony was doing there, then. Calling the Bartlebys.

"Young lady, you wouldn't understand." Winston smiled at her. "We old people can't sleep well at night. So those Bartlebys call Natasha early in the morning, they call Fred early in the morning, it's like the middle of the day to them. If those Bartlebys call

Natasha at two in the morning and tell her to look something up, and if it's something she can't do on her computer at home, something that's on paper, say, because they prefer paper, she better get over here and do what they say. It's not good for a young lady like that. No time to herself. I think lately she's taking it a little easier, though. She hasn't been in as early the past few days, and that's all to the good." And Winston paused. "And then there was something else I meant to tell the police, but I forgot."

"What?" Maybe he could tell her.

Winston shook his head. "It was someone else told me something. But I can't remember who or what. Somebody saw somebody else outside the building."

"Someone from the other part of the building? Where I work?"

"I just can't remember. It's the old age creeping up."

"Okay. I'll ask you about it later, then." And Lauren made her way up to her part of the office. So Fred and Natasha tended to hang around the office at odd hours, thanks to the Bartlebys? That was interesting. But the question of why Tony had done so remained unanswered. Would the Bartlebys be making mysterious early-morning calls to Tony? It was doubtful.

She walked over to her desk. The office was empty. Good. She could start looking for her folder. First, she should lock her bag up. She pulled the key out of her bag and opened the drawer. There, right where it should have been all along, was the folder. "Oh, my god," Lauren said aloud. Had she been hallucinating?

She pulled the folder out. What if it had been there the entire time? Quickly, she checked the contents. The article about Natasha. Natasha's resume. Tony's information. Louisa's. Nick's. Louis's. Cecily's. Jim's. That looked like everything. She mentally reviewed the inhabitants of the office. Wade. Where was Wade's information? She looked through the folder again. Wade's resume and evaluations were gone. No doubt about it. What did that mean?

Footsteps approached up the stairs, and Lauren quickly put the folder into the drawer.

"Lauren?" It was Louisa. "You're in early today." She sighed and headed for her desk. "Look," she said, sitting down and unloading a large envelope from her briefcase. "I wanted to tell you, I'm sorry about my little outburst yesterday. It's just been a very hard week. Brad had to go in to his office at five this morning, and now I have to run over to the Hill and give this to him." She gestured at the envelope.

Louisa's office phone rang. "Shit." Louisa picked it up. "Oh, Natasha. Yes. Yes, of course. I certainly will. Of course. Thank you." She slammed the phone down. "Damn. Natasha apparently just got in, and she needs me to come over now to discuss how we're going to handle the press on the survey results." She paused for a moment, before shaking her head. "But this envelope is really important. Brad has to sign these papers now." She sighed again. "I don't believe this."

"Is there anything I can do to help?" Lauren asked. Maybe she could take whatever this was to Brad and get another chance to talk to him. Maybe he would say something useful.

"Well," Louisa said, considering. "That's awfully nice of you, but I couldn't ask you to...well, so Brad and I are buying a house. And we have to sign these papers. They're supposed to be in by noon today. And Brad was so preoccupied that he left this morning without signing them. I would just send it to him electronically, but I think he really has to sign the original document. It has to be notarized."

"I'll take it over to him."

“Would you, Lauren?” Louisa looked relieved. She scribbled something on the envelope. “Thank you so much. Fogerty’s office is in the Dirksen building, all right? I just wrote the room number on the envelope for you.”

Shortly thereafter, Lauren was in an Uber. “Hey, man,” the driver said. He wore his longish hair in dreadlocks. “You work at Lens magazine?” He turned down his radio, which had been on the all-news station.

Lauren answered in the affirmative.

“I hear they don’t think the little rich girl did it. They think some guy did it now, right? Back in my country we have things like that going on. Some pretty crazy things.”

“What happened?” It seemed as if all Lauren ever talked to people about lately was death. Violent death.

“Well, it was about three years ago. And this guy, he was killed by his girlfriend right outside my house. Crazy, man.”

“That’s awful.” Lauren shivered. “Why did she kill him?” Maybe it was a love triangle, like with Anna Slinsky and the poet Petrovich.

“Another woman,” the driver said, honking loudly at a car ahead of them. “Women can be real problems, man.”

Other women did seem to be a theme of murders, Lauren thought. Could Cecily really have done it after all? Maybe she had just become so frustrated about Tony’s cheating that she couldn’t stand it anymore and her threat to kill him turned real. Maybe Tucker and McDonald had been right the first time and Natasha and the Bartlebys were wrong. And then her own investigation would be worthless. Actually, it was pretty worthless, at least so far.

“Dirksen Building,” the driver eventually announced. “Now, you be careful. Don’t go getting involved with some guy who already has a girlfriend, okay?”

"Okay. I'll try not to." She got out. He turned the news radio back up, and she thought she heard the words "murder at Lens magazine" emerging from the radio as the car sped away.

She proceeded into the building, through security, and down massive high-ceilinged corridors. As she got closer to what she presumed was the senator's office, she saw people moving around, way down the hall. They were holding large pieces of equipment. She continued walking, and realized they were reporters, waiting outside Fogerty's office.

Lauren made her way through, and eventually was escorted back to Brad's office. His desk was inundated with papers. Framed posters and signed photos lined the wall in back of him. A poster with Senator Fogerty's familiar handsome face grinned out at her. "Vote Fogerty. For All of Us," it read. Next to it was a photo of Brad and the senator, and another of Brad and Louisa.

"Hell, no," Brad was saying into the phone. "Look, I could tell you you don't know shit about it, but I won't. I'll tell you..." He looked up and noticed Lauren standing there. "I'll tell you you might be slightly mistaken." He smiled and motioned for Lauren to sit down. "Just a second," he mouthed at her. "Well," he said into the phone. "We both know the senator will be completely exonerated, now, don't we? But we respect the legal process, yes. Absolutely. Right, Tommy. Absolutely. I'll be talking to you, then, buddy. Sure. Bye." And he hung up the phone, which buzzed. He picked it up again. "I know, Eileen. Three calls now? Okay, I'll take them in just a minute." He put the phone down and let out a huge sigh.

"So." He looked at Lauren and started to smile. "Out of the frying pan into the fire, huh? But at least your office isn't as crowded as this one. And on top of everything else Lou and I are buying a house. Great timing."

"Here's the envelope." Lauren handed it to him, marveling at his composure.

"Thanks. I really appreciate your doing this." He signed the various papers and handed the envelope back to Lauren. She got up to leave.

"No, you don't have to leave yet. I actually wanted to ask you about something. This is confidential, of course. Off the record, okay?"

Lauren nodded, and sat down again. Did this have to do with Tony?

"I know Louisa's been kind of upset lately, understandably, I mean, we all have been. And I'm sure a lot of it has to do with my situation here, and with Tony's death. But I'm worried there's more to it, and I can't help thinking it has to do with that guy Wade. Lou won't tell me much about him, just that he's completely incompetent. But I'm wondering if maybe he's trying to sabotage her work." Brad scratched his head. His phone buzzed again. "Okay, Eileen," he said into the phone. "Just a couple more minutes." He put the phone down and sighed, rubbing his eyes. He looked exhausted, Lauren thought. "Now, where was I? Oh, like the Post, right."

"What?"

"Oh, nothing. I mean, do you think Wade is trying to screw things up for Louisa?"

Lauren thought about that idea. Wade didn't seem capable of doing anything like that. At least, not right now. He seemed far too preoccupied with his eating problem and the murder investigation to focus on Louisa. Although there was certainly no love lost between them. "He doesn't especially like her. But I don't think Wade really has time right now to sabotage anyone."

"Okay. It's just that you seem like a pretty observant person, and I've been worried about what's going on in your office. I was thinking of asking Jim about it, but you know how he is."

"Yeah." Lauren smiled. He'd probably get his answer from Jim next week sometime.

"Well, thanks, Lauren. Lou and I both appreciate your help. You know your way out?"

Lauren nodded, and Brad stood and gave her a thumbs-up sign before picking up his phone again. She made her way outside, where it had started to rain, and a couple of minutes later her Uber pulled up and she got in. So Brad was worried that Wade was trying to sabotage Louisa's work? And what had he said about the Post? Louisa had worked there. Had something strange happened that caused her to leave?

Maybe Amanda knew someone at the Post. She had told Amanda the previous night about Nick inviting them over for dinner, and Amanda had been amazed. "He never invites people over. At least, not me," she had said, as the two of them indulged in some tea and leftover cookies from the party. "But unfortunately, I can't go. I have to work late most nights, and then I'm supposed to have dinner with this friend of Adam and Stacy's at some point."

"Well, I'll go then."

"Go over to a potential murderer's house by yourself? Oh, no you won't. It's one thing to have dinner with him in a restaurant, in a public place with other people around. But you're not going to his house."

"But..."

"Look." Amanda gave Lauren one of her appraising looks. "I know you really like him, right? Even if you're probably still not sure you're ready for anything new. And under normal circumstances, I'd say great! Go for it! You're much cuter than Lisa, anyway. If she's even in the picture."

Lauren was grateful for Amanda's loyalty. But she knew she could never approach Lisa's level of coolness. And she could tell there was a "however" coming. She waited.

"I actually could see the two of you together, under normal circumstances. He has that same impractical quality you do. And he's kind of good-looking, in his own sensitive-intellectual way. Not that I'm interested in him. He's much too quiet. And too obsessed with his novel." Amanda took a breath. "But it probably would be good for you to have a rebound relationship, or whatever you want to call it. I think you're ready to try. I mean, Eric really messed you up, and you should do whatever it takes to get him out of your system."

Lauren agreed with some of what Amanda was saying, although she didn't like the term "rebound relationship," which sounded tawdry, and the "much too quiet" and "too obsessed" comments. And she wasn't entirely sure she was ready for anything new, because what if it only led to more rejection? And this was all completely hypothetical, anyway, because she didn't know Nick's relationship status. Or even what he thought of her. But in any case, she knew Amanda was only just winding up for her closing argument, which would turn the whole thing on its head.

Sure enough. "But these are not normal circumstances." Amanda's voice was getting louder. "Nick is a murder suspect! Tony is dead, and Nick might have done it!"

"He..." Lauren started. That was one thing she was sure of. He couldn't have. It wasn't possible.

"I'm not saying he definitely did it, but he could have!" Amanda said, steamrolling over Lauren. "And you're really vulnerable right now! I mean, first you go through the whole thing with Eric, and then you start a new job and the minute you walk in, you find Tony lying there, dead? I'm sure you must be completely traumatized."

Lauren thought about that. She probably was. An image of Tony, lying next to the copier, entered her mind, and she shuddered. It was so unthinkably devastating. Such a waste of a life.

"You're probably not thinking clearly at this point, and I'm not going to let you go over there by yourself! Find someone else to be interested in, Lauren, please! Not someone who's a suspect in a horrible murder. You're the closest thing I have to a sister, you know? I can't let anything happen to you!" And she leaned over and gave Lauren a hug. "Please?"

Remembering this conversation now, Lauren sighed. She had given Amanda some vague, noncommittal answer. She was sure Nick couldn't have done anything to Tony. But her conversation with Karel Halama hadn't been too helpful in trying to prove that point.

The car lurched to a stop outside the office, startling Lauren. She got out and saw Amanda alighting from an Uber next to her.

Eighteen

"Where have you been?" Amanda asked, as they rushed through the raindrops to the front door of Lens.

"I was doing a favor for Louisa. Dropping something off for her at Brad's office. And I found out something interesting," she continued, following Amanda into the lobby. "Or, I almost did." She briefly recounted her conversation with Brad. "Do you know anyone at the Post?"

"Yeah. I'll check around and let you know."

"Hey, young lady." It was Winston. "I remembered something. About what I was talking to you about before." He looked at Lauren, and then at Amanda.

"It was Jim," Winston said, as they came closer. "He came in and told me he was here that night. The night Tony was killed. And he said he saw Louisa, walking right in that side door. He was off down the street a ways, but he knew right off it was her. And he didn't tell anyone but me. I thought I should tell the police, but it went out of my mind." He looked sheepish. "That old age." He shook his head. "It's starting to get ahold of me."

Lauren pictured a wizened man, the personification of old age, latching on to Winston's arm and not letting go.

"Jim saw Louisa coming in?" Amanda was asking. "What time?"

Winston shrugged. "He didn't tell me about any time. He just said he saw Louisa walking in that door, that night."

"Whoa," Amanda said. "I mean, one of these days Jim's going

to have to get his act together. If he really did see something like that, he should tell the police."

A group of visitors arrived and Winston started talking to them, so Amanda and Lauren headed for their respective offices. Lauren handed the envelope over to Louisa, who thanked her effusively.

"And now I have to run over to the real estate agent's office," Louisa said. "But what if I take you out for coffee later, once I get back?" She smiled at Lauren.

"Sure, thanks." Lauren returned to her desk. Louisa was fascinating, she thought. One part of Louisa's personality was dreadful. Another part was someone Lauren could almost imagine being friendly with. And a third, mysterious, part had been seen around the building the night of Tony's death and had left the Post under unusual circumstances.

Lauren's phone rang before she could even pick up a survey form. It was Amanda.

"Okay, I talked to someone I know over there. She said she knew her and that Louisa had left in a strange kind of way. That nobody except a couple of the top editors really understood what had happened. But that everyone thought Louisa was a good reporter. Anyway, I have to go. Talk to you later."

Lauren pondered this information, which didn't explain very much. She looked around. Wade was not at his desk, and Louisa had gone out. But everyone else was in the room.

"And now we come to the section where I will ask you a few open-ended questions," Jim was braying into his phone. "Please respond to the following. How concerned are you about the state of political leadership in this country?"

Lauren realized she should talk to Jim about what Winston had said, but clearly this wasn't the best time. So she started making calls. She had just finished interviewing a very argumentative expert from the University of Texas, when Louisa appeared at Lauren's desk, purse in hand. "Shall we?" Louisa asked.

"Okay." Lauren noticed Nick giving her a puzzled look as she and Louisa left the room.

"Wade is over at the police station," Louisa said, as they walked down the stairs. "He said he had some things he wanted to talk to the detectives about. I can't imagine why they think he did it. He's the most ineffectual person I've ever encountered in my life. He couldn't murder someone if he was paid to do it." They passed Winston's desk and emerged under gray skies. At least the rain had stopped.

"Let's go to Starbucks." Louisa led the way down the street. "Brad and I really do appreciate your helping us out. You know the way things happen in life. Everything at once."

Lauren nodded. "So where's the house?"

"Arlington. We've been renting it for years and the owner finally decided to sell." Louisa started describing the house, and Lauren found her mind wandering. She had never bought a house, or an apartment, but the idea had been that she and Eric would buy a bigger apartment together at some point. They had looked around, mostly in Somerville and Brookline. But everything they liked had been too expensive.

"You know, I've often thought about teaching eventually," Louisa said, as they sat down at a table with their coffee. "Journalism is a good profession for me right now, but at some point I'll probably want a change."

Lauren nodded. "Would you want to teach journalism, or political science?"

"I need to think about it. But I admire what you're doing, trying something new. It provides a new perspective." Louisa paused, and sipped at her latte. "I certainly felt like that a couple of years ago, so I took a year off from journalism. I got a grant from a foundation, to write a book about women senators. But I never managed to finish it. I'm still working on it in my spare time."

Interesting, Lauren thought. "What made you take time off? Were you just tired of your job?"

"I was at the Post then." Louisa had a reminiscent look on her face. "It had always been my goal in life to work there, so the first couple of years I was on cloud nine. And I got a promotion. I was supposed to coordinate the paper's election coverage. But office politics got in the way. And so I decided I should quit and write that book."

"Office politics?" Lauren hoped Louisa would say more.

But Louisa's mouth was starting to purse, a bad sign. "That's right." She took another sip.

"What do you think of Detective Tucker and Detective McDonald?" Lauren asked, hoping to get Louisa onto the subject of Tony.

"Tucker is an idiot. McDonald seems a little more reasonable. But they obviously have no idea what they're doing. First Cecily and now Wade? I hardly think either of them could have murdered someone."

"Who do you think could have?" Lauren fixed her gaze on Louisa.

"I don't think anyone in the Most Admired Unit murdered Tony. The idea is absolutely ridiculous."

"But..."

"I have very little regard for the intelligence of the staff, except for Nick and Louis. And you, but you obviously had nothing to do with it. And I don't think Nick or Louis would murder anyone. The others aren't capable of coming up with such a scheme. So my theory is that Tony killed himself."

That was a new one. Lauren pictured Tony bringing the heavy vase down on his own head... "But that wouldn't work. Why would he have done that? And why in the office?"

"I can't imagine." Louisa shrugged. "I certainly never go into the office in the middle of the night unless I'm on deadline, and even when I am, I often can work from home. And with this Most Admired Unit job, I really never need to be in the office in the middle of the night."

"You don't?" Lauren thought of what Winston had said.

"Absolutely not. Why on earth would I do that? As I told the detectives, I spend enough time at the office anyway. And so does Brad. So when we don't have to be at our respective offices, we like to spend time together." She sniffed. "And then they questioned Brad too. I mean, really. Asking if by any chance I had crept out of the house in the middle of the night."

Lauren pondered this scenario. Louisa tiptoeing from the house in Arlington, leaving Brad slumbering. Or maybe not. Maybe she had taken Brad with her and Brad had killed Tony.

"Well." Louisa put down her empty coffee cup. "Obviously I had no special reason to like Tony. But I didn't kill him, and obviously Brad didn't kill him, and neither did anyone else on the staff. And that's all I have to say about it." She looked at her watch. "We should get back now. There's a lot to do."

Louisa headed straight to her desk once they returned to the office, and picked up her phone. Wade still wasn't back, and Jim, Cecily, and Louis also were gone. Nick was sitting at his desk reading, but he looked up as Lauren sat down. "Where did you go with Louisa?"

"Starbucks."

"I've never gone for coffee with Louisa." He closed his book.

Lauren glanced at it, to find that it was a beginning Dutch language book. "What did you guys talk about?"

"Careers. The office. You know."

"So." He leaned back in his chair. "Speaking of coffee, or meals, I mean, sorry, that's not the greatest segue, but did you talk to Amanda about dinner?"

"Oh. Amanda's busy all week, she told me." She took a deep breath. "But I can come over without her." She hoped she wasn't sounding too obnoxious. Maybe he only wanted to invite them in tandem.

"Good. Do you want to have dinner tonight? Or do you have plans?"

Lauren thought. She didn't really have to go to the conference tonight. And she'd much rather have dinner with Nick than spend another evening with Karel Halama, Zach Cohen, Ethan, Anna Slinsky, et al. Although the previous night's activities had been fascinating, in a bizarre sort of way. "I think that would be okay." Amanda would be furious, but she couldn't always do what Amanda told her, right? "Thanks. What time?"

"Say, seven-thirty. I'll have to clean the place up and make dinner. I'll text you the address, why don't I put your number into my phone." He lived in a converted garage, he told her, which he rented from friends.

"So did I tell you that I met a muse last night?" she asked, after they had exchanged phone numbers. "The 99-year-old woman I mentioned before?"

"No kidding. At the conference? Did you find her inspiring?"

She told him the story, which seemed to amuse him, and by then everyone had come back into the office.

"Would you all please start working?" Louisa rose to her feet and picked up her clipboard. "I have a meeting to go to with the photo staff."

"I'm supposed to go, too." Wade, who had just returned, looked quite agitated and was rubbing his head frantically.

"Are you sure you're up to it?" Louisa gave him a rather hard stare.

"Yes, Louisa, I'm up to it. Just because I've spent the day at the police station doesn't mean I'm not up to attending a simple meeting."

And they left.

"I need some tape," Jim said suddenly. He put his earbuds in and headed toward the supply room, snapping his fingers rhythmically as he went. Lauren followed him. She needed to ask him about seeing Louisa. He sat down on the floor of the supply room and started going through the bottom shelves.

"Jim?" He obviously didn't hear her. He was completely absorbed in his examination of the rolls of tape, boxes of pens and pencils, and reams of paper. "Jim." She tapped him on the shoulder.

"Huh? Oh, hi, Lauren."

"Listen, I have to ask you about something."

"Okay," Jim said amenably. He picked up a box of pencils and started looking through it. "Cool. A purple pencil."

"Could you take those out?" Lauren begged, gesturing at Jim's ears.

"Huh? Oh, yeah. Okay." He took them out. "My phone's wounded. I need to tape it together."

"What did you see that night? Did you see someone going into the building?"

"What night?" Jim stared up at her.

"The night Tony was killed." Lauren tried to retain her patience. "You were here, and you saw someone, right?"

"Oh, yeah," Jim said, light dawning. "When Tony was killed.

Yeah. And I never told the police about it."

"Well, you should. But why don't you tell me about it right now."

"Sure." Jim nodded. "See, I was hanging out down the street, and I saw Louisa going into the building. And then I left. And then I came in the next morning and I heard all about Tony."

"Was this the same night you yelled at Tony about how he treated Cecily?" Lauren whispered. She didn't think anyone could hear them, but...

"Oh, no." Jim shook his head and stood up. "Like, that was a different night. I didn't actually talk to Tony the night he was killed. I was just down the street, you know?"

"What were you doing down the street?" What possessed all these people to hang around the office at such unlikely hours? It was very strange.

"Huh?" Jim was tuning out again.

"Forget it." Lauren returned to her desk.

A few minutes later, Jim reemerged. He flipped the roll of tape up and caught it. "So, Lauren, I was just hanging out down the street for no particular reason."

"Thank you." None of this was making any sense.

Nineteen

"Okay, Lauren," Natasha said. "I don't think you need to continue the investigation." It was several hours later, and Lauren had been summoned to Natasha's office.

"What? But..."

"Look." Natasha pulled her hair back from her face and twisted it up in a knot. "The Bartlebys just called me. Apparently the police think they're close to making an arrest."

"Who are they going to arrest? Wade?"

Natasha shrugged. She got up from her desk and began pacing restlessly around the room. "I don't know. But I'd say yeah, probably. You know, there's something interesting about Wade. I'll tell you, but you've got to promise me you won't tell anyone, okay?"

Lauren nodded. What now?

"When the Bartlebys first came up with the idea of the Most Admired Unit, last year I guess it was, Bonnie Atlas—she was the editor then—told them she thought Louisa would make a good director. She's bright, she has a Ph.D., you know. And they liked her, too. That was fine. But then the Bartlebys insisted on making Wade co-director." Natasha sat down again and started fiddling around with one of the pens on her desk, taking its cap off and putting it on again. "Bonnie couldn't understand that at all. And neither can I. I mean, Wade has absolutely no managerial ability. But they insisted. By the time I got here, it was all settled."

This was interesting, Lauren thought. "Do you think he has some kind of hold over them?"

"I have no idea. I've been trying to find out, but I've been too busy to focus on it properly. But it's possible Tony knew something about it, and Wade killed him because of it. Tony did have a way of...well, I don't know."

Natasha's office phone rang. "Shit." She dropped the pen and picked up the phone. "Yeah? Oh, all right, Joanna. Yeah, I know. Fine, a couple more minutes, okay?" She hung up and turned back to Lauren. "So I really appreciate everything you've done for me."

Whatever that might be, Lauren thought. She had hardly scratched the surface.

"But I really don't need you to find out any more. I think the Bartlebys are satisfied now. Cecily's not the main suspect anymore, and all's well on the home front. So I'll be seeing you."

Natasha had already picked up her phone before Lauren was out the door. She felt a sense of letdown as she made her way back to her own office. What had she found out, anyway? She had been a disaster as a detective.

She slumped back to her desk to find that it was already six, and everyone seemed to be getting ready to leave.

"Good work," Wade was muttering. "You can leave if you want." He looked positively ashen. The brown paper bag was prominently placed on his desk.

"Don't think that because we're letting you out early today that you'll have an easy day tomorrow," Louisa snapped from her desk. "I expect you all to maintain a high productivity level throughout the remainder of the week."

"I'm going over to check out some glasses," Jim said. "You want to come, Cecily?"

"I can't. I'm supposed to have dinner with my family tonight."

"Okay." Jim departed. Louis wasn't far behind. Cecily remained at her desk, looking pensive.

"So," Nick said to Lauren. "You'll come by around seven-thirty, then?"

Lauren nodded. "Should I bring anything?" She found that she was really looking forward to this dinner. As long as she didn't think about Amanda's reaction.

"No, that's okay. See you." And he smiled at her and left.

Lauren's phone rang. It was Professor Segal. "Would you like to come and sit in the garden at my hotel? It's quite charming. Simon and Daniel and I are taking a little break from the conference, and we were wondering if you'd like to join us."

"Sure," Lauren said. The professor gave her directions to the hotel. There would be enough time to meet them before dinner.

"Lauren?" Cecily asked timidly. "Are you getting ready to leave?"

"Uh-huh." Lauren picked up her bag.

"Oh."

"What is it?" Lauren asked, concerned.

"I just wanted to ask you something."

"Why don't we walk downstairs, then. We can talk before I leave."

"Okay," Cecily whispered. She got her things together, and the two of them left Wade and Louisa working away.

"What's going on?" Lauren asked, once she and Cecily were in the parking lot. The weather had changed again. It was humid and muggy, almost like summer, and a slight breeze was blowing. The sort of weather that always made Lauren feel expectant, as if something out-of-the-ordinary were about to happen.

"It's Tony." And Cecily started to cry. Lauren patted Cecily on the shoulder, located a tissue, and handed it to her.

"What about Tony?" Lauren said gently.

"Well, the more I think about it," Cecily said, gulping, "the more I think Tony didn't really care about me at all. I think he only cared about my family."

"Oh, I don't know. I'm sure he cared about you very much."

"Only sometimes. There were all these other women. And I think recently there was one other woman that he really cared about." And she sniffed into her tissue.

"What other woman?"

"I don't know. It's just that he was always leaving in the middle of the night whenever he'd be over at my apartment. And he'd never tell me where he was going. It's like the night he was..." and she stopped abruptly.

"Cecily. Did he leave your apartment that night, and you followed him over here, and..."

"I wasn't here. Please believe me." Cecily looked at Lauren with widened blue eyes. "Really, I wasn't."

"What was Jim doing over here then? Did he come over here because you asked him to?"

"I didn't. I didn't ask Jim to do that."

"Did Jim tell you he saw Louisa over here that night?" Lauren felt elephantine again. Cecily seemed to have that effect on her.

"Yes, Jim and I think Louisa killed Tony."

"Did you tell the police that?"

"No."

"Why not? Jim saw Louisa going in there, and he didn't tell anyone? Especially when you were the main suspect?"

"I think he forgot."

"And you weren't anywhere around here yourself?"

"No, really I wasn't. I should be going. My family doesn't like to eat dinner very late." And she smiled a watery smile at Lauren, hopped into her car, and, with a roar, zoomed onto Wisconsin Avenue, narrowly missing a bus.

This still wasn't making sense, Lauren thought, as she drove over to the professor's hotel, which was down the street from the Institute. She entered the hotel, a quaint old building, to find Professor Segal, Simon, and Zach sitting in comfortable-looking armchairs in the lobby. The place reeked of atmosphere. There were fireplaces and nooks and crannies and wood-paneled walls. It looked like the kind of hotel she wouldn't mind staying in.

"Oh, Lauren." Professor Segal rose from her armchair. "Isn't this lovely? I stay here whenever I'm in Washington."

Zach, fedora on his head, glowered at Lauren, and Simon smiled. "I say. It's quite nice to see you. And shall we go outside now?"

"What a good idea," the professor said, and they followed her out into a small garden, where tables were set up and a few people were eating dinner.

"Charming spot." Simon looked around as they all sat down. "A nice change of pace, hey, Meryl?"

"Well," Professor Segal said. "The conference has been quite interesting, but one does need a break every now and then. It's too bad Ethan couldn't join us. He's with the people from his panel, discussing what they're going to say."

Lauren sighed. Hearing about Ethan's activities really upset her. But would she want to be presenting a paper right now? She wasn't sure.

"I've been so busy meeting people at the conference I haven't had a chance to do any of my own work," Simon said.

Zach fidgeted around unhappily. Lauren wondered what his problem was.

"How's Cecily Bottomley doing?" Simon said, as usual looking quite pleased with himself.

"Bartleby," Lauren said.

"Bottomley, yes."

"Well, she was kind of upset today."

"About what?" Zach asked, coming to life.

"Nothing in particular." Lauren wasn't going to tell the world, via Time magazine, about Cecily's problems.

"Oh, come on," Zach said, a wheedling note in his voice. "If you help me with this story, I'll be eternally grateful. I'll help you one day with a story."

"Ah," said the professor, raising her index finger in the air, "but Lauren's a scholar, not a journalist. At least, I certainly hope so."

Lauren smiled weakly at her and checked the time. She should leave soon.

"Yes, yes," the professor suddenly said. "About your magazine, Lauren. It was something Ethan said that reminded me. Something to do with an article. Maybe libel?"

"What was the article about?" Lauren asked. What if it had to do with Nick and Tony? That second accusation? Oh, no, please, make it be about something else, she thought.

Zach had pulled his pen out from behind his ear and was looking alertly at the professor.

"It'll come to me," the professor said.

"All this talk about investigations reminds me of something interesting I've uncovered in my study of your campaign finance system," Simon said. And he started on a lengthy discourse about campaign finance. Zach had replaced his pen behind his ear, so Lauren figured whatever Simon was saying couldn't be too newsworthy. The professor was wrinkling her brow, obviously trying to remember what it was she had heard that had so disturbed her.

"So," Simon said, "I was informed just last week that there may be an investigation into this fellow's finances. Chap's rolling in money, and he was serving on the board of this bank out in

California. He was steering his friends toward all these good investments. Making special deals for them. And furthermore, I was told that he'd been involved in some sort of tax scandal a few years ago that was hushed up by his family. Quite powerful people, really."

Cecily must have been there that night, Lauren thought. And despite Natasha's instructions to stop investigating, she couldn't. You couldn't just stop doing something like that. It was exactly like how she used to feel about her research.

"...made all their money in the oil business, decades ago, I believe," Simon was saying. "They've certainly branched out since then. This chap's some sort of nephew, I suppose, I can't really keep all the family relationships straight. Supposedly they're an eccentric lot. Never come out of their house or some rubbish like that."

This was starting to sound familiar. Lauren sat up straight and stared at Simon. "Are you talking about the Bartlebys?"

"Why, yes. Their nephew, I believe it was. He's the one involved in this whole matter, yes."

"But that's Cecily's father."

"No, it isn't." Simon smiled annoyingly at her. "Cecily's last name isn't Bartleby, it's Bottomley."

"It's Bartleby," Lauren almost screamed at him. Why was he looking so smug and self-satisfied when he was so wrong?

"Bartleby and Bottomley do sound quite a bit alike," the professor contributed.

"Is it really?" Simon said. "My mistake then. Cecily Bartleby? So she's Reggie's daughter? Why, how fascinating."

Zach had jumped out of his seat and was standing in front of Simon, holding his phone, which clearly was set to record. This must be big enough news for him to forego the pen and notebook. "Tell me more, Simon." Zach thrust the phone into Simon's face. "What a development. Cecily's father's about to be investigated?"

"Well, I don't think you should publish any of this," Simon said, seeming alarmed by Zach's journalistic zeal. "It's all quite preliminary, you know."

"What else do you know about it?" Lauren's own curiosity was outweighing her displeasure at Zach's getting to hear whatever Simon was trying to say.

"Yes, Simon, do tell us," the professor entreated.

"I don't really know all that much else about it," Simon said. "Reggie Bartleby had some problem with his taxes a few years back. I believe he didn't pay them, or some such thing. But his family managed to avoid any nasty publicity. And then a while later he became involved in this whole campaign finance matter. That's about it."

"Damn, this is great stuff," Zach said. "Excuse me, Mrs. Segal, but I'm going to check this out." And he was gone in a flash.

"Oh, no," said Simon. "Perhaps I shouldn't have said anything."

"No, no," the professor said, "it's really quite interesting. I always wish I knew more about these domestic financial issues."

"So what exactly did the Bartlebys do to avoid publicity?" Lauren asked.

"I really have no idea," Simon said. "Would that I knew more." And he spread his hands in the air apologetically. "So. We should be heading back to the conference, shouldn't we, Meryl?"

"Oh, yes."

Lauren checked the time again, to find that it was already seven-twenty. She was going to be really late. She stood up quickly. "I have to leave too."

"Well, I'll be sure to see you before I go back to California," the professor said.

"Yes," Simon said, looking pleased. "I'd say the same thing, except that I'm not going to California."

"Bye," Lauren said, and fled.

Twenty

Lauren pulled up in front of Nick's house, after making sure she had the right address. It was a quiet tree-lined street, and the warm night air felt heavy. A piano sounded somewhere down the block, and the wind was blowing just a little. Did she look okay? She probably should have changed into something a little more...well, she didn't know exactly what she should have changed into. She was out of practice. Feeling that same sensation of nervous expectation she'd felt earlier in the parking lot, she walked up the flagstone path to the door and rang the bell. No answer. It was getting dark, but the outside light wasn't on, and neither were the lights in the house's front rooms. Should she ring the bell again? She did.

"Just a minute," she heard a voice calling. It sounded like Nick, but she wasn't sure. She heard various loud scraping and thudding noises. What was going on in there? The noises ceased, the lights were switched on, and the door opened. "Hi. Come in."

Nick was wearing a worn-out-looking red Washington Nationals t-shirt and old jeans, and his hair seemed wet. He was barefoot. His general appearance was one of frazzled bedragglement. It made him seem more vulnerable, as if his usual protective shell had been ripped off his back. "I'm sorry. This isn't what I was planning."

What did he mean? She stepped inside and found herself in a living room. It appeared perfectly normal, not corresponding to the noises she'd heard a few minutes earlier.

"Sorry I'm late." She figured she should take her shoes off too, so she did.

"Oh, no, that's okay. I texted you but I'm not sure you got it."

She realized she hadn't checked her phone in a while, and took a look. "Flood in kitchen," he had texted. "Text me if I don't answer door, I might not hear u."

"A flood?"

"This water pipe burst in the kitchen. I got home, and there was water all over the place. I shut the main water switch off and moved most of the furniture out of the kitchen, and then I went and took a shower and then I was moving more stuff to make a passageway through. That's what I was doing when you rang the bell."

He was heading toward the back of the house, so she followed him through the dining room, edging around what did appear to be an overabundance of chairs and tables, and toward the entrance to the kitchen, down a couple of steps, where she paused. Water gurgled on the floor.

"I ordered some Chinese food, though." He gestured toward a bag that was sitting on a dining room chair. "I remembered you said you liked Chinese food."

"You didn't have to do that." She felt guilty. "You have enough to worry about here."

"Well, we have to eat. Although I guess we can't eat in the kitchen or the dining room. I called a friend who's supposed to come over tonight and try to fix all of this."

"How many people live here?" Lauren looked around. The house seemed fairly large.

"My friends Carol and Dennis, with their baby. They're away right now, on vacation. So anyway, last year, when things fell apart with Alissa, they said I could rent the apartment in the back. It works pretty well, even though I end up eating over here a lot of the time because I don't have a real kitchen. I didn't expect to still be here a year later, but I kind of like it."

They both stood there for a minute, looking down at the water in the kitchen.

"Well," Nick finally said. "There's nothing we can do about this right now, so why don't we eat? I guess we'll have to go to my shed, I mean, apartment, even though I don't usually let anyone see it."

Lauren nodded.

Nick picked up the Chinese food bag. Suddenly that abstracted, million-miles-away look came over his face.

Lauren started to feel uneasy.

"You know when you've done something really wrong?" he asked after a long moment of silence. "And you want people to respect you but you can't quite believe they will if you tell them about this thing you've done? Or maybe certain people still would, but not the right people, you know?"

"Well," Lauren managed to say, but she couldn't say anything else. A huge wave of panic was drowning her. She couldn't breathe. He seemed to have that effect on her, one way or another. What was he trying to tell her now?

He was opening an outer door that led from the dining room to a darkened strip of grass. Lauren fought back the panic. She was supposed to figure this whole thing out. She couldn't give up. Nick looked back at her. "It's out here. My apartment." And he gestured toward what looked like a shed. She followed him out the door and across the strip of grass, feeling the humidity close in on her. "This character in my novel. He has an unsavory past, and he's trying to redeem himself. So I've been thinking all day about what to do with him. I didn't mean to get so distracted."

A character in his novel? Was he telling the truth? Didn't people often base their fictional creations on themselves? "So this is where you live?" She hoped her voice wasn't shaking. "This, um, separate house?"

"Yeah. It's a little unusual, but it's private, so I can work on my writing without hearing Julian cry. Julian's the baby. I mean, Carol and Dennis's baby, you know?" He sounded nervous. She watched him push the door open. "Sorry about the mess. I tried to clean up, but I was busy dealing with the kitchen."

She took a deep breath and looked inside. It was actually a fairly large room, with windows lining one side. But, as he switched the lights on, she noticed something strange. "You have hardly any furniture."

"I know."

Lauren peered around the room. A mattress, covered with a faded quilt, was lying next to the far wall, under the windows. A huge pile of books and a jumble of electronic devices resided on the floor next to the mattress. The opposite wall was lined with more piles of books. A TV sat on top of a tiny refrigerator, and a lamp was perched perilously upon an equally tiny rickety-looking wooden table. In the middle of the room, Nick's laptop rested on a card table, with an uncomfortable-looking wooden chair drawn up to it. Cardboard packing boxes were scattered around the room, and a couple of doors, which were slightly ajar, seemed to lead to a closet and a bathroom. Near the closet, a microwave sat on the floor, and a bike was hanging from a hook attached to the wall above the microwave. Lauren found the whole thing completely fascinating. Her panic was ebbing away rapidly. Nick couldn't have murdered someone. What had she been thinking?

"This is really kind of embarrassing," Nick was saying as he put the Chinese food on the table, along with some chopsticks and plastic forks. He retrieved a couple of plates from inside the microwave. "They're clean, don't worry. So Alissa wanted the furniture and the apartment, and I didn't care so much about it. I do have another chair, in the closet." He pulled out a metal folding chair, which he placed near the table. "I hope you don't mind this." He cleared the laptop away. "The original plan was to eat in the dining room in the house. I was going to cook something."

"I don't mind." Lauren sat down on the wooden chair, which was indeed uncomfortable. He took the other chair, and they started to eat their Hunan chicken and vegetable lo mein. "But why didn't you get to keep anything? You really didn't care?"

Nick shook his head. "Not really. I was thinking I would move. Get away from D.C., away from all the memories of Alissa. But then I never got around to it."

"Don't you ever miss having a comfortable chair? Or what about a desk? Where do you keep all your things?"

"In these cardboard boxes." Nick gestured at them. "I know, it's really stupid. My sister and my parents are appalled by it. And Alissa would be completely disgusted."

Lauren sighed. She had loved her apartment so much. It had been small, but absolutely perfect, as far as she was concerned. Every time she had come home, she felt as if she were sinking into a comfortable, peaceful cocoon. Leaving it forever had been incredibly difficult. On top of everything else she had been dealing with. Once she figured out her longer-term plans, she could look for a new apartment. One that recreated that same feeling. She could get all her furniture and books out of storage. She missed them. Damn Eric, anyway.

"So are you still thinking about moving?" She hoped he wasn't. Although she wasn't sure how long she'd be in D.C. herself.

"No. Probably not. But sometimes I feel like I'm stuck, like I need to do something different. Pretty much all I ever do is go to work and then come back and revise my three pages, or go to my Dutch class or my writing group. Or the gym sometimes." He paused and reached for some more noodles.

The mention of his Dutch class reminded Lauren once more of that Czech language book, and of Karel Halama's reaction to seeing Nick's article. It had certainly been a strong reaction. Why? Could there really be something wrong with the article? Something Nick wanted to hide?

"It's great that you could come over," Nick continued. "I'm just sorry about the flood. It sort of spoiled the atmosphere, didn't it?" And he shrugged and smiled at her.

She looked more closely at him. "Are you growing a beard?" His unshaven look seemed to have taken on more of a purpose. She felt that sensation again. That need for physical connection. She wanted to reach out and run her fingers along his jawline. She was having trouble keeping her concentration, on the food or the investigation or much of anything. But she knew she had to try.

"Maybe. I've had one off and on for the past year. Alissa always thought I looked awful with a beard, but once she left, well, you know, why not."

Awful? Nick could never look awful, with a beard or without. What had Alissa been thinking?

"What do you think?" he asked her. "Should I?"

"Yes. I mean, whatever you want to do. You'll look good whatever you do. I mean, yeah." She trailed off. God, she was awkward. And inarticulate. She could tell she was turning red. "So are you going to be able to get your three pages done tonight?" she asked, changing the subject.

"Oh, it doesn't matter. I've been way too rigid about all that anyway. My writing doesn't need to be on that tight a schedule. It isn't as if I'm on deadline or anything. And the past week, you know, I've been getting a lot of revising done at work. The whole three-page-a-night thing, it's sort of obsessive, like, to the point of absurdity." He paused. "I almost forgot. I have something I wanted to ask you about." He went back over to the closet, where he rummaged around for a minute. "Here." He handed her a piece of paper before sitting down again.

She looked at it. It seemed to be a conversation between two people named Jack and Martha. Jack was telling Martha that he really wanted to be a jazz musician, and Martha was arguing with him.

"No." Nick sounded alarmed. "Look at the other side."

"Oh." She turned it over. "What was I looking at, part of your novel?"

Nick nodded.

"Could I read it sometime?"

"Oh, well." Nick seemed a little embarrassed. "Sure, if you want to. I'll email it to you once I'm done with the latest revisions. But look at what's on the other side. It's much more interesting."

Lauren looked at the other side, which had some scrawled handwritten notes on it. "Meeting, 10am," it said. "Lunch, Cecily. PM: talk to Lou about $$."

"So?" Nick asked. "Intriguing, isn't it?"

"What is this? Where did you find it, anyway?"

"It's a note Tony must have written. I was printing out a copy of one of my chapters at work today, to show it to Victor, you know, one of the copy editors, who's written a couple of novels so he's giving me advice. He's an older guy, old-school, and he likes to read longer things on paper. Sort of like the Bartlebys. So before I gave it to him, I was looking through it, and I noticed this. I guess someone must have stuffed that piece of paper into the stack that was sitting near the copier, and not noticed that it had something on the back."

"How do you know it's Tony's?" Lauren tried to sound properly suspicious.

"It's his handwriting. And it makes sense. Lunch with Cecily. And talking to Louisa about money. I'm not sure what the meeting was at 10am, but he always seemed to be meeting with people about all his projects. Or schemes, I should call them."

"Why Louisa? What about Louis?"

"Good point. It could be Louis. It's just that nobody calls Louis anything but Louis. Except Wade, of course. But Tony never called Louis Lou."

"Did he call Louisa Lou?" Lauren stood up and stretched. The wooden chair on which she had been sitting was really, really uncomfortable. How someone could live like this indefinitely, she couldn't understand.

Nick frowned. "I don't know for sure. But I think this could have something to do with Brad and the senator." He stopped and looked up at her. "You're trying to find out who did it, right?"

"Well," Lauren said, feeling awkward again. "I mean, we all want to find out, don't we?"

"Right, but I think you're really trying to find out who did it. Probably Natasha or Fred or someone asked you to help them, or help the Bartlebys, because you aren't a suspect. So I thought you might want to know about this." He gestured at the piece of paper.

"Thanks. Actually, Natasha told me to stop trying to figure it out. When I went to her office today." Why had she told him that?

"Really?" Nick shook his head. "That's strange."

It was, but Lauren didn't think she should tell him anymore. She'd end up telling him the whole thing, all the little pieces she'd managed to amass. And she shouldn't do that. She should be telling Amanda. Or maybe even Sonya. "Was it really obvious that I was trying to find out what was going on?"

"Oh, no. You were pretty subtle about it, I thought. Except when you'd get mad at Jim. But that's understandable."

Lauren felt uneasy. He had been watching her the whole time, then? So maybe the murderer...

"Don't worry." Although he looked worried, she noticed. "Maybe nobody else was paying attention. I just like watching people. I think you have to have a little voyeurism in you to try to write novels."

Lauren nodded. And to solve mysteries. Maybe she just didn't have quite enough. She sat down on the floor and leaned back against a stray cardboard box, filled with books, that was set against the wall. It was more comfortable than the chair, but that wasn't saying much. "Don't other people think your living accommodations are a little unusual?"

"Usually there isn't a flood in the kitchen. So on the rare occasions when I have people over we hang out in there. Carol and Dennis don't mind. You're one of the privileged few who's actually seen this room."

"Did Tony see it?" Lauren was starting to feel extremely tired. It had been a long day. The cardboard box was poking her in the back, and she sat up straighter to avoid it.

"No, I don't think so. In fact, I don't think Tony ever came over here. I went to his apartment a couple of times." He glanced at her. "You don't look very comfortable." He got up from the metal folding chair and sat down next to her. "And this isn't too much better than the chairs. I'm sorry. I wish I had somewhere more comfortable for you to sit."

What else was she supposed to ask? Nick's proximity was distracting her. About Karel Halama, that was it. "You know Karel Halama?"

"Yeah." Nick leaned back against the cardboard box.

"Did he seem upset when you talked to him?" She really wasn't in the mood for questioning anyone, especially Nick. Especially right now. "I mean, did he say anything negative about the magazine?"

"Upset? He strikes me as the kind of person who's in a perpetual state of being upset, actually. He's probably one of the most obnoxious people I've ever met. But he didn't say anything in particular about the magazine. I don't think he had ever heard of it."

His voice was beginning to fade out.

In its place Lauren heard Cecily screaming at Tony. "How dare you accuse my father of something like that? She had the vase, and she was hitting Tony over the head.

And then Brad came into the room, with Louisa. "How dare you accuse us of financial improprieties?" They took the vase from Cecily and started hitting Tony, who by then was lying on the floor.

And then Louis came in. "How dare you take my video game idea? I'll have to make sure you don't live to patent it." And he took his turn with the vase.

Jim then ran in and grabbed it from Louis. "How dare you treat Cecily like an object?" And then Wade came in.

But Tony, Rasputin-like, had risen. He most certainly was not dead. "You see? None of you can stop me." And he ran out of the room.

"After him," they all yelled, and everyone tore down the stairs of the Most Admired Unit. But Tony jumped into Cecily's convertible and sped away, leaving them standing outside.

But that wasn't everyone, was it? Weren't some other people supposed to be there? Lauren pondered this perplexing question, unable for the moment to answer it. She blinked and peered at Nick, who was watching her. She realized she was leaning back against the box again, next to him. The distance between them had shrunk.

"Sorry. I just completely spaced out. Everyone was taking turns hitting Tony over the head, except he wasn't actually dead. He drove off in Cecily's car. Everyone from the office was there, I think." She thought back. "Except you. You weren't there."

"Well, that's good." He sounded serious. "I mean, I'm glad you don't think I did it."

"I never thought you did it." Lauren still wasn't totally focusing. "I guess I liked you too much to think you did it."

"Yeah. I wouldn't have thought you did it either."

They looked at each other, both of them remaining very still. Then Nick reached over and put his arm around her. She burrowed her head into his shoulder and wrapped both arms around him, feeling that this was definitely the right thing to do. She didn't want to move, ever again. Maybe she could just stay like this, like a vine attaching itself to a tree. She wouldn't have to think about Eric, or about Tony, or about the investigation, or about her book, or really about anything. She closed her eyes and pictured a series of soap bubbles, each with a cartoonlike avatar inside it. One bubble contained Eric. Another, Tony. Yet another, Amanda. And the last, Professor Segal. They all ascended into the sky and popped. One, two, three, four.

She could feel Nick breathing. She could feel his heartbeat. It was soothing. The peacefulness she hadn't been able to achieve in the yoga class had finally arrived. They stayed like that for a while. And then the cardboard box they were leaning against started to buckle, and they slowly slid further onto the floor.

Lauren opened her eyes. Her vinelike grip had loosened a little, and she looked over at him. He looked back at her, his eyes telegraphing some kind of signal. He was staring at her like she was...like she was...she wasn't sure. Her weak-at-best signal-reading antenna was still off-line.

"I just..." he said, continuing to stare at her. "I can't...I mean, I just have to..." He carefully brushed a stray curl out of her face, tucked it behind her ear, and leaned over and kissed her. Gently, but with a kind of intensity that surprised her. She found that she was kissing him back, and while her peaceful feelings were still there, they were rapidly being superseded by a host of other sensations. She wrapped herself around him more tightly, running her hands through his hair. So what if she was making herself vulnerable? So what if she had only really known him for a week? So what if he was a suspect? None of that seemed to matter. It seemed completely irrelevant.

"Oh, my god," Nick mumbled. "You're just so incredible. You're so beautiful. I've wanted to do this ever since I met you."

"So have I," she managed to say, finding it hard to catch her breath. He thought she was incredible? Beautiful? "I just couldn't tell whether...I mean, so you're really not seeing anyone? I mean, anyone else?"

"Of course not." He sounded surprised. "Why would you think I was?"

"Oh, well." Embarrassment and joy were vying for control of her emotions. "My antenna is all messed up."

"Nothing about you is all messed up." He pulled her closer. And then she felt as if the two of them were drifting off somewhere, maybe down a fast-moving river, or maybe up into the sky, or maybe into a peaceful oasis where nothing bad could happen. After some time had passed, she had no idea how long, she realized that without her being quite aware of it, she and Nick had moved from the uncomfortable wooden floor onto the mattress, which was much more comfortable. And he had somehow dimmed the lights, which was an improvement too. His hands were roaming around in her hair and down her back, and she was swimming in a sea of satisfaction.

The Amanda avatar, once again ensconced in its bubble, floated past. It was saying something about rebound relationships and murder suspects and you're the closest thing I have to a sister and please don't do this. But then it floated out of range and disappeared.

They were on a desert island. They were on a hillside in Romania. They were in an Arctic igloo. They were back in the peaceful oasis. No matter where they went, she just had to hold on to him. Maybe then everything would be all right, and...

"...and I can't believe this is actually happening," Nick was whispering to her. By this point, certain pieces of clothing had been unfastened or tossed aside, and the whole situation was becoming far more passionate. "Oh, god, you are so amazing. This is really..." And he stopped talking and turned back to other matters.

"So are you." Lauren found it hard to say much of anything else. She couldn't believe this was actually happening either. That they were here together. That he felt this way about her. That they both apparently wanted to...

"We're all just material for that novel of his," a voice broke in. Oh, no. The Amanda avatar. It had returned, locked into its bubble.

No, she told the avatar. Go away. I don't want to listen to you. I have more important things to think about right now.

"He's much too quiet," the Amanda avatar continued. "And too obsessed with his novel."

Can't you be quiet yourself? she told the avatar. Sometimes quiet can be good.

She tried desperately to banish the avatar and devote all her attention to what was going on with Nick, not what was going on in her head. What mattered was the physical connection. Which was incredible. It was as if they were inhabiting their own private sensual grove in the heart of the peaceful oasis.

But to her dismay, the avatar kept talking, on and on. The way Amanda did in real life sometimes. "...as if he's storing up everything we say to put into his book. It's really infuriating." And then another voice came unbidden into her head. This time it was Nick's own voice. "Writers try to seek out interesting people," she remembered him saying. And, "You know a lot of really fascinating people." The two voices, Nick's and the avatar's, started blurring together in her mind, speeding up and slowing down until she couldn't tell them apart.

And then she suddenly saw herself and her entourage—the confused Romania expert complete with star-investigative-reporter ex-fiancé, disappearing Transylvanian alibi, and 99-year-old muse—showing up on the pages of Nick's novel along with Jack and Martha and Chuck Hefflefinger. No, that would be terrible. She should try to find out right now, before things progressed even further.

Following the light up to the surface, out of the depths, Lauren somehow managed to pull away from Nick's embrace. She looked into his eyes, dark fathomless pools of emotion.

"It's okay." His voice was emerging unevenly. "We can stop now if you want." He seemed worried. "I wouldn't..."

"No, I don't want to stop." Her own voice sounded equally uneven. "No, I just..." She gave him what she thought would be a short, reassuring kiss but when he kissed her back it ended up being longer and deeper and more hungry. It sent shock waves through every part of her being. When they came up for air, she gasped, and finally breathed out her question. "I just wanted to ask, you're not going to put me in your novel, are you?"

"No, no," he murmured into her ear. "I would never do that. You're too special. You're...you're...you always leave me wordless. You're my...my Most Admired. I Most Admire you."

"I Most Admire you too." She pulled him closer still.

And then a knock sounded at the door.

"Just ignore it," he whispered hoarsely. "Let's just ignore it." They did. But then his phone pinged with a text, and then the phone started ringing, accompanied by another knock on the door. "Oh shit." He groaned in what seemed like complete frustration. "Oh fuck. Oh, Shlomo. I totally forgot."

Shlomo?

Lauren felt herself abruptly resurfacing, not by choice this time. She was back on the mattress in his room. His furnitureless shed. What had happened to their oasis?

"My friend who's coming to deal with the kitchen." They disentangled themselves, both completely out of breath. "The water. Shlomo. He's here. Outside the shed. That's who was knocking. I'm really sorry." He gave her a series of apologetic kisses. "This is like the worst possible timing. I can't...I mean, I can barely talk. I can barely breathe. Do you know how incredibly sexy you are?" He kissed her again. "But I'm going to have to get this." He smiled ruefully at her and reached for the phone to call back. She pulled the quilt around herself. No, she didn't know. Or maybe she had forgotten that she could be. She knew that he was. Definitely. She sighed.

"Hey, Shlomo." His voice and his breath were still somewhat ragged. "Yeah, no, just a second, I'll let you in, hang on." He hung up and switched the lights back on, and she blinked and covered her eyes. "Oh, jeez, sorry." He partially dimmed them again. "God, you are just so irresistible. I wish...I mean, I wish we could have..."

She wished they could have, too. But the opportunity was

gone. She wondered momentarily if she should go hide in the bathroom or the closet. She felt emotionally and physically undone, completely unable to function. In a daze, she refastened and reassembled things, and then tried to smooth out her hair and her wrinkled tan pants and black tank top, in hopes of looking less disheveled. The shirt she had been wearing over the tank top was nowhere to be found. She figured that whoever this Shlomo was, he most likely would be able to guess what he had interrupted.

Nick, who had also been pulling himself together, leaned over and gave her one more kiss. "Sorry again. You really are incredible. To be continued?" She nodded. She didn't think she could speak. And he took a deep breath, turned the lights fully up again, and went to open the door. Lauren got off the mattress, quickly tried to straighten out the quilt, and settled back on the wooden chair, which was as uncomfortable as ever.

"A flood in the kitchen?" came a loud, slightly accented voice from outside, and then Lauren saw a dark-haired stocky man wearing a white sweatshirt and paint-spattered jeans. "I said to myself, how could Nick Belotserkovsky have a flood in his kitchen? This doesn't happen to great writers. Oh," he said, noticing Lauren. "Hello. I hope I wasn't interrupting anything."

"This is Lauren," Nick said. "Lauren, Shlomo."

Lauren managed a quick wave, not trusting her voice yet.

"So," Shlomo said. "You're getting to see this lovely room. Even Nick's sister doesn't see this room. Especially his sister." He turned to Nick. "I was over there the other day checking out Hannah's upstairs bathroom. The toilet wasn't working right. And I said to her, Hannah, how do you let your brother live in a shack in someone's backyard when you live in a wonderful house? And Hannah said, Well, you know my brother, I try and try but I can't do anything about the way he is. And I said, Look, Hannah, you have to keep trying. Family is family. We have an expression in Hebrew for..."

"Why don't we go look at the kitchen?" Nick said, breaking into this recitation, which Lauren had been finding quite intriguing.

"So practical." Shlomo shook his head. "Okay, let's check it out. It isn't many people I'd come over for this late at night, but I was in the neighborhood anyway fixing Mrs. Davis's gas stove." He kept talking as Nick led the way outside, where the light wind was still blowing, across the strip of grass, and into the dining room. "Yes, well, we do have a lot of water here." Shlomo looked slightly alarmed as he surveyed the damage. He opened the cabinet doors under the kitchen sink, bent down, and started poking around inside. "So, how's the writing going?" he said from underneath, his voice sounding hollow.

"Pretty well." Nick leaned against the doorway between the dining room and the kitchen. Lauren sat down on one of the many chairs crowded into the dining room. It was more comfortable than the one in the shed. Perhaps she should suggest that he move some of them in there. "I'm starting to edit this latest draft now. But I'm not sure how this character Martha comes through. I'll have to work on that."

"What about you, Lauren?" Shlomo inquired. "Are you a writer too? Or are you involved in some more respectable line of work?"

"I teach political science. I mean, not anymore. At least for now. I mean, maybe I'll go back to it. But I don't know." She stopped.

"She works with me at the magazine now." Nick gave Lauren a reassuring smile.

"You know, Lauren, I was a lawyer in Israel. And then one day I woke up and I said to myself, Shlomo, why don't you move to

America and be a contractor? It wasn't a hard decision." Shlomo's head emerged from under the sink. "So the good news is, it's just a water leak. No sewage. I'm going to have to go down to the basement for a minute to check on the situation there, how much water came through the floor. What about Carol and Dennis? Do they know about the flood?"

"I tried to get in touch with them, but no luck yet. They're in London for the week."

"Okay." Shlomo got up. "What they don't know won't hurt them. They're on vacation, let them enjoy themselves. Maybe we can get this all fixed up before they come home." His voice faded away as he went down the stairs.

Lauren agreed. She had finally received an email from her parents, who were in Hanoi and clearly had no idea what was transpiring at the magazine. She had sent them a breezy email indicating that she was fine.

"I should probably go down and see what he's doing," Nick said, and he departed, leaving Lauren sitting on the chair. She could hear noises coming from the basement, as if more furniture were being moved around. She closed her eyes and tried to recapture the peaceful feeling. But it was nowhere to be found.

"...So I'll have to come back tomorrow," Shlomo said. She heard their footsteps coming back up from the basement. "I'll bring a plumber with me. You should really write a novel about life in the contracting business, Nick. What happens to me in one week, no, say, one day, could set you up for life. Bestsellers, movies, you name it."

"Maybe I'll take a day off from work and help you out," Nick said. "Let me know if you go back to that house with all the trumpets in the basement."

"Anything new on the murder case?" Shlomo asked. "You

know, I was over at the Bartleby house the other day. Leaky gutters. Water was dripping down into their animal enclosures. What's the name of that animal they raise?" He looked questioningly at Lauren and Nick.

Lauren stared at him. He had been to the Bartlebys' house?

"You've been there?" She pulled her feet up on to the chair and wrapped her arms around her knees.

"Sure." Shlomo shrugged.

"Mongooses," Nick said. "They raise mongooses. If that's the plural of mongoose, I've never really been sure."

"Mongooses." Shlomo shook his head. "Crazy. The stories I could tell you about those people and those animals. So I was over there fixing up their gutters. I do that from time to time, and with this murder at the magazine I figured this would be a good time to show up. Maybe the Bartlebys could use someone to talk to. So the oldest brother, John, was discussing one particular mongoose that was sick. And I said, Mr. Bartleby, it's wonderful about the animals, but why don't you think about all the people in the world who are sick too? With all your money, just think what you could do."

"Wait a minute," Lauren said. "You mean, you've met them? You've actually talked to them?"

"The mongooses? Or the Bartlebys?"

"The Bartlebys."

"I've met them, I've met them." Shlomo raised his eyebrows. "They're a group of rich people sitting in their house, what's the big deal? So Mr. Bartleby said, Well, Shlomo, you have a point. And I said, Mr. Bartleby, why don't you come out of your house? I'm sure there are a lot of people who'd really like to meet you. And he said, Shlomo, you're a very smart man, I respect your opinion, but I haven't left my house in years, and I'm not going to start now. So then he asked me to fix a wire in his study, and I was in there doing that, and he got a phone call. So I happened to overhear a very interesting conversation. The stories you hear in this business, I could write my autobiography now and retire." And Shlomo sighed and started out the back door.

"Wait," Nick said. "What happened?"

"What was John Bartleby talking about?" Lauren added.

"It sounded to me like he was being blackmailed." Shlomo turned back to face them. "Something to do with his nephew, it sounded like. Financial things. So he got off the phone, and I said, Mr. Bartleby, good luck with everything. And he said, Shlomo, I won't tell you things are easy. Even if you're rich, things aren't easy. So remember that, you two. Even if you're rich, things aren't easy. Murder, blackmail, god only knows what. I'll be here at six tomorrow morning, Nick, so don't do anything I wouldn't do." This time, he really did leave.

"He's unbelievable," Nick said. "I keep telling him he should write that autobiography, but he says he doesn't have time."

Lauren, still sitting on the chair, was trying to fit this latest piece of Bartleby lore in with what she'd already heard. Simon had said that Reggie Bartleby was about to be investigated. So that fit in. Someone was blackmailing John Bartleby about Reggie's financial problems. Who could be doing that? But it could be anyone, she realized. Not necessarily anyone connected to Tony's murder. She wished Simon had known more about the whole thing.

She suddenly heard a buzzing sound, and realized it was her phone, in her bag, which she had apparently left behind in the main house hours ago, along with her shoes. Retrieving it, she found that she had no fewer than ten texts from Amanda, each one more frantic. The first had started with, "Home now. Where r u?" It progressed to, "Getting worried. Past 10, where r u? Please get in touch now!", and finally, the one that had just arrived: "Am going to call Tucker/McDonald ASAP if u don't get in touch!!!!" Amanda also had left five voice mails. Lauren checked the readouts to find that they expressed similar sentiments. She quickly texted, "Am fine, will be home soon. Pls don't worry." Then she shut off her phone. She didn't feel like explaining anything right now. She also didn't feel like going home. She felt like staying here. But she owed it to Amanda to call it a night.

"I should probably leave now. I don't want to, but Amanda's getting frantic." Lauren gestured toward her phone.

"No, that's fine, I mean, I'm sorry you have to leave, but I totally get it. But tell me you'll come back another time. Soon." He gave her a lingering kiss, which made her decision to leave seem foolish. But she had to.

"Of course." She put her shoes back on and gathered up her bag, making sure her phone was in it. The shirt would have to wait. If she went back to his room to look for it, she'd probably end up staying.

She opened the front door. "So."

"Well." He took her hand and interlaced his fingers with hers. "So, listen. Where do you usually park when you go back to Amanda's?"

"On the street, usually a few blocks away, but there are always people around so it's pretty safe." She was finding it hard to breathe again. She squeezed his hand.

"No." He squeezed back. "It's too late. I'll follow you in my car, and then I'll drive you back to your door, okay? I should have done that the other night, after we went to the restaurant. That was stupid of me. I realized later that you'd probably be walking around by yourself at night, with all of this going on. Especially if you're trying to investigate things. It's just not safe."

"But that's sort of far for you to go, there and back. I mean, it's really nice of you to offer, but..."

"Remember I told you the other day that I worry about you sometimes?" His eyes were intense. She stared back, mesmerized. "Well, actually I worry about you all the time. I don't know what I would do if anything happened to you."

Oddly enough, what he was saying sounded similar to what Amanda had told her. Although he was of course approaching the situation from a different perspective.

"Yeah, okay," she whispered. "Thanks."

He leaned over and kissed her again, and this time neither of them was at all capable of stopping, and still entwined, they retraced their steps through the main part of the house, out the back door, across the strip of grass, and into his shed. All she wanted was to be with him. Nothing else mattered. Before they could even fasten the door behind them, they had started pulling off each other's clothes, and by the time they had crossed the room to the mattress, it was just them. Their bodies. Together. There were no images in her mind or voices in her head. There was only the physical connection.

Twenty-One

"Well?" Amanda said loudly from the living room sofa when Lauren returned home. It was almost one in the morning. The TV was blaring something about the weather, and Amanda turned it off. "Where have you been? As you know, I've been worried about you. You go around investigating murders, and then you don't come back till almost one, without telling me you had any plans? I got back from my yoga class at nine-thirty, and there was no sign of you. And then when you finally answered me and said you'd be home soon, you weren't! That was two hours ago!"

Amanda really did seem upset, Lauren thought. She probably should have texted her again. But for once, she hadn't been thinking about Amanda. Or the Amanda avatar.

"I'm sorry, you're right. I should have let you know." Lauren sat down next to Amanda. "I was just over at Nick's for dinner." She didn't think she needed to say anything more specific. Amanda would completely lose it.

Amanda sighed, and frowned. "I warned you, I told you not to do that, and did you listen? No. You have to be careful, Lauren, I mean it. Tony Mandel is dead, okay? We're talking murder, okay?" Her voice was rising dangerously. "I told you before, you're probably not thinking clearly. You've been through a lot. I mean, I feel responsible for you. I'm the one who suggested this job to you, and look what ended up happening. You're very vulnerable. You could very easily be taken advantage of." She cast a disapproving eye at Lauren. "And you probably already have been, from what you look like."

"No one's taking advantage of me, all right?" Lauren was annoyed, yet wished she had been able to get a better look at her disheveled self and her wrinkled clothes before facing Amanda's scrutiny. "I know what I'm doing." Did Amanda think she, Lauren, was an old-fashioned damsel in distress? This conversation was going even worse than she had expected. She focused on a painting on the opposite wall, of a bored-looking peasant girl in an embroidered dress seated next to a goat. "Nick could never have done anything to Tony. He just couldn't."

"How do you know? I don't like to see you getting involved with some guy who might have killed someone. You're just too naive."

Was she? She didn't think so. She needed to change the subject, or things would get even more stressful. "Listen, I found out some things about the investigation." She told Amanda about the flood, and then about what she'd learned from Shlomo, Simon, and Zach.

"That's interesting." Amanda sounded slightly mollified. "So let's review our suspects. Pretty soon I think we'll figure this thing out, and you can go tell Natasha, and she'll be really pleased. Maybe you could mention to her that I helped you, and then she can promote me. I'd really like to be an editor. I heard there might be an opening on the national desk."

"Yeah, you'd do a great job as an editor. But actually, Natasha told me to stop investigating."

"She did? Why would she do that? I think we're doing well." Amanda paused, her brow creased thoughtfully. "Okay. We have Louis."

"Oh. There's something I forgot to tell you about." And Lauren pulled the page Nick had given her out of her bag and handed it to Amanda.

"What the hell is this?" Amanda said after a minute. "This guy wants to be a trumpet player but this woman thinks he's not talented enough? What does that have to do with Tony?"

"No, turn it over. That side's part of Nick's novel."

Amanda turned it over, but she didn't seem too enlightened. "Well? What's this supposed to be?"

"It's Tony's. See? He was having a meeting about money. With either Louis or Louisa. I think it was probably Louisa, since she's the one Jim saw that night, but I'm not sure."

Amanda gave Lauren a pitying glance. "How do you know this was Tony's?" Her voice was dripping with skepticism. "I've worked with Tony for years, and I'm not at all sure this is his handwriting." She squinted at the paper.

"Nick said it was." Realizing Amanda wouldn't accept this as a reliable source, Lauren added, "And it makes sense, too, don't you think?"

"No, I don't. What proof do you have that Nick didn't write this himself, and then give it to you so you'd think he was being helpful? You think Nick can do no wrong, don't you? I hate to say this to you, Lauren, but you don't always have great judgment about men."

Lauren reflected. Could Amanda be right? She imagined Nick, back at his house, saying that he didn't think she could have done it either. Saying that he Most Admired her. Saying that he worried about her all the time. And all the other things they had said to each other...He couldn't have been saying those things just to mislead her, could he? Could the whole evening have been some kind of horrible mistake?

Her mind flicked back to the previous summer. She and Eric had been on a rare vacation, to Maine for a few days. They had stayed at a romantic bed-and-breakfast, and over breakfast one morning Eric had looked at her and said that he had never been so happy. She, sharing those emotions, had of course believed him. And then three months later he had ended the engagement.

"I don't feel like talking about this anymore." Lauren turned away from Amanda toward the blank-faced girl and the goat.

"Fine. I'm going to sleep now anyway." And Amanda stomped off to her bedroom.

Lauren sighed. What was she going to do? There were just too many things to worry about. Okay, she told herself, take a deep breath and pretend you're writing an outline for a paper. Divide the problems into groups.

All right. The first problem centered on the Bartlebys. Who was blackmailing them? And could this have something to do with Tony's death? What could be the connection? She started thinking about the various people in the office and how they might have come across the information about Reggie Bartleby. But there was no obvious link. Frustrated, she moved on.

The next problem had to do with her languishing career. Ethan hadn't been in touch since he'd arrived in town, which was unlike him. She wouldn't even have seen him if she hadn't gone to the conference. He was apparently spending all his time bonding with his fellow conferees. Exchanging ideas, discussing new concepts. A flash of resentment shot through her. He was doing that, while she was sitting in the Most Admired Unit coaxing reluctant citizens to respond to surveys?

She shook her head and turned to the third problem, the one that, she had to admit, concerned her most: Nick. What if this fictional problem he had mentioned, about the person who was ashamed of something he had done, wasn't fictional at all? The thought was so monstrous that she tried to return to problem number one, the Bartlebys. But she kept replaying her evening with Nick in her mind. He couldn't have done it. Even her subconscious told her that. She reflected on her Tony-as-Rasputin reverie. Her feeling of peacefulness. Everything that had ended up happening. Her signal-reading might be messed up, but she still had some instincts, didn't she?

As if on cue, her phone buzzed. It was a text from Nick. "Back home. Shed seems empty w/o u. Sleep well! Miss u xo."

See? There was no possibility he could have been involved in anything suspicious. He was way too nice and thoughtful. "Miss u too," she texted back. "Will try to sleep but not sure I can, so much to think about!! Xoxo"

She thought and thought, the various problems swirling around. And all of a sudden, she had an idea. Wade. Wade could be the one blackmailing the Bartlebys. Maybe he somehow found out about Reggie's financial dealings, and then he went to the Bartlebys with the information. And that's why they made him co-director of the Most Admired Unit.

Not bad. It made sense. But how did it fit in with Tony's death?

Twenty-Two

Figuring out the Wade theory, however, didn't help Lauren fall asleep. Once in bed, she continued running through the entire evening in her mind. Overall, it had been incredible. Overwhelming in a good way. In the best way. But she felt unsettled. She tossed and turned, thinking of Nick. Of Amanda. Of Tony. Of Eric. Of everything she had been experiencing. Maybe it was all just too much. Too soon. Was she vulnerable? Was she naïve? Was she jumping into something that might be too intense for her right now? But then she'd picture Nick's face and feel some degree of contentment. It was 2:45 a.m. It was 3:50 a. m. It was 4:59 a.m. At one point she must have actually been asleep because she was back in his shed, on the mattress, his arms around her, and then she was awake again, back in her room at Amanda's. She thought she heard a text come in, and she reached blearily for her phone. 5:30 a.m.

"U awake? Can't sleep, thinking of u, wish u were here xo." It was from Nick.

She smiled. "Can't sleep either, same here, fell asleep for one minute, dreamed of u xo," she texted back.

"Would have dreamed of u if had slept at all, but thought of u all night," he texted, adding a red heart emoji.

She sent a heart emoji back to him.

"Shlomo & plumber here soon, need to stick around for a while but meet @ Starbucks near office @ 7?" he queried.

She replied in the affirmative. She crept out of the apartment an hour later, avoiding Amanda, and by 7 she was at the Starbucks up the street from the office. Nick was already there, standing near the door, looking tired. As soon as he saw her, though, his face lit up.

"Hey." He kissed her. "I really did miss you, you know?"

"I missed you too."

They got in line. "Did you eat anything yet?" he asked. "I had some cereal at home, but I might get a muffin or something."

"Not yet." She hadn't wanted to wake Amanda with all those breakfast noises. "Amanda's, well, incredibly mad at me." She didn't know if she wanted to tell him why. It did seem somewhat offensive, after all.

"I'm sure she is. I would be too if I were her."

They inched forward in the queue. "Really?"

"Best friend who's been through a lot gets involved with murder suspect? Yeah. Actually, you're lucky to have a friend like that looking out for you." He stopped. "You know, there's this editing job opening up on the national desk, and I heard Fred's thinking of offering it to her. He really likes her work. I mean, ultimately it would be up to Natasha, but I don't see why she wouldn't agree."

"That's great!" Lauren felt excited for Amanda, as well as intrigued by Nick's analysis of Amanda's behavior. "She'll be so happy. I'll tell her that, okay?"

He nodded. "She probably already knows, knowing her."

"So how's the flood?" Lauren asked, once they had coffee and muffins in hand. They sat down at a table in the corner, on a bench. He put his arm around her and a pulse of happiness shot through her.

"It's probably going to be an all-day repair job." Nick took a sip of coffee. "They're over there now. They got there at six, Shlomo and Damian, the plumber. I've met him a few times now, he's a nice guy. And the two of them kept giving me advice. For half an hour, until I finally left to come over here."

"Advice about what?" Lauren peeled the paper wrapper off the bottom of her muffin.

"You." Lauren was surprised. "Shlomo was very taken with you. He gave me a long lecture about how I shouldn't mess this up. And Damian said that after his marriage ended it took about a year for him to feel as if he could move on with his life, and he reminded me that it's been about a year now since Alissa left, and I shouldn't keep sitting around in my room feeling sorry for myself. And then they both kept coming up with story after story, all kinds of stories about all kinds of relationships, and I just sat there in the dining room and listened."

Lauren smiled, picturing the scene. But she did wonder about Alissa. Why had she left? Was Amanda's version correct? That Alissa had felt Nick couldn't keep up with her professionally? She wasn't sure if she should ask or if it was too sensitive a subject.

"Um," she began.

"You're probably wondering about Alissa, right?" Nick asked, with his usual uncanny ability to sense what she was thinking. "Why she left and took all the furniture and the apartment and why I'm living in a shed?"

"Yeah, pretty much." She pulled off part of the muffin and nibbled on it, remembering what Nick had said the other night, about Eric's behavior toward her. "How could she do that?"

"Actually, I don't have any hard feelings toward her," he said, again surprising Lauren. "You know, we met when we were 18 years old. Well, I hadn't even turned 18 yet. I feel like I was a different person back then. It was the first week of freshman year, and you know how things were for me in high school, and I thought I was supposed to be this type-A successful personality, and then I got to college and everyone was like that."

She pictured Nick as a college freshman. Pretty much the same age he had been when she had first heard of him. It seemed like an incredibly long time ago. "So Alissa was like that? Type A?"

"Oh, definitely." He took another sip of coffee. "She'll probably end up being the youngest partner at her firm one of these days. That would be typical of her. But that kind of thing used to be typical of me, too. I mean, being competitive and sort of known for being good at things."

She thought about it. That's how she remembered him from high school.

"I must have been pretty insufferable back then," he said, a faint smile on his face. "Right?"

"Well, I didn't actually know you." But, yes, the idea of him back then had been pretty insufferable, she had to admit.

"You're too nice." His smile broadened. "But I can tell what you're thinking."

"You usually can. But not always. So tell me more about what happened in college." It probably was best to return to that subject.

Nick nodded. "So things were really intense between us back then, and we were both editors of the paper our junior and senior years, and we spent all our time there, and then I followed her down here after we graduated when she got into Georgetown Law School." He paused. "She was really forceful. She always knew what she wanted. I wasn't as clear about what I wanted to do, but I figured it would be something involving journalism or writing, so I was a researcher on a couple of projects, and I went back to school and got a master's degree, and then Alissa and I got married." He stopped and drank some more of his coffee.

Lauren took another bite of her muffin as she thought of the New York Times wedding announcement. She probably should mention that. Otherwise she'd feel weird about it. "So the other day I saw your wedding announcement. In the New York Times. I was, well, investigating. You know."

"Investigating? You mean, part of your assignment? Digging up dirt on the suspects?"

"Exactly. Well, not exactly."

"It's okay." He gave her a half-smile. "I Googled you after I met you in the office that first day. But there are like a million Lauren Greens, which made the whole thing difficult. What's your middle name, anyway?"

She told him.

"Jennifer probably wouldn't have helped. You should have a more unusual middle name."

"My parents considered Lipschitz. My mom's last name. But they decided against it." Jennifer, despite its lack of originality, was definitely better than Lipschitz.

"Lauren Lipschitz." Nick smiled at her. "I like that. Very alliterative."

She shook her head. "I interrupted your story. I'm sorry. What happened after you got married?"

"Are you sure you want to hear all this? I feel like I've been monopolizing the conversation."

"Yes. I want to hear it."

"Okay, if you're sure. So that was around the time I started working here. At Lens. But the thing is, I was gradually figuring out that I wasn't that kind of driven type-A person, and I was also dealing with some issues with depression, and Alissa was working all the time, I mean, even more than I was, and that's when I started the novel. And things between us eventually just sort of ended. Honestly, I didn't care if she wanted the apartment and the furniture. It was fine. But the depression got a lot worse after we split up."

Lauren squeezed his hand. It sounded horrible. But at least he seemed to understand what had happened. The situation with Eric was something she might never understand. It didn't make any sense. They hadn't met when they were 18, and they hadn't grown apart. In fact, they had grown closer. At least she had thought so. Sonya's theory, that Eric couldn't deal with the idea of getting married at all, to anyone, was a little more palatable than the thought that he couldn't deal with the idea of being married to her. She sighed. "That's really awful," she said, reflecting as much on Eric as on Alissa.

"Yeah, it was rough," he said. "I didn't want to go anywhere, but I knew I had to go to work, so I would drag myself in most days, except for all the days when I couldn't, and then I'd just call in sick and stay in bed. And then I decided to go on that trip to Europe. And that helped, at least for a while. But I was incredibly lonely. Alissa had a lot of friends, and they all took her side after she left, and I had just sort of hung around with her and her friends since I was 18, so I didn't know how to fend for myself. Really the only people who pulled me through were my sister and her husband, and Carol and Dennis. I knew them from college, and they were pretty much the only ones who didn't side with Alissa. Oh, and my writing group. They've been great too. And the editors at work were understanding." He stopped. "I'm sorry. I'm going on way too much about this."

"No. You're not."

"You're a really good listener. Thanks. So I heard a few weeks ago that she's engaged. To another lawyer at her firm. I think I met the guy a couple of times at various events I went to with her over the years, and he seemed okay. I mean, definitely one of those type-A personalities, but, you know." He had a reflective look on his face.

"How do you feel about that? About her marrying someone else?" It must be strange.

He shrugged. "It's weird, in a way. But he's probably much better suited to her than I am. The novel really annoyed her, and she couldn't understand why I wasn't already, like, an editor at the Post or something. And I don't think she ever quite understood how difficult these depression issues have been. How it can take over your life."

Lauren nodded. "I'm really sorry. That must have been incredibly difficult." Or must still be incredibly difficult, depending on how he was doing now. "So how..."

"Yeah, thank you. Things are better now, I guess I'm finally on the right medication. But it's scary. I keep thinking I'm going to slip back into how I was before, at my worst points, not very functional." He stopped and shook his head. "So here I am telling you all these things and it's as if I only care about myself and not about everything you've gone through. And that's not true. At all. I mean, Amanda did tell me some of it, I get the sense she told me more than you would have wanted her to, but I do want to listen if you ever feel like talking about Eric. If you don't, that's fine too."

"Oh, that's nice of you." She mulled over the situation. Amanda probably had said way too much, as Lauren had feared. And she wasn't sure if she felt like talking about Eric. Even just thinking about Eric made her head hurt. There was so much that still seemed too raw. Too confusing.

She went back in her mind to what Nick had said about loneliness. She had enough of her own friends, unconnected to Eric, that she had not gone through what Nick had. The only person who had abandoned her, of course, was Eric. And he had been her friend before he was anything else. It was all so complicated. She tried to imagine Eric marrying someone else, but no pictures were emerging. What kind of person would this woman be? What would this woman have that Lauren somehow didn't? Had he even started seeing anyone else? Sonya had said no, but Sonya was often so wrapped up in her own projects that she might not have noticed. And then Nick...was she the first person he had been involved with since Alissa left? It seemed unlikely.

"So did you see any other..." she began.

"There were a couple of women, yeah, that I was sort of seeing, one a couple months after Alissa left and one a few months later. But it wasn't very meaningful, in either case." He seemed somewhat uncomfortable. "Not to belittle them or anything, it was more just a question of feeling lonely and, well, you know. Not like what happened yesterday."

She wondered if one of them was Lisa from the art department. "Was..." she started. But for once he didn't seem to know what she was about to say.

"Was what?"

"Was one of them..." This was a little awkward.

"Was one of them who?"

"Lisa," she blurted out. She glanced around to make sure no one from the office was nearby. Fortunately, she didn't recognize anyone.

"Lisa who?" He looked confused.

Seriously? But he had said they had a bond. And Amanda thought there might have been something.

"From the art department. That Lisa." She pictured her, clad in tight black leather, entering Nick's shed and slinking her way onto the mattress. It was an upsetting image, to say the least.

"Lisa?" Nick started to laugh. He looked around and lowered his voice. "You thought Lisa and I...no, of course not, we're just friends. I mean, she is striking-looking, I guess you could say, but she's not my type at all. And vice versa, I'm sure."

"But you said you had some kind of bond with her." Lauren felt ridiculous. "You know, at Amanda's party."

"Oh, my god." He momentarily planted his face in his hand and shook his head. "I said that to you at Amanda's party? I really am an idiot." He looked at her. "I didn't know what I was saying that whole night. Everything was coming out wrong. I probably just meant that Lisa and I had started working at Lens the same day so we had that in common. All I was thinking about at that party was how great you looked in that dress and how I wanted to take you off somewhere and cover you with kisses. I just felt like, maybe it was too soon for you and you weren't ready, or maybe you had someone else in mind, or maybe I, you know, just wouldn't be someone you'd be interested in. I guess my radar isn't too good either." He paused. "No, one of the women was a friend of a friend of my sister's, and one was someone I met on my trip. But they didn't mean anything to me. The whole thing just made me feel worse."

"But I..."

"You, just the opposite." He pulled her closer to him. "I mean, last night was incredible. Really. I mean it. I've never experienced anything quite like it."

"I think so too." It had been incredible. She reflected briefly on her several Romanian boyfriends, and on Eric, concluding that the previous night had surpassed anything else. "And I never have either." She whispered into his ear, "You're the one who's very sexy."

He shook his head. "No, it's all you. Or maybe it's us when we're together. I'm not exactly some kind of expert. Until last year, the only woman I had ever been with was Alissa. Ever. And, like, this is probably too much information, but things didn't go all that well with either one of those women last year. It's you. You're very,

very special."

She could tell she was blushing. "No, you are," she said, overcome.

His phone rang, and he looked at it. "It's Shlomo." He smiled at her. "Interrupting again. I should get it, sorry." He squeezed her hand and answered it. "Shlomo? Yeah, she's here. I'll tell her." He turned back to her. "Shlomo says hi." Lauren waved at the phone. And then Nick settled in for what seemed to be a lengthy update on the flood situation. He was slowly eating his muffin. Lauren had finished hers a while ago, and as much of the coffee as she wanted to drink.

"I think I'll go in to the office now," Lauren whispered to him, kissing him quickly on the top of his head. She wanted to see what was happening. If there was anything else she should be doing. She headed over to the Lens building.

"Good morning, young lady," Winston said, beaming at her as she passed his desk.

She smiled back. "Hi." She headed for the passageway.

"Winston?" It was Amanda's voice, calling from over near the elevators. Lauren stopped. "I just wanted to leave this package at your desk. Someone's supposed to pick it...Oh." She saw Lauren standing there.

"Hi," Lauren said, wondering how Amanda would react.

"Hi." Amanda handed Winston a gigantic envelope.

"I'll keep an eye on it," Winston said.

Amanda thanked him, and retreated back toward the elevator, Lauren following. She couldn't keep fighting with Amanda anymore. It was silly. "Why don't we..."

"Listen." Amanda pushed the elevator button. "I'm really sorry about last night, okay? I just want you to be careful." The elevator opened, and Amanda got in. "Come up with me, all right?"

"Sure." Lauren proceeded into the mirrored elevator.

"I simply think that you're dealing with a potentially dangerous person, and you should be aware of that."

Lauren sighed. "He's not..."

The elevator opened on the third floor. "Look." Amanda pulled Lauren into a recessed area. "You're dealing with a group of murder suspects. One of those people killed Tony. And Nick wanted to work in the Most Admired Unit. It's like he was following Tony around, keeping an eye on him. The minute Tony was assigned to the unit, Nick went and volunteered to work there, okay? And I told you how none of us wanted to work there. It's practically the worst job at the magazine."

"Well, thanks for suggesting it to me, then."

"You didn't have to do it. You said you wanted to do it. And I'm sure you're only here temporarily anyway, until you find another academic job." Amanda paused, her eyes narrowing as she looked at Lauren. "But it's a little strange, don't you think, that while everyone else was running as fast as they could from that job, Nick went and deliberately offered to do it? I mean, I'm not saying he necessarily did anything to Tony. But he could have. That's what I keep telling you. He could have. And until someone proves that he didn't, I'm going to keep trying to help you make good decisions, because, as I also keep telling you, you're not thinking clearly. Okay?"

Lauren wasn't quite sure what Amanda expected her to say. "Okay, then. He's a murderer, all right? Are you satisfied now?"

"Oh, please." Amanda turned on her heel and walked away. "I'm only trying to help you."

Amanda had an incredibly annoying way of trying to help people. What was so strange about Nick's wanting to work in the Most Admired Unit? Maybe he just wanted an easier job that would provide more time for his writing. Maybe it had to do with his depression. And so much for getting to tell Amanda about Fred and the editing job. She hadn't let Lauren say much of anything. Annoying, annoying, annoying.

But then an image of Nick, standing in line with her at Starbucks, appeared in her mind. "You're lucky to have a friend like that looking out for you," he was saying. Right before the whole discussion about friendship and loneliness.

And another image, from the previous September, came into focus. It was Amanda, crowded into a dressing room with Lauren and Lauren's mom at the shop in D.C. where they had gone to look for a wedding dress. Lauren's mom was even more fashion-challenged than Lauren, so Amanda had taken charge. "No," she had said, as Lauren tried on one dress after another. "That's not right for you."

Just as Lauren had started to despair that nothing would ever be right, Amanda had left the dressing room, returning shortly thereafter with yet another dress, the shop attendant trailing meekly after her. "This one," Amanda said. "This will be perfect."

Lauren had looked dubiously at the dress, which at first glance seemed more likely to fit someone shaped like Amanda. But when she tried it on, she could tell right away that Amanda was correct. It fit perfectly. It transformed her. She stared at herself in the dressing-room mirror. She had never realized she could look like this. "Oh, wow, Lauren." Amanda took a deep breath and clasping her hands together. "I was right. You look so beautiful. You're going to be the most beautiful bride ever." All four of them, Amanda, Lauren, her mom, and the attendant, had tears in their eyes. Lauren was about to cry now, thinking about it.

And once Eric had dropped his bombshell, and Lauren and her parents had been rendered immobile, Amanda had been the one who negotiated all the wedding-related cancellations, returns, refunds, and other financial transactions left in the rubble. Including the dress.

"Hi, Lauren." It was Natasha. Lauren snapped back to the present, feeling disoriented. "You know, I'd give anything right now for a cigarette." Natasha frowned. "You're lucky you never smoked. I have these moments when I feel like the pressure is too much and I just need something."

"Why don't you try a mint?" Lauren tried to regain her focus. "Or maybe some gum?" She found a piece of gum in her bag and handed it to Natasha.

"Thanks." Natasha had an absent look in her eyes as she popped the gum into her mouth. She pulled her phone out of her pocket and glanced at it, before focusing on Lauren again. "So you must be relieved that your little project is over. And when are you planning on going back to academia?"

"I don't know yet."

"All right, then. Did that folder ever turn up?"

Lauren nodded. "But Wade's..."

"I thought it would." Natasha turned back in the direction of her office. "It was nothing to worry about, was it? So why don't you give it back if you get a chance?" And she headed down the hallway.

Lauren returned to her own desk. Nobody else was in the office yet. She unlocked her drawer, removed the folder, and looked through it again. The article about Natasha. Tony's resume. Louisa's, Louis's, Jim's, Cecily's, Nick's, Wade's. What was this? They were all here again. Was she going crazy? Hadn't she locked the drawer? How could someone have replaced Wade's resume? "How could they have done that?" she said out loud.

"Done what?" It was Nick, who had suddenly appeared at his desk.

"Oh, nothing." She was glad to see him. But she wasn't sure about public displays of affection, given that the others might be about to walk in. And it really wasn't any of their business.

He seemed to be thinking the same thing. He reached out and squeezed her hand for a second, before letting go.

Her mind returned to the troublesome folder. Why shouldn't she tell him about it? She had to talk to someone about it, and Amanda probably wouldn't even listen to her. "Well, okay." She took a deep breath and told him the folder's history of disappearing and reappearing.

"What's in it? Secret documents? No, wait, why don't we come up with a scenario." He paused and got that now-familiar faraway look on his face. "Okay, so a beautiful Romanian spy has been sent to infiltrate a troubled American news organization, charged with uncovering the truth behind a terrible crime that's been committed there. The head of the news organization hands her a series of incriminating files on each suspect, and she zeroes in on one particular suspect, who seems unbelievably suspicious, but she's completely overcome by his...by his..."

"Amazing smile? Sex appeal?"

"No, by his lack of comfortable furniture. So she's led horribly astray, and meanwhile her handlers back in Romania are demanding information, pronto. Straightaway. However you'd say that in Romanian. And she carefully considers all the suspects, one by one, and sets up appointments in restaurants and coffee shops to interrogate them. And in the end, after all the interrogations, she keeps coming back to that one incredibly suspicious suspect. But she can't believe he could have had anything to do with it. He seems so nice. Not like a murder suspect at all. Blinded by...um..."

"By her fascination with his flooded kitchen?"

"Exactly. Blinded by her fascination with his flooded kitchen, she overlooks certain important clues, and...oh, wait, my phone's ringing, hang on." He pulled his phone, which was buzzing, out of his pocket, and looked at it. "It's my sister. Do you mind if I get it?"

"No, go ahead."

"Thanks. Hey, Hannah. What's up?" He paused. "Oh, really? Oh. So they're staying with you guys?" Another pause. "Right, I mean, obviously they can't stay with me, yeah. I know."

Lauren turned her thoughts back to his interrupted story. What was that about overlooking certain important clues? Was he trying to tell her something? Or was she reading too much into it? Why couldn't anything ever be straightforward?

"Tomorrow night, okay," he was saying. He listened for a while. "Yeah. I can't really...not now, like, yeah. Okay, talk to you later, bye." He ended the call and sighed. "So my parents are coming down for the weekend. Tomorrow. They're staying with my sister and her husband."

"You don't seem too happy about that." He seemed really tense all of a sudden.

"They're very competitive. And very argumentative. They really stress me out. Would you come with me tomorrow night when we all go out for dinner? It would definitely help."

"Oh." Meeting his parents? Already? And competitive, argumentative parents, no less? She wasn't sure. It seemed premature. As well as terrifying.

"No, forget it. Forget I said anything about that. I shouldn't have said that. Now I'm stressing you out. Sorry."

"No, I mean, I don't know. Let me think about it."

"No, you don't have to think about it." He shook his head. "Bad idea on my part. Let's just move on. So back to the secret documents. Is that really what they are?"

"Sort of." She was relieved to return to the topic of the folder.

"It's actually all of your resumes and personnel evaluations. And it was Wade's resume and evaluation that was missing, and then was returned. Unless I'm going crazy and it was here the whole time." She paused, something tickling at the back of her mind. "Um, so you know your story about the Romanian spy? What important clues was she overlooking?"

He looked puzzled. "Important clues?"

"Right, you said she was blinded by her fascination with his flooded kitchen, and she overlooked some important clues."

"Oh. Yeah. Well, I hadn't gotten any further in the story yet. It was kind of improvised on the spot. So I'm not sure." He thought for a minute. "Maybe a clue about the overwhelmingly intoxicating effect this beautiful Romanian spy has on him? Or maybe a clue about how he'd like to take her out for dinner tonight? No parents or anything, don't worry. The story could have gone in various directions, really. But those are a couple of clues." He stopped. "So would it be okay if I looked at my information in that folder?"

She smiled at him. She must have taken the whole thing the wrong way. Obviously he hadn't meant anything problematic. "The overwhelmingly intoxicating effect is mutual. And dinner tonight would be really nice, thanks. Sure, here's the folder." She retrieved it and found the relevant pages.

He glanced at them and seemed to relax slightly. "Thanks," he said after a minute or two, handing the papers back. "It's a relief to see that. This latest evaluation was right after the whole incident with Tony, so I remember I was kind of worried. Fred said I didn't have anything to worry about, but...."

The incident with Tony. What had Amanda said? That Nick was deliberately keeping an eye on Tony after that? And that he had asked to be switched into the Most Admired Unit once he knew Tony was in it? "Why did you want to work in this unit anyway?" She put his evaluation form back into the folder with the rest of them.

"So that one day I could meet you."

"Since you missed your chance in high school. No, I meant, knowing that Tony was here."

"I didn't mind working with Tony. I told you, we got to be pretty friendly once the whole investigation was over." He looked at her. "You seem to find that really hard to believe." A perplexed expression crossed his face.

"I do." Male friendships were often hard to fathom. "Not that I don't believe you, but I can't imagine being friends with someone like that."

Nick shrugged. "I suppose. But Tony really wasn't that bad." He paused. "You know, speaking of working in the unit, Fred and Natasha wanted to move me and Tony out of here soon, like move him back to the Hill and me back to the Justice Department. With all the news breaking, they thought we should have more people on those beats. They've already hired a new reporter to help Frank McCloskey cover the White House."

"Really?"

"Yeah, I've actually been helping out with some of the FBI stories for a while now, because I still have some good sources over there. But Louisa and Wade didn't want to let us go, and neither did the Bartlebys. So whether they move me is up in the air right now, given, you know, Tony."

Could a dispute over this proposed shift have something to do with what happened to Tony? But why would it? Would shifting beats somehow lead to getting hit over the head? That made no sense. She sighed. Things were getting even more complicated. "So is that something you'd want to do?"

He smiled at her. "I'd rather stay here with you. I mean, it would be an incredible time to be covering the Justice Department, though, and I think I'm feeling better enough that I could handle it now. But we'll just have to see." He pulled his laptop out and opened it. "I think I might do a little revising. Not that I'm really functional enough today to do anything coherent."

"Is Tony in your novel?" Maybe that was why he wanted to spend time with him. Research purposes.

He looked at her thoughtfully. "Not really. Well, sort of. It's hard to explain. Sometimes something will strike me that I think would work well for one of the characters, but it's not that the character is actually Tony. But now I feel as if maybe I should take out anything that even somewhat resembles Tony. Considering everything that happened. I just feel really bad, as if I'm using him or something. So I'm not sure what to do."

She nodded. She probably wouldn't know what to do in that situation either. "So what about Alissa?"

"Yeah. I didn't want to put her in there, but one of the characters is going through a divorce and little bits and pieces of things that happened to me ended up in the novel. So it's not actually Alissa, but there are a few Alissa-like things that happen. Does that make sense?"

"I think so."

"And I'm really, really not putting you in there, if you're still worried about that. I hope you believe me. Although I have to admit that the Transylvanian alibi and the 99-year-old muse are hard to resist."

"Okay," she said, convinced for the second time that he meant it. He smiled at her again and turned back to his computer. She heard footsteps coming up the stairs, and a minute later, Cecily showed up.

"Hi," she said softly. "Lauren, do you want to go for a walk?"

"Sure." Lauren got up. She didn't feel very functional either, but maybe the fresh air would help. Did Cecily know about her father's financial problems? Was that what she wanted to discuss?

"Lauren?" Cecily asked once they were standing outside in a quiet corner of the parking lot. "I'm really worried about something. I just can't stop thinking about all these awful things." She cleared her throat nervously. "I just wanted to ask your advice. I feel sort of like I can talk to you about things like this."

"Of course. I really want to help."

"I don't think Tony was going to break up with that other woman," Cecily said, sniffing. "Remember, I told you that Tony kept leaving all the time in the middle of the night and going off somewhere? So the night he..." she choked back a sob and continued. "The night he died, you know, we had a big fight."

Lauren nodded.

"I told him he'd have to stop seeing her. That I couldn't stand it if he was seeing someone else he really did care about. Maybe as much as he cared about me." Cecily pulled a tissue out of her pocket and blew her nose. "So he finally said he would break up with her. That I was the one he really cared about."

"Mm-hmm," Lauren said encouragingly.

"Tony went to take a bath at that point. He really loved to take baths. So then I called Jim. While Tony was in the bathtub." She sniffed once more. "And I asked Jim if he'd follow Tony. Find out where he was going. I mean, this thing with the other woman had been going on for a while, and I really wanted to know who she was. So Jim said he'd do it. He drove over to my apartment, and followed Tony when Tony left. It was really late by that point, after four in the morning. Jim followed Tony, and all of a sudden he realized Tony was going to the office." Cecily stopped and reached for another tissue. "He was going to the office, not to the other woman's house," Cecily said, sobbing again.

"Why would he be going to the office in the middle of the night?" This really was the central question. "He wasn't on deadline, was he?"

"No. But, you know," Cecily said, regaining her composure somewhat, "Tony always had all these things going on. He never really told me about them, but he was something of an entrepreneur, you know?"

Like stealing someone's invention? Or accusing people of things they probably hadn't done? Great.

"So I think he was never going to talk to the other woman at all. He was just going to the office to meet someone, to talk about one of these projects of his. Because Jim hung around there for a while, down the street from the magazine, you know? So he wouldn't seem too conspicuous if Tony happened to come out? And he didn't see anyone come in except Louisa. And we all know only one person went in there."

"Have you and Jim told the police about seeing Louisa?" It would fit. Talk to Lou about money, that note of Tony's had said. Did she have it with her? She reached into her bag, which she'd brought with her, and started searching.

"And, I mean, there's no way Louisa was the other woman." Cecily started to laugh behind her tissue.

Lauren pictured that. Louisa, sneaking off to an early-morning rendezvous with Tony in the magazine office. It was implausible.

"No," Cecily continued. "I mean, Jim and I haven't told anyone about it except you and Winston. We don't really trust anyone else."

"If I were you, I'd tell Jim to tell the police."

Here it was, all folded up. Tony's note. She unfolded it and handed it to Cecily. "Do you know what this is?" she asked, hoping she sounded a little like one of those detectives in a classic movie.

"It looks like part of a short story or something," Cecily said, not betraying much curiosity.

Lauren sighed. "No, turn it over."

Cecily gasped. "Oh, my god. That's Tony's writing. Where did you get this?"

"From the copier." So it was Tony's writing, or a good enough facsimile to fool Cecily.

"I think this is from the Friday before he...I don't know about this first meeting. But we had lunch. And then this discussion about money? With Louisa, it must have been."

"What about Louis?"

"No," Cecily said, surprisingly firmly. "Tony used to call Louisa Lou sometimes. I guess because Brad does, and he first knew Louisa in the context of her being Brad's wife. He never called Louis Lou. Louis would have been really mad." And she giggled.

"What were they meeting about?"

Cecily frowned. "I don't know. I guess it was another one of his projects." She sighed. "But Lauren. Tony wasn't going to break up with that woman. It was the last time I ever saw him, and we had a fight." She sniffed again. "I thought he really loved me, that he'd tell her that. But he wasn't going to." And Lauren saw a couple of tears roll down her cheeks.

"Oh, Cecily." Tears were springing to Lauren's own eyes. "Maybe he was going to. Maybe he went to the office to take care of whatever this thing was, and then he would have gone to her house and told her it was over."

"I don't think so. I don't think Tony ever really told me the truth about anything."

"Well," Lauren began.

"No. I'm finally starting to realize that Tony was a total shit. And it's hard to deal with, because he's dead." Cecily wiped her eyes with the tissue. "I guess we should go back in now. It's almost nine."

Twenty-Three

"I was just saying," Louisa said as Lauren and Cecily returned to the office, "that tomorrow is Founders' Day, and the annual party will be tomorrow at noon in the front lobby." Everyone was back at their desks. "For anyone who doesn't know, it's the anniversary of the day the Bartleby family founded the magazine. Which means, of course, that we have a lot of work to do by noon tomorrow."

And she launched into a description of various surveys. Lauren glanced over at Nick, who was typing something on his phone. Her mind jumped back to the previous night in his shed. Part of her still couldn't believe it had actually happened.

"...new survey," Louisa was saying loudly. "Our Most Admired American Author."

"Well, at least that's interesting," Lauren heard Nick mutter.

"I'll have the surveys ready in a few minutes," Louisa said. "I just have to go over a couple of things."

Lauren heard a text come in, and she checked her phone. "So it turns out secret office romances are the best! #mostadmired," it said, with a heart attached.

She glanced at Nick, who was smiling at her. She smiled back.

"Very old-style Eastern European of us, right?" she texted, adding a heart and a smiley face. She saw him look at his phone and then back at her, giving her a slight nod and another smile.

"What about me?" Wade was complaining to Louisa. "Don't I get to see the surveys?"

"I thought you did already. Didn't you tell me you saw them?"

"Oh, yeah. You're right, Louisa." Wade got up and started pacing around the room.

Lauren looked over at Wade, and then around the room, and tried to focus again on the investigation. Would she ever figure out what had happened?

Suddenly, Amanda appeared in her mind, standing in the recessed area near the elevator. The regular Amanda this time, not the avatar in the bubble. "I'm not saying he did anything at all to Tony. But he could have," Amanda was saying. "That's what I keep telling you. He could have. And until someone proves that he didn't, I'm going to keep trying to help you make good decisions."

Until someone proves that he didn't. Of course. That someone would have to be her, Lauren. Right? She'd have to figure it all out, as soon as possible. Redouble her efforts. Come up with the proof. Wouldn't that make things better?

"Here you go." Louisa loomed suddenly over Lauren's desk. "This is another survey where we'll be calling random people, not experts." She dropped a large stack of papers onto the desk.

Lauren skimmed through a copy of the survey. "We'd like you to respond to the following questions," it said. "Do you enjoy recreational reading very much, somewhat, not very much, or not at all?"

"And how many hours per month do you engage in the act of recreational reading?" The survey made reading seem like a furtive, subterranean sort of activity.

"Recreational reading?" she heard Nick say. "This is ridiculous."

Lauren picked up her phone and began dialing. She was in the middle of interviewing a woman who felt that recreational reading was not as much fun as skiing, when out of the corner of her eye she saw Wade run out of the room, flinging surveys and crumpled candy wrappers behind him.

Louisa, not batting an eye, continued to sort through some surveys on her desk. Louis kept on with his computer work, and Cecily and Jim with their phone calls. Nick, who seemed to be between calls, got up and followed Wade.

Damn, Lauren thought. She was trapped in the middle of this endless call. "Well," the woman was saying. "I'd have to say somewhat. Somewhat expresses how I feel about that question, ma'am."

"Excuse me," Lauren said. "There's something important going on here, and would it be all right if I called you back a little later?"

"Of course. I'll be right here waiting. This is the highlight of my day. I've always wanted to be called by one of these survey outfits."

To each her own, Lauren thought. She hung up and hurried out of the room.

"They went that-a-way." Winston gestured up the street. "First Wade came running out of here, holding that bag of his, and then Nick came after him."

"Thanks." Lauren followed the direction Winston had indicated. And there they were, Wade and Nick, the only two patrons of the ice cream store up the block. Was this only a food crisis? It couldn't be. She opened the door.

"...Detective McDonald," Wade was saying, an edge of panic in his voice. The two of them were sitting at a table. Wade was furiously spooning ice cream into his mouth. Nick was leaning back in his chair, his ice cream neglected. "I don't know what to do. They're about to arrest me, I know it."

"Lauren?" Nick noticed her presence almost immediately. "I thought you might show up."

"I didn't do it," Wade said. "Really, you both have to believe me. I didn't do it." He had finished his ice cream by now, and he reached into his bag for a piece of candy.

Lauren glanced over at the guy behind the counter, a vacant-looking young man with long stringy blond hair pulled back in a ponytail. He was wearing a vintage gas-station-attendant-style jumpsuit with the name "Joe" stenciled across the right pocket. Lauren wondered if Joe was actually his name. The uniform looked ancient, like it had been sitting in a thrift shop for several decades. He had the radio turned way up, and fortunately didn't seem to be paying any attention to Wade's plight. "And if you can tell us what's similar about these three songs, and remember, the clue has to do with the lead singers, call us up and if you're the eighth caller, we'll give you two tickets to see the Eternal Peons Saturday night!" the radio was blaring.

"Will you two help me?" Wade asked piteously. He bit into a Snickers bar.

Lauren sat down next to Nick, across from Wade. Maybe she'd finally get the real story. "Why don't you tell us what happened. Were you anywhere near here that night?"

"No," Wade said. "I don't even know why I'm telling you two about this, but I don't know who else to turn to at this point. Nobody believes me."

"It's okay," Nick said. "Just tell us why this witness thinks he saw you there."

"I'm being framed." Wade expelled a shuddering breath.

"Framed?" Nick looked startled. He picked up his spoon and swallowed a soupy spoonful of ice cream.

"I'm sorry, Lauren." Wade craned his long neck in her direction. "I've been very rude. Would you like some ice cream?"

"No. I mean, no, thank you." It made sense. Wade was being framed by the Bartlebys, because they could use this murder investigation to get rid of a troublesome blackmailer. There had never been any connection between Tony and Wade at all.

"I'm just so embarrassed." Wade's eyes shifted between the two of them. "You two will probably never speak to me again if I tell you what I did."

"You blackmailed the Bartlebys," Lauren said, without thinking. "About Reggie's financial misdeeds, right?"

"But...but..." Wade looked at Lauren in amazement. His look was nothing compared to Nick's. He was staring at her, mouth open.

"So what did you tell the police about all this?" Lauren asked.

"Well," Wade said. "Look, I'll tell you guys the whole story." He glanced nervously at Joe, who seemed absorbed with the radio. "It all started when I was covering legal and financial issues. I wasn't very good at it. You know that I flunked out of law school, which was extremely humiliating. Then I went to business school, and I quit that. And then I went to journalism school, which seemed to suit me better."

Oh, Lauren thought. That accounted for the missing years on his resume.

"I didn't know what to do after that, but I did some freelance writing. One thing led to another, and there I was, at Lens, finally working for a halfway decent magazine. Things were looking up." He sighed and finished the Snickers bar.

"Then one day I stumbled on this evidence that Reggie Bartleby hadn't paid his income tax for five years running, and also that he had been involved in various questionable campaign finance situations. I sat there thinking about what I should do. I knew I couldn't write a story about it, because the magazine would never run it. I didn't want to make some kind of principled stand and lose my job, because it had taken me so long to get a good job in the first place. So what did I do? I called the Bartlebys and made an appointment to go over and meet with them. At their house. It was amazing, actually seeing them in person. And they agreed to pay me if I didn't say anything about Reggie."

"So that's how you got to be the co-director of the unit?" Nick asked.

Wade nodded. "I know Fred doesn't think much of my reporting abilities. But the Bartlebys made sure I got a good raise, and then this promotion. Plus they've been paying me a large sum. I put it all in a savings account. I didn't want to change my lifestyle or anything." He frowned. "I think I'm going to get another ice cream now. Either of you want one?"

They declined.

"Okay." Wade approached Joe. "A small scoop of pistachio." He turned back toward Nick and Lauren. "I just can't eat very much more. I might burst at any minute."

"Wait a minute." Joe raised one hand. "I have to listen to this song. I'm about to...Oh, shit. Oh, shit. What's the first name of the lead singer in the Eternal Peons? Shit."

"I have no idea," Wade said, rubbing his head. Neither did Lauren. She had never heard of the Eternal Peons.

"Isn't it Nathan?" asked Nick.

"Yeah, Nathan!" Joe smacked a fist into the other palm. "All right. Hey, thanks, dude. That's the clue I needed." He picked up his phone and jabbed at it frantically.

"How did you know that?" Wade asked, abandoning his quest for pistachio ice cream and returning to his seat.

"I have all this useless trivia crammed into my head," Nick said. "Every now and then I can impress people with it."

"Anyway," Wade said. "I've been blackmailing the Bartlebys for over a year now. And I really don't enjoy it at all, Nick and Lauren, not at all."

"So now the Bartlebys are framing you?" Nick still looked

incredulous.

"That's right. The way I see it, they panicked when Cecily was under suspicion, and they needed someone to take the fall. So they figured this would kill two birds with one stone. Kill two birds with one stone."

Why would someone want to kill a bird with a stone? Much less two birds? Lauren had never understood that expression. Were the birds eating the person's crops? Were they large birds that were attacking the person's livestock?

"Yeah," Joe was screaming into the phone. "My name is Joe." His voice sounded incredibly loud, and Lauren realized that Joe was on the radio.

"Well, you're the eighth caller, Joe!" the DJ bellowed. Static from the radio filled the ice cream parlor.

"All right!" Joe said.

"I was wondering if his name was actually Joe," Nick said musingly.

"Joe, please turn down your radio," the DJ commanded. "Please turn down your radio. We're getting a lot of static here."

Joe adjusted the volume.

"Can you tell us the connection between these three songs?" the DJ asked. The radio was so soft now, Lauren had to strain to hear it.

"Yeah, man. The lead singers' names all begin with the same letter."

"You got it, Joe. The lead singers from these three groups all have names beginning with the same letter!"

"All right!" Joe jumped up and down. "All right! This is awesome!"

"You've won two tickets to the Eternal Peons concert Saturday night!" the DJ said. "Just stay on the line, Joe, and we'll get all the details from you." And a commercial for a new type of chocolate bar replaced the DJ's voice.

"Maybe I should try that chocolate," Wade said thoughtfully. "It sounds pretty good."

Joe was shouting his name and contact information into his phone. He was still jumping up and down.

"I've always wanted to see someone win one of these contests," Nick said, his eyes glued to Joe. "This is fascinating."

Lauren looked at Wade, who seemed forlorn. "So, is there anything else..."

"Oh, yeah." Nick switched his gaze back to Wade. "Go ahead."

"Well, they must have found some guy that owed them something, and he went to the police and told them I was at the office that night, and the police believed him. So they're about to arrest me, I know it. They're about to arrest me." He twisted his hands together nervously. "They have my gold pen, with blood on it. The same type as Tony's blood. But I haven't seen that pen in weeks. And they have some pages that must have fallen out of my journal. All these things about feeling guilty. But I wasn't feeling guilty about Tony, I was feeling guilty about eating high-cholesterol foods."

"Why didn't you just tell the police that you blackmailed the Bartlebys?" Lauren asked. "I mean, it's better to be a blackmailer than a murderer, isn't it?" His story sounded right to her. She didn't think he had killed Tony. Although Amanda would probably tell her she was being gullible again.

"I didn't want to. I didn't want anyone to know I blackmailed the Bartlebys. But now that I'm about to be arrested for murder, I had to tell someone about the blackmailing. I could never murder someone. And I had no reason to kill Tony. I never did. Even you have a better motive than I do, Nick. Everyone has a better motive than I do. So the Bartlebys wanted to kill two birds with..."

Joe had detached himself from his phone. "Hey, I won!" He bounded over to their table. "I actually won. Do you know how many times I've tried to win one of those contests? So I was wondering, man, you want to come to the concert with me?" He looked at Nick. "I never could have gotten that clue without your help. And I just broke up with my girlfriend yesterday, and none of my friends like the Eternal Peons. They think they're too intellectual. So you want to go? It's Saturday night."

"Sure, thanks," Nick said, smiling. "That sounds great."

"All right!" said Joe. "I'll meet you here, then, around six-thirty on Saturday?"

"Okay," Nick said. "I'll get you a ticket, too," he whispered to Lauren. "And this means I don't have to spend all of Saturday night with my parents, which is probably a good thing for my sanity." He paused. "So how did you know that anyway? About the blackmailing? You're just so unbelievable."

"I'll tell you later."

"Hey," Joe said, looking at Lauren and Wade. "I mean, if I'd won four tickets, I could have taken all of you."

"Don't worry about it," Wade said gloomily. "I'll probably be in jail by Saturday night."

Joe laughed. "That's a good one, man."

"Maybe we should go back to the office now," Wade said. "I shouldn't have run out that way. But I just panicked. I just panicked."

"See you Saturday," Joe said, as they left.

"That was amazing," Nick said. "I really like the Eternal Peons."

"The police are up there," Winston said as they entered the lobby, gesturing above their heads. "Those detectives."

"Oh, no," Wade said, trembling. "Oh, no. Oh, no."

"Look," Nick said, "you're going to have to deal with this sooner or later, right? So why don't you just go up and tell them the truth?"

"But..." Wade stammered. "But..."

"Come on," Lauren said, noticing that Winston was staring curiously at them. "We'll go up with you, right, Nick?"

"Yeah." Nick nodded. "Just tell them what really happened, okay?"

Wade shuddered, but he let them lead him past Winston's desk and up the stairs to the Most Admired Unit.

Twenty-Four

"Mr. Wood," Tucker boomed, once Wade, Lauren, and Nick appeared in the office. He and McDonald were leaning against the wall across from the door. McDonald was looking rather impatient, while Tucker looked as if he could happily spend the rest of the day there. "It's nice to see you again. Beautiful weather, isn't it? I often wake up on a morning like this, and feel glad to be alive, don't you, Mr. Wood?"

Wade gave Tucker a sickly glance. "Just get it over with, detectives, just get it over with."

"Good idea," McDonald said, glaring at Tucker. "Mr. Wood, we're..."

"Hang on a second, Mac," Tucker said, holding one hand up. "I'd like to explain to these folks why we're here."

"Please," Louisa snapped. "We've had our routine disrupted quite enough over the past week. If you're going to tell us something, tell us. And if you're going to arrest Wade for Tony's murder, that's completely absurd."

"Why, thanks, Louisa," Wade quavered.

"There's absolutely nothing to thank me for." Louisa gave Wade a scornful look. "I don't think you'd be capable of committing such a crime, because I don't think you're capable of doing much of anything at all."

"Yes, I am." Wade glanced at Lauren and Nick. "I am capable of blackmailing the Bartleby family." And he settled into his chair, looking relieved.

Cecily gasped. "What? You're blackmailing my family? About what?"

"Oh, sorry, Cecily," Wade said, his voice shaking again. "That wasn't very nice of me to say with you in the room. It wasn't very nice of me to say."

Cecily jumped up and ran over to Wade's desk. "What are you blackmailing them about?" Wade didn't answer.

"This is all just routine questioning," McDonald said. "Mr. Wood, we'd like you to come down to the station with us again, please."

As Cecily quivered by his desk, Wade started trembling. "I'm being framed. It's all because I blackmailed the Bartlebys. I'm being framed. I'm sorry, Cecily, but it's true. I've been blackmailing them for over a year now."

"I don't believe you." Cecily turned her back on Wade and returned to her desk.

"Ask them, they'll tell you." Wade gestured at Nick and Lauren.

Everyone turned to stare at them.

"And what do you two know about this?" Tucker asked.

"Well," Nick began. He glanced at Lauren.

"Wade told us his story, about blackmailing the Bartlebys, and we think he's telling the truth." Lauren didn't feel like saying anything else at this point.

"Nobody would blackmail my family," Cecily said, softly but fiercely.

"Damn right," Jim said, nodding.

"Well, I can imagine..." Louis began.

Tucker sighed. "Okay, Mr. Wood, will you come with us, please?"

Wade, looking half-alive, struggled to his feet. "Okay. Do whatever you want with me. I don't care anymore." And he departed with Tucker and McDonald.

Cecily ran after them. "Wait! What are you implying about my family?"

"Wait, Cecily." Jim sprinted out of the room, Louis following.

Lauren heard their footsteps echoing down the stairs, and then the sounds faded away.

"For once," Louisa said from her desk, resting her chin on her hands, "I wish I could just run a normal office. Where nobody was murdered, and everyone wasn't always being taken away for questioning, and things weren't stolen, and people got along with each other." And she walked out of the room.

Lauren's phone indicated an incoming text. She picked it up. "In neighborhood, lunch?" It was Simon.

Lauren looked at her watch, to find that it was, in fact, lunchtime. "Where r u?" she replied.

"Downstairs," he answered. "Outside Lens building."

"Do you want to go to lunch with Simon?" she asked Nick.

"I'm not sure. My stomach feels a little weird. I couldn't eat my ice cream before, you know? When we were talking to Wade. I think it might be this stomach thing again."

"Oh, no." She hoped that wasn't the case. She reached for his hand. "Then I won't go either. I'll stay and keep an eye on you."

"No, why don't we go. I'll probably be all right."

Lauren texted Simon back, and the two of them met him outside the building.

"Hello, hello." Simon looked pleased. "I've just been watching the dramatic events down here. That Wade Wood chap being hauled away in a police car, and Cecily Bottomley, or Bartleby, I should say, running along after, with her entourage trailing behind. Quite fascinating, really."

By mutual agreement, they headed over to the nearby Chinese

restaurant.

"So," Simon said once they had started eating. "What exactly is going on with the investigation? I'd wager that Wade Wood didn't do it. He's as bad a suspect as Cecily was."

"Why do you say that?" Lauren asked.

"Oh!" Simon said, helping himself to some more kung pao chicken. "I was meaning to tell you something. Meryl Segal and I were at a fascinating session on comparative legal systems, and after the session ended, Meryl mentioned that whole thing again. Libel, or whatever it was. Some terribly serious matter, I understand. She thought it possibly concerned fabricating quotes? Stealing story ideas? Possibly plagiarism? But I can't quite remember. I'll have to look into it."

"Stealing story ideas?" Lauren felt tired all of a sudden. Not that again. She glanced over at Nick, who had turned white.

"Um," he said, standing up, his voice shaking a little. "I really feel sick. I'm going to have to leave." He reached into his pocket, took out his wallet, and put some money down on the table. "I hope this is enough. I'm really sorry about this. It's just that whenever I get this stomach thing, I have to go home and lie down."

Lauren sighed. She didn't know what to think. "Do you want me to..."

"No, it's okay, I'll check in later."

And he left.

"Hmmm," Simon said. "Poor chap. He does seem to have a problem with his stomach, doesn't he. Now, was it plagiarism?" Simon mused. "Or was it something else?"

And Simon continued chattering away, while Lauren tried to block certain unpleasant thoughts from entering her mind.

"Oh, yes," Simon was saying. "And how's the tech world?"

Lauren looked up to find Louis standing beside their table, a take-out bag in his hand.

"Great. I have a hell of a lot of work to do, though. The Monster says I can't leave until I work out a lot of formulas, so I have to get going if I want to make it to the theater tonight."

"All right," Simon said. "I'll see you, then."

"Okay." And Louis ran out the door.

"The Monster, I presume, is Louisa?" Simon said. "You see, I'm starting to decipher the cast of characters here. Although I didn't find her to be too much of a monster, I must say."

"Only sometimes." Lauren realized she had torn her paper napkin into shreds.

"Do you ever get up to New York? You know, I'll be returning there next week. You could come and visit, and I could introduce you to some of my friends. They're rather an interesting group of people. I think you'd like them. So anytime you wanted to come up, maybe at the weekend some time, just let me know and I'll organize something."

Was Simon asking her out on some kind of date? As usual, she had no clue. She thought she should inform him that she was unavailable. But maybe he had only meant it in a friendly way? "Well," she said, not sure what would be appropriate. "Thanks. Actually, I should be getting back to work now."

"Yes, so should I, come to think of it. So I'll see you before I leave for New York, I'm sure."

"I'm sure," Lauren said, and returned to her office. Only Louis was there, hunched over his computer. Okay, she told herself. If Wade didn't do it, and Nick didn't do it, then who did?

They could have done it, a voice in her head said.

I don't want to believe that, she said to the voice. Nick couldn't have.

Oh yes he could. Until you prove he didn't.

All right, then. What should I do?

That's easy. You simply make it crystal-clear to each of these people that you're not satisfied with the police's investigation, and that you want to know once and for all whether they killed Tony.

But then I'd be putting myself in danger.

Well? You want to know what happened? You can't keep tip-toeing around the edges of this thing. You have to plunge into the middle of it.

"I guess you're right," Lauren said out loud.

"What was that, Lauren?" It was Louisa, back at her desk.

Lauren was alarmed. She'd really have to stop talking to herself. "Nothing. No, I mean, it's not nothing. It's important." She went over to Louisa's desk. "Louisa, I have to ask you about something."

"What?" Louisa looked tired.

"You know how you said you didn't think Wade did it? Well, who do you think did it then? I mean, someone had to. Someone who knew the combination to that door."

"I told you. Tony did it himself."

"But someone came out of the building that night. And if Tony did it himself, then who came out of the building?"

"Isn't it possible," Louisa said, giving Lauren a cool green stare, "that someone came in, found Tony dead, and left again? Perhaps this person had nothing to do with killing Tony."

Lauren thought about it. Could Louisa be referring to herself? Maybe Jim saw her out there, and she had, in fact, gone up the stairs and found Tony dead by the copier. And then she had left the building. But why would Tony hit himself over the head with a brass vase in his office in the middle of the night? And what about Tony's note that mentioned talking to "Lou" about money? "Did Tony ever talk to you about money? Did he talk to you about it the Friday before he died, for example?"

"Money?" Louisa looked puzzled. "You mean, did Tony want a raise?"

Lauren realized she had no idea what money-related topic Tony had planned to discuss with the mysterious "Lou." "Well..." she began.

"Lauren, I understand you want to find out what happened. We all do. But for now, I think we'll feel more settled if we focus on our work. Not that anyone's here to do the work." Louisa looked angrily around the room. "I know Cecily and Jim went running after the police. I don't really expect much from the two of them anyway. But I can't imagine where Nick's gone. He doesn't usually disappear like this."

"He said something about his stomach."

"Oh. That's right, he does have stomach problems. Those parasites can be pretty bad. Brad had some problem like that years ago, before I met him." Louisa tapped her pen against her clipboard. "Academia. That's the way to go. I don't think I can deal with crazy news organizations anymore."

"Academia can be crazy too."

"You're right. But if I were you, I'd go back there. This job is too full of nonsense. I have to take these charts over to a meeting now with Natasha and the art department people. What a waste of time." And Louisa stalked out of the office.

"Lauren," Louis said, the minute Louisa's footsteps were inaudible. "I found something else interesting. Just a couple of minutes ago."

"What?" Lauren felt drained of all energy.

"Remember what I told you about the whole thing with Tony and Nick? You know, about how Tony was..."

"Yes."

"Well, I checked my T-man email again, and reread that

message Tony meant to send himself, and way down at the bottom was this note that said Talk to N. about money. I missed seeing it before."

"Talk to N. about money?" Lauren sat down in her chair. "What's that supposed to mean?"

"It's obvious." Louis looked smug. "He was going to talk to him about money. Nick, I mean. Like, blackmail money or something, you know?"

"Do you really think Nick stole Tony's ideas?"

"Well..." Louis frowned judiciously. "I'd like to think he didn't. I'd like to think Tony was full of shit. I mean, I know Tony was full of shit in general. But I just don't know about this."

"Can I see it?"

"Sure, I just printed it out. Here." He handed it to her.

Lauren looked at it. Talk to N. about money. It sounded like that piece of paper from the copier. Talk to Lou about $$. "Did Tony ever talk to you about money?"

"Money?" Louis said, a wary expression on his face. "Why would he do that? I don't have any money. Of course, I will have some fairly soon, I think, but for now, no way. He talked to me about tech, not about money."

"Some fairly soon? What do you mean by that? And why did you go to a lawyer the other day?"

Louis looked away from her toward the window. "Just some business."

"Did it have to do with a video game that Tony was about to steal from you?"

"Look, Lauren," Louis said, looking extremely worried, "I'd seriously suggest you stop whatever it is you're doing, or you could get in real trouble, okay?" And he returned to his computer.

Twenty-Five

Lauren considered what to do next. Maybe call Karel Halama again. It was time for a fresh round of insults.

"Yes?" He sounded as angry as ever.

"It's Lauren Green. I wanted to talk to you again about that article? In Lens?"

"No. No and goodbye." And he slammed down the phone.

Well, she might as well go outside. She was far too upset and bewildered to get any work done. So she sat down on the front steps of the building. She texted Nick: "How r u feeling?" But there was no reply. Was he asleep? She was so confused.

A text came in, but it wasn't from him. It was from her old friend Melanie, up in Boston. "L, I don't believe it!!" the text said. "Just heard about murder at ur magazine! R u ok? Also wanted to let u know about fellowship for next academic year u applied for, possibly will work out, should know soon, will keep u posted M."

Had she applied for a fellowship for the next academic year? Something that would start in September? She honestly couldn't remember. Much of what had happened in the month or so after Eric's abandonment of her was hazy. Undefined. As if it had happened to someone else.

"Am ok, it's awful though. Thx, hope u r well," she texted back. Should she ask which fellowship she had applied for? Where this fellowship was located? No. She'd seem too spacy. Even though Melanie had seen her at her worst. Could this fellowship be at the research center where Melanie worked? Did she want to go back to Boston if she even got the fellowship? She had no clue what she was doing, clearly. Or what she wanted to do. She also had to reply to the sponsors of that month-long Romania fellowship and let them know what she'd decided. Except that she hadn't decided anything, so she had no idea what to tell them.

And on top of everything else, she wasn't getting along with Amanda. She'd have to stop by Amanda's desk and try to remedy that. But going inside didn't sound too pleasing. The sun slanted against her face, and she closed her eyes for a few minutes. She really did feel so tired.

Just then, her phone rang. Was it Nick? But no. It was Melanie's mother.

"Lauren? It's Norma. Oh, my god, Melanie just told me you're working at Lens magazine!" Melanie's parents lived next door to Lauren's parents, and their mothers seemed to talk every day, so it surprised Lauren that Norma hadn't known. "I guess Sally was so busy getting ready for their trip that she didn't have a chance to tell me. Are you okay? Can I do anything? Do you want to come over for dinner?"

"I'm okay. It's really horrible, and everything is awful here at the magazine, but I'm all right, thanks." The job had come up suddenly, and her parents had indeed been preoccupied with trip preparations, which probably explained why she hadn't been inundated with worried calls from their friends. And she hadn't told many of her own friends about her new job, either, come to think of it. She had been too overwhelmed.

"And your parents..." Norma began.

"My parents don't know anything about this, so please don't tell them, all right? I don't want them to worry." That was the last thing she needed.

"Yes indeed. They should just enjoy their trip. So I would have called and checked in with you sooner, but I didn't know that's where you were working, and Melanie didn't know about the murder, and the two of us just were talking and we figured it all out, and oh, how terrible! After everything else you've been through! I feel dreadful that we weren't there to be supportive, but I guess you do have that wonderful Amanda, right? Such a fantastic young woman."

"Um, yeah." The wonderful Amanda who wasn't even talking to her. Honestly, she didn't feel like discussing any of this with Norma, even though she was very fond of her. She certainly didn't want to get into a conversation leading to the revelation that she, Lauren, had been the one to find Tony. A detail Norma didn't seem to know, fortunately.

"Well, please call us any time, and we'd love to have you over for dinner, okay?" Norma continued. "I'll let you go now, but I mean it, all right?"

After thanking Norma and ending the call, Lauren reflected once more on how fortuitous it was that her parents were far away right now. Apparently they were not reading the Post or any other local news sources on the ship, or she would have heard from them. She settled back and closed her eyes again. She felt as if she might fall asleep right here...

"Lauren?" Startled, she looked up to find Cecily, her blue eyes red-rimmed, standing in front of her. "Can I sit down with you?"

"Of course." Lauren gestured at the space next to her on the concrete step.

"I heard the whole story." Cecily sat down. "About my dad. It's all so upsetting, I don't know what to do." She pulled out a tissue and blew her nose. "I'm sorry I keep crying like this. It's just that all these horrible things keep happening to me. I mean, I know my dad isn't a very responsible person. My brother and I had a sense he was involved in something he shouldn't have been, but my dad never tells us much about what he does anyway. And my mom hates him. She's probably not surprised about this at all."

"Do you think Tony knew about this?"

"No." Cecily leaned back on the step. "He would have mentioned something. He probably would have made some nasty comment to me about it, you know?"

"So do you think this has anything to do with Tony?" Lauren persisted, feeling a little guilty. Hadn't Cecily been through enough lately?

Cecily sat up and frowned. "I don't know. I haven't had a chance to think it through. Actually, I think I should go home and talk to my family. Oh, and Jim and I did tell the police about seeing Louisa. But I'm not sure they were paying attention to us."

No sooner had Cecily sped away in her Mercedes than Jim showed up.

"Hey, Lauren." He gestured at his face. "You like them?"

"Your glasses?" Lauren figured that must be what he was talking about. The glasses were large, with tan-colored frames. "Yeah, they look good."

"I was, like, dubious at first." He flopped down onto the step and stretched out. "I mean, I've never had glasses before. But I really like them. They're just so legit. It's cool to be able to see so well." He took them off and held them out in front of him, and then put them back on.

Lauren nodded.

"So, Lauren, what did you and Nick mean when you said you believed Wade?"

"I don't think Wade did it. I think he was blackmailing the Bartlebys, but I don't think he killed Tony."

"So who did?" Jim asked, wide-eyed behind his new glasses.

"Do you know?"

"No. Do you?"

"Huh?" Jim raised himself up on one elbow. "Do I what?"

"Do you know who did it."

Jim looked pensive. "Well, I could have done it."

"What do you mean by that?" Lauren looked closely at him.

"I could have done it," Jim repeated. "But if I had, would I tell you?"

Was this conversation real? "I don't know, would you?"

"I might tell Cecily. Maybe I'd tell you. I doubt I'd tell Louisa, though, you know?"

"Are you trying to tell me something? I mean, right now?"

"No." Jim looked puzzled. "What would I be trying to tell you?"

"Forget it. So do you think Tony knew Wade was blackmailing Cecily's family?"

"Like, totally. Tony always knew everything that people didn't want him to know. He knew some stuff about me, like how a couple of times I blew my work off and went to an intern party or a Nats game or something. But that was a long time ago now."

"You're talking about when you worked for the senator, right?"

"Huh?" Jim took off his glasses and twirled them around. "These are so cool."

"So tell me about the night you saw Louisa going into the office."

"Louisa? When?"

"The night Tony was killed. The night you saw Louisa going into the office."

"Okay. Like, I was just hanging around in the neighborhood. And I saw Louisa walking into the office. I was like, what's the deal? I mean, I knew Tony was in there too. I was totally freaked.

Why would everyone be hanging out in the office in the middle of the night?"

"Exactly. Why would they?"

"Yeah. Really. It was just too weird."

"Why were you there? Do you always hang around the neighborhood at four in the morning?"

"Really." Jim laughed. "Totally."

"Did Cecily tell you to come over here?" Lauren said, hoping to confirm at least one thing. "Did she ask you to follow Tony to find out where he was going?"

"Cecily?" Jim twirled his glasses around again.

"Stop that, you'll break them." A couple of weeks ago, she had accidentally sat on her glasses and broken them, forcing her to rely solely on her contact lenses. She really needed to get the glasses repaired, but there hadn't been time.

"Good point." Jim folded his glasses up and put them in their case.

"Well?" Lauren asked, feeling slightly obnoxious.

"Yeah," Jim said, nodding obediently. "I'll be careful with them."

"No, I mean about Cecily."

"I'm not sure." Jim brushed a few stray pieces of hair out of his eyes. "I'll have to get back to you on that one. Like, tomorrow we'll get to eat a lot."

"What?" Lauren was baffled by this response.

"At Founders' Day. Nick told me there's a lot of food and stuff."

Not that Nick could eat any of it, with his stomach problem. "I'm sure he can't eat anything by tomorrow, though."

"Why?"

"His stomach. He had to leave."

"Stomach?"

"You know. His stomach problem."

"I don't think he has a stomach problem," Jim said, more definitively than anything Lauren had ever heard him say.

"Oh, really?" Lauren wished she'd never come to work here. Would that she were back in Boston, safely ensconced in her apartment with her books about Romania.

"No way, man. Hey, there's Wade. He's back already?" Jim pointed down the street, where a distant figure was hurrying toward the Lens building.

The figure came closer. "That's not Wade. That's Fred."

"Hey, you're right. Hi, Fred. How's it going?"

"Hi, Jim, Lauren," Fred said, approaching them. "I can understand why you're sitting out here." He looked up at the cloudless blue sky. "It's beautiful today, isn't it? I had the Lyft driver let me off a couple of blocks away, so I could enjoy the weather."

"Yeah," Jim said. "And there's like nothing for us to do today, with Wade at the police station and all."

"Mm-hmm," Fred said. "Things are a little crazy around here."

"Do you really think Wade did it?" Lauren asked. She might as well ask anyone she ran into, she figured.

"No." Fred shook his head. "I've just come from the police station, and I don't think Wade killed Tony. I do think Wade blackmailed the Bartlebys, though. I've thought for a while now there was something strange about Wade, and now I know what it is. But my instinct tells me Wade's no murderer. Not that the police listened to me, of course. They seem pretty convinced Wade did it. I think it'll take some hard evidence that someone else did it for them not to arrest him."

"Well, who do you think it was, then?" Lauren asked. "That did it, I mean."

Fred pulled out a tissue and wiped his sweaty pink brow. "I

have no idea. It's frustrating. I've been dealing with the police for more than a week now, and I feel completely steeped in this whole thing. It's all I ever think about. Well, I mean, besides the nonstop news pouring out of the White House and the Hill and so forth. Somehow we've managed not to get too far behind this week on all these stories, but I'm not sure how long we can keep it up." He sighed. "I've been trying to get to the bottom of this awful business with Tony, but the solution escapes me."

"Hey," Jim said. "Like, what kind of food are we having tomorrow?"

"Food?" Fred asked. "What are you talking about?"

"For Founders' Day."

"Oh, and that's another thing. I've been talking to the Bartlebys about postponing Founders' Day, because of Tony. But they insisted it had to take place tomorrow." Fred sighed again. "Anyway, I should be getting back. I think Natasha's expecting a report on my latest trip to the police station."

Lauren decided she should return to the office too, and Jim followed her inside. Louisa and Louis were both there, working.

Jim settled down in his chair. "Hey, Louisa, do you mind a lot if I listen to some music?"

"Go ahead. At this point, I don't really care what you're doing. I just want to make sure Louis is finishing up the data. At least I can say we in the unit have done our part with that." And Louisa sniffed and looked over at Louis.

"I'm working, I'm working," Louis said, his fingers clicking away over the keyboard. "I've calculated all the formulas, and I should be done by six-thirty, okay?"

"Very good," Louisa said, sounding distracted. She walked over to Lauren's desk. "Well, I don't know what we're supposed to do now. What do you think of this? I was giving Natasha an update on our progress with the surveys, and she acted like she didn't give a damn."

"Really? After all those meetings and all those surveys?"

Louisa nodded. "In fact, when she finally did pay attention, she said maybe we wouldn't move ahead with the surveys as soon as she'd thought. That maybe we'd wait for a while. It's so frustrating." She frowned. "You know, Lauren, why don't you just go home? We're not going to get anything done today, and there's no point in your sitting around here. I'm sure you have better things to do. And you, too, Jim."

"Cool," Jim said. He grabbed his belongings and ran out the door. Lauren followed, more slowly. She sent Nick another text, but didn't get a reply. She took the elevator up to the third floor, and made her way to Amanda's desk. There was no sign of her.

"Amanda's covering a press conference," said a vaguely familiar-looking woman at the next desk. "I'm not sure when she'll be back."

"Thanks." Wandering back down the hall, Lauren texted Amanda, telling her she hoped to see her later, that they shouldn't stay mad at each other. Soon she found herself near Natasha's office. And there was Natasha, heading in her direction.

"Hi, Lauren. How are things?"

"Confusing." Maybe she should talk to Natasha about it. Natasha had started her off on the whole adventure in the first place. "Do you have a minute?"

"Make it quick." Natasha turned toward her office and led Lauren past Joanna, who was screaming something into the phone about someone who hadn't shown up for a meeting.

"Well," Lauren said, once they were inside the office. "I just don't think Wade did it. I mean, he had no connection to Tony. He was just blackmailing the Bartlebys. He didn't murder anyone."

"Lauren, Lauren." Natasha started to pace around the room. "I told you you didn't have to worry about this anymore, didn't I? The Bartlebys are satisfied, okay?"

"But I don't think he did it. It just doesn't make any sense."

Natasha sat down. "I'd drop it if I were you. Wade probably did it. I mean, the Bartlebys told me his pen had blood all over it and his diary talked about how guilty he felt. And someone saw him going into the building. What more do you want?" And she raised her hands helplessly in front of her.

"What if he was being framed?"

Natasha smiled and shook her head. "I don't think so. And neither do the Bartlebys. So I'll be seeing you, okay?" And she picked up her phone.

Lauren left, still confused. How could Natasha be so sure Wade had done it? How could the police be so sure? What should she make of the email Louis found? She texted Nick for a third time. "Am coming over," she wrote. "Need to see how u r." No reply.

Half an hour later, she pulled up in front of the house. She could see Nick's car, but there was no sign of any other vehicles. She supposed Shlomo and Damian must have left for the day. Looking around the side of the house, she found a gate, and she pushed it open. There was the strip of grass, and there was the shed.

She knocked on the door. "It's me. Are you in there?" What if he wasn't there at all? But his car was there. So where could he be? She looked back and forth across the strip of grass. What about the email? What about that legal issue Professor Segal kept mentioning? What about Nick's story about the overlooked clues? What about Karel Halama? What if Amanda was right? What if she really wasn't thinking clearly and was gullible and naïve and had bad judgment about men?

She felt as if her eyes might close. The lack of sleep was really catching up with her. She knocked again. Nothing. Where was he? What if she never solved this? What would happen? Which clues might she be overlooking? What if she kept making mistake after mistake, year after year?

She sat down, unable to stand up anymore, and leaned back against the doorway. What if Eric had been right and she was worthless? Disposable? Not platinum at all. A wave of dizziness hit her, and she decided it made sense to lie down on the grass. She couldn't keep going. She couldn't figure anything out. The grass felt soft underneath her. She was outside the shed, and then she was inside. Back on the mattress. Asleep.

Twenty-Six

Lauren opened one eye. Where was she? A pile of cardboard boxes loomed in the distance. She shook her head and opened the other eye. She could see the uncomfortable wooden chair. How had she ended up in Nick's shed, on the mattress, asleep? And where was he? She checked her phone, which had been in her pocket. Nothing from him, but a reply from Amanda, who seemed grateful for the message, agreed they shouldn't fight, and wished she could meet Lauren for dinner but had already made plans with the guy from Stacy's office. Lauren texted back to say she'd see Amanda later. She realized she must have been asleep for a few hours. It was already past seven.

Her phone rang, and she checked to see who it was. "Unknown," it said. Probably one of those solicitation robocalls. But what if it had to do with the investigation? She answered it.

"Stop interfering where you don't belong," an echoing machine-like voice said. "If you want to end up like Tony, you're on the right track, Lauren." And the phone went dead.

Lauren dropped the phone and it clattered to the floor. She was shaking uncontrollably. The voice had been inhuman, chilling. This was like a nightmare. Should she leave the shed? She didn't know. Maybe the person was outside waiting for her.

She should call the police. Trembling, she picked her phone up, dialed, explained her situation, and was eventually connected to Detective Tucker. She would rather have talked to McDonald than Tucker. But she was in such a state of panic that even the booming sound of Tucker's voice comforted her.

"Well, Ms. Green. My colleague here tells me you've had a threatening phone call?"

Lauren told him the details. "Can you trace it?" Her voice was shaking.

"Let me see what can be done. And please let me know if the caller tries again."

"Okay," Lauren said, still quivering.

"You have no idea who this caller could be?"

"No." Lauren's brain was starting to click back in. "But doesn't this mean that someone besides Wade killed Tony?"

"Well, all options are still open. I don't like arresting innocent people. You didn't happen to catch me on the news earlier, did you? Mr. Wood had something of an impromptu press conference outside the station earlier, and I hovered around the edges and got into some of the camera shots."

"Oh, sorry I missed it." The idea of this press conference almost made her smile.

"So we'll be in touch, Ms. Green. We're working on this case, you don't have to, okay?" And Tucker hung up.

So who could have made that call? It could be anyone from the office, Lauren realized as she curled up on the mattress, anyone she'd talked to about the murder. It could be Nick. Suddenly chilled, she pulled the quilt around her. No, it couldn't. But where was he? She felt as if she should leave, but she wasn't sure she should go outside. Was the shed even locked? She should check on that. She stood up, and another wave of dizziness crashed over her as she tiptoed to the door, still huddled in the quilt. But before she could reach the door, it opened. She screamed.

"Oh, my god, Lauren, are you okay?" It was Nick. "What

happened? I should never have left you here by yourself. I just had to go into the house to get some more medicine. For my stomach. Are you all right?" He put his arm around her and led her back to the mattress. She lay down, still feeling dizzy. "I'm so sorry I scared you. That's the last thing I would want to do."

She glanced at him. He looked pale, all washed-out, with dark smudges under his eyes. He was wearing old blue sweatpants and a gray Georgetown University t-shirt with a couple of holes in it. His hair was standing on end.

"I found you out there a few hours ago, and I brought you back in here half-asleep and let you keep sleeping. What were you doing there?" He kissed her on the forehead. "For a minute when I saw you lying there, I thought..." his voice trailed off. "I was so scared."

"I wanted to check on you." She was almost whispering. She couldn't speak any louder. Her head was aching. "See how you were. You didn't answer any of my texts. And then you didn't answer when I knocked on the door. And then a few minutes ago I got this threatening phone call. A voice that was disguised. Sort of like a terrifying robot. It said I should stop interfering or I'd end up like Tony." She felt like crying. It was all too much.

Nick's eyes widened. "Oh no." He lay down on the mattress next to her and wrapped his arms around her. "That's so awful. That's the kind of thing I was worried about." He shook his head. "I never should have gone in the house for the medicine. I mean, that wouldn't have stopped this person from calling, but at least I would have been with you when it happened. Did you call the police? Do you want me to call them?"

"No, you don't have to, I did just a minute ago."

She described her conversation with Tucker, and Nick nodded. "I wish I wasn't feeling so sick, or I'd be a lot more help. And I feel terrible that I didn't get your texts or hear you at the door. I was asleep. This stomach thing always really knocks me out." He looked as if he were about to pass out, she noted. "I wonder who could have made that call. I guess you talked to pretty much everyone, right? They all know you're trying to figure it out?"

"Yeah." She thought about her latest round of questioning. "By this point, I think they probably know."

"Why don't you just stay here tonight?" He twirled a piece of her hair around his finger. "I mean, you're already here, and I'd worry about you too much if you left. And I should be feeling a little better tomorrow, so we can figure all of this out together then, okay? I really want to help you."

"Thank you." Her head was spinning. She closed her eyes. It didn't really improve the situation, so she opened them again. "I appreciate it, especially when you're feeling so sick."

"Of course." He seemed surprised. "Sick or not sick, I care about you, Lauren. A lot. I just wish we could solve the whole thing right now and be able to move past all this awful stuff. You know?"

She nodded. Speaking of feeling sick, she wasn't feeling well herself. She turned away from him and buried her head in the pillow, which was soft and cool and soothing.

"Are you all right?" she heard him asking, as if from far away. "I mean, beside the phone call, which is bad enough."

"No," she managed to say. "My head hurts, and I've been really dizzy. And so, so tired."

"Oh, wow, that's too bad. Do you want an aspirin or something?"

"I have some Advil in my bag. And some water, I think." Her bag had been outside with her, but she realized she had no idea where it was now. Yet another problem.

"I brought it in here before," he said, to her relief. "It's over by the door. Let me get it for you." He got up slowly, looking dizzy himself, and retrieved it. She raised her head a little and swallowed a couple of pills.

"Thanks." She felt guilty. "I'm sorry to be making you wait on me when you're sick too."

He smiled, and then started laughing as he collapsed next to her on the mattress.

"What's so funny?"

"It's just kind of ridiculous. Like, we had our moment of amazing passion last night, and now we're both sick and totally wiped out. Completely incapacitated. I could maybe see that happening if we were a lot older or something, but what are the odds?"

"Yeah." She smiled despite her headache. "It is pretty ridiculous."

"Well, I hope it doesn't happen again. The getting sick afterwards part, I mean. I hope we have a lot more moments of amazing passion. Once we're both feeling better. You know. I mean, I hope that part happens again, definitely." He looked at her. "Am I making any sense at all? Probably not. I think everything I'm saying is coming out wrong. I tend to do that when I'm around you, in case you hadn't noticed."

"No, I understand what you're saying. It makes sense to me." And she reached for his hand.

"So you'll stay here?" He entwined their fingers together. "Especially if you're dizzy, you shouldn't drive anywhere. I'd drive you, but I'm probably not in good enough shape right now either." He sighed. "And I'd been planning to take you out somewhere really nice tonight. I'm sorry."

"It's okay. I'm sorry too. But about staying over, I don't know." She tried to sit up, but the dizziness was too much. And her head felt as if it would explode. "I need to go back to sleep. But I think I should go home. I have a feeling Amanda wants me to come home."

The next thing she knew, she was still lying on the mattress, the quilt draped over her. Some time must have passed. The shed had grown dark, but she could see that Nick had burrowed under the covers and was sleeping. She tried again to sit up, testing for dizziness. It seemed better. The headache had almost gone away.

She stood up, found a piece of paper and a pen, and scribbled a note, "Going home to sleep, hope you feel better xo." Then she made her way to the door, quietly opened it, and slipped out into the night. He needed to rest. She didn't want to wake him. On the walk back to Amanda's apartment from the car, she startled at every noise. She noted each person who walked by. Who had made that call? Could she really trust anyone? Even Nick? By the time she opened the door to the apartment, she was shaking uncontrollably again.

"Lauren? Is that you? I just got home a few minutes ago. What an awful date! The worst ever! I mean, who reminisces over dinner, with someone they've only just met, about dissecting a fetal pig in middle school? Completely unappetizing!" Lauren could hear Amanda's familiar voice, her familiar footsteps moving around in the kitchen. "Where were you, anyway?"

"Sleeping." Lauren closed and double-locked the door. "I'm just so tired." Her teeth were chattering. It was hard to say anything more.

"Holy shit," Amanda said, having made her way to the living room. "What on earth happened to you? You look terrible." A concerned expression appeared on her face, and she guided Lauren to the sofa. "You're shaking. What happened?"

Lauren's defenses finally collapsed and she started to cry. "A threatening phone call," she managed to say between sobs. "There was a disguised voice, and it said I'd end up like Tony if I didn't stop interfering. Detective Tucker's going to try to figure it out."

"Whoever's doing this to you is going to be sorry," Amanda said, a tone of absolute fury in her voice. "I'm going to call Tucker right now." She pulled her phone out and dialed. Lauren heard her identify herself and ask to speak to Tucker. "I'm on hold." Amanda drummed her fingers impatiently on the coffee table. "Hi, Detective Tucker. Yes, I'm calling about this phone call Lauren got? You guys need to get on this right away! This is unacceptable. Yes, I know." There was silence for a while. "Yes. I know you're doing what you can, but you need to do more, okay?" Silence. "What exactly are you doing? Why hasn't an arrest been made already?" More silence. "Okay, please do that, thanks." And she hung up. "Jeez. Total incompetence. And now it's time to get you into bed."

Lauren's sobs had subsided. "You're the best friend anyone could ever have," she said, as Amanda tucked her into bed. "You're like a superhero or something."

"So are you." Amanda gave Lauren a hug. "Do you want the lights on or off?"

"I think on." She had slept with the lights on every night for a month after Eric had abandoned her. It was hard to sleep that way, but it banished some of the scary thoughts from her mind.

"Do you want me to stay here in your room with you, or will you be okay?"

"No, it's okay. I'll be all right."

She could hear Amanda in the hallway. She was talking on the phone with her mother, something about a trip to Vancouver that Adam and Stacy and the kids were planning. "No, I'm not going along. I can't take off right now. Too much work. Although I've never been there, so it might be fun."

Lauren had never been there either. But she had been to Europe, many times. Over and over. Eric hadn't gone to Prague with her, but he'd gone to Maine. And they were sitting on the steps of the romantic inn, and it was a beautiful day, just like it had been today. Jim was twirling his glasses around. There's Wade coming down the street, he said, but it hadn't been Wade. And the DJ was yelling, All right, you've got it, these names begin with the same letter, free tickets to the concert Saturday night. But Lauren couldn't go, because she had a stomach problem. She'd have to give the tickets back. She could give them to Sonya. Maybe she could take Anna Slinsky and Petrovich and the other woman. The love triangle. Natasha was sticking her lip out, imitating Karel Halama, complaining about how hard he was to interview. Lauren handed her the article, and all of a sudden Natasha really was Karel Halama, recoiling in horror. Out! he shouted. But was there a problem with the story?

Everyone had stories to tell. Shlomo could tell stories about the Bartlebys, and so could Simon. Amanda could tell stories about Tony and Nick, and so could Louis. And Wade wasn't a murderer, he was a blackmailer. And Tony wasn't going to meet this woman, he was going to the office.

She woke up, hours later. She could hear the noisy morning birds communicating with one another. Her head felt clear. She remembered her dream. And she thought she had figured the whole thing out.

Twenty-Seven

She sat up, switched the lamp off, and reached for her phone. It was 7:15. A text had come in from Nick, apparently a few minutes earlier. "How r u?" it said. "Worried. Slept till now. Please let me know how u r doing? Xo"

She thought through everything she would need to do. It probably made sense to keep it to herself for now. Not sound as if anything had changed. See how it played out.

"Am fine, went back home to sleep, hope u r feeling better, see u at work xo" That sounded normal enough. She shut off the phone.

Amanda knocked on her door, already dressed for work. "How are you doing?" she asked, as Lauren opened the door.

"Okay. Much better."

"I wanted to wait for you." Amanda perched on Lauren's bed. "I think I'll drive you in today."

Lauren nodded. A ride would be good. She still wasn't sure how things would go. She didn't want to say anything more, but there was something she was supposed to tell Amanda, wasn't there? On a different topic? Oh, right, the editing job.

"Yeah, thanks. That would be great. So, guess what I heard?"

"What?"

"Fred's thinking of offering you the editing job. On the national desk. Apparently he's very impressed with your work, understandably enough."

"Really?" Amanda looked excited yet skeptical. "Who told

you that?"

Lauren didn't want to reignite their argument by mentioning Nick. "It doesn't matter who."

Amanda shrugged. "Well, okay, thanks for telling me. I hope your mystery source is right." She paused for a minute. "And of course the Bartlebys still want to have the Founders' Day party today? Insane!"

Lauren agreed. She spent the drive to the office thinking about her plan, and by the time she and Amanda arrived, she felt it would work. Sitting down at her desk, she quickly glanced around, noting that everyone was present.

She reached into her bag, turned her phone back on, and considered a few last details. The only question was whether Tucker and McDonald would believe her and would come over to the building at the appointed hour. And whether Jim would pay attention to her. She would need to talk to him as soon as possible.

"Hey." Nick looked at Lauren. "How's it going? Are you feeling better?"

"Okay. Yeah, thanks."

"Did anything more happen? Any more calls?"

"No." How could she talk to Jim alone? Furthermore, how could she make Jim listen to her for long enough to get this plan off the ground? There were so many variables. She sighed and rested her head in her hands.

"Is everything all right?" Louisa frowned at Lauren from across the room.

"I think so."

Lauren returned her focus to Nick, who was looking at her quizzically. "I'm sorry, I should have asked you how you're doing, too. I've just been distracted. How are you feeling, anyway?"

"A little better, thanks."

"Great," she said, although she didn't really think he looked much better at all.

"Did you..." he started.

"Please," Louisa entreated. "To your phones, everyone. I would appreciate your doing some work for a couple of hours at least, please."

Lauren realized she'd never called back the woman she had been interviewing the previous day when Wade had rushed out of the room, so she dialed her number.

"Hello!" The woman sounded delighted to hear from her. "I had just about given up on you."

"Sorry about that," Lauren said, belatedly continuing with the survey. If she could talk to Jim before the party started, maybe it would all work out. She finished the survey and hung up, whereupon her cell phone signaled an incoming text.

"Thinking of stopping by your office @ lunchtime w Meryl & Ethan. OK?" It was Simon.

"OK," she texted back. Then she remembered the Founders' Day party. It would have started by then. Oh, well, so they'd get something to eat too. Nobody would notice a few extra people. And by the time they got there, everything would have been resolved. Or so she hoped.

"I don't have too much time for recreational reading myself," Jim was bellowing into the phone. "But I've got to say, that's one of my favorite books too. I really liked the part with the sea serpent, didn't you?"

Cecily was whispering something into her phone. She looked as if she hadn't gotten enough sleep.

Lauren completed a few more surveys, and then she heard Louisa again. "I am leaving for my meeting with Natasha. Louis, you've done an excellent job. I'd like you to come with me, to tell

Natasha exactly what you did."

"Really?" Louis looked pleased.

"Certainly. You deserve a lot of the credit."

"I'm coming too, right, Louisa?" Wade got up from his chair.

"Only if you want to." Louisa sailed out of the room, Louis in her wake.

"Well, if you and Louie are going, then I should, too," Wade grumbled, trailing after them. "Just because I'm a blackmailer doesn't mean I shouldn't get to go to a meeting."

"This place is too weird sometimes," Nick said to Lauren, putting down his phone. "I have to go to CVS and get some more medicine. I'll be back soon." And he left.

Cecily stood up and blew her nose. "I'm going for a walk." And she, too, departed.

"I've really enjoyed talking to you, too," Jim said into his phone. "Maybe we could get together and discuss books some other time, you know? You live in Omaha, right? Oh, well, I'm thinking of driving across the country at some point, so let me get your street address. Yeah, sure. Like, that's great. Bye." He put his phone down. "Man. You get to talk to some totally cool people with this job. I just spent like an hour talking to this old dude about literature. He's a retired Air Force guy, and he spends all his spare time engaging in recreational reading. It's amazing."

Lauren wished she could get as much out of the job as Jim seemed to. She took a deep breath. This was going to be tricky. "So, Jim. I have to talk to you about something very important."

"Huh?"

Oh, no. He was in one of his more spacy moods. "This is incredibly important."

"Okay. Go for it."

And she told him her plan, after asking him a couple of

questions.

"Cool, man. Let's do it. I'll be back by then. I just want to find Cecily." He ran down the stairs.

Now she needed to call Tucker and McDonald and see if they would come over to the building. Neither of them answered their cell phones, so she left messages, and then dialed the police station.

"No," a woman's voice said. "Neither one of them is available right now, ma'am."

"Are they out of the office? Or are they there but they're busy? Because..."

"They're not available right now, ma'am."

"Could I leave a message?"

"Look, ma'am, I have five other lines ringing. Just give me your name and number."

"But it's really important."

"Name and number, ma'am."

Lauren left her name and number and started to relate the rest of her message, but the woman cut her off in the middle and hung up. Lauren sighed exasperatedly and looked around the office. Fortunately none of them had returned. Her phone rang shortly thereafter, and she picked it up. It was probably one of the detectives calling back.

"Did you listen to what I said last night, Lauren?" the voice said. Lauren felt chilled. It was the same voice, inhuman, metallic, distorted, and terrifying. And now she thought she knew who it was. "Did you listen to me?"

Lauren reached out tremblingly to her office phone, lifted the receiver, and dialed the police again.

"Just stop trying to look into things that don't concern you," the voice said.

"Hello?" It was the same woman again.

But the cell phone call had gone dead.

"Hello?" the woman asked again.

"This is Lauren Green. I called a few minutes ago?"

"I'll pass your message on to Detective Tucker and Detective McDonald when they're available, ma'am."

"No, wait. I just got a second threatening phone call. Detective Tucker told me to call him if I got another one."

"You'll have to speak to Detective Tucker or Detective McDonald about that. And they can't come to the phone right now, ma'am."

"I know Detective Tucker and Detective McDonald can't come to the phone," Lauren said between clenched teeth, hoping she wouldn't completely lose her temper. "I can't stand this anymore."

"Well, ma'am, that's not my problem. I'll give them a message when they're available." And she hung up. Lauren hurled the receiver back down and seethed.

"What was all that about?" Nick had reappeared at his desk, without her even noticing.

"Stupid bureaucratic idiots."

Nick looked closely at her. "What exactly are you doing? Are you trying to..."

"It's party time," Louis called, coming into the room. Louisa and Wade walked in a moment later, followed by Jim and Cecily.

"We should all start downstairs," Louisa said. "Fred said I should make sure all of you showed up."

Lauren started to panic. She hadn't planned on the detectives not being there. She knew that once she was in the lobby, her cell phone reception would be spotty at best. What if they called back? And Jim couldn't do his part of the plan without the detectives. It wouldn't be safe. If her plan backfired and someone got hurt, it would be her fault. She should try to figure out a way to stay up here, where she'd be able to use her phone.

"Come on," Louisa said. "Nick, Lauren, everyone, let's go."

She sounded like a kindergarten teacher, Lauren thought, through her own growing dread of what was about to happen.

"It's really a lot of fun." Wade rubbed his hair. "Lots of food. Lots of food."

"Sounds great," Louis said. "And I deserve some food, too. I mean, Natasha didn't even show up for the meeting, after all my work."

"Well, Fred did," Louisa said. "He was very impressed with our efforts, I thought."

"So did I." Wade nodded.

Louisa pursed her lips. "Okay, let's go. All of you." She looked at Lauren. "You, too."

Reluctantly, Lauren got up. She pulled Jim aside. "I have to talk to you." Everyone else, except Nick, was heading down the stairs.

"Are you trying to call..." Nick began.

"Nick?" Louisa's voice interrupted. "Lauren? Jim? Where are you? I have to ask you something about one of your surveys, Nick, all right?"

Nick looked puzzledly at Lauren, and then followed Louisa.

"Jim," Lauren said. "We can't do what I told you to do, at least not right now."

"Huh?" Jim stared blankly at her.

"Pay attention," Lauren snapped at him, feeling terrible. "This is important."

"Jim?" It was Cecily, who had come up the stairs again. "You have to come with me. I can't face all this without you."

"We can't do what we planned," Lauren shouted at Jim. "Don't do what I told you to do, okay?"

“Sure thing,” Jim said, and he and Cecily left.

“Lauren?” Louisa called, her voice echoing up. “Please come down now.”

Lauren reluctantly went down the stairs and emerged into the lobby, to find it transformed. Buffet tables lined the walls, and people were swarming around, collecting food on large plates. One table was covered with platters of shrimp and bowls of cocktail sauce, another held small tea sandwiches of different varieties, and another was filled with fancy chips, vegetables, and dips. And then there was the dessert table, packed with elegant pastries and tarts. In the middle of the dessert table was a huge sheet cake decorated to look like a Lens magazine cover. Lying next to the cake was a large, sharp-looking cake knife. Lauren watched as Wade sliced himself a piece of cake.

The food looked amazing. But Lauren felt far too nervous to eat anything. Jim and Cecily had disappeared, as had Nick. She wondered if Jim had comprehended her message.

Maybe she should go to the police station, stake out the two detectives, and drag them over here once they appeared. But no, she couldn’t. She had to stay here and make sure Jim didn’t do anything. If only she could be in two places at once. If only the Bartlebys realized that a news magazine’s lobby should have cell phone reception.

She sighed and looked around. Louisa was over in the far corner, talking to a group of people Lauren didn’t recognize, and Louis was chatting with Lisa from the art department and Winston, who was away from his desk for once.

“Ladies and gentlemen,” Fred called from near the dessert table, as he banged on a glass with a fork. “I want to welcome you to the annual Founders’ Day party. First, we’ll have our annual greetings from the Bartlebys, and then I think Natasha wanted to say a few words, right?" He glanced at Natasha, who nodded.

Amanda was making her way over to Lauren. "How are you doing?"

"Um, not great. I got another call."

"Oh, no." Amanda gave Lauren a hug. "I'm so sorry."

"And I can't..." Lauren began, just as Fred shouted, "Attention, everyone." The room fell silent. "Mr. Bartleby?" Fred queried respectfully into his phone. "Are you there?"

An elderly-sounding voice emerged. "Yes, Fred," it said, coughing politely. "Hello, and welcome to Founders' Day. I am John Bartleby, and on behalf of my brother, my sister, and my entire family, I am glad to talk to you today. Thank you for your hard work, and especially during..." the voice droned on.

Lauren wished she could go outside, or upstairs, or anywhere that had cell reception, to try to call the police again, but everyone was fixated upon Fred's phone. She could only hope Jim had listened to her.

"...thank you very much," the voice said, apparently finishing.

Everyone smiled at the phone, and then resumed eating. The noise level instantly returned to normal.

"Wait a minute," Natasha called, banging on her glass. The gathering turned quiet again. "I want to say a few things. I want to thank all of you for keeping things going during a very difficult time."

Lauren felt someone poke her in the shoulder and saw Simon grinning at her. The professor and Zach brought up the rear. They were all still wearing their nametags from the conference.

"What's he doing here?" Amanda whispered to Lauren, gesturing at Zach, whose nametag clearly identified him as an employee of Time magazine. Zach was gazing around the lobby and pulling his pen out from behind his ear. "And what's up with the fedora and the pen behind his ear anyway?"

Lauren shrugged. Zach was hard to explain even under less fraught circumstances.

"Who's she?" Zach pointed at Natasha, who was still speaking.

"Shhh," a couple of people around them said.

"Natasha Wise," Lauren whispered. "The editor of the magazine." Surely it couldn't hurt to tell him that much.

"Why are you here?" Amanda whispered at Zach. "You're not supposed to be here."

"Be quiet," someone said.

"Natasha Wise?" the professor said. "Now, why does that name sound so familiar?"

"Thank you, and now you can all enjoy the party," Natasha said, concluding her remarks.

"Why did you have to bring him with you?" Amanda asked Simon. She scowled at Zach, who was scribbling in his reporter's notebook. "He works for the competition."

"Oh, yes," Simon said vaguely. "You're right. I had forgotten. The three of us were together at the conference, so he just came along over here. And Ethan was with us too."

Lauren noticed that the professor was talking to Louisa. Everyone seemed occupied, so she seized the opportunity to run over to the phone on Winston's desk and call the police again.

"Yes, ma'am, Detective Tucker and Detective McDonald are still not available."

Damn, Lauren thought. "Well, could you tell them, or tell someone, to come over to the Lens magazine building as quickly as possible? Or could you send someone else over here? I think something's about to happen."

"Yes, ma'am," the woman said tonelessly.

"Listen, could I please talk to someone else?"

"Will you hold, please?" The woman put Lauren on what seemed to be infinite hold. Finally Lauren hung up, completely exasperated.

"Problems?" Winston asked, returning to his desk. He smiled kindly at her and bit into a piece of cake.

"Yes." Lauren sighed. She still couldn't see Jim anywhere, or Cecily, or Nick for that matter. "Have you seen Jim?"

Winston shook his head. "Not for a while."

"Hi, Lauren." Ethan appeared suddenly at her side. "Sorry I haven't been in touch. I've been really busy meeting people. And my panel's scheduled for this afternoon, just before the closing session. The scheduling's really screwed up. And did you know Jose's going to be in D.C. next week? I'll remind him to contact you when he gets here."

Lauren nodded absently as Ethan headed toward Professor Segal. Still no police. She didn't know what Jim was going to do. And she didn't know if that woman at the station would send anyone over. She needed to call again. But Winston was on his phone. She'd have to run up to her desk to call. It would only take a minute. She glanced around. She could slip out, and no one would see her.

She left the lobby and rushed through the passageway and up the stairs to her desk. The Most Admired Unit room was quiet. But she felt a prickle of fear. What if...but no, she had looked around, and she didn't think anyone had seen her leave. Still, she had to hurry. She had to get back to make sure Jim didn't do anything he shouldn't. She picked up the phone and called the police station again.

"Ma'am, Detective Tucker and Detective McDonald left, just a minute ago."

"Where were they going?" Lauren tapped her fingers nervously against the Kis book, which was on her desk, mostly unread. "Were they coming over here?"

"I don't know where they were going, ma'am."

Lauren hung up, fuming. So now she'd have to rush back to the lobby. Maybe everything would still work out. But then—oh, no—she heard footsteps coming up the stairs. She caught her breath. Oh, my god, she thought, picking up the Kis book and clutching it to her chest. A huge wave of fear hit her, worse even than that of the previous night. She looked around. There was nowhere to hide. Except maybe the office supply room. She ran into the supply room and quietly shut the door.

"Lauren?" She knew who it was. This was horrible. What would happen now?

"Lauren?" The voice sounded louder. "I think you're up here somewhere, aren't you?"

Lauren huddled in the pitch-dark supply room, still hugging the Kis book. What could she do? There was nothing in the room to use as a self-defense weapon, just a lot of paper and pens and rolls of tape and old magazines. She couldn't breathe.

The footsteps came closer. Lauren felt like screaming, but she managed to control herself. And then the door opened. Lauren gasped.

Natasha was standing there, holding a plate with a big slab of cake. And the large cake knife from the party. "So, Lauren." Her eyes looked feverish. "I thought maybe a little chat was in order. Maybe tidy up some last-minute details about your investigation. Cake?" And she sliced a piece for herself.

Lauren shook her head. Was there any chance she could reason with Natasha? Could she run past her somehow, and get back to the lobby? Maybe by then the police would have arrived.

"You think you're so smart, Lauren, don't you." Natasha moved away from the supply room door and started pacing back and forth between the supply room and Lauren's desk. "I was such a fucking idiot to get you involved." She slammed the plate with the cake and the knife down on Lauren's desk. "So what exactly do you know?"

"I know you were secretly meeting Tony at night here in the office." Lauren took a step out of the supply room. Jim hadn't seen Louisa that night, he had seen Natasha. He had just thought it was Louisa, because he couldn't see very well. "And I know Karel Halama's about to sue you for misquoting him in that Czech series you did for Synthesis." Tony hadn't been referring to Nick in that note, he'd been referring to Natasha. And Professor Segal must have heard something about it, too. It was only a guess, but it seemed to fit together. Lauren took another step toward the stairs.

"God damn it." Natasha grabbed the cake knife and started stabbing Lauren's empty chair. "Shit, shit, shit." Her voice was getting more and more out of control as she kept stabbing the chair, and suddenly she wheeled in Lauren's direction. By this point, Lauren had made it halfway to the door.

Without thinking, Lauren hurled the Kis book at Natasha, and ran down the stairs, not even waiting to see if it had hit its target. She bolted through the passageway and into the main lobby, where Jim, standing near the front door, was holding forth to a transfixed crowd.

"So, like, it actually wasn't Louisa that I saw," Jim was saying. "It was Natasha. And Lauren figured it all out."

"Jim," Lauren shouted. "Be quiet. She's..."

And Natasha ran into the room, looking disheveled, the cake knife still in her hand. "What the hell are you talking about? Who's going to believe a word of this anyway?"

"Jim," Lauren implored. "Please be quiet. The police aren't here, and she's already tried to..."

"It's true," Jim said over Lauren's pleas. "Like, you and Tony were having secret meetings in the office."

"Oh, please." Natasha looked furious. She strode back to the dessert table and thrust the cake knife into the cake. "Secret meetings with Tony Mandel? Give me a break."

"Natasha Wise," the professor said suddenly. Everyone turned in her direction. "I remember where I heard your name. I heard that you're about to be sued by someone claiming you misrepresented them in an article. In Synthesis magazine, that was it. Not an article that appeared in Lens. It's just that you're the editor of Lens now. Now, who was it?"

"Please, Professor Segal," Lauren begged. "It's Karel Halama. But be quiet, please?"

"Look, whoever you are," Natasha glared at Professor Segal. "You seem to know a hell of a lot more than you should about something that's totally irrelevant, okay?"

And then Cecily burst through the front door. "It was you all along, Natasha." Tears were running down her face. "Tony was sneaking around with you. And I never guessed it. But he really was going to break it off with you that night. I understand now."

"You stupid little idiot." Natasha pushed her hair back angrily as she turned away from the professor toward Cecily and Jim. "Tony never cared about you. He just cared about your family's money."

"That's not true. I told him to break it off, and he said he would, and then I told Jim to follow him, and Jim followed him over here."

"Cecily, stop!" Lauren ran toward Jim and Cecily. Everything was out of control. "Wait till..."

"Yeah," Jim said. "Like, we couldn't figure it out. But Lauren did."

Natasha turned her wrathful gaze upon Lauren. "You bitch."

"He didn't care about you, really," Cecily broke in, an edge of triumph in her voice.

"God damn it." Natasha turned back toward Cecily. "It's you he didn't care about. He wasn't going to break it off with me because he cared so much about you. It was because he knew I might be in a hell of a lot of trouble with this stupid Synthesis thing she was talking about." And she glared at the professor, who shrank back against Louisa.

"And you killed him," Cecily shouted. "You killed him because he was rejecting you."

Natasha ran forward, grabbed Cecily, and started shaking her. "Stop it. Stop saying that."

"You killed him," Cecily shrieked.

"Stop shaking her." Jim pushed Natasha.

"Don't tell me what to do." Natasha let Cecily go and latched on to Jim's shirt collar. Cecily fell to the floor, and Lauren helped her up.

"Stop it, immediately," a commanding voice sounded from the front door. "Break it up." It was McDonald, with Tucker and Nick behind him.

"She did it." Cecily pointed at Natasha, who was still struggling with Jim.

"All right," McDonald said, separating Natasha and Jim. They faced each other, quivering with anger. "Let's..."

"He never cared about you," Cecily broke in. "He used to tell me things about you. I mean, I never knew that it was you, but he used to tell me he really didn't love you at all."

"Shit," Natasha said. She gulped, and blinked a couple of times. "Shit."

"I don't get it," Zach said. He had his phone out and was

surveying the room. "Who was in love with who?"

"I didn't mean to kill him," Natasha said, gulping again. "Oh, shit."

"But you did?" Fred mopped his brow, a stunned look on his face. It was a look shared by pretty much everyone else in the room. Including Nick, who was still standing near the door, gazing back and forth bewilderedly between Natasha and Lauren herself. She felt bad. Maybe she should have filled him in ahead of time, after all.

"It was an accident." Natasha expelled a shuddering breath. "It was self-defense. I didn't mean to do it. Really, I didn't."

"All right." McDonald shook his head. "There's no need to say anymore, Ms. Wise. We'll have to take you in now." And he started reciting her rights.

Natasha looked drained. She stumblingly followed Tucker and McDonald toward the door, just as another contingent of police, uniformed this time, showed up. They looked around, seeming confused, before conferring with Tucker and McDonald. McDonald and a couple of the uniformed cops stayed behind, while Tucker and the others departed with Natasha. Everyone stared after them.

"Well," Simon said after a minute, breaking the silence. "You Americans certainly know how to throw a party, don't you?"

Twenty-Eight

"Where's Fred?" Louis was bouncing up and down in his chair with impatience. "I can't wait anymore. I'm supposed to be going to a tech convention this weekend, and I really wanted to try to get out of here a little early today."

"You can wait another few minutes," Louisa said sharply. It was a couple of hours later, and the Most Admired Unit's staff, along with Amanda, Simon, Ethan, and the professor, were seated in the lobby amidst the party leftovers waiting for Fred to return from the police station. Antonio was sitting at the front desk, reading a copy of the magazine.

Everyone else had drifted off, many of them returning to their desks because despite the chaos, the news didn't stop.

Lauren, taking in the scene from near the elevator, was feeling rather dazed. The events at the party hadn't gone quite as she had expected. It ended up okay, but there had been a few scary moments. She had spent the past two hours giving statements to the police, mostly about the cake knife episode, and had just been told she could join the others in the lobby. She checked her phone, to find a text from Amanda.

"Congrats, u did it!!! U r the true superhero(ine). And u have my blessing to pursue whichever *former * suspect u'd like." Amanda had attached a couple of smiley faces.

"Couldn't have done it without u!" Lauren texted back. "Thanks. U r the best."

She looked up, and saw Amanda giving her a thumbs-up sign

and a big smile, just as Fred came through the door.

"So?" Louis leaned forward. "What did she say? Why did she really kill him?"

"Did she do it on purpose?" Amanda asked.

"Are they going to offer any apologies for harassing me?" Wade asked, an aggrieved look on his face. "Obviously I didn't murder Tony. I don't know what they were thinking. All I did was blackmail the Bartlebys." And he reached for a piece of leftover cake and ate a mouthful.

"Well..." Fred sat down in an empty chair. "Actually, they didn't say anything about you, Wade. But here's what Natasha said. She and Tony had been secretly meeting in the office for a couple of months."

Lauren glanced involuntarily over at Cecily, who was, for once, not crying. Jim was sitting next to Cecily, looking contented, and Nick, still quite pale, was leaning back in his chair, his elbows on the table behind him. He smiled at her and gestured at the empty seat beside him. Lauren sat down and smiled back. It had been very resourceful of him to track down Tucker and McDonald, especially given that she had kept him in the dark about her plans. Of course, those other police officers would probably have shown up in time, but still.

"I'm so proud of you," he whispered, reaching over and squeezing her hand. "You seriously take my breath away, in so many ways."

She wanted to bury her head in his shoulder and wrap herself around him again. She wished no one else was there. She pulled her chair a little closer to his. "Thanks," she whispered back. "For getting the detectives over here, and for everything. And I'm sorry I didn't tell you anything ahead of time, I just, well..." She realized she didn't have a very good reason for not telling him. She should have told him. Was she somehow still focused on not allowing herself to become vulnerable or attached? On not letting her guard down? But hadn't she already let it down, in a pretty significant way, a couple of nights ago?

Of course, she hadn't told Amanda about her suspicions of Natasha either. And both Amanda and Nick had, separately, been eager to help her. Maybe she had wanted to prove to herself that she could do this on her own. And there was nothing wrong with that, was there? Well, but what if something had actually happened when Natasha came upstairs...

"Oh, no, that's okay," he whispered, shaking his head. "And that was the least of it. I mean, getting them over here was the least I could do for you. That thing with the cake knife, holy shit." He squeezed her hand again, and then released it, pulled out his phone, and started texting something.

"Why couldn't they just go to her flat?" Simon was asking curiously. "Or to his? I can't imagine why they would have been indulging in secret assignations at the office."

Fred shrugged. "It is a little strange. But Natasha worked late a lot of nights, and she liked to come in early in the morning, and she didn't always feel like going home. So it became a habit."

"But why did she kill him?" Louis asked, one foot jiggling up and down, and then everyone started talking.

Lauren felt her phone buzz and she pulled it out of her pocket. "Next survey: Our Most Admired Detective," Nick had texted.

A second text followed: "Experts agree, that would be u! #formersuspect #grateful #thankyou"

She texted back a smiley face.

"If u need a Dr. Watson-type figure to help u, can I apply?" he texted.

"Definitely!" she replied. It was finally starting to sink in: He wasn't a suspect anymore. She felt some of the heaviness surrounding her start to dissipate a little.

"Okay, a quick summary coming up," Fred said, mopping his forehead again. "According to Natasha, Tony called her that night and said he needed to see her a little later than usual. Around a quarter to five. That he had something important to tell her, and she should come to the Most Admired Unit. So, once they were both there, he told her he had heard about this potential lawsuit. Karel Halama had been talking about it, and word got around. She thought it was crazy, because she said she didn't fabricate any quotes or misrepresent anything."

It was possible, Lauren thought. Karel Halama, with his choleric temper, could easily have misinterpreted something in Natasha's article. Especially with the language issues. But then she thought of Natasha stabbing the chair with the cake knife and felt less charitable.

"So," Fred continued, "according to Natasha at least, Tony started threatening her. He said he'd tell people that she did misrepresent what Halama had said, that she'd told him she'd done it. Then Natasha started getting upset. And then Tony announced that he wasn't going to see her anymore. She told him he was a despicable person, and she jumped up and hit him. He picked up the vase from Cecily's desk and threatened to smash her over the head with it. They were both yelling and screaming. Natasha ran up the stairs to the third floor to get away from him, and the next thing she knew she had somehow grabbed the vase away from him, and she thinks she must have hit him over the head, and then he fell down and didn't move, and she was so frightened she didn't know what to do. So she ran out of the building and threw the vase into the dumpster. And then she came in for our early-morning meeting a couple of hours later. I thought she looked tired, but I knew she'd been working very hard."

"But then why weren't her fingerprints all over everything?" Nick looked puzzled. "Like the vase?"

Fred nodded. "McDonald asked her the same thing. You remember how it was really cold that night? And the heat's never turned up very high in most of the building at night, except where the overnight staff works. So Natasha was wearing gloves when she came over here, and she never took them off."

"What about my missing data?" Louisa frowned at Fred. "Did she have anything to say about that?"

"No," Fred said. "But the police did. They found it in Tony's neighbor's apartment. Tony had dropped off some magazines for this neighbor to borrow, the same night all of this happened, and he had put the data inside them. The neighbor just realized the other day that it might be important, and he finally told the police about it."

"Well, really." Louisa pursed her lips. "He stole my data. He was trying to get back at Brad through me, I suppose. Tony always hated Brad."

Lauren noticed another text. "Did u figure that out about the gloves?" Nick had written. "U r so incredible."

Actually, no, she hadn't really thought about the fingerprint issue. She probably should have. "Well, not really," she replied, and then she noticed everyone had stopped talking. She looked up.

"What I'd like to know is, how did you figure out Natasha had done it?" Fred had turned toward Lauren, as had everyone else. She felt a little embarrassed.

"Lauren was one of my best students." The professor beamed at her proudly. "I would have been quite surprised if she hadn't figured it out."

Lauren took a deep breath. "So I really didn't discover anything all that big, at least not all at once. But I kept finding out all these little things, and gradually they started fitting together. At first I didn't think Natasha could have had anything to do with it. She actually asked me to help her investigate the whole thing, because the Bartlebys had asked her to help them exonerate Cecily."

Everyone then transferred their gaze to Cecily, who looked down uncomfortably.

"There were two sides to the whole thing," Lauren continued, beginning to feel a little more confident. "Part of it was professional, and part of it was personal." She paused, reflecting for a moment. It actually was sort of incredible, that she'd figured the whole thing out. Everyone was looking at her, waiting to hear what she would say next.

"Why don't we start with the personal side?" Simon suggested. "That's always the most fascinating."

"Okay. So Cecily and Tony had a fight that night, and finally Tony agreed to go tell the other woman he wasn't going to see her anymore."

"Maybe Natasha's right," Cecily said, doubt in her eyes. "Maybe Tony just told her that because he thought she'd be in trouble with the lawsuit, and then she couldn't do anything for his career anymore. Maybe it wasn't because he really cared about me at all."

"I'm not sure." Lauren shook her head. "But then Cecily asked Jim to follow Tony, and Jim followed him over here, which puzzled Cecily and Jim. They assumed he hadn't been going to see the other woman after all. And then Jim thought he saw Louisa going into the building, which made sense if Tony had been talking to her about some business deal, but it didn't make sense for Louisa to be the other woman."

"Certainly not." Louisa looked thoroughly appalled.

"And then Jim called me and I did come by here," Cecily said. "I didn't tell the whole truth before. But I didn't go inside. And then Jim and I left. We must have just missed seeing Natasha come out of the building. Except we thought it was Louisa."

"Right," Lauren said. "When Jim thought Fred was Wade yesterday, all of a sudden, I realized Jim couldn't have seen who it was very well from down the street. And then I was thinking about this friend of mine who's always discussing love triangles. All of a sudden, I wondered if maybe Natasha could have been the one Jim saw at the door, and that Tony could have been meeting her in the office at night. But I wasn't sure, because she had asked me to try to help her in the first place. If she really had done it, she would have been perfectly happy to see Cecily arrested for the murder. And then I realized that maybe she was trying to balance pleasing the Bartlebys and keeping her job, versus seeing someone else arrested for killing Tony." Natasha had been acting very strangely the entire time.

"I guess she didn't think you'd figure it out, Lauren." Fred wiped his forehead. "She must have underestimated you. And I'm so sorry you had to go through that whole thing upstairs with the cake knife."

"Thanks." Lauren shivered at the thought of the cake knife. "Well, I didn't know for sure that Natasha had done anything at all. But then there was the professional side. Louis told me he had found some things in a computer file indicating that Tony was about to accuse Nick of copying one of his stories again, that there was something wrong with the Central Europe story."

She deliberately didn't look at Nick. She couldn't. She felt terrible that she had doubted him, even for a moment.

"So I talked to this Czech writer I know who was quoted in Nick's story, and I remembered that Natasha had also interviewed this guy for her story last summer. And then Professor Segal kept hinting that there was something wrong with a story that had something to do with Lens."

"And they thought I did it." Wade reached for another piece of cake. "And they thought I did it."

"But there were a few things I didn't figure out." Lauren turned to Louisa. "Was Tony talking to you about money the Friday before he..."

"Oh, yes, you mentioned that yesterday. I checked my calendar and sure enough, Tony asked me for a raise that day. I told him in no uncertain terms that he wasn't getting one."

"Oh." Lauren remembered something else. She looked at Wade. "And does anyone know who borrowed a file Natasha had given me?"

"I did," Wade said, right on cue. "But I put it back."

"That's true."

"And how did I know about Louie's invention, you might ask?" Wade brushed at his hair. "Good journalism. Tony told me about..."

Louis glared at him. "There's nothing suspicious about my video game. Tony couldn't have copyrighted it anyway, he didn't understand it. He just thought he did."

"How much did Brad really know about the senator's financial dealings?" Simon asked loudly. "Someone told me he really masterminded the whole thing."

"Who told you that?" Louisa turned to face Simon. "Brad certainly did not mastermind anything of the sort. He tried to steer the senator away from those people."

"Daniel, I believe. I mean, Zach. Wasn't it Zach who told us that?" Simon looked at Lauren and the professor for confirmation.

"Do you mean Zach Cohen?" Amanda looked disgusted. "He left. He said he had to go back to his office and file his story. He's probably got the whole thing up on their website by now." She frowned. "So on top of everything else, we're getting scooped by Time on our own story. I really thought..." She turned to Fred.

"You were right, Amanda. We should have put something up on our website, but the Bartlebys didn't want to."

Amanda shook her head in frustration.

"Lauren," the professor said, "the last session of the conference is this afternoon. Would you like to come? Part of it has to do with Romania, you know. At least tangentially."

"I'm going to be presenting my paper," Ethan added. "I'd really appreciate it if you'd be there."

Lauren pondered it. Romania. Did she want to go? Actually, she wouldn't mind going to Romania itself, but a conference still didn't sound so great. "Okay. Sure, I'll go."

"Well, hello, folks," came a booming voice from the doorway, and Tucker strode into the lobby. "I bet you all thought you'd seen the last of me for the day." And he nodded majestically as his eyes swept the room. "Mr. Wood?" Tucker focused on Wade. "That witness recanted what he said, after we told him Ms. Wise had confessed. You're off the hook."

"Oh, good," Wade breathed.

"But the Bartlebys may have a few questions to answer. And you, Mr. Wood, are now under arrest for blackmail. Would you come with me, please?"

"But..." Wade spluttered. "But..."

"What do you mean, questions to answer?" Cecily asked, her voice starting to shake.

"Questions," Tucker said sternly. "And did you think nothing would happen to you if you blackmailed someone, Mr. Wood? Will you please come with me, now? You do have the right..." his voice faded as he left the room, Wade reluctantly in tow. A quivering Cecily followed, Jim at her side. Louis trailed behind them.

Lauren settled back in her chair, watching them leave. She spent a few minutes thinking about everything that had just happened, and then she looked around the room.

Fred and Amanda had retreated to the corner, where they appeared to be having a serious talk. She wondered if he was offering Amanda the editing job. She hoped so. Ethan, Simon, Professor Segal, and Louisa were gathered near the door, discussing Ethan's upcoming presentation.

Lauren turned to Nick, who was looking thoughtfully at her, and she gave in to her impulse to lean her head on his shoulder and wrap her arms around him. Just for a second. And he wrapped his arms around her. And then they let go of each other and pulled apart. She noticed that the thoughtful expression had turned into one of those smiles of his. Directed right at her. She wasn't completely sure what he was thinking, but she felt she might possibly be picking up something.

Still, she knew that the issue was deeper than piecing her flawed signal-reading capabilities back together. It was a matter of trying to piece her entire life—the professional and the personal—back together. And that would take time. On the professional side, at least she had a job, assuming Lens survived for a while. She had some breathing room to figure out her academic career.

And the personal side wasn't something that could be rushed. It was something that would require patience. Maybe making a serious effort to sort through her feelings and come to terms with what had happened to her over the past half year. And maybe, perhaps, ending up with something new that could last. Even after the chaos and intensity of the past ten days had long since faded away.

"So," Lauren said.

"Well," Nick said.

"Do you think you might consider going to the conference

with me this afternoon?"

"Yes, I'd like that."

"And if you still want me to have dinner with your family tonight, I will. I mean, I'd be glad to." Maybe glad was an overstatement. But if she could solve a mystery, surely she could handle some competitive, argumentative people who undoubtedly would be scrutinizing her. Right? She gave him a smile that she hoped conveyed confidence.

"Well, we can figure it out later." He sent back a smile that she could tell conveyed gratitude. "But thanks."

And they followed the others out the door.

Acknowledgments

I started working on a version of this novel more than three decades ago, and have been revising it on and off over the years. It's an incredible feeling to know that it's being published after all this time. There are probably hundreds of people I could acknowledge who read drafts of my manuscript, and I apologize for not listing all of you. Dear friends and colleagues, your contributions mean so much to me, and I greatly appreciate your willingness to read the manuscript and offer thoughtful suggestions. I would like to thank Apprentice House Press for providing such a wonderful publishing home the second time around! My appreciation goes out to Kevin Atticks, Chris Kimani, Sarah McKoy, Aminah Murray, Eleanor Salvatore, and Nick Kelly. Many thanks to Mary Bisbee-Beek. And I am eternally grateful to my family for their ongoing support. Huge thanks and much love to David Levitt, Aaron Kalb Levitt, Madeleine Kalb, Marvin Kalb, Judith Kalb, and Eloise Ogden.

About the Author

Deborah Kalb is the author of the new mystery novel *Everything She Most Admired*. Her other books include the novel *Off to Join the Circus*, also published by Apprentice House. She's written fiction for kids and nonfiction for adults, is the host of the book blog *Book Q&As with Deborah Kalb*, and is the co-host of the podcast *Rereading Our Childhood*. A former longtime D.C.-based journalist covering Congress and politics, she lives in the Washington, D.C., area.

Apprentice House is the country's only campus-based, student-staffed book publishing company. Directed by professors and industry professionals, it is a nonprofit activity of the Communication & Media Department at Loyola University Maryland.

Using state-of-the-art technology and an experiential learning model of education, Apprentice House publishes books in untraditional ways. This dual responsibility as publishers and educators creates an unprecedented collaborative environment among faculty and students, while teaching tomorrow's editors, designers, and marketers.

Eclectic and provocative, Apprentice House titles intend to entertain as well as spark dialogue on a variety of topics. Financial contributions to sustain the press's work are welcomed. Contributions are tax deductible to the fullest extent allowed by the IRS.

To learn more about Apprentice House books or to obtain submission guidelines, please visit www.apprenticehouse.com.

Apprentice House
Communication & Media Department
Loyola University Maryland
4501 N. Charles Street
Baltimore, MD 21210
Ph: 410-617-5265
info@apprenticehouse.com • www.apprenticehouse.com

www.ingramcontent.com/pod-product-compliance
Lightning Source LLC
LaVergne TN
LVHW010601100826
845148LV00014B/2793

* 9 7 8 1 6 2 7 2 0 6 4 2 6 *